ANYONE LIKE HOPE

YEAR TWENTY

NOAH STEPHENS

Year Twenty

thanks to A.R.

PART I

1

Extremely sleep-deprived when he finally fell asleep—for seventy-plus hours he had been awake due to Adderall—during the nearly nineteen hours Stanley slept he experienced an oneiric epic, a visceral tragedy; dreamed a dream long and terrible, one that thankfully he would not remember...

He was sitting at a dialing station—a chair, a table with a monitor on it, and tower beneath—in a long line of these each with a person wearing a headset sitting in it, each separated from the other by a thin divider consisting of a metal frame upholstered with mottled gray fabric.

What the fuck? What is the point of that? To draw attention to himself? Why wear shit like that to work, it wasn't a fashion show. Why did so many of the girls there dress, dye and style their hair as colorfully and outlandishly as they did, tattoo and pierce themselves to the excessive extent they did? For attention, in an effort to evoke desire?

Variety was the spice of life; he didn't look down on these choices, he just didn't understand. Really they made it less drab there, the people who treated each day like a costume contest, who modeled their appearance on clowns.

There were plenty of reasons it wasn't fun to be a man. It wasn't fun to be a man that had not been with a woman in any sort of man-woman way for at least five months but more like twelve, and among the many causes of his exceedingly sad state, along with his lengthy-feeling recent resignation, a general resignation, was that he'd not had any level of physical—hell, even emotional—intimacy anytime in the last year. It was no fun to be a man, one sexually and emotionally wanting, one who needed a woman to fulfill either need (want?), especially when the cubicle you choose to sit in at work is adjacent that of the one chosen by a young woman you find sexy— similarly aged and with a personality and lifestyle maybe similar— and given the proximity you unexpectedly notice she is sexier than you'd thought, or is sexier to you at present than ever previously.

She was his current physical favorite there (the only place he spent significant time around others), a redhead he'd become at- tracted to earlier. She had short red hair and looked amazing with short hair and her red-lipsticked lips were erotically but not over- ly pierced and, worst, best, she was wearing a short skirt and gray stockings that her ideal legs looked very, very good in—he couldn't stop stealing glances at them. And he couldn't stop because for the first forty-five minutes of the shift she was either turned all the way around in her swivel chair so he could see them easily (constantly in the peripheral vision of his left eye) or actually turned toward him so that her biologically appealing legs were even closer and nearly touching his chair: and he could not concentrate, could not think about anything despite his effort other than how hot this girl was; he was overcome, mentally incapacitated by lust, pure warm lust, his brain capable but of firings that created conscious desire. *Oh woman beside me*, he thought, *I pine for you; I want to know you, to the extent I ever could.*

She was not nameless to him, and they had spoken from time to time, but he did not anticipate their relationship going beyond that, despite his being reasonably certain she did not have a boyfriend, even if he tried only to evolve their relationship (or lack of one) to friendship.

Sometime during his twenty-sixth year, the same year that he became convinced (perhaps not for the first time) he would never have sex again, and the year he'd last had sex, last been in a relationship, he came to think that he'd never really cared about, given enough attention to, or even known what mattered, mattered ultimately, spiritually—that he'd been his entire adulthood, and perhaps since early childhood, what to his mind was a bad person. Not in every way but in general. Unenlightened, unthinking on many occasions or immoral in his behavior. Overall, judging himself retrospectively based on what he'd come to think was the correct basis for evaluating a person's life, evaluating the character of a person's actions and (though he had access only to his own, and that access partial) a person's thoughts.

He was sick of course, mentally, spiritually, and had come to realize that at some point previous—though this didn't cause him to become any better, the sickness's severity would fluctuate, symptoms change. And as a rule with few exceptions he wouldn't be conscious of the acting up of the illness—which reared its head, many heads unpredictably even for him—for what it was while it was acting up, to his detriment. And if he did couldn't intervene on his own behalf was like a computer that had given itself a command, and would execute it even if conflicting commands followed, would do so unless it was unplugged or destroyed. The illness *was* him. A facet. A face. Causes, its origin not entirely known or understood. A nonphysical disease that seemed to have the overall effect of thwarting him; perhaps self-defeats and -alterations had all along been its motive, a secret of his subconscious.

Well, it had worked. Many times. And now he felt he was less sick and would continue becoming less sick; was not so bad a person and would be daily becoming a better one. No, he was not so crazy anymore as he long had regarded himself. He was merely a bit anti-social, bookish; his self-esteem was a bit low and he intermittently felt lonely, sometimes very; he still drank too much perhaps, was a pothead and cigarette smoker.

⊸((◦))⊸

To his mind he was a drunk (albeit a sometimes teetotaling or to various degrees functional one) and always would be, even if some-day he became a permanent nondrinker. A depressive nature had something to do with it. And sometimes he experienced a feeling that seemed to emanate from the core of him, to be him. But it was a feeling foreign too, ultimately ineffable, and disliked by him. A cold wave—a feeling that ruled out life and love while it controlled him, a feeling of no feeling at all, other than emptiness, and perhaps a vague bewilderment and feeling of being ill at ease. His face was stern when it was affecting him and he had the sensation of being inhuman. Nonhuman, on the inside something starkly other. Closer to an insect, robot.

He didn't much like himself, didn't much like his life (to him it was generally unpleasant, there was probably a fair amount left, and he saw it continuing to be unpleasant, getting worse. And among a multitude of problems, many social, he had gotten to the point with his longtime job that the more hours he worked the more he hated it (and the more his quality of life declined, the more he drank) but the less he worked the more he dreaded work, the worse he was at the job, and the poorer he was), but had become a survivalist; was, he thought, in the habit of surviving—of course he was, he was alive—whether he wanted to or not (did so instinctually, as a wild animal, and was good at it). And he felt he had to, sometimes felt he wanted to, and guessed he would be making up for the previous bulk of his life for whatever remained of it, perhaps another, larger bulk.

He also over the last half-decade plus had come to hold other people in a lower regard, often thinking less of them than he did himself. He didn't expect from them anything that would impress him, didn't expect surprises—like meeting someone, a woman, comparably aged, who was totally different, and totally right for him, who would surprise him, make him feel again the fiction of romantic love, whatever such a hypothetical person would be like. (Damaged goods, he speculated cynically. A real nutball. Probably clingy.)

Maybe he would change then, maybe his life would be better.

For now though he felt a little dead, inside, and physically also he was sure he was in fact fast dying. He felt a little hopeless, that he was and long had been trudging through a drudge existence, a pointless, stagnant term. His life was primarily waking up, going to work, working, coming back from work, watching TV for hours, taking sleeping pills (he had a problem sleeping, or getting to sleep in time to get a full night's rest before work; sometimes he suffered from insomnia for three, four days in a row. He'd get during this stretch some shuteye, two to five hours a night, but it wasn't enough, and created a sleep deficit that increased throughout the work week. The sleeping pills, over-the-counter, which he ingested six nights a week, helped a little, but he'd taken them for years, was addicted, and had a high tolerance), going to sleep, doing it over. He felt a yearning for adventure growing within him, a yearning he felt too old for for what seemed too vague, a yen he'd not felt at all recently.

With the aim of changing the quality of this existence, or how he or others regarded it, but truly more to find someone new, he was sincerely going to attempt to do new things he didn't do typically or ever, things he didn't like to do nor he suspected ever would.

<hr />

At home he was thinking about how he hardly had any friends anymore, wasn't even thirty yet and he was somehow quite isolated in the world, somehow. (No, that wasn't right. He knew how everything had happened: for some reason, he had isolated himself.) He sat alone in his one-bedroom apartment on the fraying drab olive green sofa striped various shades of brown that held a limited sentimental value for him though it was ugly. The TV was on, muted; the radio played sixties to nineties favorites. He wasn't watching the set, the glowing screen so hypnotic, was just in his mind. Looking at it he noticed consciously for the first time it was an NBA game, one of the teams the local one. He switched around, found a hilariously bad movie that looked to be about three decades old, *Bare Knuckles*, left it soundless, laughed for a while, went back into his mind more, came out a bit occasionally. Eventually, after he'd hit his marijuana pipe a few times, he began considering coming up with someone to call, to see what they were up to tonight. It was Friday evening earlyish and he was off weekends.

He decided he would go through the phone numbers written on little scraps of paper he'd accumulated over the past year or so, some of them numbers without names, numbers that would now be a complete mystery to him (if he dialed any of these he'd have to say something awkward like, "Do you know a Stanley Northrop? Yes? Oh great, well I'm he and I was going through some things and found this number. There was no name written on it so I thought I'd call it and see whose number it was." Probably, to avoid this, he would only consider the numbers with names, depending on what the names were; some of them he might not recollect anyway).

He slowly rose—too slowly for a yet young man, but deliberately, maybe to feel older than he was—and went into his white-walled bedroom, small, in the center of which was an old and unappealing-looking mattress (the cover not on it) on a box spring also old (and too two times larger than the mattress). It was a room with books, an upturned milk crate in a corner, clothes hung in a closet and folded in a squat plastic dresser there, a lamp, and little else. He began looking through the pile he kept there of these phone numbers. There were about ten. He separated those with names and those without;

one, in his own hand, had one too many digits (*must've been drunk* he thought)—and there was a name, Katie (*oh well*). There were five other scraps with names, and numbers of seven or ten digits. Two of the names were unambiguously male monikers and, with the notion of finding a "wingman" to go with him to a bar perhaps (though he found it more likely he'd wind up occupying that role himself), he chose from among these to call first. Only one was local and it was the number of a guy he'd spoken to many times and known awhile, someone he used to work with at his present job, a job he'd been at going on five years (the other number a personage unremembered).

They were dissimilar in that he was the sort who dyed and styled his hair, had piercings, probably tattoos, but they had seemed to click in the past. The guy was about two years younger, his name Bartholomew.

Back in the living room he dialed, the muted network on commercial, radio now tuned to the classical station, sipping from a mug of red wine. He drank a slim bottle of the same—the nearest store's cheapest bottle of merlot—almost every day.

"Hello," Bartholomew answered, sounding stoned, after four rings.

"Hey, Bartholomew," he said sounding casual and chipper (he felt depressed but at least was high). "It's Stanley. Remember me?"

"Stanley. Of course. How ya doin', man?" Bartholomew likely remembered he didn't at all like *Stan*, just as Bartholomew, Stanley remembered, did not like *Bart*.

"Pretty good, man, how are ya?"

"Not at all shabby."

"What's new with you? It's been a while."

"Just going to school, hanging out with my girl. That pretty much, uh, occupies my days."

"School, girl—cool."

"Yeah. Lot of homework."

"Uh-huh, hear that. Well, it's been a while, uh, and I just thought I'd see if you wanted to get together some night this week or whatever, maybe a bar."

"Yeah. Yeah, actually, uh, Satur—tomorrow night I was going to go to The Touchstone." He called to his girlfriend. "Babe, when's that thing—when's that band playing that we're going to? ...What time though?" Stanley faintly distinguished a female voice say, "They're supposed to play at nine."

"Yeah, we're going there to see this band at nine tomorrow, her friend's in it I think. You could totally meet us there if you want to."

"Touchstone. Yeah—"

"There's probably a cover."

"Oh that's no problem. Yeah, that sounds good. I don't know if I'll like them—"

"Neither do I, man."

"Yeah." He chuckled. If he thought about it it was pretty much a false laugh; convincing though most likely, as it was automatic. "Yeah, that sounds good, man, cool. I guess I'll see you there."

"Sweet."

"Well, alright, man, I'll see you soon. Good talkin' to ya, hope you don't have too much homework this weekend."

"Oh, not too much, man."

"That's good. Well, good talkin' to ya. Have a good night."

"You too, Stanley. See you soon, man."

"Peace." Click. Click.

He was going to be the third wheel, but it likely wouldn't be an issue since they'd probably be in a crowd, listening to the band or bands, hardly able to hear anything else. To Stanley's benefit Bartholomew didn't know Stanley especially hated that bar, particularly would on a weekend night, and generally disliked going to live shows. He meant to do though what he hated to do, or thought he'd hate, and he was going to. They might be musical at least he told himself. Probably be hot girls, dancing maybe, maybe in the band. Maybe if people did dance and he worked up the will, had enough alcohol to let go enough, he'd dance too, try dancing with a girl even.

He finished the wine over the next two hours, watching a few sitcoms, muting the electric cube ubiquitous only during commercials, eating a TV dinner (corn, ribs in barbecue sauce, rubbery green beans) and two pieces of toast, continuing to hit his pipe, to smoke rollies. Eventually, after the bottle was empty, he pointed a device known as a remote at this weird futuristic device that he sacrificed so much of his time to over the years while pressing a red button that made its glow die. He switched to AM radio, to a show he'd listened to on and off more than a decade, a late-night program the main focus of which was aliens, conspiracies, the supernatural and the like. Frustratingly (two to three nights a week it seemed the topic dissatisfied him) tonight the guest talked about America/the West's age of terrorism, about the manufactured event that precipitated the new paradigm; the problem being the guest called that late summer attack the result of Islamic fundamentalists—no treasonous public sacrifice, no false flag, no ongoing deception campaign to commit the country, and others, to two illegal imperialist wars.

About three A.M., shortly before he fell asleep, BBC news coming softly from the radio at the head of his bed, not having masturbated in four days (though he wasn't horny), he jacked off mechanically, the fantasies he relied on never forming fully in his mind, did so briefly but to his overdue physical relief. And, in darkness, without first managing to turn off the radio or crack the window open as he liked to, the astral body, released on a leash, floated from the physical to recharge; a stream of disconcerting and sometimes enjoyable dreams ensued that may have spanned centuries in minutes and that would be largely forgotten on awakening—which felt like the next minute.

When he groggily, somewhat reluctantly, returned to the physical realm, feeling like he'd lost time; and he remembered moments of dream, of one, three people partially nude and engaged in sex play, all of whom looked like or were supposed to be crackheads: an overweight black woman with a mouthful of silver crowns whose eyes were unfocused and smile idiotic, skinny white trash man who pulled down his shorts and she grabbed his pecker from a forest of black pubes, fat white guy hair growing on his shoulders.

He defecated, urinating first while sitting, came out and prepared via the microwave a cup of green tea, which he then poured more sugar into than he would have liked (he discovered on tasting it), though he typically added the equivalent of three teaspoons, maybe more—he rarely used a spoon, and this was the reason he often put too much in (resulting in hot green tea-flavored sugar-water)—stirring this in with some cold water from the faucet so that it was immediately just the right temperature (due to this step never filling the cup to the brim prior to nuking it). He sat on the sofa, NPR on, drinking it slowly and smoking a cigarette, the best cigarette of the day (especially when he'd slept ten or twelve hours—which he hadn't just now, had gotten about eight). An avalanche had killed a number of military men in India. A woman had come home from work to find her Afghanistan veteran husband and their two young children shot to death in a murder-suicide. A bomb had killed nearly a score of U.S.-trained Iraqi soldiers in an insurgent attack, along with one American one. It droned: the casualties, the far-flung calamitous incidents; he was externally stimulated nearly always, but not always giving his attention to this stimuli. Why did he do this, always having the TV or the radio going or both?

It was the way he had grown up. The omnipresence of the TV even as a young child, the omnipresence of movies, of forms of entertainment electronic, as music was for the most part in the current era. And things were just going to get weirder as technology got better. Just think, the public at large was only ever supposed to know about technological advancements at least a few years old, and that technology they wouldn't find alarming, that wouldn't shatter their perceptions. (But technology (or its absence) would be used to shatter or manipulate those, and certain applications of technology by the government(s) were not be known to, recognized by the people; sometimes, often for what was thought to be the greater good, it was used on the public in ways that would be seen by most as unethical or immoral (or governments did not allow them to know of particular technology/utilizations of it for the sake of their subjects).)

After he finished his tea and smoke and without making a conscious decision to but because he was a pothead who was presently supplied (and usually was, could afford to be—but made only about an annual fourteen grand) he got stoned, really stoned. He turned off the radio, on the way back to the couch turned on the TV, with a remote turned on the digital box, grabbed the remote for the TV for adjusting the volume and placed it on the couch, and half sat half lay there flipping through the stations (which with the switch to digital had increased in number for non-cable subscribers).

He continued, for hours, watching TV, with or without the sound, or not watching it but having it on; listening to NPR or classical, or hits sixties to even the aughts; every now and then reading a paragraph to two pages from the book he was working on, more often a novel than nonfiction. The whole time he was at intervals hitting his sole pipe, which he had had for three or so years; much of the time he was thinking about alcohol, desiring some. At some point he decided that at five he would leisurely start readying himself for going out: a shower, a shave, an attire change; putting sufficient food on his stomach, brushing his teeth; and mental preparation—years past he had developed or became aware of agoraphobic (and antisocial) qualities within himself, that were now as extreme as ever.

2

He locked the door and shut it behind him, his pockets filled—though he was glad not to be wearing the black backpack he always took to work, and usually when he went to the grocery store on the other side of the thoroughfare that buzzed daily behind his building, which he was crossing presently at the crosswalk.

It was drizzling; three cars were lined up to his right waiting for him to get onto the sidewalk, and where it sloped into the street there was a small puddle when it'd been raining for hours or raining heavily. One had developed there and he avoided it as he stepped up on the curb, ceasing to legally impede the driver of a big square car from turning right, and went past a gas station beyond which to his left was the sheltered bus stop that was on the route of four city buses and his destination. The store lie beyond the stop—a few benches in a line under an oblong steel roof painted the same color—and dark figures were entering and exiting its doors and dark vehicles with bright beam eyes were going into and leaving the lot. Five figures more visible from his location waited, two of them sitting on adjacent benches, from left to right a middleaged woman who was groping in her purse and an elderly motionless man. Stanley stayed some yards from the shelter as the people accumulated there, moving to the right of the man on the bench and remaining a bit behind him (from which vantage he noted that the geriatric stooped creature's big nose had the appearance of dripping from his face); in front of him stood another man, who would stand in place a minute or two looking to the left (the direction the buses approached from), move to another spot a few feet away, glance quickly to his right and then look off in the other direction, repeating this series of actions every minute or so, impatient maybe.

A bus came, the one he was waiting for, the one of those that stopped there that took the second longest getting to where he was headed. He was taking and usually did take this bus downtown because, unlike the more direct two, if it filled up it was not until it was near its destination—and he didn't like crowded buses, crowded anything. No one but he boarded, after a solitary passenger disembarked, an old lady with a two-wheeled cart, the bus with the hiss of air expulsion across its length having been lowered for her.

He went up the steps and the driver, a blonde past her prime, looked at him a moment and said hello; he replied "hi" (the first word he'd said to anyone since getting up) as he fed dollars into the machine next to her and she handed him a piece of paper with the day and month printed on it in yellow, a pass for the rest of the day.

As was his habit when it was unoccupied he took the seat in the midpoint of the vehicle behind which was no seat and the back exit. The digital screen attached to the inner roof of the bus that cycled through time, date, and route info indicated there was a minute till the bus departed. He thought about how he didn't have a book with him so would have to pass the thirty-minute ride people-watching and looking out the large window, perhaps (he didn't think consciously) shutting his eyes for a while from time to time as he'd gotten in the habit of doing on bus rides whether he was or wasn't sleepy (and he wasn't).

Aboard, two folks that he noticed because they were seated in front of him, one either side of the aisle, were a woman who appeared to be in her sixties and asleep but not at peace, and a man maybe mid-fifties who was inaudibly muttering or appeared to be. As the bus went along and their bodies swayed with it, as it gained a patron something like every one point five stops and lost one every three, the woman seemed to intermittently and for but a second open her eyes, then lapse once more into sleep or faux-sleep, a sleep that revealed itself to be genuine (or her to be an Oscar-worthy actress) as the person-conveyor, that departed going in the direction opposite downtown, progressed on the route—for her head kept dropping, and she seemed to lift it involuntarily, not waking (which seemed to occur randomly) with eyes that from the side were perplexed and glossy.

It got there, and seemed a less lengthy trip because he knew he was heading to the sort of environment he had for much if not all of his adult life avoided; more accurately in the earlier part of that life coming to feel he wanted to avoid and learning to identify such settings, activities, people, and thereafter always doing so—except occasions when he was seeking something he thought he might find there (at such a place, by accepting an invite to do such a thing—whatever it might be), sometimes seeking what he could not name.

It arrived and he was one of the last getting off though he sat so near a door—because he made a point, as per his custom, not to shove himself in the flow of the eagerly debarking—but when he did he experienced to his surprise a brief rush of what might have been happiness, though it was a sensation almost unfamiliar and he wasn't sure; he thought maybe it was actually a surge of anxiety, which would have been explicable.

The bar he was to meet his friend at, his acquaintance, was a five-minute walk from the city's main depot for buses local, an unnoticeable place (although the site of regular debauchery) sandwiched between a specialty clothing store and an office building and closed in the day. There were three people outside The Touchstone's front door; one or more of them was smoking. One of them, a male in his early or mid twenties, expectorated; Stanley told himself to do his best not to seem apprehensive or out-of-place, to seem to enjoy being there—by, through sheer will, being at ease, an inconspicuous member of the crowd, enjoying himself. He could hear an unsoothing sort of music before he opened the bulky black-painted wooden door, a door covered in nicks and scratches. At the forward end of the hall that led into the dark zoo, pen in a zoo, where against the left wall the bar was visible and he could see a strobe was moving, was a heavy bouncer sitting on a stool checking IDs and taking money. Stanley's was inspected and the cover, five dollars, handed over and he went past, on to whatever experience awaited, as a man passed leaving; Stanley, having a decent amount of money on him for drinking all night and whatever, decided to go straight to the very crowded bar before looking for Bartholomew—the noise of music and many people mixed was blaring—and order a drink, an endeavor he expected to take a minimum of three minutes. When finally he had squeezed himself up to the bar and the bartender, a tattooed musclebound type, got around to him he said, "I'll have an IPA please." After paying and receiving change he took a sip—enjoying the bitter taste of alcohol, the first he'd had all day, later in the day than usual—and got immediately out of the especially dense pack at and near the bar, got off to the side a bit and looked into the crowd, some dancing, filling a large area terminating in the stage most were facing. He glanced at the band up there and saw a trio in tight pants and torn tees, two males, one female, all sweaty. The strobe above searched aimlessly, up, down and around. He didn't know exactly what time it was but knew the bus had gotten in about fifteen minutes till and so it was probably nine or nearly, so Stanley began searching the faces, the frames, for ones matching Bartholomew's. He thought it'd take a while, despite the young man's being six-three, but he spotted him shortly, about simultaneous to the music ceasing with an electric echo and one of the twiggy male young adults saying thanks in a microphone, after which the ensemble he was a part of gathered some things from the stage. The beam had passed over the side of his face visible to Stanley as he looked at the man from five or six yards, across part of the lower sea that presently seemed to be dispersing in all directions, some of whom held drinks; there were tables about behind and to the left of him that were filled like the floor, drinks spotting them. Bartholomew moved closer to his position, a girl beside him much shorter, more than a foot he was thinking as he got over to them. She was petite, her hair was a white-leaning blonde (unbeknownst to him given the light it was pink-tipped, dark roots showing). His friend—acquaintance really—spotted and greeted him seeming happy to see him (though Stanley wondered, for no reason other than that they perhaps weren't full-fledged friends, if in actuality he was ambivalent about his arrival). He introduced his girlfriend, whose name was Shelly; Stanley had to put his ear near to Bartholomew's head to hear him. Bartholomew's head was topped by black hair partly dyed green and presently spiked; he wore a necklace of silvery objects interspersed with what appeared to be teeth; there was a silver spike through his lower lip, a stud in a nostril, a ring in an eyebrow. "How long you guys been here?" "Twenty or fifteen minutes," answered Bartholomew. "You just get here?" "Yeah, pretty much. Did you like that band that was just on?" Stanley asked him, or them. They were moving toward the bar, Stanley doing a lot of people-circumventing, especially conscious of the pint glass he held, the beer within which had been drunk down to such a level he felt it would not splash over were he lightly bumped. "They were okay," he replied. "Not really," said Shelly. "Nothing special," said Bartholomew. "It's a disharmonious kind of music but they didn't do it very well." Stanley sincerely laughed; they were in the crush, of many colors all dimmed, about the bar. A short stocky seemingly drunk guy as he left the bar bumped Stanley's shoulder, the one descending to the hand holding the dark brown brew, with force enough to cause the latter's ire to drowsily open its eyes, but his beer experienced a spill-less tsunami, and soon Bartholomew was ordering a Jim shot for himself and his girl; Stanley, helped next, decided to follow their lead, and the three took them simultaneously, back-less, facing a wall of liquor bottles and pressed by a vocal swarm against an oblong polished-wood protrusion, behind which was also a bustling burly biped. It went down smooth, Stanley savored the taste; he'd considered ordering also another IPA, feeling mildly, expectedly, uncomfortable, but refrained— and when he'd had the shot felt better and buzzed, and glad he'd not ordered a beer too, especially since he was sure to go back forthwith to the swarming crowd filling the dance space facing the stage, the crowd which was growing dense again. They were headed back into it smacking their whiskey lips, a short woman sandwiched by tall men, as a number of young ladies of the modern-cool sort came on leisurely from audience right, one in an above-the-knee flower-print skirt, one in form-fitting pants of black leather, another baggy cargo pants worn low on revealed hips, the other in corduroy bell-bottoms; all of them doing grunge but clean-looking, the wardrobes seeming the opposite of spontaneous. "That's them. I want to get closer," said Shelly, and they followed her single-file as she bore into the pack, Stanley thinking he wanted a cigarette, his head filled with an electric hum, the vocalizations of the pack. The woman in corduroy—her hair straight, black or dark brown and choppily cut, bunches different lengths restrained by elastic, the longest of it shorter than shoulder-length, her upper half garbed in an unbuttoned suede vest over an aquamarine sports bra—came confidently to the mic and enunciated "We're the Cunk Rock Punts." She pivoted and took a Y-shaped white guitar hooked to an amplifier from a stand stage left, returned to the elevated bulb of the microphone. On the other side of the platform was the girl in the skirt, attractive like all of them, wearing a bass, and behind the bassist and guitarist sat the operators of a synthesizer and a drum set electronic. But most attractive to him, magnetizing immediately, was the frontman, the one with dark eyes like tractor beams and vacuums who was now strumming with intensity, the only one on whose face no makeup was discernible, the mic and stand splitting her fit figure, guitar hiding her midriff. The drummer bounced on her stool behind an arrangement of assorted-sized black saucers, the bass player contorted soulfully to her part, the music was competent though unmemorable and not to his taste, but the charismatic choppy-haired vocalist, who had begun to sing (in a manner that probably didn't suit her voice's strengths), had Stanley uncharacteristically captivated. Without choosing to he took in each motion, nuance, as best he could, as if they were an extension of his consciousness too, if only because his consciousness was unasked so attuned to these. He was in a dream of abstract sex with a somewhat unlikely other, unexpectedly, his pupils enlarged by her presence, the fact of his being able to see her. And he felt suddenly stupid, strange, self-conscious, felt the fool again, old-young unwanted Stanley. Overwhelmed by an entity as good as make-believe, good as a nonentity—a glimpse of the desirable unobtainable by a sad neurotic fuck.

In her performance, this separated phantom, she was attention-drawing he was sure, that was a part of it. She was full of energy, even passion; was damn talented. To him she seemed the embodiment of perfection even from the distance, was, across a gulf, natural as the sea and as hypnotizing.

They did three numbers; during the last she called to Stanley's mind a female, differently styled Maynard James Keenan. After this final harsh but poetic song, as the musicians gradually toted off their equipment, the trio headed toward the bar with a crush of others mostly perspiring and half or fully (as they said in Hemingway's day) tight, a lot of typically attired women and men primarily twenty-one to twenty-four. "I liked them," said Stanley. "I like them too. My friend's the drummer," said Shelly. When it came time for them to order Bartholomew conferred with her before requesting another two shots of the previous, handing a Hamilton; Stanley after a moment's deliberation took the same, and he felt the after-sting with a removed self-destructive happiness.

And soon after he wanted a cigarette, badly. He heard Bartholomew say, "I'm kind of getting tired of the bands, babe, how 'bout you?" and Shelly say, "Yeah...I'm getting tired of standing more than anything, but I want to wait and meet up with Chelsie. I'll text her." The three stood to the side of the bar, Bartholomew's arms akimbo, facing but not really looking at a many-visaged conglomerate, components of which were ever moving to and from the source of drink. Stanley saw a portly guy go past in the direction of strong beverages who had long sideburns and a bald head; another, coming from the entrance, only slightly more hair, who wore a bulky emblem on a chain that swung pendulum-like, Stanley thought hazardously. "I can't see in here," said Shelly, cell in hand. Stanley followed them outside, immediately lighting up a pre-rolled smoke he extracted from his paper pouch of tobacco; they positioned themselves before the façade of the specialty shop, Bartholomew smoking a Crush (crush the filter for menthol); five or six people, all males, were speaking loudly in front of the bar, inebriated-seeming; there was dried vomit low on the far end of the shop wall, sort of a tan color.

After a few minutes, during which Stanley maximally enjoyed his long-longed for cigarette, Shelly said: "Chelsie's gonna meet us outside." It was another few minutes, Bartholomew and Shelly talking about recent events and pressing issues in their shared lives (Stanley heard them but did not, could hardly have listened), and then emerged from the din, the unnaturally lit darkness, a cute blonde with dreads in an unzipped hoodie over a top that just reached her navel, leaving a sexy portion of midsection visible above cargo pants—and behind her was the woman Stanley's interest had been so strangely piqued by (and he didn't think it was because of her crazy hair, which looked good—she looked good); they made immediate eye contact that caused Stanley to avert his eyes, but not quickly (for despite this reaction he felt his eyes being held and he wanted to continue looking), and his throat to feel constricted. He at once inwardly cursed himself for yet again breaking eye contact, when he would have preferred the message of maintaining it, and despite his efforts in a matter of seconds.

These women were introduced to Stanley without any hands being extended and then Hope lit a cigarette. The five stood outside the bar, the women doing most of the talking. He felt a bit awkward or aimless, he didn't want to stand too close to everyone or too far; Bartholomew just stared, it seemed, at his girlfriend; Stanley found opportunity to insert something into the women's conversation every once in a while, trying not to look at Hope any more than he did anyone else...but he unconsciously tracked her right hand to her mouth...she took a drag and he was thinking about and looking at her lips—and then she was looking at him and their eye contact compelled him to say to her, to say something, since they were talking about bands he hadn't heard of, "I don't really listen to much new stuff, like last couple years new."

"I don't either exactly," said Chelsie. Hope had smiled.

"My musical knowledge, or horizons, are pretty limited. I need to hang out more often with people who know more about music, like you guys. Take notes or something," he said to her. She chuckled, falsely or emptily he thought.

"I need to hang out more," he added.

"I don't hang out much except over the summer," said Chelsie. "School."

"I pop into bars fairly often," said Hope.

"I definitely do a fair amount of drinking," Stanley said.

"Don't we all," said Shelly.

"What do you prefer—" he queried Hope, surprising himself mildly while thinking that what he was saying, or how he was saying it, was somehow stupid (feeling self-conscious), "wine, liquor...?"

"I just try not to mix them," she said, her demeanor he speculated, since Stanley hadn't consumed enough alcohol to quell his anxiety, gradually putting him at ease.

"Of late I've been drinking a lot of wine."

"I like wine. I also like sake," she said.

"Oh—so do I," he said, happy to be conversing with her and pleased to learn she was also a fan of rice wine. "Sushi?"

"Are you asking me out?" she said smiling. Simultaneously they burst briefly into laughter, Hope revealing an upper row of healthy teeth. (For a moment he very vividly imagined himself sexually engaged with her. He was standing, wearing a Hawaiian shirt, his forehead beaded with sweat; she was wearing a low-cut blouse, a skirt hiked up to her hips. Her panties were on the floor at their feet, her legs wrapped around his back, her mouth next to his left ear, her vocalizations of pleasure increasing the intensity of his desire, his own pleasure; her body glistened with perspiration, smelled mildly of perfume. They seemed to be in a small space, like a booth or closet.)

A group of three, youngish males clad in dark clothing, exited the bar, passed between them. The night was going well, better than he'd expected (though he'd had no positive expectations). He interpreted in eye contact with Chelsie that he was getting along with Hope, maybe that he'd been deemed normal, been accepted by them—but, he thought, this was in his mind: he was, in truth, crazy (crazy, sad animal. Pathetic man-boy who wanted to feel like a full man, whatever it meant; to embody or convincingly portray a vague idea. Neurotic tightly wrapped sonuvabitch desperately needing releases plural. What was he? An animal in a shirt, constantly containing its animality). He'd make a bit of conversation, he was already successfully doing so, despite his not being the best in social situations. He'd get to know them a little; especially, he hoped, the unusually sexy intriguing one. It was good exercise if nothing else—the needed exercise of his ability to meet and communicate (well) with new people, to get along with them; to go out with people even if he didn't know any of them and do things and go places he didn't often or never had, maybe didn't like doing (or just didn't think he did or would); to be natural in, perhaps even enjoy doing such activities.

He felt, for the first time in quite a long time, invigorated. He was somehow, suspected Stanley, invigorated by Hope, by possibility. Life, he seemed to be remembering, was full of possibility, even his—that of a man crushed over years by himself, society.

A burlyish fellow, comparably aged, came out of the front, immediately greeting Bartholomew and putting his hand up for a high-five; it was a guy who worked in the bar, a guy of a sort (like most he encountered among peers) that he immediately guessed he had little in common with, liked sports. The most popular sport in the area, due to the successful local team, seemed to be college football. Stanley had tried to understand football for a while, some years earlier, and made strides, but was never able to be excited by it, to care about who won. This guy, he thought, was probably a fan of the local team; and then he wondered, is he Bart's real friend, or the friendly-when-paths-cross kind? But did it matter? Bart wasn't his real friend—and what was his definition anyway? Maybe it was mostly about time known and time spent together.

"I just got off a little bit ago," the probable sports fan was saying to Bartholomew.

"How do you like working in a zoo like this?" Stanley heard in his head, followed by a confident but crazy-sounding laugh, then considered what might have been the effect of actually vocalizing this while the guy talked, then looked at Hope who, fuck, made immediate eye contact with him (sexily, or her eyes were just sexy). The guy, garbed in a t-shirt in the chilly evening, was smoking a cigarette he held overhand. He thought, though he didn't want to, *I hate his haircut. I hate the way he holds his cigarette.* The haircut was a crew cut, the dialogue between he and Bartholomew he could not concentrate on. He wasn't trying hard enough, didn't want to.

It was an eternity, felt like it, and then Stanley became conscious of a change in the group's demeanor, the group he was a part of but, as usual, felt somehow removed from. The bartender or bouncer had just invited them all to his house to continue drinking.

Stanley, a bit surprised, was especially averse to going until he heard Hope say, "Okay. Sure," and then he was compelled to, in fact genuinely wanted to, and Bartholomew and Shelly were going to. And also-cute Chelsie had been included in the invite, but she had declined (something about her boyfriend), which meant that Hope would perhaps only really have Shelly to talk to—and maybe Stanley. And perhaps Hope, despite her societal attractiveness, was single, as Stanley had an inkling she was. And maybe—if for the time being he could convince himself he had a shot with her, and he made conversation with her—he actually would have a chance.

The dude had asked if anyone needed a ride and Bartholomew had said he and Shelly would; he then asked Hope specifically, with what Stanley read as lust in his eyes.

"My car's here," she responded.

"I'd need a ride too," said Stanley.

"I've still got room," the guy said.

"There's room in mine too," said Hope.

"Well, yours'll be less full," he said to her.

"Cool. I need to drop Chelsie off first, hope you don't mind." Then to the inviter she said, "If you give me your address I can find it."

"It's 340 James Street. It's a big blue house and my big black SUV'll be in the driveway. Do you need directions?"

"It's on this side of town. No, I can find it. Okay. I should be there pretty soon, Chelse doesn't live very far." To Stanley: "My car's around back." To the others: "See you guys there."

"Bye," said Chelsie as the two turned to go.

"See you guys," said Stanley as he started to follow them.

They crossed the street, Stanley walking behind the women trying not to stare at their asses. But hot as they both were—and maybe it was mainly because Hope's pants were tight above the knee—he couldn't keep his eyes from returning again and again to the tight buttocks of on the left the brunette he'd immediately fixated on, admiring its shape and the way it moved, a slight side-to-side motion, as she walked. A guy, early or mid twenties, approached on Stanley's left crossing from the other side, a guy who walked exaggeratedly, like a thug, legs wide apart, a posturer, clad in attire black and boots clunky, steel-toed. A short man mentally underdeveloped, likely negligibly dangerous (if so because more ego-ruled animal than mature man). He passed close to Hope who turned her head and saw Stanley, internally irked, move inches to the right to avoid him.

"You shouldn't have done that," said Hope.

"Huh?" said Stanley, fairly sure he knew what she was referring to.

"He had the whole street. You shouldn't have adjusted your course. He moved into yours."

"You're right. He looked at me, it wasn't not paying attention, which would have been very unobservant. It just would have caused a problem though. Because he wouldn't have moved."

"He was asking for a problem by getting in your way for no reason." They got into the car, Stanley in back.

"That's true. But I try to avoid fights, altercations—with idiots without courtesy, who are intentionally rude. I'm quite accustomed to them. I'd be getting in fights all the time." Seatbelts were stretched, snapped secure.

"I'm accustomed to shitty people too. You should stand your ground sometimes though. And if that results in a fight—fight." She looked back at him, then turned her attention to the matter of maneuvering.

"Easier said than done. Actions have consequences."

"He showed a lack of respect for you. Which is a good reason to stand up for yourself. Besides...I bet you'd fight him if we promised to fuck your brains out."

The girls looked at each other smiling; Chelsie giggled, glanced back. Stanley immediately had an erection, hot against one leg.

The car came to a stop at a signal glowing red above them in the night, one car motionless in front of Hope's blue-gray beater.

3

Hope parked her vehicle in the driveway of what was indeed a large blue house, two stories, and she and Stanley, the former's friend having been taken home, emerged from the auto and headed for the artificially illuminated front door. Music blared inside, hip-hop, a genre Stanley liked plenty of but not what he was hearing (the volume seeming to amplify his feeling of being out-of-place and also excitement). If he had more to drink he would feel better. He wished he were closer friends with Bartholomew. How was he here? No—why? There were, thankfully, plenty of beers and not that many people really, thirteen in total, three of whom were sexy young women (two of them in skirts). He moved to the kitchen and grabbed two brown bottles of umber ale from the counter, saying hi as he walked out to a guy with a trimmed red beard who was walking in. Stanley handed Hope one of the beers and they, Bartholomew and Shelly sat on one of three large expensive-looking couches in the living room, the one facing a gigantic flatscreen television—Hope's leg, thigh in contact with his own. The bar employee guy (Aaron apparently) he might not have been much akin to (he was a gamer, worked out daily, was a sports fan, was trained in a martial art, probably wasn't much of a reader...), but the variety of the guests, some of whom were perhaps his housemates, surprised Stanley slightly, and he found himself in conversation with a few of them, including the bearded redhead, aided by his gradually declining inhibition. The bouncer or bartender guy was a drug person judging from the large quantity of cocaine and weed he saw (Stanley speculated he may have been a seller), the latter of which he abstained from. But the blow got going round by the time Stanley had had two of the ales and he partook each time, and the guy, Aaron, had said it was really pure, and it felt it, and everything was faster, what the strangers sitting and standing around said more interesting—Stanley continued to down beers, began going through them in short time, was starting to feel he was being overindulgent (but could hardly bring himself to care)—and the bar employee, if it was all his coke, was far from stingy with it (no money changing hands), maybe because of the good-looking ladies.

They inhaled the blow off a big mirror using a rolled-up President Grant. They moved on to green bottles of Rolling Rock when the beer in the brown bottles, which there had been a few cases of, ran out. By this point Stanley was drinking quickly, nonstop, feeling each was hardly having an effect after four thick lines; feeling perfect despite not being particularly interested in anyone other than Hope, or at least not very engaged by the subjects of their chatter (but then Stanley generally wasn't big on conversation). But maybe he found the conversation uninteresting mostly because he did not relate, could hardly have constructively participated in it.

It had been ninety minutes or two hours. Bartholomew and Shelly appeared to be considerably high, their eyes bloodshot. Hope, who seemed happy, did not look high however, although she must have been. She blended in effortlessly. She and Shelly, perhaps just Hope, were like magnets. It slowly grew annoying how much everyone—except Hope and (especially) Stanley—was talking.

Presently Stanley felt a heightened sense of his social/conversational noncontribution; also, slowly, he'd started feeling not that he wasn't a part of the group but that he didn't want to be.

But then again the music had changed to techno, more than just tolerable since he was so wired. And though he cared little he did care that the music, and the coke, the alcohol, had seemed to inspire some of the ladies to start dancing in the middle of the room, joined in minutes by Hope. And then someone turned the overhead lights off and some others on and brightly colored beams probed the space, allowing Stanley to watch the women with undetectable licentiousness. And he thought about the fact, as he admired feminine contours, that his mood had shifted again within a short time, a bit surprised and very high and excited in a way that was only partly sexual. He didn't think he was feeling the beer, consumed in copious quantity and which he continued to drink at a slackening pace. It was as if all the other girls were in the background and Hope under a spotlight, yet the others (and doubtless the coke) seemed to serve to heighten Hope's desirability, or sexuality. The way she moved was controlled yet natural, as natural as her haircut and attire, although he couldn't imagine feeling that way about another with the same cut, in the same clothes. It wasn't long before Bartholomew was looking comatose, a part of the furniture they sat on, and some stocky dude with a shaven crown was doing magic tricks in front of them; and the Rolling Rock was gone; and Hope said she wanted to take off—and asked Stanley if he wanted to come with her, causing him to feel like his heart was thumping out of his chest and to wonder seriously if he was dreaming (as he felt his dick moving as he said yes independent of thought, of being present, as he experienced the sensation of floating a bit above his body).

But was she only going to take him home? It occurred to him this was a possibility; after all, she'd brought him. Though no, his impression was that she'd been inviting him to go home with her, or to wherever she was going.

4

He'd asked her if she was fine to drive and she'd said she felt pretty alert due to the premium blow and so they'd said goodbye and gotten in her old beater and in no time (Stanley was outside of time) they were pulling into the parking lot of her apartment building, and his heart got to thumping again, more palpably than before.

Her unit was number 4, on the ground floor. He walked just behind her, again attempting and failing to not look repeatedly at her perfect posterior as he did.

By this point his initial shock, and arousal, due to the invite had subsided and he was thinking *Realistically she's not going to sleep with me. Even if for some reason she would, or is attracted to me anyway, she's not going to sleep with me tonight, hours after meeting me.*

The place was messy. About what he expected. He was one of the tidiest people he knew. Even undergarments, sexy ones (pink polka-dotted panties, a lacy blue bra), lay on the living room floor, oddly (to Stanley, who was aware of the thought just on the border of consciousness) causing Stanley to think his chances of sleeping with her—if not that night in general—were remotely better. The mess—giving him the impression that a number of quite different people lived there or a person with very eclectic tastes/interests—was of a random sort (some of the randomness trash, utensils, attire): music/movies, knickknacks, posters, antiques, art—a hodgepodge more than pop cultural, in every room miscellany (Hope gave him the brief tour, then changed). Despite her having mentioned she had a roommate the place was only a one-bedroom, a reasonably spacious one, the roommate (apartmentmate) sleeping on the couch in the living room, in which room were the signs (though Hope hadn't indicated) the absent occupant was male.

The blue bra had also caused him to think about her underwear; about the fact that she wore, not necessarily exclusively, sexy underwear. As they talked about the music they liked—a varied selection, from pop to death metal to classic to tribal—she seeming (unsurprisingly to him) more knowledgeable on the subject—he was thinking less about the music that she liked (finding—also to his lack of surprise—that their tastes there were largely the same, only she was familiar with more musicians) than about the quite unanticipated notion that this beautiful, apparently (strangely) available young woman, maybe twenty-five, was interested in him, *him*; why? All signs pointed to that conclusion. And this comparably-aged, confident, interesting—magnetizing—single woman was not only arousingly attractive but he was developing the idea that they had a lot in common, anyway on a level that could form the basis of a friendship (though it was a sexual relationship he was the most interested in being in with her).

She offered and he accepted a cold beer. Her fridge was stocked with these, and there was an assortment of magnets splayed on it. They drank their beers standing in the kitchen.

"So how long have you played with the Cunk Rock Punts?"

"About three and a half months. Did you like us?"

"Yes, very much so. In fact it was a pleasure just to watch you."

"Oh, thanks."

"I loved the music," said Stanley, feeling he shouldn't have said the last sentence.

"It's just a hobby." After a moment: "Among others."

"I wonder, are you anything of a renaissance woman? If the apartment's accoutrement are any indication it seems you're a collector too at least."

"All that stuff's mine. Yeah, I guess I'm something of a collector. They're just things I've accumulated over the years. And the weird abstract paintings I did myself. Hey...do you work tomorrow? Do you wanna split an eighth of shrooms with me?" She made a dramatized gesture toward the refrigerator. "Besides brews there's orange juice in there."

"Oh shit. Damn. I'd definitely like to. I don't work tomorrow, but...I don't know how I'm going to get home. I don't live close."

Said Hope, much to Stanley's delight, "My apartmentmate isn't here tonight. Not that it matters. He's out doing something strange, committing crimes, burning someone's housecat; I don't know what he gets up to. You can definitely stay. I mean, we're going to be tripping balls for hours, if you want to."

"Well. Shit—that's awesome. My place's on the other side of town. And I'm a ways from sober. Yes, I want to. Yeah. Of course." She moved to the fridge.

"It's weird, unusual, just randomly meeting someone, someone cool, who you end up doing shrooms with the same night."

"*Life* is cool that way. From time to time. Depending on oneself."

Stanley—who could hardly believe the way the night had turned out, was turning out; who almost thought he was dreaming the domicile he stood in and the woman across from him; whose self-esteem was below par and who, he thought, even women unattractive to him weren't attracted to (anymore)—stood, as a portion of hallucinogenic fungi was placed on the counter in front of him, ruminating on the possibility that, inexplicably, the absurdly hot girl not a yard away from him was interested in him, or anyway might sleep with him.

He was happy, unexpectedly even ineffably happy. Clearly, he said to himself, all the serendipitous surprises of his life were not behind him, joy was not an emotion exclusively of his past.

5

Sitting on her beat-up sofa as she channel-surfed, Hope eventually sticking with a nineties comedy-drama starring Robert Downey Jr. as a reluctant redeemer of souls, the duo had waited to begin to feel the effects of the mushrooms washed down with chill citrus libations that forty-five minutes later were beginning to kick in.

"This movie just became...more engrossing. At least visually."

"I've been kinda zoned out for a while," said Hope. She looked about the room cursorily. "Everything's become more interesting visually."

"Including you."

"Ha."

"You've got some interesting stuff in here. Your apartment's cool. Cool apartment."

"Thanks man." She giggled.

"Do you shroom very often?"

"Now and then."

"How old were you when you started playing guitar?"

"Sixteen. Kind of old really. It's just a hobby though."

"You're excellent. Even if you were otherwise totally uncool you're a talented musician. It's awesome that you're way cool period."

She laughed, looking at him.

"I feel like I have mouth diarrhea all of a sudden."

On TV the screen was filled by the pink flower petals of an

antidepressant advertisement.

"That didn't sound right."

"I know what you mean. Happens to me."

"Where have you been all my life? How long have you lived in Oswald?"

"I've lived here for a little over two years," she said, Stanley subconsciously thinking of the smile still on her lips, feeling so close to her—other than physically—that it was as if incrementally, wonderfully, they were melding into one another (which was his highest desire, the coalescence of yin and yang). "I've lived in this apartment for six months or so."

"I like what you've done with the place. There's a lot to look at."

Stanley's eyes inadvertently found a porcelain elephant in a pink tutu mid-pirouette; it stood on a wooden shelf, the third from the bottom shelf of a bookcase the tiers of which were occupied by small objects Hope had accumulated over the years.

"I like to shop at thrift stores," said Hope beaming, eyes twinkling, her body turned toward him now. One knee (she had changed and, hairless, it was visible through the hole in her worn jeans) was on the couch and Stanley was adjusting the language of his own bodily positioning to hers as he said—as before, joyful—"I like thrift stores too. A lot."

A phony-smiling dentally-perfect actor in a Colgate commercial penetrated his consciousness via his peripheral vision.

"I like antique stores a lot also."

"I was just going to say that," said Stanley.

"I hate to ask but...would you mind turning the TV off? Unfortunately the ads are seriously harshing my mellow."

"I was just going to say—I can't handle these commercials."

She reached for the remote; the appliance became a black screen.

"Thanks."

They sat there looking at each other.

"I like that you're the kind of person who can sit in silence with someone and not feel awkward."

"I feel the same way, stranger."

"Your eyes are amazing."

"Thank you. You have nice eyes too."

"Thank you, stranger."

She giggled in a way Stanley found sexy and enigmatic.

"What an unpredictable night. I feel like a million dollars. I guess my life hasn't turned out so bad after all."

"It's a journey not a destination."

"And what happens while you're making other plans."

Both chuckled. He was sitting next to, in the apartment of, a presumably single, comparably aged woman with a perfect body, a woman who was probably more intelligent and more interesting than he was, or most of the girls he lusted after that he saw fleetingly on the street, in the bars; or year-round at work. He had a serious chance with her, right then, and he was really there; and his mind was going a mile a minute yet he was in a state of supreme serenity.

"Who do you prefer," he asked, "the Stones or The Beatles?"

"Oh, The Beatles. Definitely. You?"

"Absolutely."

"So would you characterize yourself as a renascence fellow?"

"I don't know if I'd go that far. I write. I bet you do too."

"I'm a dabbler. A merry dabbler, small and sweet."

"Ha. Are you much of a foreign film fan?"

"Only squares aren't," she laughed. "You know strange birds like me like a lot of things."

"I'm...gradually beginning to realize I am occupying a different than usual dimension of consciousness at the moment."

"Model airplanes and modern art. Kombucha and Big Macs. Exhibitionism and violence."

"What?"

"Exhibitions and science. You're cute," she said leaning toward him slowly, then kissing him wetly on the lips, hers soft, as ideal as everything about her. (Explosion, dopamine flood, conceptualized mind sparks.)

The seratonin pounded in his brain; an overdose of it, the

moment of the kiss (the fact of it), whatever would come next, he thought were maybe going to kill him.

"*You* kissed *me*."

Their faces were a few inches apart, his olfactory organ intaking her perfume; in the quiet room with off-white walls a cheery dwarf looked on lifeless.

"Yeah." Her bare knee was against his thigh. His body felt light; it was a sensation like disconnecting from it.

"That...makes this all less fathomable."

"All what?" She kissed him again. "You and me and my apartment? That I find you attractive?"

"That. The first part. Am I sweating?"

"Not that I can tell."

"I probably shouldn't be asking you this now but, how long has it been since you were in a relationship? It's...difficult to believe you would be single for very long. Unless you wanted to be."

"Oh, it's been four or five months. They're not really my bag. I'm not too good at them anyway."

"Me neither. But maybe I didn't put forth my best efforts. I feel lightheaded. And warm. And," Hope moved in, kissing him a bit longer, one of her firm breasts against his chest, "I love it when you kiss me. And...to say I'm attracted to you is a gross understatement."

Stanley ripped off his sweatshirt and kissed her, putting his tongue into her mouth where it collided with hers.

As they frenched ferociously he put a hand on one of her firm breasts, pressing her into a corner of the couch. Squeezing her left mamma he broke off to kiss her neck and ear, clavicle, then went back to her mouth.

Hope and he stood, connected via suction, she moving toward the bedroom, guiding him while walking backwards. The floor was covered with clothes. They fell, he on top of her, onto the bed, which creaked.

With a swift motion he pulled her t-shirt over her head; she threw it aside. The tops of her C-cups were visible above a white bra.

He removed his top with one motion of his left hand while Hope unhooked her plain brassiere, revealing breasts anything but. Stunned a few moments by their extraordinariness, the perfection of their shape, of the pink nipples, by their tautness, he gripped the left one with his right hand.

In a matter of seconds more he become conscious of the fact that he was in a lucid trance of ecstasy, pure, true (if drug-tinged)—and that a throbbing erection was pushing forward the front of his pants.

6

Stanley remained at the job he'd had the majority of his adulthood for only about three more weeks. He didn't quit, just stopped going. (On the final day of his employment at his silly telephone research vocation of over a half-decade—a long-anticipated day—he noticed on the wall of the men's room at his depressing workplace (brown outside, gray inside), above the urinal, someone had written messily in pen:

PEOPLE = SHIT
HUMAN = TRASH
LIFE = DEATH

He had been reminded that a number of months earlier on the same spot—sloppily, shakily—a seemingly different hand had written the soon painted over prose

> fat whore
> likes food)

It was much too quickly, Stanley knew it, but Hope had become, really almost immediately, the only part of his life he truly cared about, and a part of his life he cared about to what if he were to reflect on it he might characterize as an infinite degree.

Even self-preservation he had become less heedful of, had stopped caring about in the same way he basically always had; now, subconsciously, being with Hope was the reason he wanted to live. (If anything because she was in his life he actually cared about being, about staying alive more, even if he was less proactive about his own welfare than he had been.) *After all*, he said just below his perception, *what was left to desire with a woman like her? What else was there to care about?*

One night, while she was fairly sober, Hope (the human specimen of no physical parallel, who gave him the impression of being eerily wise but who he yet barely knew; who for Stanley fulfilled something deep inside him—had brought him a fulfillment which, currently expanding, developing a life of its own, produced joy in him, a response he had been worried he might have become incapable of feeling and that he'd felt certain he would experience very rarely in his future) randomly offered to support him, urged him to let her. Strangely. And so that was that.

Later, as Hope drank red wine and Stanley domestic beer, they had watched a French movie from the sixties, a film about a relationship of slow-building tension. Then they migrated to the bedroom where they had sex that was (in his opinion) as good as sex could be—twice—Stanley, disappointingly to him, not lasting more than a few minutes the first time. (So far he generally finished too quickly with her. But she was so sexy—unbelievably for a guy with no substantial bankroll, no bankroll at all; with average good looks at best; no surplus of charisma or other traits women seemed to gravitate to—and they'd been together less than a week, had had intercourse at most fifteen times.)

And he woke the next morning with his arm around still sleeping Hope (clad in a tank top and panties) feeling like a man, like a success, like he was living out the best days of his life—the end of those days not in sight, if he and Hope stayed together he thought never to arrive.

7

Hope's offer—to essentially be his support system—had come only five or six days into their relationship, which, though neither had discussed commitment, had basically begun the first night; the night they'd first copulated, in a dream realm that was tangible reality (ego-gratifying, fantasy-fulfilling), psychedelic-altered, at its best. Thirteen days later he failed to show up for a scheduled shift, and moved, with his relatively meager possessions, into Hope's.

What made the offer (of the new girlfriend of one Stanley Northrop—lately feeling better about himself, life) stranger was that to his knowledge her only source of income was from working twenty or so hours a week at a restaurant in town. To have spending money without having to ask Hope for it, which unfailingly made him feel guilty (besides the fact he didn't feel like she could really afford to just give him money), he asked her apartmentmate Troy if he could join him in selling weed, and he unhesitatingly said yes.

Troy was a veteran who had served in Iraq as part of the fallacious 'war on terror.' He had nearly died there and some of his friends had not been so lucky, either being visited by the grim reaper or sustaining severe injury. He was diagnosed with PTSD, sent home. His massive rat habitat was located in the living room—when Troy wasn't around and Stanley was trying to fall asleep on the couch, having had a lot to drink and/or a lot of coke the previous night, knowing he'd be recovering or sleeping all day (or needing to), the sound of them scurrying and squeaking often kept him from doing so—and Troy spent hours watching them, learning rat society. (He once told Stanley he liked theirs more than human society. "For me it's like watching TV, but more engrossing and rewarding.")

Stanley wondered whether Hope had ever slept with him, but never asked her. He was a musclebound fellow, had a prominent facial scar (jagged, ugly), was approximately Stanley's age, and knew a lot about weapons, combat, survival. He once referred to himself as a pornography addict, talked often of suicide and homicide, and on one occasion since occupying the apartment, sober he said, intimated he'd seen spider-like creatures ascending the walls, each with a single-digit number for a body. Troy also frequently spoke of government conspiracy theories (as Stanley he knew that 3/27, as presented to the public, was a fabrication) and went on long middle-of-the-night walks and week-long meth binges. "There's an evil, insane little voice, little man in my head that won't ever shut up," he told Stanley not long after they met. "It's always saying the worst things—things that don't come from me; that I think don't, hope don't—usually over and over, at the most inopportune times. It really stresses me."

He was also writing (or attempting to write, or wanted to write) a bizarre novel centering around a charismatic, comical, but socially awkward man-boy—Russ, age twenty-two—who lived with his wealthy parents (distant to him and each other) in their mansion and who was possibly an idiot (potentially even a genius who had all along been putting on an act—for whatever reasons), whose father was obsessed with a network of large tents turned into mini greenhouses behind the mansion that were filled with an array of well-tended plants.

In fact it turned out he had a great many projects planned, the bulk of them literary, and most of them apparently entirely existent in his scrambled skull... A novella about a microscopic organism of extraterrestrial origin that grew to an ever-larger vibrating, chirping mud-like mass from feeding on not human bodies but human souls, which it had the power to vacuum free of bodies; an hour-long one-man play (to be performed by Troy only) that sounded like the unreliable recollection of a bad acid trip in a Middle Eastern desert; a screenplay about the specter-haunted, worse-for-wear longtime occupants of a moldering hotel in downtown Los Angeles that maybe wasn't real; a short story he said he'd recently begun about a friendless recluse, twenty-fivish, who had the nasty habit of masturbating and wiping his semen on public objects, who graduates to smearing it on pedestrians at random, being dubbed by the media The Sperm Slimer...and he could go on and on, perhaps inventing it all as he spoke (his eyes glistening, animated—magnetic, disquieting).

—◦《◉》◦—

"Can I give you one of my stories to read and get your opinion on? It's super short," he one day asked Stanley.

"I'm not really a critic," the other man said, thinking "God no."

"You don't have to be. Besides, you told me you dabble in writing too. That makes your opinion more worthwhile than a critic's." He was already proffering him a stapled story.

"Sure. I'll tell you what I think," said Stanley, taking it with concealed reluctance. "As long as I don't have a deadline for reading it."

"No. No deadline, man."

As he placed it on the sofa beside him Stanley saw the piece was titled *Unicorn in the Ice* and on the inside laughed heartily, derisively, not realizing the work of fiction was a comedy. Its plot: a cyborg unicorn is found at the North Pole a hundred-some feet underground and in suspended animation by biologist-archaeologist-adventurer-womanizer Jameson Holtz—tan, fit, thirty-six. The awakened unicorn turns out to be named Emmek, two hundred-three years old, and a refugee from world-at-war Tmicc. Located in a neighboring galaxy, its civilization millennia more advanced, Tmicc is the site of a 160,000-year battle for planetary domination between its invaders—a hairy dwarf-like race with oversized feet, hands, ears and noses; an unpleasantly disposed and rather bellicose race comprised of clever and well-trained warriors—and the autochthonous cyborg unicorns. The unicorns are outmatched by the dwarf species, the Uwlo, which come (in endless waves) from the planet Uupoy, located in a star system bordering that of Tmicc. They therefore long ago sent craft in all directions in search of lifeforms that might aid them in liberating themselves from the Uwlo. Holtz is eventually convinced by Emmek to accompany him to Tmicc to aid in the fight against this foe. Holtz enlists a top-of-his-field mechanical engineer to build a light-speed starship from Emmek's instructions. Along with a Special Forces friend of Holtz's the latter enlists for his battle expertise, sexy *New York Times* reporter Ana Hargraves joins them on their journey. British, busty, and brash she is a woman willing to do anything for the right story. Her substantial sex appeal and cunning are among the weapons that have brought her much success and she knows when she gets wind of the discovery of the alien Emmek that the biggest story of her career, of all time, has fallen in her lap. She uses Holtz to get herself on the ship. And soon afterwards the foursome has landed on Tmicc and copious cheesy sci-fi action ensues—the end result of which, somewhat refreshingly, is the heroes' defeat rather than victory.

In their cannabis-peddling enterprise Stanley and Troy mostly operated downtown, primarily standing around the outdoor mall—six square blocks of businesses, most on the upscale side; tiled sidewalks; a plethora of potted plants, local artist-created sculptures and statues; a high panhandler population. They sold from Troy's oversized military-issue backpack, dime bags only.

Leaning against a wall between a boutique and an internet café—both of which, like most of the businesses making up the rough rectangle that was the mall, had opened within the last year—the two were one afternoon on the job. The streets were slick and fewer people were out, an extended downpour having let up about a quarter-hour earlier. They had arrived some time before then and were both drenched—Troy, due to a waterproof jacket, less so than his new associate. "Trees. Trees. Got trees? Need trees?" he called out, frowning, to passersby whom he judged to be potential clients, the eave over them still dripping rain a few inches from their feet.

A man in his mid-thirties to early forties who appeared to be homeless approached, stopped in front of them. "Selling weed?" he inquired. He was wearing beaten-up tennis shoes, black gym pants which dragged on the ground, and over a too-big collared cotton shirt a tattered, dirty olive-green coat—everything damp. His hair was a medium-brown mass with some organic debris in it, his eyes wide and blue, his face permanently sunburnt-seeming.

"Yes," said Troy reluctantly, irritation in his tone.

"Nice. Nice. I like weed, I smoke weed."

"So do I," said Stanley. He looked over at Troy, who obviously wanted the man to leave them alone.

"Do you know God? Do you know what God is? I know what God is." Troy attempted to interject but he elaborated. "God is me and you and you. And," he glanced down the street, "her"—he looked the other way—"and her." Some fifties-ish businessman passed them. "And him. And a squirrel, a monkey, a cat, a rat. A bug, every plant. Everything that is alive. God is divided up among all of them—all of *us*. We are all God, and all the same. All part of the oneness that is God. If I stab you, I stab myself."

"Nobody's gonna stab me, buddy," said Troy, perturbed.

"I'm not going to stab you," he said, quickly pulling a blood-stained blade from the folds of his soiled outer garment. "I told you. I'd be stabbing me." And then—before either of the salesmen had time to process what he'd produced, simultaneous to his victim's visible astonishment—he plunged the weapon deep into Troy's abdomen simultaneous to his victim becoming clearly astonished, returned it to his waterlogged coat, and briskly crossed the street without looking for cars, continuing at the same pace down the art-tile walk toward the city center.

"He hit a bad place," said Troy, already woozy and evidently weak in the knees, putting pressure to the bodily breach.

"I agree," Stanley responded, perhaps nearly as surprised as Troy, who was likely in shock, as he braced him with his right arm. "We need to get you to the hospital."

Then it occurred to him that it was some fifteen blocks away. "I don't have a phone anymore. Too poor. Is yours in your pocket?"

"No. Out of minutes," said Troy, wincing, as they progressed slowly in the direction of their destination, Troy's midsection expansively red and the area that was soaked with sticky blood growing larger quickly.

"Someone'll call an ambulance for us. I can't believe that...crazy motherfuck stabbed you for no reason." He said this though a part of him could believe it.

"Me neither."

As they moved slowly along the path, Stanley supporting the much larger Troy, Stanley was conscious of being indifferent about whether his acquaintance lived or died, indifferent in fact as to whether he died in front of him or not. He did not dislike him—rather he liked him a little, although also found him a bit creepy, under ordinary circumstances a bit intimidating—he simply was unconcerned. He even caught himself having sexual thoughts about the first person they came across—a woman no older than twenty-three in form-fitting pants who, seeing them, was perceptibly dismayed.

"Can you call 9-1-1 for him?"

"Oh god. Of course," she said and whipped her phone out of her purse.

Stanley lowered Troy to the curb, where the two of them sat, as the lady called—her day having just become more eventful too. And Stanley kept having carnal thoughts about her, a girl to him less attractive than his girlfriend (as all others were), while she waited with them for the appearance of an ambulance—which, all lights, siren, and speed, arrived four or five minutes later.

8

Troy had survived, somewhat expectedly. A few days after the event, Stanley was laying on Hope's bed. The song "In Your Eyes" came on the radio, Hope sitting across from him. And he began thinking about the spark of life in her lovely eyes, the animating nonphysical that he believed survived death, energy that seemed so strong in her, as he examined them—seeing, he believed, quite the quantum of power, a hint of wildness.

She intoxicated him. He could understand phrases like *drinking of her presence, drunk from her proximity*. He was a neurotic in love and a relationship with someone who, while a bit crazier than he was perhaps, was more than he had ever hoped for, like a dream figure as real as anyone he'd ever encountered. A paradox in the most pleasant package. The once in a lifetime type.

Gone with Hope, since he'd been with her, was the feeling Stanley sometimes—at points often—experienced of waiting for the time when he was no longer, had finished doing whatever activity he happened to be (non)engaged in; gone was having the thought in the forefront of his mind at times that at some point in the near future (a point he was subconsciously or consciously looking forward to) he would not be 'engaged' in whatever he happened to be doing.

In the past were the days of not being in, not appreciating, not enjoying the present. Stanley had ceased to be disinterested in everything he recently had been, despite neither approving of nor understanding his lack of interest.

Maybe, he speculated, a factor that contributed to this perceived phenomenon was attention deficit disorder, which along with damn-near everyone else he probably, supposedly, had. But probably low-level depression was partly to blame, hence Hope's positive effect; this change obviously correlated regardless to a tremendous happiness increase he couldn't help but be conscious of.

⸺ ((◦)) ⸺

Stanley was in love with Hope. Already. He loved everything about her—from what (it felt like much) he'd so far ascertained about her as a person.

She was a compliment to, seemingly quite compatible with him. And he had to include, when it came to compatibility, the wonder that was her womanhood, small, silky—which, the first time they'd had sex, perhaps because of the shrooms, he'd actually managed to last four or five minutes inside. (Perhaps with time he'd even be able to last more than ten minutes, despite how good she felt, despite the fact she was to young Stanley—and no doubt so many others—ridiculously attractive.)

He could yet hardly believe his change in fortune, his life's unpredictable rapid transformation. It'd been a little over a month since the night he'd met Bartholomew at The Touchstone, but he was sure of his love, unsurprised even. It may or may not have been obvious to Hope, who assuredly did not love him, though no doubt existed in his mind.

Am I being a fool? he wondered. Had he been a fool when before he'd been in love? Had he ever really loved before?

While (though it'd been but a short time) they were very close, or Stanley felt they were—he even felt they were soulmates of a sort—perhaps Hope, beknownst to him, had herself never loved anyone. Possibly he didn't actually know much about her and ought to be disquieted by this. But he had been swept into an emotion

⸺ 45 ⸺

and existed within it. His feeling centers had relieved his calculation center of its command.

***

That night Stanley lay supine on the bed, Hope having already gone to sleep. The Bee Gees' "More Than a Woman" started playing and his mind was filled with her, his newfound treasure, the mysterious beauty who had come out of nowhere; his chest with a sensation akin to or the same as an adolescent-seeming near-forgotten one.

9

At the end of Hope's hall, on the right of which was her untidy boudoir, to the left of which was the bathroom, there was
a small closet filled with miscellaneous volumes Hope had already
read, some on wood shelves, some stacked on the floor. The thought
occurred to Stanley they seemed to have similar taste in books,
though judging from the accumulation he was scanning as he spoke
to Hope in the other room, the TV on low, her tastes were broader.

"I get through one, depending—on length and difficulty—in
three to ten days; if I stick with it," Hope was saying. "But I'll go
three or five days between books. Usually. They're a lot more colorful
for me than they are for most people."

"Colorful?"

"Yeah. Not figuratively. Due to synesthesia. Letters have colors
for me. It's really weird." She took a bong hit, coughing as she exhaled. In front of her on the coffee table was a mirror with a pile of
pink dust on it, previously a tablet of Adderall Hope had crushed
with her lighter. There was a sofa behind her but she was sitting on
the floor.

"Holy shit. I think I've heard of that. What an interesting
condition."

"L's are cerulean and M's magenta. H's are lemon-colored and
Z's dark purple. They're random to me, the associations."

"That's certainly very out-of-the-ordinary. How long have you
had that?"

"As long as I can remember."

"Huh. Do you know what causes it?"

"I don't. I usually don't even think about it I'm so used to it. I usually don't mention it to people either."

"Well, I feel privileged." He smiled.

"You should." She laughed, perfect-looking teeth flashing, then took another—a smaller—bong hit, finishing the bowl.

Stanley continued looking at her assemblage of books as his companion loaded a bowl of the same sparkling, strong marijuana, an indica.

"I see you have some Schopenhauer here. I'm a fan. Not as versed in him as I am with some others though. Have you read much philosophy?"

"Not really. Not sure it's my cup of tea. Maybe it's depressing to me. Anyway, I prefer living to reading about life. Even if I've done plenty of reading."

"I get the impression you're fairly into living," he said, chuckling, as he moved into the living room, where a cloud of fragrant smoke lingered in the air. "I've mostly read Nietzsche. I've actually been reading some Schopenhauer recently though. I agree with most of what I've read—except the misogynism."

"Seems like the ratio of basically worthless women to men is pretty even. The only way one gender is unequal to the other for me is sexually, because women don't turn me on as much. I feel no need of men, or anyone else really. Except for that I guess, sex. I don't know, maybe if I were the only person alive I'd end up dying sooner rather than later though—or going mad." They now both sat on her beige carpet. Hope seemed distracted, seemed to be looking at the purple-painted toes of the foot in front of her.

"Are you more of a reader than a liver, Stanley? Stanley with the old man's name," asked Hope, having directed her attention toward him.

Her boyfriend chuckled. "I have been these last years," said the young man who felt like the old man. "These days I hope there's—I'd like there to be—a balance."

"Balance is good. My life could be more balanced. But I'm not very good at balance...and I don't think I want to be really. I think I prefer indulgence to moderation. Wild to civilized. The lion to the worm."

"It's nice to meet someone who can have an intelligent conversation and who I'm attracted to."

"To phrase it differently it's nice to meet someone you want to fuck who has an IQ over ninety."

"Yes."

She smiled, looking at him the way she might a creature in a zoo that she pitied a bit due to its plight but would not bother to free no matter if without consequence she could—which look Stanley did not even begin to perceive.

⚫

He woke, groggy, momentarily without a sense of setting or time. After a moment, an odd feeling engulfing him, he realized the source of the sensation was that Troy was hovering over him, staring at him. Hope's apartmentmate having been out, Stanley had decided to go watch TV in the living room when he found himself lying awake in Hope's bed after she had drifted off. At some point he had fallen asleep on the couch and now it was the early morning and Troy had returned home from wherever he had been and was giving him the creeps. Hungover, having dreamt of having sweaty sex with Hope in a photo booth—she wearing only shoes, socks, a black miniskirt, and a piece of black ribbon around her neck, her nipples pierced, both of them panting, he for some reason mustachioed and wearing glasses—Stanley pulled his glued together lips apart to speak.

"Hello...uh, Troy. What's up, man? How's it going?"

"Alright."

He continued to stare.

"That's good," said Stanley, starting to stir. "I'm going to clear out of your spot here. Sorry about that. Didn't mean to fall asleep on your bed."

"No problem."

Stanley had come to his feet and was moving slowly toward Hope's door. "So you're healing up pretty well?"

"What? Oh. Yes. Healing up good."

"Nice. Good. Well, man, I'll talk to you again soon no doubt."

He didn't respond.

Fucking weirdo Stanley thought. And that thought reminded him of another weirdo who would sometimes come by in the early evening unannounced: Thaddeus, a neighbor and former manager of the apartment complex next to Hope's who she and her friends familiar with him privately referred to as Death. A bespectacled man with thinning brown hair and a near-unibrow who professed (the first time Stanley met him) to having no friends, who stated he had never really been accepted into a group throughout his quarter-century on Earth. A man who was either possessed of little social intelligence or who cared not at all about being socially awkward. A man who, Stanley judged, overcompensated for his oddness in such a way that he came across as a jackass, alien, arrogant, vibrationally off, just below a polished mask. He might bring over a bottle of wine but he was always peripheral and unwanted. ("I don't know why he comes over here," Hope had said after he'd left the first time he came by since Stanley'd moved in. "I was never friends with him. I don't know him that well. You know, besides knowing he's odd.")

As Stanley snuggled sleeping Hope, his new incomparably good-looking significant other, he thought with a kind of malicious smirk this Thaddeus seemed to have every reason to feel lonelier than most of his peers. He would likely always be a stranger to everyone else and to himself. He was twenty-five and about to receive his master's (in, what was it—computer science?), and on the inside lie a self-pity-tinged cavern that by sheer will was largely ignored. Never would he have the interpersonal success Stanley had found, nor even the moderate people savvy. His psyche and penis would never know the pleasure of a woman such as Hope. Stanley was the apex animal beating its chest in the jungle on some vegetation-blanketed ridge; and Thaddeus was some timid creature below that crept through the undergrowth, surviving on scraps left by the hunters and poisonous to the touch.

10

"I guess Troy moved in with his dad who lives nearby. He said he was going to try to get his shit together." She was standing in the kitchen looking as sexy as usual. Wearing a logo-less tee, no bra, and a pair of wide-cut dark blue jeans the legs of which were pocked with holes of various sizes. They had just come in from having a cigarette out front and now Hope was preparing to make a vegetable and beef soup from scratch, her eyebrows arched in contemplation.

"Good for him. He could stand to get his shit together. Kind of a strange fellow. Not a bad guy. Odd though."

"I concur."

"Can't say I'm exactly bummed he won't be living here anymore."

"Yeah," she said absently.

They occupied the space a moment unspeaking, in their own minds, Stanley striped by five P.M. sunlight coming in through the blinds, Hope in the kitchen.

"How old are you, Hope?" he asked her impulsively; it'd just occurred to him he'd never asked, and he felt strange not knowing, not having inquired, having remembered to. In the living room, where he sat, his posture poor, the TV was on but neither of them had been paying it any attention.

"Twenty-five."

"Two years younger."

"Huh?" She was cutting a steak into small square pieces.

"I'm two years older than you."

"Oh, you cradle robber."

He laughed; a moment later he became aware for the first time that a sitcom starring David Spade was on. "Your birthday's soon though, so you're only about fifteen months younger." He remembered she was an Aries.

"Yeah. It's in a couple weeks."

"We're supposed to be compatible, romantically. I'm a Sagittarius."

There was no response, just the sound of chopping—and of David Spade braying for some reason in the direction of a tall (or comparatively tall) brunette with a sports coat on and a mole adjacent her upper lip.

And then it was Hope's birthday and they went via taxi at about six-thirty in the evening to a local strip club, The Satyr's Grove, to celebrate.

"Going to a place like that with you makes me feel a bit uncomfortable," he had said, when Hope broached the idea.

"Why?"

"I don't know exactly. It makes me feel—or I'm worried I would feel insecure, or abnormally anxious, or both."

"No one's going to be looking at me. They're going to be looking at the nude women under the lights."

"Yeah. I suppose. It's just the atmosphere. All those dudes, a lot of libidinous dudes, drinking and ogling women—hot women like you are. Except you're even hotter."

"If someone does check me out we can ignore it. That's the kind of thing that can and does happen anywhere anyway." She kissed him, on the lips, closed mouth.

"Are you bi? Is that why such a place interests you?" he asked her, feeling a bit less apprehensive about the outing.

"I wouldn't use that word."

"Then why do you want to go to a nudie bar?"

"It just seemed like something fun for us to do together."

In the dark interior, sitting at the stage, they watched the girls dance, none of whom were disappointing, and compensated them with dollar bills that both of them stuffed in their g-strings. Later, when Stanley and Hope were half-drunk (he from beer, she from cocktails), she leaned into him and said "Let's migrate to one of the private rooms in the back."

"Uh...why's that?"

"I'm going to buy you a lap dance, babe. Watch another woman rub all over you."

"Ha. That sounds great, but...it's your birthday, babe."

"So? I'll enjoy it! Don't you want one?"

"Sure. Of course."

"You've had one before, right?"

"...No."

"What? You've got to get one then!"

He smiled at her. "I sure lucked out with you."

They sat watching the person in front in them, pubic hair an up-side-down triangle above a slit that disappeared between her thighs, move her hips side to side, turn and repeatedly squat, then head back toward the pole.

"So which one do you want?"

"Let me think," he replied as his smile widened.

He considered the girl currently on the stage, a blonde with large breasts and a round posterior (introduced by a guy in a booth with a mic as Clementine), then glanced at the others sitting in various spots—all of whom he had seen perform, many of whom were seated at the bar, a beverage before them—settling after a few minutes on a slim-waisted flowing-haired Latina with Cs, the nipples of which were particularly protuberant.

"You're cute," she had said as she climbed on him, nude again, the scent of her floral perfume almost too strong. "Your girlfriend's cute too."

The darkness of the room they occupied, while there was something vaguely repugnant about the space, had the effect of intensifying the psychic excitement the woman's body caused Stanley.

Hope started sucking on his left earlobe as the woman rubbed the area from her neatly trimmed vagina to her lovely brown butt along his crotch.

"Looks like somebody's waking up," she said, Hope laughing and suckling, the stripper continuing to massage his crotch with her lower body while with both hands holding on to the back of the plush sofa Stanley was sitting on, an arm on either side of his head—sometimes rubbing his face between her exotically shaped breasts, a chemical but not unpleasant floral smell going into his nostrils (the aroma actually increasing his arousal, his penis seeming also to pulsate all the more because of the—to him—highly desirable woman simultaneously doing things to an ear with her mouth).

But he couldn't help looking over at Hope, at her choppily cut dark hair, at her engaged though ever unrevealing visage that was like an animate mask, and thinking *Who are you?*; thinking of her as some all-too-close (yet distant) stranger (a stranger just like the woman riding him with a smile, whose life he had briefly speculated about); and as he did his erection slightly subsided. The dancer though continued to move her hips rhythmically forward and back, her smooth well-formed flesh rubbing his crotch, her uncommon mammaries in his face, and soon he was as hard as he had been, Hope—unsettling enigma in a pleasing package—kissing the side of his face.

And that night in bed she pleasured him until he ejaculated down her throat—the thought repeating itself in his mind as he watched her fellating him that he couldn't believe how fortunate he was. That perhaps—he tried to banish the notion from his head but didn't quite—there was a catch. Some unforeseen price or punishment that would come later as a consequence of the relationship, result of his association with the person that was responsible for his current happiness.

He didn't know how many times now he had climaxed in her mouth but each time his orgasm was so intense he let out a loud vocalization, guttural, primal. And always afterward, for some while, he would feel submerged in a warm sensation of complete, heavenly satisfaction. Such orgasms with her, his dream woman from nowhere, were every time unusually powerful, incredibly fulfilling. The lady of his dreams gave dream blow jobs. Sometimes in her—now their—dimly lit bedroom at night; sometimes during the day, out of the blue, while he was sitting there half-dressed, zoning out while stoned.

They fell asleep after—he nude, she in panties—lying on their backs, uncovered, his left arm around her, his left hand gripping her left breast.

But that morning he had a horrific, unexplainable oneiric experience though he fell into slumber in a state of bliss:

He dreamt that he had just come home and stood in the living room, looking concernedly at a Hope who had an odd, unreadable expression on her lightly made up face; who was sitting on the carpet in sock feet, medium blue socks on her small feet, but leaning her head on an arm propped on the sofa behind her (her eyes faraway as they occasionally were; also appearing glossy).

"Stanley. I have something to tell you," she said, moments after he'd shut the door behind him.

Immediately he was petrified. *Why was she talking that way? What could she have to tell me? Definitely something bad. But how bad? What* kind *of bad?*

"You know I'm really into you. But—I mean because I am, I feel...compelled to open up to you about myself more. And what I plan to tell you...will probably bother you."

He could see, mentally, his face turning a color it seldom did, see its form transmuting horribly, sense it was even beginning to slightly but perceptibly (and uncontrollably) twitch. *Was her face a pretty trollop face?* was a peculiar question, surprising sentence that came into his mind.

"Here it is. ...I can't stay faithful, to you, when I'm really high on coke or ecstasy. And...Lana and the other girls I said I met a while ago, who I went to that party with, are all former or current porn actresses. And I met a guy at that party that does porn. He's about my age, a year older I think, light brown hair, sexy. And I just get really horny when I'm coked up. And I love sex way more than usual when I'm on E. I'm sorry, Stanley, I know this is hard to hear. And maybe it might not have happened if you were a little more typical or more exciting, or didn't have an old man name—I don't know. I accept you for you, but—you realize, I'm sure, you are a little odd. So am I. But you're not the most desirable kind of odd. In my opinion. Anyway—what we have is special. You're special. The way we came together was really cool. And our sex life is pretty good. But recently...I was hanging out with that guy again, and did a lot of coke with him. One of his girlfriends was there and we were all snorting lines and drinking whiskey and listening to music. She's really good-looking and she was wearing a short skirt and a silk blouse without a bra and her breasts were basically falling out of it. She was hanging all over him. And at one point he started kissing me, even though his girlfriend was draped on him. And then I noticed his cock was hard. And it was fine—I wasn't going to have sex with him no matter how much I wanted to and even though I was wet. I just kissed him. I kissed back."

"Hope. ...Hope," Stanley—sweaty, feverish, his lips seeming to hardly open, his will almost unable to make his mouth vocalize—was barely able to interrupt. "Please. Don't do this, to me."

He felt impotent; his voice seemed soft—so soft, practically inaudible; he felt he was fading away, disappearing backward; dissipating into soft focus. He was disappearing, in his mind, into an approximately peanut-sized shell that would hover, just large enough to be perceivable, in about the spot his upper torso was located.

"But Stanley—there's more. I need to tell you this, the whole story. To tell you about me, real Hope. Confess."

Stanley's head dropped; on each side a hand moved to support it, the veins in his somewhat squeezed forehead a map of worst anguish.

"...We were making out on the couch. And then, while we were, his girlfriend unzipped his fly and pulled out his penis. Which I really didn't see coming. But I still resisted temptation. I watched his girlfriend jerk him off while we were kissing but was determined not to touch him—I didn't want to do that to you. Anyway, his girlfriend stripped down to a g-string and suggested we take our clothes off too—and we did. A little skin-to-skin contact's not a big deal when you're sucking someone's tongue. At first I kept my panties on but he said it was a little pointless and I agreed. He said 'You have a great body' and I said thank you; then he said 'I can tell you're really turned on,' and I admitted I was attracted to him but I told him: 'I have a boyfriend. Sex is not going to happen.' That was about when his girlfriend leaned over and started giving him a blow job. And, it surprised me, but I felt very envious, so horny I was miserable." She stopped a moment, making sure Stanley was listening; then continued, gravely. "Nonetheless, I didn't do anything. I just continued to feel what I was feeling, without taking action. He started to kiss me again but I said I'd rather just watch his girlfriend. And that was all that happened. I watched him come and then I noticed a bunch of people had been watching us—which was sort of hot too. And I slowly put my clothes back on and pretty soon I left the party."

"Jesus Christ," said Stanley, his face purple on white, feeling queasy and weak, defeated and humiliated, cornered—the tormented young man experiencing yet a sensation of evanescence, a sensation akin to having an O.B.E.

"I know it sounds bad." She sighed, and through his trauma-induced quasi-delirium he thought it was a false sigh, a calculated gesture. "I wanted him so much it hurt. Consider that. I realize what I did was wrong but it could have been much worse." She looked at her boyfriend as if she expected him to commend her. There was an upswelling of the sickness within.

"I think I'm going to vomit," he said looking at her face (an expression of somewhat irritated anticipation on it), into it, into what he regarded as essentially a void, a window into a human nonbeing, as gradually—simultaneous to whole-organism tension diminishing—it faded away.

The next image he saw, only moments later, was an image from reality. Sweet, unnauseating reality. In which, to his knowledge, his beautiful girlfriend was not unfaithful and promiscuous; was not some kind of possibly malevolent monster who would destroy his psyche.

And the real-world view he woke to was a close-up of a white pillow; saliva-wet, a bit scratchy. The bedroom was immersed in sunlight and he was in a better mood than he otherwise would have been because he was no longer (he thought) living a nightmare. Instead he occupied the bedroom, now his too, in the domicile (also his) of an uncommon gorgeous woman (she was now absent and he was partially covered by a wrinkly white sheet; he didn't know where she'd gone)—one who, he admitted to himself, worried him a little, for some unspecifiable reason, but who he thought looking back over the recent past had so far only been a positive force in his life.

11

"Why do you prefer Stanley over Stan?" Hope asked some days after the person addressed's highly unpleasant dream of her as they laid beside each other in bed, minimally clothed, under a thin blanket. It was a Monday, forty minutes to noon.

"Stanley reminds me of Stanley Kowalski or Stanley Kubrick," he responded, still waking up. "Stan reminds me of Stan Laurel or the character from *South Park*. The former set of associations is more favorable to me. And I think Stanley's the stronger form of the name."

"Stanley is also the name of the black guy on *The Office*," she said.

"There's two black guys in *The Office*. There's also the character played by Craig Robinson. ...Craig Robinson is funny. The guy who plays Stanley is funny too. I've never known his name. Craig Robinson is a little funnier though." He turned toward her. "Have you ever seen the British *Office*?"

"Yeah. Some. I liked it, just not quite as much. Ricky Gervais is great though."

"My feelings are the same." He smiled at her, curled his toes under the blanket luxuriantly. "What's your favorite show of all time—favorite comedic show?"

"*Seinfeld*."

"Mine too! Totally. So rewatchable."

"Absolutely."

Stanley yawned. "Do you mind if I make some coffee?"

"No. Of course not. You don't need to ask. Sounds good."

———((◉))———

A little later both were sitting in the living room, Hope wearing socks, panties, and an extra large t-shirt featuring a big lethargic-looking smiley face (bright yellow on medium blue) that came down to the middle of her thighs. A cup of steaming coffee on the table in front of her, she was loading her bong—around a foot tall with a green-yellow base decorated with a similarly hued toad, its glass eyes alert and orange, forever padding around the pipe's spherical bottom toward the person partaking. Stanley, seated beside her, held a hot mug of unsweetened/-diluted joe with two hands, occasionally blowing on it.

"Have you ever been in jail?"

The TV was activated, the volume down so low the show that was on—*Cops*—was barely audible.

"Amazingly no. There've been a couple of times when I came close to getting arrested, but no—I've only gotten tickets. Have you?" She took in a substantial volume of smoke, clearing the tube, then passed her device to her boyfriend.

"Yes, but only very briefly. I got caught smoking this stuff in public. I dislike it more than I thought I would have. I also learned, relatedly, I like freedom more than I thought." He lit the bowl, sucked, pulled out the stem, inhaled the remaining smoke, coughed for a second, placed the apparatus on the table before Hope. "I have to say—in my limited experience a lot of cops are control freaks. I can understand someone, some ex-con—somebody who spent a lot of time in prison anyway—wanting to cut the throat of every cop alive. Not that I think that would be alright, or that such a hypothetical individual isn't a psychopath."

Hope chuckled in an odd way. "You're funny. Yeah, I understand it."

She was looking through the partially lifted blinds at the sunny outside world. "To slit a pig..."

She laughed more naturally, but seemed elsewhere, absent.

After a while she picked up the book that lay on the coffee table in front of her, a Saul Bellow (*Henderson*...), which she was seventy-five or a hundred pages into; Stanley, a few minutes later, went into the bedroom to grab the book he was in the midst of reading, a brief and darkly humorous history of American imperialism—looking up from it every few minutes to see Hope, stoned, still engaged; or perhaps two stocky European American cops with crew cuts chasing and, with the aid of an excited German shepherd, catching a thin African American in a t-shirt and unhelpfully low-hanging trousers; perhaps a commercial for hemorrhoid cream, in which an unexceptional woman, forty-fivish, went from a put-on look of pain on sitting to a toothy smile at table, surrounded by friends.

⸻

She was, Hope, in Stanley's unexpressed opinion, somewhat strange and mysterious—even after three months—but he loved her, and he loved their conversations (if anything it Stanley felt he likely loved her all the more because he did not totally understand her, because she was a bit peculiar—due to the fact that there was something, he couldn't even identify the category of that 'something,' so-to-speak off about her, and maybe what it was wasn't positive). They could, it seemed, converse at length about anything; and they had so many opinions and interests and affinities in common. She was even on the same page as him when it came to 3/27, which subject Stanley had apprehensively broached one afternoon while, as was often the case, they were sitting around not doing much of anything—the TV on but neither of them really paying it much attention, smoking the weed that Hope seemed to never run out of.

"What were you doing when 3/27 happened?" he had asked over

the low sound of *Judge Judy*, fairly stoned, after looking at her for some time—which look Hope had not met, though he was positive she was well aware of being observed.

"Oh, I was in Tempe."

"Oh, right. ...So you moved from there to Olympia. And didn't you live in Seattle for a while too?"

"Yeah."

"How did you end up living in Seattle?"

"I moved up there with a boyfriend after I dropped out of Evergreen State."

"You've sure lived in a lot of different places. I mean including when you were a kid."

"Yeah."

"Some pretty interesting places too. I know there's plenty about you I don't know still, but it seems like you've had a pretty interesting life."

She smiled. *She's so beautiful* thought Stanley. *It's really pretty strange I'm with her. That she chose to be with me. Why would she choose that? Is she just bored? Unparticular? Does she truly see something in me? I'm not the most common guy, but it seems like most really good-looking women prefer assholes—which are common.* "Compared to many," she responded, before her gaze went back to the television, her eyes seeming to drain of life a moment after they did.

He watched her. "As a kid you lived in Maryland and Iowa and Arizona, right?"

"And Idaho and Kentucky. And North Carolina. Yeah. I spent the longest in Tempe."

"Damn. The only moving my family did as a kid was within, and around, Oswald. But my dad wasn't in the army."

"What was he like?"

"Slender. Taciturn. Liked to drink. Rather dull really."

"My father was also thin and didn't talk much. He was a tall but stooped, sort of gray, almost milquetoast man. He had been, no doubt, cowed—rendered timid, hollowed out—by my mother; who I confirmed as an adult had been slyly unfaithful to him." Hope made eye contact for a moment. "She was a kind of masculine woman. More masculine than he was perhaps. I'm not sure if she stopped doing it for my father or the other way around, if my dad just didn't ring her bell after a while, but she got around I discovered. As I had suspected at the time. Anyway they got a divorce when I was fifteen, and I got an emancipation the next year. ...I think they had been reasonably content, for a decade or so."

"My mother was pretty quiet, like my dad. Religious. Was she, like, bossy? Like kind of a bitch?"

"Sure. Overbearing, verbally abusive. She was not unattractive but had a permanent frown; glittering, tiny, mean eyes. And she was definitely addiction prone, at least when it came to substances. She liked the sauce. She liked pretty much anything that would relieve her from sobriety."

"Sounds like it's safe to assume you didn't like her overmuch."

"No."

On the TV a geriatric judge with dyed hair spoke briskly words that could not be heard. Her face too displayed the etched lines of a grimace.

"What about your dad?"

"Eh. He was okay. But if you were sitting in the same room as him you tended to feel no less alone."

"I get that."

"So you stayed in Arizona until you were eighteen, but then you ended up living in both Peru and Chile?"

"Yeah."

"How did you manage to do that anyway?"

"I was in an accident when I was twelve, involved in an accident. An accident involving a Coke truck."

He laughed. "Interesting. My brain is now frantically trying to figure out how that relates to your living in South America in the first half of your twenties."

"Ha." Their eyes were bright; Stanley found himself very engaged.

"I'm going to give you the medium-length version."

"Okay..."

"This Coca-Cola Company truck backed into me when I was on my bike, breaking my left hand. It was basically the driver's fault, even though I wasn't exactly being sufficiently aware of my environment. Anyway, the company's lawyers made a deal with my parents' lawyer and I was awarded a settlement of twenty thousand dollars. Which I gained access to on my eighteenth birthday."

"So that's how you financed fourteen months in South America?"

"Yes."

"Did you spend it all?"

"No. I spent about half. I still have approximately a quarter of it in the bank. I was living off of it in part when I was in Atlanta too."

"Didn't you have like a million jobs while you lived there?"

"A lot. Eight or nine in two years."

"And from there you moved to Oswald?"

"Yeah."

"And you've been here about as long as you lived in Georgia."

She thought. "Three months longer."

"Why did you leave Atlanta for here?"

"I'd heard good things about this city. And I was sick of it there. I'd never really liked it."

"How did you come to live there in the first place?"

"I was basically financially able to start fresh wherever, so when I came back from Chile I blindfolded myself and stuck a pin in a map of America and moved to whatever part of the country fate decided."

"You literally did that?"

"Yeah, literally."

"...And now you lead a more or less unassuming existence working part-time at a family-owned café as a waitress. Few if any of your customers perhaps knowing that you are the remarkable human specimen known as Hope Brownen. That despite being the tender age of twenty-six you have, compared to your peers, lived a life rather extraordinary."

"Wow. Aren't you being flattering. And inaccurate."

"You're just modest. One thing's undeniable: what a lot of bouncing around you've done."

"I've been a bit bounce-happy I suppose."

Stanley stared at her a moment, thinking of Hope just at the edge of consciousness as some sort of prize he had won for unknown reasons, or maybe by luck, then looked at the bong, considering taking another hit, if only to have something to do with his hands. He still wanted to get to why he had brought up the topic of 3/27.

"So, do you recall exactly when you heard about the planes crashing into the towers that day?"

"Definitely. I was eating breakfast, with the TV on, when the news came on talking about the first plane."

"...What did you think about that particular infamous—most infamous—terrorist attack anyway?" he asked squinting slightly, not looking at her full on.

"I thought it was convenient."

"Hm."

"I mean it made sense to me that certain people in high places would have wanted a war—particularly with an epicenter in that part of the world, oil-rich, strategically positioned—that might never end. A war against not an enemy per se but a concept. An abstraction."

"Absolutely. That is to say you thought—think—there was something fishy about it?"

"Certainly. It is something I know." Her beautiful eyes, dark in hue, were looking into his own.

"Any idea how they did it?"

"Well, for one thing the video evidence seems to point to not-so-good computer-generated imagery as regards the so-called airplanes."

"I know!" shot out Stanley, excited. "It's such an important aspect of the crime. But part of it that definitely isn't widely recognized."

"Seems pretty clear the towers, and building seven, were wired to be demolished. And that a missile, perhaps a winged one, hit the Pentagon—and in Shanksville, P.A. As to what happened to the actual planes—more importantly the passengers on them—who's to say. They were probably flown to some secret hangar where the people on board were all dispatched one at a time via a bullet to the cranium."

Stanley, smiling widely, sat in awe of her. "You're great."

"Aww shucks," she said cornily. "I'd say it's better to shut the fuck up about it, the real story, than be too open. I mean this is the black op of all black ops we're talking about. A bigger deal than the public splattering of Kennedy's brains. Its repercussions are major, ongoing. People, Americans, don't—won't—accept the truth; don't even want to consider the *possibility* that 3/27 was a complex covert action executed at least in large part by elements within the U.S. government and utilizing the mainstream media to sell the lie. And these...people—these conscienceless murderers—their, you could say, memory about you is better in ways than your own. They know events and dates you've forgotten, and a lot of what you've ever done on your computer, your magic phone. They're great at deducing, if they choose to put any time into it. Finding things out about you, your fears, desires, convictions, that you wouldn't think they could know is not outside their purview nor would the quick creation of a comprehensive dossier on someone deemed troublesome to the State be a task they wouldn't be bothered with. You don't want to be a target, really. Not while you have a body. Not if someday they might decide to fly you out to a secret prison with a sufficient number of sadists on staff. You know, armed with not just specific physiological but psychological knowledge."

"Yeah. Pretty chilling stuff." His eyes, wide, were focused on nothing but his gaze was directed at a point on the coffee table. "We are the subjects of a frightening master."

"Someone with no power they can destroy with the ease of smashing a gnat, only they have many more than two hands to do it with. For the practice of their art of chaos, terror, they have a million hands, a hundred means."

———————

Later during that calm day of mild weather and no plans, a day the pair had spent the first part of indoors and aimless—young and free—Hope, feeling boredom creep upon her, spontaneously suggested they go for a drive, though they had no destination. After a while she didn't feel like driving anymore—they were on a highway headed north, a cow pasture with low mountains in the background on the left, houses and a barn on the right—so she asked Stanley if he would take over. He agreed after hardly a moment's thought despite being unlicensed and having never had a license, in part because it would be the fourth time he'd driven her car and he'd accumulated a little confidence behind the wheel, which had been previously nonexistent. And his sense of adventure had been at maybe maximum since she'd come into his life, Hope the enigma; for whom he would do anything asked he felt, and probably really would, with the same lack of deliberation.

They approached a medium-size city forty-five or fifty minutes out of Oswald and decided to get off, maybe figure out some way of occupying themselves there. Stanley had some trepidation about turning off the highway but accomplished the task smoothly enough. They drove, still destinationless, along a main boulevard in town, the sun on Hope's creamy legs, recently shaven, not skinny but neither those of a voluptuous woman; the wind ruffling her thin floral-print skirt, lavender on pink, and his wavy hair. He felt as happy, he speculated, as he was capable of feeling, legitimately; because of the woman beside him, the bright clear day, his lack of responsibility; because he was carefree (unless he considered the possibility of losing Hope) and had an ideal partner in carefreeness, ideal because she was in his mind as unhindered and directionless as possible—a free spirit without attachment (except, he hoped, to him)—and as attractive to him. *Attractive* seemed an empty word, a gross understatement; she was: stomach-stirring, impenetrable, superior to any opiate, any chemical or compound. She nearly made him hard with a glance, gave his heart g-force jolts; she was as an alien that had appeared in his lifetime unannounced and about as unknowable, perhaps.

The radio was on FM, tuned to the '80s/'90s station. On came The Fine Young Cannibals, "She Drives Me Crazy"—a song Stanley remembered liking as a kid; that he still liked, he guessed mostly because it triggered a sensation of nostalgia. And because as the song was playing Hope was sitting next to him—sunlit and gorgeous, Hope who was his girlfriend—and he was relating it to how he felt about her (she did drive him crazy, and he couldn't help himself), and he was experiencing a happiness, a joy, that was the greatest he could recollect ever having known, that rather than being brief (a moment's ecstasy) he was present in, he enjoyed the track more than he ever had.

12

"Have you ever had a threesome?" Hope asked Stanley one night as they were sharing a case of PBR on the back porch, both of them having begun to feel the loss of sobriety.

"No. Have you?"

"Yeah. Quite a few times with another girl. Only once with two guys." She cracked another beer, a porch light illuminated yellow behind her, drooping trees and dark sky before her. "If you've never had a three-way you should. I have a couple of friends I can call who might be interested."

"Wow. Really? I definitely am, and have been, interested. ...You wouldn't get jealous?"

"Nah," she responded nonchalantly, taking a drag of the Camel Wide in her hand and looking forward into the darkness.

Stanley wondered if that was maybe a negative indication—a sign she wasn't all too invested or interested in him. The thought though that seemed to for the time being trump that one was less a thought so much as a highly sexual vision—a flash dream of carnal pleasure, of a suddenly possible reality that he had not imagined he would ever live.

Chelsie, the fit blonde with dreadlocks he'd met the same night as Hope, had said she thought he was cute Hope informed him; and, she said, Chelsie—who was in a relationship—had in the past clandestinely cheated. And so she planned to phone her about meeting up sometime for a ménage à trois.

"I think your chances are good. You think she's good-looking, right?"

"Yes. Yes, of course," he replied smiling, only half-believing what had just transpired.

***

As it turned out Chelsie, one of Hope's best friends, found the idea intriguing—and her significant other was out of town for two weeks. So three nights later Stanley and girlfriend made a scheduled trip to her apartment, Hope dressed rather seductively, Stanley (dressed a bit nicer than usual, and wearing cologne) flooded with dopamine.

"Heelloooo," said Chelsie exaggeratedly, greeting them at the door in a mostly transparent piece of pink lingerie and with some sort of like-colored feather wand in one hand. Though the toy didn't do anything for him Chelsie's body, and anticipation of the impending threesome, did—and Stanley had an awareness of being halfway hard already (though, he noticed, the thin garment she wore did not reveal the nipples of her reasonably sized firm breasts).

"I hope you guys don't mind that I'm pretty kinky," said Chelsie as she led them into her boudoir, in which some time earlier a scented candle had been lit.

A heart-shaped canopied bed with maroon silk sheets and an inordinate number of plump pillows on it occupied the center of the space—a bed Stanley regarded as rather silly.

"I already knew that about you, sexy," said Hope, removing her top as Stanley resultingly became erect.

"Oh look," Chelsie said pointing at his crotch and then pulled her shapely pink-nippled mammaries out of the top of her negligee-like garment.

Hope looked at Stanley's erection saying "Somebody's ready to play" as—events taking on a dreamlike quality from that point—Chelsie knelt in front of him and slowly unzipped his fly. "I want to see it and then suck it," she said as Hope sidled up to his right shoulder and Chelsie gently removed his penis from a plaid pair of boxers with her soft hand.

———⟨⟨◊⟩⟩———

"I can't wait till you come in her pussy, baby," Hope was saying some time into their bacchanal and after Chelsie—beautiful breasts intermittently touching his (clothed) inner thighs, head of blonde dreadlocks moving rhythmically—fellated him fairly skillfully (her tongued pleasantly studded—a first for him) for five or seven heavenly minutes as a precursor to his entering her, initially from behind.

She was on the tight side, excited but not overly wet, but more arousing than how good she felt was the fact that Hope was watching, also turned on, and that Chelsie was new. He also, he admitted to himself, was even more turned on because their intercourse was secret, illicit.

He was going in and out of the moist grip of her vagina, a small upside-down triangle of soft, curled blonde hairs just above it, at a steady pace in the missionary position. Hope, nude and rubbing her womanhood, stood behind him and to his left, where she had a good view of their copulating and occasionally made sexual remarks— "You guys are hot together," "I like seeing you bang my friend's little pussy"—that further aroused him. Chelsie moaned softly, having removed the lingerie, her nipples stone-like on slightly jiggling teats, and Stanley—fully without clothing now too, his rigid appendage glistening with her juice—was beading sweat, making a concentrated effort not to climax, had occasionally stopped palming Chelsie's breasts for that reason. It had only been about fifteen minutes and he never wanted the experience (which maybe was an *actual* dream) to come to an end, an end he knew became nearer.

And soon, inevitably, the physiological conclusion did occur.

And the perspiration-drenched ejaculator was very loud, the intensity of the recipient's moan increasing as a copious amount of semen was ejected into her deeply; Stanley exhaling blissfully afterwards, still connected to his girlfriend's sexy friend, her knees raised and his posterior between her smooth thighs—finding himself thinking only moments post-climax, before he even pulled out, that he wanted to be inside her again sometime, ideally soon. "That was so hot, baby," said Hope, twisting his head and kissing him wetly, Stanley in a pleasure-induced stupor.

"Did you like that? I did. ...I *almost* came," said Hope, putting on her bra.

"Oh fuck yeah. That was fucking amazing," he answered, finding his gaze going to his viscous and shining, no longer blood-flooded member.

Without choosing to he began taking inventory of what had occurred, in the room with the improbable giant heart bed topped by silken covers—with the woman he hardly knew and the one he loved.

I fucked Chelsie doggie-style for a while, until I got wary about finishing; then I looked over at Hope, who wanted me, and entered her from behind while she had one leg propped on the bed; and she kept looking back at me with lust in her eyes and kissing me as I fucked her deep; then she sucked me briefly before I reentered Chelsie, who was supine and had been biting her lip watching us fuck. And now my warm seed is flowing from between her legs as she hurries to the bathroom. Because I just shot a huge wad into my girlfriend's sexy friend's pussy.

The hallmarks of reality were there, but the events were nonetheless almost indistinguishable from the material of his most licentious fantasies. Such that accepting them as true, though he'd been there and they had so recently happened, was surprisingly difficult. However, the experience and the fact of its having occurred he found extremely gratifying.

He was back at home soon, the two having said goodbye shortly after everyone had re-garbed, but really the dream wasn't over. He was still with Hope—more attractive than Chelsie, more interesting, and all his (or as much as she might ever be maybe). Alone and cozy in their bedroom after Hope had dozed off, as he pondered the recent turns his life had taken, Stanley thought aloud, his eyes scintillating with joie de vivre, "Hope...has given me hope." And out of pure happiness he began to laugh.

For some reason he remembered an incident then, at an off-the-beaten-track bar mid-evening, that had been very strange and in retrospect was more disconcerting even than it had been at the time; an event he had not thought about for some while, that he did not know what to make of but that in the weeks after it occurred he had replayed and pondered many times.

He was standing next to Hope, near the bar, when a mangled cripple of a man who looked to be in his late thirties to mid-forties and whom no one would ever have guessed was twenty-three years old, with a look of mingled great horror and surprise on what served as his face—clearly long ago mutilated—emerged (becoming more and more the focus of people's attention) from the kinetic mass of humanity that was the establishment's centrally located dance area (the majority of the patrons situated there, most in their twenties, grinding one another or rather artlessly close-dancing with pint or cocktail glasses in their hands) with an ominously outstretched finger, pointed directly at her head; his attention and finger and movement through the throng all directed toward Hope, who having become aware of the disfigured pointer seemed gradually to become disturbed by him. "Call the police!" the stranger yelled urgently as he neared her, wide eyes displaying recognition and fear. "It's a wanted criminal. A homicidal nutcase!"

"Are you talking about her?" Stanley—shouting, motioning to Hope, although it was obvious—asked the deformed, difficult to behold hunched human who, at the edge of the pseudo-dancing mob, appeared to be keeping a safe distance.

"She's no 'her.' She's a demon, a thing, inhuman. Your worst nightmare. She's a witch from Hell! Call the police! It's a fugitive, a dangerous criminal!"

Lots of people were looking—not at Hope but her accuser—and doing nothing else.

"Mary! Mary the evil one. She'll ruin you. She'll kill you."

"This girl's name is Hope," yelled Stanley over the din. "You have her confused with somebody else. You're confused."

"Her name is Mary. I'd know her anywhere and always. At least Mary was what we knew her as. But it's her. You can see the malicious glint in her eyes a block away.

"I...know...her," he said eerily, gutturally, a bit triumphantly.

Stanley looked over at Hope, whose countenance was reminiscent of a headlights-paralyzed woodland creature, and the moment he looked back to the seemingly psychotic unfortunate a pint glass whizzed past his left ear on its way to his girlfriend. Its trajectory seemed to line up with her face, and had Hope neither moved or deflected it the projectile likely would have damagingly hit where intended. But, in a (Stanley thought) remarkable manner, Hope did the latter, and *punched* the glass when it came within range—doing so in such a manner that it was sent flying into the right side of the face of a woman on the edge of the dance-floor crowd. Bleeding, holding the injured area as blood streamed through her fingers, the shocked young woman started screaming.

An eye had gotten a small piece of glass in it and she had no idea what had hit her, had hardly been aware of the bent man yelling at a girl at the bar, and had basically been rendered temporarily insane, lost to pain and confusion. As she was—one hand incarnadining, her boyfriend trying unsuccessfully to be helpful—while the irate stranger was forcibly removed by two imposing bouncers (stunned Stanley and a crazy-eyed Hope watching from the bar).

His body had been badly broken many years ago but the accusatory enigma demonstrated an amount of strength difficult to believe as he struggled against his captors while being gradually dragged toward the front door, the whole time ranting, or thinking he was, about Hope.

"Her name's Mary. She's a liar. The best liar. She tried to kill me, and she drove my mother to lunacy, and because of her my dad killed himself!"

"What...the...fuck?" Stanley asked Hope, who looked more serious than he'd ever seen her, once he had stopped staring at the door the troublemaker had finally been ejected via.

"I have no fucking idea," said Hope, looking in the direction of the entrance, through which the security personnel not had reentered. "Fucking crazy people. I'm glad I didn't get hit."

"That was quite the move. Too bad it sort of backfired."

"There she is," said Hope, her attention now directed at the distraught girl and her conspicuously concerned boyfriend, whose arm was around her, as they walked toward the exit. "Looks like, luckily, I avoided negative consequences for inadvertently fucking up some girl's face. ...She probably just wants to get the fuck to the hospital."

"I hope your accuser doesn't come back. He was honestly kind of a scary guy. And scary-looking."

"Me too."

"I need a drink."

"I want a drink," Hope said.

———— ◈ ————

More to Stanley's than Hope's surprise about a half hour later the physically wrecked man did come back, as crazed and single-minded as before—and he was toting a container of gasoline, plastic and red.

He approached Hope briskly, fury burning in his pupils. His relatively relaxed target only became fully aware of his return at the point at which he was close enough to douse her with the fuel he'd come back bearing. And when he was he already had the yellow nozzle off that capped the three-fifths-full container of inflammable and was splashing her, his mouth gaping, its appearance that of an unnaturally wide frozen smile.

Hope, in a state of instant dismay, immediately backed away (into people—bewildered, gas-soaked neck to mid-thigh on one side). Simultaneously the man permanently contorted pulled from a back pocket an oblong campfire lighter, compressed one button while pressing another (a safety) downward, and thrust its flickering flame of orange toward Hope's fuel-wet dress, failing (but not by much) to extend it far enough to set his perceived nemesis's garment ablaze; failing and then with a brutality not yet exercised getting rushed and pinned down until the arrival of police.

Soon after, once Hope had stopped hyperventilating—something her boyfriend had never witnessed her do—Stanley left with the victim of the monstrous man's verbal and physical attacks (her flesh tingling unpleasantly under the dress that clung to it), the shaken duo circumventing the pile at their feet comprised of bouncers and the immobilized assailant (almost rendered incapable even of wiggling), all of whom looked like possible circus runaways. Local law enforcement arrived a few minutes later.

⚫

When they got back and had stepped into the apartment they both stood just inside the living room a few feet in front of the door, unspeaking, looking and feeling dazed.

Stanley chuckled nervously, breaking a long silence. "You're not really a wanted criminal named Mary, or something other than Hope, are you?"

"Jesus. Of course not. That guy was out of his gourd. I've never seen him before. I can't believe you would even have to ask."

"I'm sorry. God, that was fucking insane."

"You're telling me! ...First time anything like that ever happened to me," she said, going farther into the room and slowly lowering herself to the sofa as if wearily, her purse falling off her shoulder.

"Same here. Needless to say I think."

"Yeah." She laughed. "Well, I guess I'm going to *try* to think about something else. If at all possible."

"I think I'm going to be thinking about that incident for a while to come," Stanley said, joining her on the couch. "Are you sure you're okay?"

"I'm fine, yeah. Oh shit—I should have changed out of this fucking burning dress before I sat down. Now the sofa's going to smell like goddamn gas." She got up in a rapid movement, headed for the bedroom.

Stanley sat there thinking, wondering if he fully believed her, until maybe twenty minutes later—after she had showered—when Hope, looking more than a little different due to her hair being damp, peeked her head in and said "Feel like hanging out in the room? Maybe putting a movie on?"

"Okay," he replied, really hoping—close to certain—he wasn't cohabiting, and much else, with a stranger.

13

They'd been together for a while and Stanley, whose life had changed rather drastically because of her, had come to the conclusion Hope was desirable to many people not only due to her being considered very physically attractive but often also because she was easygoing or gave off that impression, because she was smart and they liked what they felt they perceived about her. She got along with people seemingly effortlessly, and always had she said, had always fit in, despite or perhaps as a result of being a unique and complex specimen—though, he hypothesized (in a dark recess of his mind, in a part of it where he stored thoughts he didn't like to be reminded of and certainly preferred not to examine), she was potentially sinister, too. By adulthood, she confessed to him, she had come to unethically employ her popularity, her social talents; had developed the (to his thinking immoral) habit of using people, sometimes to get a foot in a door somewhere or stay on the side of a door she wanted to be on. She also engaged in the manipulation of others to satisfy her desire for excitement—she was she told him "hooked on adrenaline," and the roots of this went back to an early age.

"How did that start?" he'd asked her during the impromptu self-revelatory session in which this had come up.

"When I was still a young girl I discovered I was really kind of fearless, comparatively. And that I got high, a high I liked, from like placing myself in dangerous situations and surviving them. That sort of thing. From shoplifting and successfully committing other minor crimes; vandalism, cruelty to animals, criminal mischief. Throwing shit off overpasses, random assaults. Making bombs. Train-hopping. Eventually stuff like coming onto guys only so I could get into their house and steal from them."

"You can hurt people quite badly by dropping stuff from overpasses onto their cars. You can kill people."

"That never happened. More than one broken windshield happened."

He sat there, internally stupefied, a bit frightened—but more taken aback than anything.

"Wait, so you would just beat people up for no reason or something? People who were walking down the street?"

"Kind of, yeah. People who were walking down alleys or were sitting somewhere isolated. Like homeless people."

"Wow. Like what was the worst one, the worst you ever fucked someone up or whatever?"

"I stabbed a guy once. But it was with a Swiss army knife, in the side, and not very deep. He almost grabbed me actually."

"Just randomly stabbed him, huh?"

"Yes, Stanley," she answered with a measure of irritation.

"And then he tried to grab you and you ran away?"

"Yeah. He was this overweight, sixty- or sixty-five-year-old, bearded, ball cap-wearing, stinking—alcohol-reeking—garbage bag-surrounded red-faced transient. Rotting teeth and a gray beard with yellow hairs in it. He was very surprised, and needless to say not terribly agile. I still remember his swollen-looking hand, grasping; his bloodshot eyes opening suddenly to the pain."

"Was he asleep?"

"He was in the midst of a late-morning nap."

"...Quite an unpleasant awakening no doubt."

There was a silence that for Stanley, if not for Hope, was filled with contemplation.

"That was pretty mean, my love."

"I've changed a lot since then. That was not a recent event."

"What about the animal cruelty?"

"That was longer ago. When I was thirteen, fourteen. Even younger."

"Tell me about an instance of your abusing an animal," he said, feeling a person was being introduced to him he ought to've known—the identity of whom he wished he'd realized had all along been obscured, perhaps intentionally hidden—and wary about what he would find out.

"My parents had a pet rabbit that was very neurotic. I mean I know rabbits are usually timid, but this thing was ridiculous—it'd hop away or spasm if your hand got anywhere near it. And I disliked it. I didn't see the point of having it. And its existence seemed miserable besides. Anyway, I guess I made its life more miserable, briefly. I chloroformed it and put Tabasco in its eyes. My mother couldn't figure out what was wrong with it. And it was kind of funny. The thing really flipped. And as I say, it already acted near psychotic."

"That's a weird, fucked up thing to do."

"Yeah. I guess I was a so-called troubled child. But not as bad as many."

"Yeah."

"I mean some kids at that age are cappin' fools or molesting younger kids, gangbangin' or knockin' up some precocious preteen from the neighborhood."

"Right." He looked at the sociopathic stranger whose boyfriend he was, face impassive. "Of course it'd be pretty hard for you to knock anyone up though."

"Well aren't you a comedian today."

He smiled broadly, sitting near her in the untidy living room of a generally messy apartment, worried now about the turn—represented by Hope—that his life had taken.

"So...you also stole from people's houses?"

"Yeah. A couple times. Once—it was crazy—the guy ended up still being home. I was pretty high. It was stupid. He was high too, but unfortunately only on cold medicine, so he wasn't exactly immobilized. I was in the attic, where I knew he kept these, like, antique gold-plated dishes from Hungary or someplace, and I heard him below me, upstairs, lumbering around—he was kind of a fat dude. Ill-tempered, basically a total loser; had a Confederate flag hung up in his bedroom, was minimally employed, had lived with his parents for like forever. I pretended I was potentially romantically interested for a while, like two weeks, and had first come over after two dates. Anyway, I thought if I was quiet he'd go away and I'd just have to wait up there until I heard him leave; but then he pulled the attic stairs down, so I started looking for a weapon—assuming he knew I was up there, not that there was really anywhere to hide.

"I found a heavy wooden candlestick. About two minutes later—he was moving slowly, due to the two aforementioned factors—I saw his head emerge in the opening of the attic floor, eyes bleary, a combination of upset and confused. Without wasting time I swung the candlestick, before he had even seen me or processed my image I think, as powerfully as I could into his fat stupid skull, sending him crashing down to the hard floor. I remember he uttered a loud groan the moment the thing smashed his head, remember the substantial thud his body made hitting the second floor. Remember the look of his unconscious awkwardly situated corpus down below.

"I climbed down to take a closer look at him to try to determine how injured he was, if at all, and how long he might be out—trying to decide my best course of action, whether to pillage quickly or just to evacuate right then. What I chose to do, after reaching the conclusion that he was concussed and had a small forehead gash but might awake any moment, was to make sure he wasn't going to be able to do anything when he did come to and then to take my time collecting the plates and whatever if anything else I found that was valuable. So I located some duct tape in a drawer in the kitchen and brought it and a dirty hand towel upstairs to gag him and secure his hands and feet, hoping while I was looping the roll of tape around his appendages that he would not start to stir. Unfortunately though he did begin to awaken almost as soon as I'd started—I began with his feet, which were encased in fucking clunky shoes like Timberlands or something—and within a few seconds I had abandoned my task and he was grabbing at me, though his feet were thankfully pretty well secured, buying me some time. From the blow, the concussion—combined with the cough syrup or whatever—it was as if he was fairly groggy, and I was fast and comparatively highly aware, so he did not get ahold of me. I darted into the next room and soon he was hopping in that direction, in feeble pursuit. It seemed briefly that he was too out of it to free himself and that I would escape easily—although sadly empty-handed—and so I was thinking of just finding myself another weapon and going after him, but then he appeared in the room with the tape just trailing from one foot and fire in his eyes and my adrenaline got pumping, I really went into go mode.

"He goes after me full bore—but nonetheless kinda slow mind you—and I run as fast as I can in the space, making it downstairs. But then—and I shit you not, and this would pretty much be the end of the story if I hadn't been, I guess, dumb—I'm practically at the front door and he's coming down the stairs, fast (for him) and not being at all careful, like not watching his footing at all, just fueled by rage, and he trips, on the stairs, with like a lot of staircase to go, and ends up falling all the way to the bottom—like a sailing through the air sort of fall—and lands, *hard*, on his face. His face meeting the floor making a dull impact sound. And he's totally motionless, this is his second bad fall in a matter of minutes basically and this one was a good deal worse than the first, and this pool of dark red thick glossy liquid appears under his face and starts to spread, circular, across the hardwood floor. And I'm like, *Oh fuck. Is he fucking dead?* And, foolishly, after a minute of just watching this puddle of blood expand under this unmoving guy's face-down head—short, sweaty blond hair growing out of a pink scalp, pink rolls of superfluous tissue above his thick neck, this goddamn retarded profusely bleeding cookie-cutter redneck's meaty neck—I go over to him and bend down to check the carotid for a fucking pulse. And then, without even a hint of his still being conscious, in one swift motion he grabs my leg at the ankle with an extremely firm grip—his mouth, which his front teeth have been broken out of, pouring blood; his expression like he's an infuriated demon. And I cannot get free, and he's starting to pull himself onto me, really freaking me out—because I know now he's for sure going to kill me with his bare hands if he's able to. And so I kick him in the head, have to kick him twice, three times, and finally that does it, the fingers come loose, though he is only stunned long enough for me to open the door, and before I'm out he's gotten to his fucking feet and grabbed me in a bear hug and brings me to the floor, all of his weight on top of me, blood dribbling on to my head and clothes as he sweats and grunts saying like "Fuck you, bitch. I've fucking got you, you crafty cunt, I've fucking got you." And then I see a clenched up hand being cocked behind his head and the force of his large arm and white-knuckled fist being released into my eye—then blackness."

"Jesus. This is fucking insane. This is real?"

She shook her head to indicate the positive, seemingly exhilarated by the telling of her tale, an event she had likely not recollected in many years. "I woke up with him above me, still sweating and bleeding on me, on a cold floor covered with garbage and miscellany, a small oblong window below the ceiling of the dim room I was in, which I realized was his basement. I was kind of woozy but didn't feel that hurt, and felt pressure but didn't feel restrained, but something did feel weird—I wasn't sure what. It took me a minute to process all the stimuli. Then I understood that what I was reacting to was the sensation of a penis in my vagina, and noticed that my body was intermittently being pushed upward slightly, my back sliding rhythmically on the chilly concrete—that I was being fucked, I had no idea for how long. That my weakened body was being rocked on a cold floor below some house as I was raped by a borderline hillbilly with a bad haircut, and that said person would maybe be able to do whatever else he wanted to me, to my body, at his leisure, hate-filled, leaking blood. That I possibly would die there, aged sixteen, in a dim messy basement in an suburb of Tempe on a fucking midweek morning.

"For a second I felt incredibly disgusted, actually nauseous, but that changed very quickly into a feeling of violation—which really pissed me off. I didn't care so much that he was inside me I cared that I hadn't allowed him to be.

"Realizing that I wasn't actually tied or anything but only being pressed to the ground by his body I tried to force him off of me, but he punched me in the face again—with about a third of the force as the previous time, not hard enough to knock me out.

"...I remember...drops of his acrid sweat landing on my lips, a drip hitting me in the eye. That his penis was neither big nor small but fairly thick. That to me he was like an injured paleolithic man in a t-shirt dampened and stained by body fluids, starved for sex and incapable of gentleness, self-awareness, higher thought. And that the degree of arousal I came to feel as he rather brutally fucked me, seemingly endlessly—eventually ripping my shirt and bra, staring at my moving breasts drooling bloody drool onto them as he rammed me—just caused my thoughts about him to be the more hateful and violent.

"'Now I'm getting that hot pussy you were holding out on me' I remember him saying. 'I bet you're a real slut bag. Hot fucking bitch' I processed him saying, trying to be somewhere else, mentally, as he kept fucking me, as roughly as he could, while I was totally helpless.

"It was all infuriating. My partially liking it, the violation, the inability to stop it. My pussy was feeling sore, from the force, and perhaps also because he had been raping me for quite some time before I gained consciousness, his dull eyes which now read venomous looking down at my unanimated face, my tits, the left one definitely bruised."

She stopped, Stanley staring at her intently but feeling as though he was barely hiding a level of disgust toward Hope that he didn't understand completely though felt was somewhat undeserved.

"And?"

"And...it really sucked."

"But how'd you get free?"

"He climaxed, finally—it felt like hours—said 'That was real nice,' smiling, degradingly, making me want to extract his remaining teeth with the claw of a hammer, and released me into the wild."

"You mean outside?"

"Ha. No actually. I mean it was outside, yes. He drove me out to like a desert area fifteen minutes away, drug me out of the vehicle, and his parting words, before punching me in the face really hard, were: 'I hope you have to crawl out.'"

Stanley, experiencing a sensation of being nearly psychically overloaded by her recounting, after a few moments directed his eyes to the table in front of him, covered with assorted items—some marijuana-related, many drug-related—his eyes seeing its contents but not taking them in, his mind's activity solely devoted to the taking in of that which he had just been told; he in socks, pajama bottoms and generic white tee, not long ago having finished his morning coffee and internally near aghast at the now clearer picture of his partner, a picture that with some gentle prodding she had herself made more clear, without any identifiable indications of shame or a like result—regret, horror.

Hope seemed to be lost in thought too. "I can picture myself staggering wearily through sand, falling repeatedly, finally giving up and resting then resuming my trek, being picked up before long by a kind couple passing in their Jeep. ...It had a rack with camping stuff on it; the guy's teeth were very white; his girlfriend or wife looked like someone from a woman's fitness magazine. I felt ravaged—bodily, psychologically—though I wasn't in particularly bad shape. I calmed down a bit on the criminal activity after that. Though I don't think it made me a better person." She laughed. "More the opposite."

He watched her lean over to grab the bong, filling it from a film canister-type bottle, wondering if he was in some way—or rather for some reason—her prey. A captive—emotional captive—of a monster, in highly pleasing form.

Her self-stated pattern of rampant people usage, maybe anti-societal behavior made Stanley uncomfortable. Made him seriously wonder if, for whatever reason (he didn't even have a guess what it would be—unless she was just entertaining herself, got off on her own power), she was merely manipulating him. But her revelations caused him to want to learn more, as he assumed there was more—probably a lot more—to know about the dark past, the perhaps extant dark side, of his new love; the sexiest one he had ever had, the one who was still the most the stranger to him, though about whom he had recently gained much information—regarding the negative aspects of whom Stanley was it might've been destructively compelled to discover more about, yet afraid to.

However, it was that same day—they were in the living room, still lounging, as they often were—when his angelic-looking if more internally demonic partner, the girl from everywhere with the choppy haircut, opened wider the door into her.

He and she were stoned, both drinking bottled beer, fridge-chilled. Smoke hung in the air, pungent, a cloud above and in front of the couch. Stanley was perturbed and his forehead showed it, his fingers on the sides of his head showing it, despite the substances that were meant to make him feel good. Hope, though her eyes were not glassy as Stanley's, was oblivious or indifferent to his state.

No longer content to do nothing or to let the whole of his thoughts stew within, he looked over at the woman beside him, a warm cipher, his body like it was filled with quivering water; took a moment, deliberating; then spoke.

"I really feel—after this morning, and I already had kind of, sometimes, felt this way—like I don't know you. Or I'm finally starting to, and from what little I know even now you aren't who I thought."

"Well then, sweetie." She met his eyes, her dark irises devoid of distinct emotion. "I promise: I'm going to totally open up about myself. Tonight. Maybe you just haven't been inquisitive enough."

"You haven't been exactly forthright," returned the other, half-indignant, in the hazy room it seemed they spent so much time in. "You've made yourself sound...like. I don't know. Like sorta crazy."

"My past hasn't been the most typical maybe. My life has maybe been more adventurous than many people's. I've been more experimental, as far as my choices, than some. I grant you that."

As he stared into her vacuum eyes, eyes he sometimes saw as that, at the object of his affection who perhaps was more of an object (for him) than he wanted to believe, he was trying to come to some definite conclusion by simultaneously studying and listening to her.

"I can assure you I'm quite sane."

"Ha." His response surprised him, but he was not in a typical frame of mind. He altered his posture on the couch. "But. Hope. As you know, I think, a quote crazy person would likely not think of themselves as insane, and even if they somehow had that insight I don't think they would admit their condition to others, as a matter of preservation."

She took a big hit, placed the bong back on the cluttered table, saying at length, as Stanley observed her coldly, "I am not responsible for what goes on in your brain."

"So how does this begin? Self-revelatory session número dos."

"You could tell me what you want to know."

"You could tell me what I don't know."

"Don't you think you need to narrow it down a little, realistically?" (laughter) "I mean you want me to read *War and Peace* aloud to you too?" She took a swig of brew, laughing again but in a new way; a foreign, obnoxious laugh he thought was a bizarre sound to've come out of her. A kind of laugh like he would expect from a perverted sixty-something-year-old man in a nightclub stand-up set.

He was feeling a bit irritated. "Fine. Uh...how many boyfriends have you had?"

"Eleven or twelve before you probably. Something like that."

"How many of them did you love?"

She seemed to ruminate. "None. I don't think I really loved any of them. I don't think I had time to love any of them anyway."

"Have you ever cheated on someone?"

"Yes."

"How many of the people you've been with have you cheated on?"

"Only three I think. Not counting a guy who basically asked me to. To do stuff with other guys."

"*Only* three? You make it sound like that's something to be proud of. For one thing that's like a fourth."

"I didn't say I was proud of anything. I've never implied that I consider myself a paragon of virtue."

Again hardly believing the words that were issuing from her lips he was shaking his head just perceptibly. "So you had a boyfriend that you were in an open relationship with?"

"I wouldn't say open relationship so much as he liked to watch me give other people head. I sucked off a lot of guys while I was with him, even publicly a couple of times. In fairness I had actually been cheating on him anyway, but I stopped counting it when I found out he was into that sort of thing. The way the whole thing happened was I admitted it to him and then he ended up telling me he would get off on seeing me perform fellatio on random dudes. I thought the idea of blowing guys in front of him was pretty hot, so it was a win-win. But eventually he broke up with me, because I kept fucking other guys too." She laughed. "At first he tolerated it, but it got to the point where he'd come home to me getting banged almost every day. He wasn't so into me fucking other people.

"One time he walked in on me bent over the couch, nude, getting the shit fucked out of me by some hot dude I had met that day, and he just lost it. I never saw him again."

Stanley was pinching the bridge of his nose. "I think we need to stop for now. Stop the...session, revealing session. It's too much."

She looked at him with a smile part quizzical and part

condescending, as if she regarded him as a curious, perhaps pathetic, alien creature that'd found itself disoriented and helpless in a strange land.

"You don't know anything about me," he heard her saying, song-sing, as if in a nightmare, through a fog.

"Jesus. It literally horrifies me to hear that," he managed to say. "I need another beer," he said going to the kitchen for that purpose.

"Are you afraid of me or something?"

"Something like that, yeah, Hope. You're like a bottomless container of mystery. And the more I discover the less I wish I had." He deliberated whether to return to the sofa, deciding on doing so.

Looking at him intently she said, "You started this."

"Curiosity killed the cat."

"...Are you calling yourself a pussy?" She snickered, happy, at ease, in her world.

Stanley wasn't amused, felt quite the opposite of cheerful. "What else?" he asked.

"What else don't you know?"

"Exactly."

"Again: that's really not narrowing it down at all, but, for one thing"—she took a gulp from her bottle of beer, a green bottle, the beer inside going warm—"I know this guy."

His heart sunk a bit, preemptively. "You know this guy? What guy is that?"

"His name's Emile."

"Emile? And what does Emile have to do with anything? Who is he?"

"He's, say, a business associate. I have a...business arrangement with him."

"How did you meet Emile?"

"The café. He used to come in."

"Okay. And what sort of business do you conduct with Emile?"

"Entertainment services, loosely, I suppose."

"What the fuck does—entertainment services? What does *that* mean?"

"I know you're not going to like this, but...I let him use my body, for money. On occasion. Set times."

Stanley felt his face flush and, at the same moment, the room seemed to start to spin: he experienced the space as if it really were in motion, as if he were suddenly having a strong and unpleasant hallucination or strapped into a whizzing carnival ride.

"Three hours once a week. In the early evening."

She looked at him, gauging, trying to gauge, how he was handling the information—the instant of heartbreak. "I know what you must think. But it's just for money. The agreement is that I am sexually at his disposal, with some rules, for that block of time. But we basically just have sex—regular non-atypical intercourse—and I am generally out of there inside ninety minutes."

His fingers were on his temples. His face was lightly coated in perspiration. He had entered into another realm, internally—a dimension in which he felt at once intensely inside of but also removed from and objectively observant of himself, a sweating newly broken man-boy, reduced swiftly to rubble psychologically by a so-regarded girlfriend who was nothing more than a literal prostitute. Whose body, far from being a temple or what only she, he, and a physician had access to, was actually something that this woman opted to sell to any adequately bankrolled bidder. Who was a sordid, probably deranged, cipher—certainly a psychically unwell person—with whom he'd been sharing a bed, and a life, and was now completely dependent on; and emotionally enslaved to.

Hope was, she elaborated, as she became higher and—going repeatedly to the fridge—approached drunkenness (a state Stanley seldom saw her in, and one which on this occasion seemed to render her somewhat crude and annoying), three weeks into a nine-week arrangement with a European immigrant, himself apparently something of an entrepreneur; also, she told her beaded-skinned horror-filled partner, income was earned by occasionally running deliveries for him. The morning following each meeting with Hope, she explained, he transferred one-ninth of one hundred thousand dollars into her bank account—and after nine rendezvous the terms of their agreement would be fulfilled, and Hope's checking account balance would be substantially augmented.

"He certainly finds you valuable. Your pussy. What does your fucking john look like?" Stanley asked barely managing not to choke, his eyes watery and unable to focus, the spinning having yet not entirely ceased, after he had had a minute for this information to set in.

She laughed heartily. Another unfamiliar, grating laugh. The kind of sound one might expect to emanate from a devil-may-care, seventy-three-year-old man who smoked cigars and lusted after teenagers. "Medium-height, stocky. Dude in his mid-thirties. Pretty generic."

"Does he wear a condom?" Stanley inquired, knowing she had a IUD.

"No. But he's clean."

He felt something warm, moist, streaming down his cheeks, a slow droplet per—realized by feel rather than mental state that he'd begun crying. (And for a split second he actually imagined Hope chomping on a cigar, sitting in a masculine manner, saying "So I fuck other men. Are you really surprised? Stop sobbing you girl.")

"Have you ever been a prostitute before?"

"Oh god. Are you actually shedding tears?"

"YES YOU FUCKIN WHORE. I'm a person. So yeah."

She guffawed. "You're being super emotional about this. And you oughtn't whore shame. After all," she winked, "it's the world's oldest profession."

"Answer, you evil fucking nonhuman."

"Stanley, I'm sorry you're hurt. Okay? I get it. I'm not who you assumed I was."

"Yeah. Well have you?"

"I've given some guys blow jobs for money."

He was looking at her through a veil of saline, using eyes plugged into puffy pink-red circles. "How long ago...did you last do that?" Stanley inquired, trying to gain some hold on his emotional state.

"Um... About seven or eight months ago maybe. I've only done it when I found the guy really attractive."

"How many guys would you say you've done that with, for pay?"

"A dozen or so."

"Jesus." The tears flowed afresh, snot emerging clear thick and bubbly from both nostrils, as he failed to retain any control. "You're such a terrible person. How have you been able to do this, seriously?"

She exhaled exaggeratedly, as if vexed; then took a drink of beer, the last of the bottle. "Stanley? All prostitutes are, in your opinion, horrible people?" Her reply was synched with another return to the kitchen.

"No. You are." His wet, swollen eyes had followed her. "Because behind my back you've been doing this. You knew what you were doing to me. You've been not only cheating on me but literally *whoring* yourself."

"I never said I wasn't going to sleep with other people."

Stanley, watching her come back into the room, emitted a sound of exasperated incredulity.

Hope drank of her just obtained beverage then began singing, looking at him from the corner of her eye. "She's a tomboy, tomboy. Got herself an ego, ego."

Stanley was watching her puzzled, feeling drained of life.

"She's a supervillain's hero, hero." She hummed. "She's a liar, she's a cheater, she's a curser." Humming. "If she knows you, then she owns you. You can't get far, you leave her." She took another gulp of green-bottle beer.

"What are you singing?"

"She's a rebel, she's a rival, she's a walking Inquisition. She ain't got mercy, she's just thirsty, and she's filled with ammunition."

"What are you doing? What is that?" Wiping his cheeks.

She looked at him disapprovingly. "Gonna trick you, and pick you, but just don't be defeated. Gonna leave you, deceive you, you'll never feel so mistreated." She broke off to answer, "Habibi," then continued. "If you see her, you should fear her—don't fall for her cooing."

———

"What's the longest relationship you've ever been in, Hope?" her beleaguered boyfriend asked, his eyes' redness reduced over the previous few minutes of recuperative silence.

"About half a year. Why?"

"Because we've been together for nearly four months and I just found out that you are and have been a whore. That you are actively a prostitute. Doesn't that seem a little fucked up...to you?"

"Does the thing with the Emile guy really bother you?"

"Uh, yeah," he said, his renewed amazement partly evidenced by the collection of creases between his eyebrows. "I'm officially doing terribly. I mean you just told me you've been fucking another guy a quarter of the brief time we've been together. That you started fucking him *after* we got together." He laughed pathetically, hopelessly, cathartically. "I don't want you to sleep with him again," he added, feeling his emotions regathered to some extent by force of will. "If you want 'us' to continue to be in any way a thing."

"We never discussed being monogamous. And I have no feelings for him, certainly not of a romantic sort. And I need the money. Plus even though I basically loathe him...we are very sexually compatible. ...And having sex with people for money kind of turns me on."

It came on quick, unexpected, on the heels of what he had thought of as an ultimatum (though he didn't honestly expect Hope to accept his condition), but Stanley had probably never been more enraged. His jealousy and obvious anger seemed to cause a smile to form on Hope's face, which smile her significant other read as purely malicious, and served merely to tip him mentally into a state of near psychotic ire. He wanted to rip her face off (a beautiful work of genetics plus time untouched by tragedy—until he sunk his adrenaline-strengthened hands into it one day in her living room when she was twenty-six), or his scarlet own—to feel flesh being torn by his tightening fingers.

"What do you mean by sexually compatible?" He was barely holding off tears. "...You awful cunt." His windpipe was tight; nausea was another result of his consuming anger, a tremendous unprecedented anger that frustratingly was without expression—and, it seemed to him, short of committing unplanned homicide would remain unexpressed, unpurged from him.

Hope cleared her throat, cast her eyes across the room. "Well, if you really want to know. I mean he's good in bed, and—on just an animal level—I'm pretty attracted to him."

"Fuck you."

She giggled, girlish now, extending her right arm to reach his manhood, which, Stanley wasn't consciously aware, had become erect. "You asked."

He pushed it away with his own arm, almost reflectively, a little ashamed at his arousal, offended she would make sexual contact with him.

For some time he was staring at the table—disappeared into it, into himself—as he considered the various ways that his body had reacted to his emotions; while too he tried processing as objectively as he might the new reality (new to him) that this Hope person (*If that was her real name* he thought with a sad internal chuckle) was a malevolent likely mentally ill individual, maybe a psychopath, and that so many of the positive attributes about her, roles she had filled, were fabrications of his mind, assumptions proven false.

"So it doesn't bother you to be a whore, that is an actual whore?" he asked, thinking he had achieved a certain clearness of mind after a period of lucid reflection that'd been for him duration-less.

"I honestly like being a whore," she responded, verging irritatingly on self-satisfaction. "I don't advertise the fact but I'm not ashamed of it. I don't feel I should be. Besides: It's getting paid, very well in the case of my deal with Emile, to do something that I always get enjoyment out of. That I'm good at. And it's a profession that serves an important societal need."

Beside her, Stanley's seething was revealed by his face, which appeared preliminarily puckered for a pending eruption.

"I can tell you're really jealous. I'm sorry." She pecked him on the lips.

Regardless of his desires it was clear his supposed significant other was planning on continuing with her confessed arrangement, that very possibly she had never had any interest in a committed relationship, and therefore he would be terminating whatever so-called relationship they had had. (Though that hardly seemed to matter having learned that she was more or less inarguably a terrible person, maybe insane, definitely a total mess psychologically, and a proud harlot.)

"So is there a certain day you've been fucking him?"

"Tuesdays," she responded in a manner she might've if he'd asked what she was preparing for dinner.

"Wait." His face was a radish hue again; he was conscious of his heart pounding unpleasantly and its beat seemed loud, audible— even to the attractive prostitute he loved, thought he had, but in fact was only in the last hours coming to meaningfully know, only now seeing beneath the pleasing mask of. "Is that why you've been too sore to have sex sometimes?"

"Yeah." Still, while seemingly attempting to hide it, she read as pleased with herself. Stanley's brain, consequently, took him on a fast journey along an imagined street paved by moving images of Hope's face and/or whole body being ruined by violence, sometimes inflicted by him (sometimes with results unsurvivable). "I know that's lame, baby. But I promise from now on to always go down on you when I'm too sore."

Now two fingers were massaging his penis, its warmth steadily increasing. Stanley was too aroused to elect to stop her.

"Does he have rough sex with you?"

"No. Aside from pulling my hair a little. But he's not gentle either. He throws me around sort of too I guess. Not to the extent I get bruised or anything. And anyway I kind of like that also. I'm pretty sure that despite his sexual interest and the fact that he trusts me he doesn't particularly like me either, or any other woman. He's a piece of shit. Who I'm sure gets off on treating women like objects." She looked at him with an expression he perceived as apologetic. "I always want to fuck you you know...it's just that I'm not used to having sex with someone who's so big, down there. And it's usually pretty athletic sex, that lasts a while...and I typically orgasm a couple of times. So I have to recover a little."

He wanted to explode, emotionally, or just die, immediately cease to be alive in order to never again experience pain—but he also wanted to fuck her. Really hard. Rage fuck her. Fuck her with a ferocity like never before. His demented whore of a faux girlfriend. His amoral sex worker girlfriend. Who had during most of the third of a year of their relationship (a word he thought he had never heard her say) been sleeping with someone else. Who he now thought was probably a nymphomaniac or some variety of deviant (perhaps more than one variety). Who he now thought much, much differently of. Negatively so.

It wasn't that he necessarily had an issue with Hope's being possibly a nymphomaniac, though he thought the truth was likely something more commonly considered undesirable; but: *Who wanted a nymphomaniac girlfriend if they were going to sleep with other guys?*

He wasn't special, he could now see, even if his purpose for her remained a mystery; she was a dirty slut and there was something wrong with her head. Maybe she had been touched young by a special uncle who enjoyed the company of children far too much. Maybe cutting her hair choppy and weird and her having intercourse with local businessmen she didn't know in exchange for financial gain had a root cause in common. Maybe she was completely insane. And a sadomasochist who had brought Stanley into her life only to own and then emotionally and otherwise annihilate him. Because it gave her pleasure to destroy, to destroy people. It alleviated her boredom, an ennui intensified by her superior intelligence. Perhaps having sex with strangers served that function. Perhaps she was of the sort—and she had basically said she once was—that got in car crashes just to feel. Maybe by the time she was forty her body would be as wretched as she was on the inside, would offer a record of her violence, her nihilism. *And then she would only be fucking ugly people,* Stanley cogitated darkly. *It might so happen that by then she's a heroin addict, puncture marks up her thin, scarred arms. And her unhygienic johns, two or three daily, finance her habit and a bed in a motel, barely. And she hardly eats and has an irremediable incapacity for enjoyment or levity. And she dies, forgotten, at forty-three in said room of a malnutrition-linked heart seizure.*

The unhappy future he imagined for her had brought a smile to his face—a kind of twisted, malicious grin—and caused him momentarily to forget why he felt he now hated her (though that probably wasn't accurate; his true feelings were at least more complicated— but for the moment a feeling akin to hatred, or a temporary hatred, radiated from within; and he enjoyed it, wallowed in it, imagining further: he pictured her run over but still alive, her body mangled, all of it save one arm immobile, and her one not completely ruined arm reaching out to him desperately, shock in her eyes, as she mouthed "Help me," a ruin of blood and fat and bone and muscle, an askew face and head above topped by dark brown hair matted with expelled bodily fluid—Stanley standing over her motionless, looking down with the same cold grin and finally spitting on her face. Pictured her diving into a shimmering springtime river, and coming up after a moment with blood gushing out of her skull, gasping, bobbing helplessly, having hit her head—hard—on the muddy bottom. And again, standing on the bank, was an unsympathetically observing Stanley, enjoying the show, waiting for her to sink after a minute or two of useless struggle, her final seconds of consciousness after a lifetime of bad deeds and apathy spent in futile panic).

Far more than when he and Hope had met and practically at once become an item he felt he was in an alternate universe. And the dimension he'd thought a paradise had, in mere minutes, turned into a realm more akin to the Twilight Zone, like a version of Hell (that somehow, it seemed to him, back of his mind, was a version only he could have inadvertently tailored for himself—which thought caused a twinge of mental agony and regret).

"It's just one guy. And just for six weeks more," he heard her saying, his pleasant trance of envisioned deaths interrupted. "That's only six more times. I don't care about him at all. Only his money."

It was as if someone far away—but coming nearer—was trying to propel him into inconsolable depression using merely their voice, and was gradually succeeding. He thought this semiconsciously. Then she was opening his fly with a soft, smallish right hand the nails of which had recently been painted azure and pulling his manhood, red and athrob, from the leg of his pants and his boxers. He was seeing her do this, feeling the pleasure of it, as in a fog; mentally hating it to a large degree, but surrendering to her actions.

He watched, again experiencing a sensation like he was removed from himself and yet physically present and stimulated, as Hope bent her head down to the level of the blood-rushed appendage beating in her smooth hand. She put his fully erect member, all of it, into her mouth, then much more slowly raised her head until the very tip was at her lips, then went back down to the base, at molasses pace, his penis pulsating in her throat briefly before she began to gradually lift her head again.

Stanley involuntarily closed his eyes and let his head fall back against the wall above the couch, letting out a moan. She moved from the sofa to between his legs, jerking him off for a moment before slowly moving her lips down the veiny apparatus sticking out of his khakis until once more its head was touching the back of her throat and the entirety of his shaft was in the warmth of her mouth;

the moist mouth, saliva-wet canal, of a whore with oral expertise and a choppy haircut, a woman with an ideally curved posterior and silky tight vagina that she might offer up to anyone for a price, enough little pieces of thick green-printed paper. As he sporadically moaned, sporadically watched her perfectly formed lips move up and down on him, as she sporadically made slurping noises, continuing to fellate him, she imperceptibly quickened the speed at which she moved her mouth over his glistening and inflamed-appearing member, coated thickly with her the secretion of her glands. She was bobbing quite briskly when with what felt like tremendous force he shot semen down her throat, after some ecstatic minutes, the new nightmare of her again for that time gone from his conscious mind. "Oh fuck yeah," he said, hardly aware of speaking, feeling after he had somewhat physically recovered, somewhat returned from a plane of sexual heaven, immense satisfaction. Only then did he remember all that had just changed, in such a horrific way, in regard to Hope. Remember her frankness as she tore him open where he was most vulnerable, an insensitivity that had made it all the worse, all the more infuriating. Remember that she had been not only, to his mind, unfaithful on numerous occasions but was additionally the very definition of a prostitute—and derived satisfaction from this fact. Realize that he probably would not be able to bring himself to break up with her. That if he stayed with her he would probably be unable not to frequently imagine her having sex with another man for a long time to come, and be internally rent every time he did.

"Do you go down on him?" he decided to ask her. He had zipped up but was still on the sofa (he felt almost sunken into it, or perhaps just unmotivated, too sad to will his body upright). Hope was in the kitchen.

"Don't ask questions you don't want to know the answer to."

"I want to know."

"Yes." She thought for a moment, yet another beer in her hand.

"He always wants me to deepthroat him. Which is impossible. For me. It's like he's a mutant or something." She laughed, and the laugh along with everything she was saying became etched permanently in Stanley's mind, in a place in it where the worst memories were stored. "I can only fit two-thirds of it in my mouth at most. I have to admit, I like it—but...more than anything I think it's because he treats me like trash. I like feeling used, being used by men. I like being a whore, and being treated like one. I like having intense sex with a guy I barely know and don't like, for money, in a really nice apartment. I like it when the only sound is the sound of me choking on his dick. He doesn't play music or turn on the TV or anything so all he can hear is the sounds of us fucking. He likes that too." She ingested some beer, contemplative. "I just like sex in general, like most people, but he's particularly good at it. And because I don't like him I try to stop myself from coming, which I'm pretty sure makes me come harder, and faster, more often." She giggled as she absorbed, looking pitiless, his twisted face. "I can't help it. I've learned that getting efficiently banged by a well-hung guy makes me have a lot of orgasms. I had so many the second time I lost count. I was shaking by the time he finished. But. Baby. Remember:" She smiled toothily. "I'm not doing it because I like it I'm doing it for my bank account. There's nothing wrong with liking your job though, right?"

Stanley—more stunned than repulsed, paralyzed—felt sure he never had nor ever would meet such a heartless person, a person he could evermore only view as one of the lowest kinds of degenerate.

"No. There's nothing wrong with liking your job," he responded with easily detectable iciness through gritted teeth. *Psycho bitch*, he was thinking. *Psycho whore. Gross, disturbed whore.*

"You realize that you told me about a hundred times too much, don't you? If not a thousand?"

"I'm really honest... I was just talking. To my boyfriend."

"But not honest enough to tell me you're fucking somebody else."

"Then what are we talking about?"

"Hope." He was exasperated, his new depression a coat of lead. "I think you're a disgusting, extremely foul, utterly mentally ill reprobate. You know that, right? Or would that be expecting too much?

Or do you just not care at all, about what I think of you? Is self-reflection or self-awareness beyond you? You're not that fucked up—are you? I mean I know now you're pretty *goddamned* fucked up, but not in that sort of way. Right? I mean thanks—really, thanks—for that amount of detail. Do you think you could have talked any more about the penis of the guy you are fucking?"

"I really don't see what the big deal is. It's just sex. A perfectly natural part of the human experience. And I'm not exactly some malevolent beast, incapable of seeing myself or outside of myself."

"Well"—his posture was all tension—"it's a big deal because even though you've been letting someone shove their member in *numerous of your slut holes* I'm basically your fucking BOYFRIEND," he screamed across the room. "And for another thing because I don't want to hear about some dude's dick—especially in relationship to your mouth."

He almost broke down once more. "Goddammit. Don't you get emotions? The attachments people form to other people? Simple, human, typical social stuff?"

Taken aback still by his outburst as she stood in the kitchen bottle in hand Hope looked genuinely perplexed.

"Of course. I guess I just wasn't thinking about it. I'm sorry."

She walked over to him and kissed him on the lips.

Stanley spat. "Fuck you. Go away."

"Want to go to bed?" she asked, laying on the sultriness, as if not having seen nor heard his reaction, as though nothing had transpired, as if nothing was transpiring.

"I want to throttle you, to be truthful."

"Wow." She made long eye contact, her eyes placid and glossy. "How about you hug me instead? Hug my vagina with your penis." She grinned, her merriness in full contrast to the condition of the psychologically battered man she leaned over. "Think you're up for it?"

Stanley let out a deep frustrated sigh, shook his head, said "No. But if you wiggle your hot ass in my face anything's possible," and, moving like a man in his late sixties, took her hand and accompanied her to the bedroom that was now his only bedroom. The bedroom of a vile specimen who Stanley had the misfortune of loving.

He determined himself to be a bit helpless, hopeless; felt already resigned to his fate, of staying with her (whatever that meant), to the quantum of his attraction. The fate of being the partner of a beautiful woman whose head there was something terribly wrong with. A prisoner to aspects of his animality.

————————

That night he dreamt of dead cockroaches in the walls and under the floor; he thought of VHS copies of direct-to-video sequels to modest commercial successes. Of pureed food-stained bibs and striped rattles and rubber huge fake light-brown nipples known as pacifiers; of a mobile that played brief looped lullabies and from which dangled spinning hollow plastic clowns, red spheres for noses and red circles for dimples, with frizzy orange hair under brown derbies and yellow umbrellas in their hands—hung rotating above an infant respiring as through a screen of mucus, winter air coming in an open window through soiled gauze curtains. A musty living room barely lit by a tall lamp's yellow bulb, a decaying armchair the centerpiece, its hanging strings of fabric like clinging dead skin, and on shelves behind it in front of book collections untouched for twenty years dusty picture frames with photos of dead middleaged people inside, the enclosure all earth tones.

14

*F*ucking *whore bitch*, Stanley was thinking, not having yet really processed everything the individual he was ruminating on had said the previous night. *How did I end up in love with a fucked up bitch whore?*

For one thing because you knew almost nothing about her, nothing important, he answered. *Love is irrational anyway. Maybe you would have fallen for her regardless. You never know. She is quite unique, intelligent, sexy, charismatic; and even yet mysterious.*

"About how many people would you say you've slept with, Hope?" her embittered boyfriend asked, nearly scowling.

They sat—Hope still in her sleeping-rabbit-spotted gray pajama bottoms, a trio of Zs emanating from the compact bunny—on opposite sides of the couch, drinking coffee that steamed from mugs, hers plain orange, his white with an illustration of a corpulent cartoon cat on it.

"Slept with? Probably about forty or forty-five. ...What about you?" she asked as if the question were an afterthought she didn't care to know the answer to.

"Seventeen."

"I'm lucky number seventeen, huh?"

"You are. And I love you. Which is a very unhappy reality."

"Ahhh," she said with a winsome smile and, though likely not to be unkind, condescendingly.

"You heard the last part, correct?"

"Yes." Hope distantly sipped java.

Something occurred to Stanley then, something he didn't like. "You haven't had sex with more than forty-five people?"

"Sort of, yeah."

"What do you mean by sort of?" he asked, fearing the answer—oddly, since he didn't really think he could be further damaged by her.

"If you count oral sex."

"About how many guys would you say you've done that with, just that?"

"A lot, like I've said. Definitely over fifty. I don't know how many really. ...Look, the only guy I'm going to have sex with, besides you, is Emile. And only six times. ...Stanley, I love to fuck. I love it. More than anything. And a lot of guys find me attractive. So the fact that with this one exception I've only been having sex with you is very meaningful."

"Super." He ran his hand over his forehead and into his hair. "Fuck. Fuck me. Fuck. You are one unlucky man's girlfriend. Since it's exactly like you don't care about anyone but yourself. Not that it matters that you're my girlfriend, given your unfaithfulness."

"It's just a job. We could have talked about this before I made a deal with him."

"But we didn't. I didn't have the chance to say definitely not, because you never brought it up to me."

"I didn't think you would care. I didn't think it was an issue. We talked about this last night and I didn't know you were under the impression this, the 'us' thing, was a committed thing."

"Even if you are so stupid as to've been unaware that was my expectation—my, fucking, understanding—how could you think it wasn't an issue? You can't even have sex with me the day afterwards."

"I had no idea to expect that complication."

"Jesus Christ. This is so fucked up." Spit flew from his mouth. "I thought you were someone halfway—a quarter normal."

"I wasn't going to back out of it once I had agreed to a certain number of meetings, given how much money is in it for me. I'm going to be practically rich."

She drank carefully from the mug of hot dark brown bean juice. "All this comes down to is that I have a job you didn't know about."

Stanley guffawed. "A job that involves somebody's penis being in you! ...I don't even feel like I can trust you to not fuck—or fellate—anybody besides me and your john. I mean how could I? You're insane. You're some kind of insane nymphomaniac. Seriously. You can't even say how many guys you've blown for god's sake. Or fucked. How does being extremely, maybe psychotically promiscuous fit into leading a healthy lifestyle?"

"It's certainly not healthy not to have sex, I can tell you that."

"Yeah," he said with exaggerated snideness. "So what would your guess be as to how many guys you've sucked off anyway? Sixty? Seventy?"

"I don't know," she said, seeming mildly irritated. "Between sixty-five and seventy-five, yeah."

He exhaled substantially, looking at the floor—flabbergasted, stressed—then looked back at Hope, who above a plethora of slumbering rabbits was wearing a white tank top over a white bra. Whose look seemed to say *What?* with eyes of sincerity.

"How do you expect me to trust you—when it comes to fidelity?"

"To be honest, baby, I don't expect anything from you. That might be the way I'd prefer it stays." She got up—flashing a look over her shoulder that was alluring, vexatious; which said *I can and will do whatever I choose. You don't matter*—finishing her coffee in the kitchen then placing the bright orange cup in the sink.

"Has Emile ever come in your mouth?" His rage was at full burn within. He watched her with narrowed eyes, judging, loathing.

"Once. Because I asked him to. He prefers to come in my pussy.

"I like swallowing come," she added casually, unconcerned with his internal experience and not noticing the color of Stanley's face nor aware he was approximately as internally irate as possible. "I'm going to the supermarket in a sec," said Hope, on a trajectory from the kitchen to their bedroom.

15

Some meditation on Hope, on the state of their relationship, had led Stanley to decide that the only way to cope even minimally with the fact she had been and was sleeping with someone else was to himself sleep with someone else—as soon as possible. And ideally he was going to enjoy it; would definitely not be guilty about it in the least—for he had absolutely no reason to have mixed feelings about it, though he didn't intend to inform her of his dalliance. So, that afternoon, Stanley, determined to engage in meaningless coitus with another woman, quickly put back a couple of pre-outing brews, put a little of Hope's weed in a baggie without asking, put that in his more than half empty pack of smokes, and left for a bar downtown, any bar, saying nothing to Hope of his departure, thinking merely *Fuck her*.

He ended up in a joint across from The Touchstone, sitting at the bar in the dim environs milking a pint of medium brown ale that was about eight percent alcohol he had ordered with a shot of rotgut he'd already downed.

There were few people inside the establishment. Two guys who looked to be about ten years older than they actually were, which was probably about thirty-five and forty-five, playing billiards; a woman with a belly and small breasts wearing a teal halter top and drinking a domestic, down the bar to his left; and another lone male, similarly aged, sitting in a booth with what might have been a Jack and coke. He was drinking slowly, hoping someone might come in he actually found attractive to some degree.

An hour later no one had. But the woman in teal, who maybe was in her early forties, was still present and working on her third beer since he'd been in the place. Behind him he could sporadically hear pool balls clacking together as the poorly aged duo—the older one with oily-looking longish hair and wearing a snug jacket of black denim, the younger one with a wide but sharp-angled face—continued their green-felt-table-based battling. He for the first time considered how it would be to have intercourse with Teal Woman, and did not like what he envisioned, but nonetheless left himself open to the possibility of approaching her, should no other, better prospect enter the tavern during the next few hours.

As one sixty-minute block became three he found the low light of its interior progressively more depressing, an effect attributable in part to his alcohol consumption, which by the beginning of his fourth hour in the unremarkable bar consisted of (since he'd been there) three pints of strong brew plus one Pabst and one he had just started working on, an elbow on the glossed wood spotted with rings from where coaster-less beverages had stood.

"Buy you a drink?" he said to Teal Woman, four barstools away from him, who seemed slightly inebriated and presently a somewhat more viable sexual partner than she had two hours earlier.

She smiled, showing enough of her front teeth that Stanley saw one was a bit brown, though they otherwise appeared to be in reasonable condition. "Sure, pilgrim," she said, the addressed one thinking her John Waynism peculiar.

He turned his attention to the fat redheaded man about twenty-eight or -nine years old on the other side of the bar. "Can I get a... What'll you have?"

"Damsel in Distress," she responded, the request a cocktail he had never heard of.

"I'd like to get a...Damsel in Distress for the young lady," he told the rather expressionless employee.

"Come here often?" he asked, continuing to be consciously unoriginal.

She laughed, her voice sounding a little scratchy, like the smoker he knew from her numerous trips outside she was. "Yeah. I do. Almost daily actually." With a phlegmatic countenance the bartender was concentrating on mixing the drink, which had five ingredients and which Stanley knew would be expensive. "What about you, sugar?" she asked and chuckled good-naturedly.

"No. Quite rarely. But I go to The Touchstone every so often, among other such businesses."

She flashed her teeth again. "You sound smart."

He smiled back, was trying to think of something to say besides 'Thanks' when the bartender said "That'll be eight-fifty" on his way to deliver the beverage requested, curly pink straw and wood and paper umbrella in it, to the woman down the bar.

"Well, thank you, sweetie!" she said to Stanley as the drink was placed on a coaster before her. "What a treat. I love these!"

"You're welcome. Glad to hear it," he responded, fearing an impending conversational lull, having placed a ten in front of him for her colorful libation. He surmised he likely had little in common with this woman, but could bed her; and, having decided that he was unlikely to have an opportunity with someone else, the hour become late, he resolved to work on doing so.

Stanley went right into boldness, figuring her signals were positive and he was the more attractive human being anyway. Taking a big gulp of his beer and getting up from his stool, beverage in hand, he said "Mind if I sit with you?"

"Be my guest, guy."

"So what's your name, stranger?" he queried the perfume-wearing woman—lines on her face visible now that weren't from the distance, and the foundation on her face visible from nearer too, a flaky-looking pinkish white layer over epidermis prematurely aged and with a few medium-sized moles—consciously thinking *I don't like her perfume. It's kind of strong and unappealingly floral.*

"Delilah. And yours?"

"That'd be Stanley," he said with a degree of artificial aplomb.

"Kind of an old man's name, isn't it?" She laughed, took a sip of her drink.

"Well, I don't know. But with a name like yours I'm worried if I fell asleep around you I'd wake up with my head shaved."

"Ha ha! You're funny. Smart and funny. And a generous gentle-man, for buying me my favorite drink. ...Hey, wait a second: Are you trying to get me drunk?" Laughter. More teeth, including the one brown one.

This is actually going pretty well so far, thought Stanley, whose eyes then momentarily went down to her stomach, reminding him he didn't like the look of it. "No, no. ...Maybe." He laughed, sipped his Pabst, his eyes having journeyed up to her breasts for a quick evaluational glance. One thing he did like was her lack of a brassiere, and that he could see the outline of her nipples. And he had noticed she had a decent, good-sized posterior. *Yeah. She wouldn't be too bad* he thought.

"And why would you want to get li'l old me drunk?" she asked flirty, leaning into him in a bodily expression of mirth.

I'm just trying to weasel my dick into your pussy he heard in his mind. "Maybe to find out what the *real* Delilah's like," he answered winking.

"Ha. You just met me!"

"And you just met me. But already I'm laying my heart bare to you," he said bringing clasped hands to his chest and turning on sac-charine corniness.

"You're *weeiirrd*, Stanley." She lightly placed a hand on his shoul-der a moment, then sucked some seconds on her straw. "Yummy," she said.

"You're not too bad yourself. ...Oh. You were talking about your drink."

She cracked up, even snorted, bracing with both hands on the bar, a bracelet on her right wrist made of plastic beads of myriad colors. *Score* thought Stanley.

"So do you have a place anywhere near here? If you felt like maybe continuing this elsewhere I could call a cab for us. We could order some food if you're hungry. Watch TV and smoke a bowl maybe. If you partake."

"Hmm." Her face became serious quickly. "Yeah. My apartment's not far. Just blocks. I still live with my ex, but he's out for a while." She examined his face. "Do you have pot? I haven't smoked for a while actually. Like a couple weeks."

"I have a little. Enough to get us stoned. ...We can get a head change going, maybe watch *The Land Before Time*, eat some cheese puffs. Whatever we want." He smiled his most inviting smile.

She laughed, seemed won over, looking into his eyes with a tilted head, brown-yellow eyes luminous.

Within ten minutes they were walking side by side to the woman's domicile, the subterranean bottom apartment in a huge house divided into six residences—hers, #1, being a two-bedroom. The place was messy but reasonably spacious. She gave him a beer from the fridge (an import, seven point five percent alcohol and with a lemon-honey flavor), also opening one for herself, and placed some corn chips and dip out on the kitchen's center island; then they settled cozily onto a comfortable couch (although the kind one's skin stuck to as if it were glazed with something viscous, which material annoyed him) across from a flatscreen TV she told him her ex had purchased for them the previous year. At fifty inches the appliance was enormous and had crisp resolution. She had turned it down to barely audible after activating it via remote and the cable channel it was tuned to was airing a show that seemed to be about a sweaty, red-faced, maybe fifty-five-year-old owner of a store that only sold Halloween-related merchandise that a goth twentysomething with a bad attitude who was probably his daughter worked at, and the man seemed always stressed and on the verge of cardiac arrest. He heard him say "I don't know why I still do this. I don't need the money."

"How long ago did you guys break up?" he asked Delilah, leaning into him on the sofa, her left breast pressed against Stanley's upper arm.

"Three months ago about. But neither one of us is really in a position financially for him to move out. He's working on it though. He's been saving. He makes alright money. He's a mechanic. We don't really get along anymore though."

He shook his head in acknowledgement, looked at the perspiring guy, who seemed perturbed and was talking to his daughter—behind a glass counter at the front of the store and apparently mentally elsewhere.

"This is a good beer," he said after a gulp.

"Yeah, I like this stuff."

"This is the biggest Halloween store in central Illinois" he heard the reality show's glossy-faced star say.

"So..." she moved a forefinger slowly down his forearm, wrapping it around two of his fingers, the bottle of beer in her other hand. "What do you want to do now?"

A graphic flashed briefly—BLOOMINGTON BOO STORE—before a commercial for Prilosec started. Stanley turned into her, their lips meeting in a simultaneous kiss, their mouths opening, tongues connecting, his penis getting blood. He could feel the entirety of one breast against his chest. She without looking set the bottle on the table in front of them, released his fingers, and pulled her small teal garment down enough for her breasts to be exposed—they were not firm but her brown nipples were, a mole above the left, and something appealed to him about their unexceptional shape—both of which she pressed into him as they explored one another's oral cavities.

The door opened with a whoosh. Stanley saw a tattooed, lightly muscled guy in a sleeveless shirt maybe nine or ten years older, hair blond, apparently dyed, enter briskly; an instant later he saw his male appendage was fully engorged. The woman responsible pulled away a foot, tugged her top up. "What fucking—? Nice, Li," he said moving with a kind of exaggerated swagger to the kitchen, where he laid a grocery bag on the island. "Didn't think to do that kinda shit like at least in your room?"

"Dan. Goddammit. What're you doing home already? You said you'd be a good four hours."

"I think you were at the bar a little longer than you thought, alchie," he said venomously. Stanley, stiffness subsided, felt blood going to the top of his body, anticipating conflict; he also realized, having not eaten all day, he was a little drunk.

"Let's go," said Delilah, her mood soured, taking his hand. She began to lead him toward the back of the apartment, where her boudoir was located.

"Looks like your standards have dropped even lower," he said— Dan the ex—watching them migrate.

"Hard to do worse than you," retorted the woman, shooting a harsh glance back at him. "'Sides: he's funny."

Dan pulled a box of Bisquick out of an upper cupboard. They were at the threshold to her room. "I know how you like dumb ones. I'm probably smarter'n him even if I had a lobotomy."

Delilah was pushing her door open. "If she likes 'dumb ones' then by your own admission you must be dumb," Stanley said, surprising himself. "Unless you weren't her type."

He could see the man's temper flare. "Fucking smartass. If you had half a brain you'd have kept your mouth shut. You guys just go fuck and keep it down. I'm gonna try to let your new boyfriend hold on to his ability to walk."

"There's something comical about you to me," said Stanley, experiencing a fearlessness at least partly related to his blood-alcohol level, as Delilah pulled him into her room and he offered slight resistance.

"Better go with her 'fore you get cracked."

"Make your pancakes, Dan," Delilah said closing her door. "Sorry about that." She pushed him backward in the direction of the large bed in the center of the room and lowered her shirt again. He sat on the edge of it and she came over kissing and then mounting him as they scooted toward its middle, Stanley becoming aroused again. "He's a real dick," she added, breathing heavy, before suctioning his mouth again. "I'm going to fuck you good."

He unbuckled his belt, unbuttoned and unzipped his pants, sliding them down to his shoes. His erection was full but as the woman dry humped him while they made out her jeans rubbing against it began to feel uncomfortable. "Take off your pants," he said.

She moved backwards off the bed and removed them while making eye contact in an exaggerated shimmying way that was intended to and succeeded in being sexy. "Turn around," he commanded once they had dropped to the carpet.

He took in her round, pleasingly large posterior, clothed in thin magenta and bright red panties. "I really like your ass," Stanley told her. "Get on," he instructed, motioning to his erection.

She got back onto the bed and crawled over top of him, sliding his penis into her vagina, fairly wet and a reasonably good fit, above it a trim forest of sparse black hair over unsunned skin.

"Your pussy feels quite good," said Stanley as she started to move slowly, rhythmically on his engorgement, pleasure beginning to light up his brain, her large buttocks intermittently making contact with his testicles.

Just then there was a very loud sound, a continuous sound, from the living room. It was almost immediately clear that it was rap music. It was emanating from the massive TV, the volume of which was maxed out.

"Fuck, man. That's fucking terrible," he said more to himself than Delilah at almost the same moment she lifted her body, terminating their connection, saying "Fucking bastard. Motherfucker" as she dismounted the bed and began putting her pants on—Stanley meanwhile feeling a carnal longing for her barely experienced seat of femininity mixed with an anger at tasting before being denied it.

He watched from the bed, his lower half unclothed, as Delilah stormed out of the room, leaving the door ajar. "Why are you fucking turning your goddamn music all the way up?" he heard her yell.

The guest pulled his boxers and jeans back on. Knowing it was a bad idea he nonetheless decided to exit the room, to needlessly—to doubtless no positive end—insert himself into the situation. Maybe he was just uncharacteristically, because upset about the coitus interruptus and not sober, interested in a confrontation.

Entering the living room, where Delilah and her ex were in each other's faces and both clearly perturbed, the rap still blaring from the television, Stanley's focus went quickly to the source of the noisome noise: a music video starring a moderately famous hip-hop artist named Thugg Pott—a morbidly obese but energetic black man in probably his early thirties, the video being at the point when the oversized appliance was within his view at which Pott—his sidekick in the production beside him, a midget with gold-capped teeth and a backwards- (and crookedly-) worn red ball cap with a pro baseball team logo on it (the head of a ferocious shark, its jaws wide)—was flicking through a large wad of high-denomination bills in his hand; then throwing them all onto a trio of voluptuous and attractive black women laying on floating cushions in a kidney-shaped natorium below him, the women for a moment upset then pleased, fighting among one another as they plucked wet bills from around them with hands full of cash. Cut to: Pott, wardrobe no longer urban but formal, sitting at the wheel of a limousine or limo-like automobile with gold rims, fender, bumper, flowing in rhyme about how everywhere he went ladies smiled and guys gave him space; and then from the back the midget, gold grille shining, appeared over his right shoulder rapping something about his agreement with his big buddy's assertion.

Stanley shifted his attention as if snapping out of a trance. "So were you trying to thwart us from fucking?" he asked Dan calmly, the man's anger-contorted furrow-filled visage slowly turning from the woman's face to the other man's as the previous expression drained from it and was replaced with a new sort of quizzical yet still somehow hostile one.

"What the fuck did you just say, little shit?" he responded, drawing out the sentence with the exception of his uninspired epithet.

"I wondered—Dan—whether you chose to pump up this *Atrocious* music," Stanley said, blood rising with a warm rush, "because you were trying to interrupt, or preempt, sexual activity between your ex-partner here and I."

"I'm going to ruin your stupid face," retorted the physically anachronistic man, veins in his sun-touched forehead inflated by rage, as he moved rapidly toward Stanley, who in response moved agilely toward the kitchen where pancakes were blackening on a burner-situated pan and there was a pitcher of thick off-white batter on the island.

Feeling Dan approaching fast behind him he impulsively grabbed the container of cement-like prepped Bisquick and half-turning hurled it at his head, which it hit with a degree of force sufficient to knock him back a bit and momentarily stun him—gluey batter painting his head and exploding in all directions behind him. Stanley heard Delilah, standing approximately where she had been, gasp; saw her bring hands to her mouth agape in surprise; a few bubbles of flapjack mix had made it onto her creased teal top.

Then though, with the same lack of forethought and in the name of self-protection, he saw and grabbed an empty but previously used and grease and food debris-coated frying pan off the stove and taking two sizable steps toward his moment's enemy, still stunned by batter, swung with no little force the sideways pan at Dan's head—immediately causing consciousness-suspending cranial trauma and a troubling vertical gash that appeared deep and was bleeding profusely before the wounded resident heavily hit the floor—the back of his head striking a shelf on the way down—coming to rest half on the linoleum of the kitchen area and half on the carpet of the den area.

"Fuck, dude," Delilah—psychologically overwhelmed—said rushing to, bending over her ex but only observing helplessly as the blood of his head gushed onto the purple-red carpet beneath it. "What the fuck did you do? Do you want him to *die*?"

"I don't care about human life. Despite my best efforts. ...Or maybe I do. Care about children, the impoverished, the hungry, the abused," he said quietly, not intending for her to hear, his eyes deadened by the visible reality of his rash actions, as he stood motionless, also watching the blood flow, staring at the unanimated face of his onetime antagonist.

"You better hope he's alright, motherfucker, if you don't want to be in prison in the 2020s," she said rising and heading for her bedroom. A few moments later she emerged staring abstractly in the vicinity of Stanley's visage with her cell phone to her ear, the same expression on her face that she had worn when she called him *motherfucker*, one of mingled concern and anger. He heard a faint ringing emanating from the device as she directed her gaze down to her unconscious ex's head, the man looking somehow worse to his attacker as the seconds ticked by.

Stanley—feeling as if the quite negative state of his life had suddenly, surprisingly, been dropped heavily on his hunched back at Delilah's mention of penitentiary time—experienced a jolt of panic akin to the preliminary pang of a heart attack. Only then did he realize (and think how it might have looked) that he was still slackly holding the dirty frying pan in his left hand.

"No—" he called out feebly, or he felt enfeebled, preemptively, as he thoughtlessly swung the pan he had only just become conscious of again—swung it, weakly he thought, at the woman in teal's face.

She made a sound like *Huhhgh* as it connected, with substantially more power than he anticipated, hitting her in an upward arc from the right front of her chin to the opposite side of her forehead—propelling her away and leaving a light red mark like the track of something that had traveled aslant over her face. Delilah—a middleaged woman who a few hours earlier he had never spoken to nor seen but whose life he was now spontaneously drastically affecting—seemed shocked and simultaneously there was an apparent diminishment of consciousness. After being initially sent backwards by the force of Stanley's second kitchenware strike she continued to stagger away from her assailant (still inebriated, dead-eyed, and once again unmoving) due to momentum, lack of bodily control, and after a few awkward retreating steps into her living room sat, slowly, with what resembled poise, on the carpet—her eyes rolling up into her head once then twice before she shut her eyes. Stanley, aware of his unwilled-feeling and to him alien actions though with the sensation of watching rather than being inside himself, went over to her where she had started to slump as she sat, knocked out it appeared, and checked for a pulse by gripping her left wrist.

There was one. But, that wasn't good, thought Stanley, since Dan gave him the impression of being dead—a possibility that would make him a murderer, and one Delilah could identify.

By his estimation his mind wasn't functioning in typical fashion, he wasn't thinking as clearly, as rationally—as well—and it had to have much to do with what he'd done to the man on the floor, that action had started him down the wrong path. Or maybe speaking up to him had, some idiot; or picking up Delilah; or cheating, malevolent girlfriend damned setting out to hook up with anyone at all—or, or ever getting together with Hope in the first place. *That evil whore* he cogitated, putting a hand on either side of his consternated sweaty forehead. Holding his head at the temples hopelessly in the foreign downtown apartment of some strangers, both of whom were unconscious in front of him, as a result of his lunacy.

I could use some more booze thought Stanley, the string of words passing through his brain lethargically, and he turned and started going through the wooden cupboards, a grin forming when he found a nearly full bottle of whiskey in a high one, which container he opened and took a hearty swig from following a fleeting reticence about consuming whiskey having put no sustenance and many beers in his belly.

He held it loosely, uncapped, feeling the fire of the liquor journey downward in its progression toward the center of his body, feeling low on energy, as he stared at the Teal Woman, slumped to one side—trying hazily to come to some decision about her fate, holding onto the belief that to leave her as she was might spell doom for the unemployed twenty-seven-year-old who was in the process of drinking himself insensate in her living room.

As he was deliberating, as if through a fog, Delilah's eyes began to flutter behind lids spider-webbed by thin red veins.

The idea occurred to him to find some chemical to knock her out (so he wouldn't have to by striking her again) in order to buy himself some time to continue pondering what to do with her, if anything.

He was brisk, knowing he had perhaps less than a minute, and started by looking under the kitchen sink for a suitable substance. He saw a large plastic bottle of dishwashing soap; a cylindrical can of Comet made of thick cardboard, green on the outside; a tall container of dark yellow Lysol; scour pads in a bag; a spray bottle of window cleaner.

Opting to examine the latter he read the ingredients on the back label of the transparent polyethylene that contained it, his eyes fixing on the word *ammonia*. Stuck by a dangerous notion he went to find the bathroom down the hall, flipped the light on, opened the cabinet under the sink, and took to his knees to root around in it—almost immediately finding what he was after: bleach, a big white container of it, which he took with him back into the kitchen.

Maybe this'll work he thought, standing presently before the woman, Delilah—whose eyes were half-open and bleary, who seemed unable to focus and unaware of her surroundings, whose body he had briefly been inside of—with the ammonia-containing chemical blend he had gotten out of the kitchen in his right hand and the bleach in the other. Then, watching more Delilah's face than the piece of carpet on which he was making a blend he presumed would be noxious, would render her unconscious again, he poured out first the window cleaner—unscrewing the nozzle top and dumping the whole bottle on the floor in front of his victim—and on top of the puddle of chemical a fair amount of bleach from the big jug, retreating quickly.

It took a moment but a thin yellowish mist arose from the spot, ascending toward vulnerable Delilah's woozy-looking countenance—while Stanley, who had exchanged the household cleaners in both hands for a whiskey bottle in one (though not yet drunk from it), watched for the interaction of the apartment's tenant with the poisonous fog with dark curiosity and a comparatively worried countenance.

Breathing involuntarily but barely conscious of the miasma about her face Delilah, taking some of it inward, coughed mightily, sounding as if she were going to bring up a piece of lung. She ceaselessly continued coughing, in a similar alarming fashion, as the lemony mist engulfed her slack, seated body, which soon fell over to her right—hair brushing the sofa they had recently sat on as her head arced toward the burgundy-colored carpet.

"Fuck," Stanley uttered, his eyes bugging, the smell of the gas reaching him, as he decided to flee rather than stay and see what actually would happen to her, taking what remained of the whiskey with him and heading at a rapid clip out the front door.

On the street he felt somewhat relieved for no good reason, but the sun seemed unnaturally intense; he had the sensation of being uncomfortably bathed in bright orange light, light oppressive and overly illuminating. He walked, aimlessly, disoriented—oddly, for he was extraordinarily familiar with the area he occupied—the way he moved, slowly, unsteadily, making him appear drunker than he was.

It took him the better part of five minutes to become normally conscious of himself and his spatial orientation, which included realizing that he had a bottle of liquor in his hand—prompting him to take a big pull from it, bringing his consumption of the container's fiery amber liquid to about twenty-five percent.

The quality of the light of the day, though sunset was approaching, still struck him as oddly vivid; and people, to the extent he absorbed their passing, seemed more indifferent and their expressions more hostile than usual. He kept experiencing very brief episodes of derealization, and during these the mean anonymous faces and trees overhead and apartments and houses and parked vehicles and painted asphalt swirled together into a whirlpool of dreamlike quality—an unpleasant dream that he was the bodiless center of. Then, after mere seconds, he would come back to the static actuality of being a probably dazed-looking guy standing on a sidewalk as the sun waned laggardly, holding a bottle of booze and focusing on nothing—purposeless, disconnected.

"Alright, where am I going?" he said aloud, a small twentysomething in black yoga pants going by with her phone in one hand and earbuds in, two white cords becoming one below her minimally expressive face. He looked to the north, the direction she was walking, his eyes glossy, a forlorn feeling taking hold.

16

"Where have you been?" asked Hope, sitting facing the door, her clothes changed, as soon as he walked in—the walk having seemed to've taken much longer than it would have normally, which due to Stanley's state (now worse in that he was far drunker, having nearly finished the bottle along the way) it had. "I didn't know you'd left."

It was surprising to him, though he was unconcerned, that she read as slightly perturbed. He was conscious of his physical attraction to her seeping into his thoughts, but said, nonetheless, "None of your business," surprising himself.

She sighed, looked away, tried to find something to focus on. "How long are you going to be an asshole? Any timeline in mind?"

"For at least as long as I don't want to fucking touch you," he slurred.

A sparkle in her eyes he perceived as meanness mixed with amusement she said, "We're intoxicated? Not how you usually operate. ...Oh well, drama queen." Mouth now dismissively downturned, her eyes went searching the immediate surroundings for something to fix on again, locking on *Henderson the Rain King*. "You'll be missing this very fucking soon I know."

"Yeah, whatever," he retorted, thinking it pathetic he could come up with nothing better and thinking too that he really was quite soused—his belly full of swishing fire, not feeling exactly well—as he began turning toward the door, having decided he had no desire to be at home around Hope.

And then he was out in public again, this time destinationless—oddly with no thought in his mind of the up to two people he had just murdered, murders it seemed totally plausible could be traced to him. But he did find himself thinking of the twain in the downtown apartment, with a rush of adrenaline-laced sickness, and held out hope that either both would be fine or neither; though he admitted to himself what seemed logically likeliest was that he was sooner or later going to be in serious trouble for what had very recently transpired.

Out of doors a sunset had come on and its orange-purple had and was altering the appearance and feeling of all and everything. The world had a vividly hued fuzziness, a beauteous blurriness to his eyes that was the result of his alcohol consumption and the late spring day's hour. He felt light but moved awkwardly. He felt, lest he remember his victims or who he had discovered Hope was, care-free, in every way unburdened—but, too, unhealthy and out of place. Where was he off to amid these empty or malicious visages atop bodies that were sometimes fit, often overweight, and covered in garments of a plethora of cool-weather styles—the physical baggage of people who tended to be engrossed by something electronic but were occasionally merely walking a dog or out with their family? He had no idea; however, he had an awareness of wanting to have sex, a want probably, Stanley supposed as he clunked along the gray darkening sidewalk, intensified by the taste of intercourse he'd had earlier as well as his intoxication.

Ambulating, mindlessly self-directed downtown again (perhaps with the notion of visiting another bar), he lost time. The blur became blackness, thick and forever lost. When the blackness temporarily cleared he was standing—in an expansive fashion shifting his weight leg to leg in an attempt to stay upright—in front of another woman in her forties (she was garbed in a stained and torn sleeveless shirt, aquamarine, with gold lettering that read ONE TOUGH COOKIE in flourishy cursive; there was a band-aid on her upper arm, and scabs and small spots that had not yet formed scabs or that the scabs had come off of or been scratched or picked from along both arms—and maybe along both legs, she was wearing shorts but he couldn't really tell—and here and there on her face), who stood with her back to a port-a-potty blue-green in color and which read 'Honey Bucket' on the unlatched plastic door, dusk having become early evening.

Unlike Delilah she was the sort of unattractive person that most human beings if privately asked would likely describe as ugly. She was also rank, her body odor scent (a sour mixed with musky armpit stench—a stench of old, accumulated body odor) easily discernible from five feet—though Stanley could not consciously smell anything and stood three feet away, apparently speaking to her, or more accurately being spoken to.

Her teeth too were in an amazing state of disrepair—all of them partly or completely rotted out and some of what remained coated thickly with medium-brown plaque, teeth remnants one might become nauseous to behold—their condition obviously the result of long-term and based on her mien ongoing methamphetamine use; another consequence of this being the classic shrunken jaw her face tapered into.

Overanimated, in constant motion, side to side, forward and back, she was saying, wide eyes glued to Stanley's, drowsy-looking: "...always wondered where they kept the other feature, the hidden one—the nose for trouble—if there was a compartment on the face that could not be seen. Like the way you can't see a person's crotch except sometimes some kind of outline of what it is, except this wouldn't be something under a covering, a garment, this would be another appendage somewhere, secreted somehow though but not by cloth. A specially powered biological tool; there—maybe under the hair?—but hard to perceive."

She seemed to search his eyes with her bouncing own for answers.

"The phrase kept bothering me—like I couldn't get it out of my head ever since I heard it—'nose for trouble.' Like because where is this nose, the other nose—unless it's an auxiliary function of the one facially centered, the regular, smelling one. You know? Where is it?"

She abruptly cackled quite frighteningly, an otherworldly kind of brief, sharp, haunted laugh that seemed to emanate from deep within. "I mean I'd like to see a crotch—ha, ha—I haven't fucked since I used to go to the bars and a guy—usually a fat guy—ha, har—would come over to me and ask if I wanted to have a good time, like in the back of his car—but what I'd really like to see more than that is this nose they were talking about that could detect trouble like it has an aroma the other people aren't aware of and go to it or away from it, choosing, knowing where it is, where it will be." Her purposeless fast footwork continued, her sockless feet encased in stained off-white Keds knockoffs with mismatched laces.

"I think it's just a fig-gure of speech," Stanley slurred heavily, involuntarily leaning forward a little. "They don't have another nose anywhere they jis have a special sense. ...Like Spider-Man." He planted his right foot with a thunk to stop him from going forward toward the box-stepping addict as his ability to stand stationary wavered.

She laughed another short, disturbing laugh of explicit desperation. "I've just always wanted to understand," the woman continued as if he hadn't been heard. "Like my Uncle Linus who was afraid of birds. His wife left him when I was a girl. But she didn't have any birds. So why? He was nice and gave me candy when I came over and I didn't have to ask. On occasion I washed his car and he gave me money that I used to buy a lot of candy: gold-wrapper-wrapped chocolate, fruit-flavor bright stretchy stuff in long packages you would pull until it came apart. I don't know why he was afraid of birds. Maybe a bird attacked him sometime—when he was little. We both lived in Chestnut, Illinois. Me and my mom, and he lived next door. I remember a bird flew at his head once and he made a sound like a girl. It was small and so boring. I ran away when I was sixteen." More human laugh. "I had never kissed a boy and went to church each Sunday. Twice sometimes."

"Church, huh?" His mind seemed to shift gears. At the moment he felt he could see himself; he had the appearance of an ugly, sleepy man who was unsteady on his feet and barely recognizable. He was bathed in darkness and stationed middle of the sidewalk, a passerby or group walking from left or right going behind or before him something like every five to ten seconds. Minimally was he aware that the woman about a yard from him was insane, though he did not know or speculate whether her insanity was temporary and drug-induced or permanent, and possibly drug-induced in that case as well.

"So you wantto see a crotch?" he asked with a giggle.

"Har," she replied toothily, an evident monster, with eyes enlarged, otherworldly in their expression.

"How long 'as it been since you had sex?"

"Four years, feisty!" she answered enigmatically and repellingly, Stanley being taken aback despite his extreme anesthetization.

"Back when they usedta fuck ya in automobiles in front of tavenns, long after your church dayss were over?" he slurred, his body again trying to come forward due to diminished coordination.

"Yeah. I had a boyfriend named Mitch before. We used to hang out. I liked him. But he lost his money. And I found ways to get my stuff without him. I don't know where he is now."

"How'd you want my crotch?" he asked, seeing about one and half of her now and having difficulty keeping his eyelids up. She still looked pretty bad to him, despite hardly being able to see her, but he had lost any lingering ability to think rationally.

The streets woman's circular movements became a mere pronounced shifting of her weight from foot to foot, her face no longer communicating that she was beyond high but that she was serious, deliberative (and wide awake).

"You give me money?" she inquired like a suspicious ape or long-extinct Homo sapiens ancestor, her matted medium-brown hair, a bit of organic debris in it, backlit by a near orange-bulbed streetlamp.

He reached into his right pocket stuffing his hand with too

much force into it and pulled out a wadded up five and one-dollar bill that he couldn't see but held near his face, in a wrinkly ball, staring at confused.

"I have money for you," he said looking back at her, constant-motion woman of drug and street life.

"How much for sex?" she inquired, continuing to bob laterally to either direction and look at him with a shrunken face of sober single-mindedness.

Stanley began to unfold bill one from the wad he brought up again to his face holding it as if it were something alien. After much too long and having to examine each piece of crinkled green and white paper a few inches from his face with a lighter that lit his dark synclinal eyebrows and white face in the night he answered "Six dollars" with a mouth that felt overly lax to have been able to properly form words, and perhaps he hadn't.

The woman regarded him like he was crazy but almost immediately gestured and turned toward the portable plastic john behind her, Stanley seeing then her buttocks, clothed in athletic shorts, for the first time—their general appearance roundish, inexplicably lumpy, and fairly firm.

It was hot inside and tight for two and the stale air within smelled strongly of feces and urine, and distinctly the excreta of many people rather than one. The other removed her shirt, remarkably dropping it to the floor, and began to attempt to turn awkwardly toward Stanley but he physically stopped her, grabbing and turning a shoulder saying "No" and then pulling out his semi-erect penis and tugging her shorts down, which fell to her ankles as the smell of the surroundings and the woman herself—a worse aroma, an aroma that so close seemed to also contain hints of used tampons and band-aids—caused him to retch.

His penis was making contact with her bare butt—she hadn't been wearing underwear—and her stiff-feeling lower-jaw-length hair kept brushing against his face and ill though he was the sensation of his manhood making contact with her unwashed posterior had caused it to become harder, hard enough to be sexually functional.

It went in forcefully, slightly painfully; her vaginal lips having a crusty texture, the inside dry but moments after entry quite wet and feeling overly sizable, its scent like decaying cave fauna.

At a result there was a distinct lack of friction—but it was the aromatic medley his nose was communicating, fighting through his extreme inebriation, that did the most to subdue his arousal; though he made the wise decision to close his eyes in the small warm blue-walled stall and think, rather than of the beast a part of him was inside of (who thankfully little in the way of sound was issuing from), of the woman he had momentarily also participated in sexual intercourse with earlier in the day—a person who by comparison was a great beauty on the level of Helen of Troy.

He heard the sound of his penis going in and out of her sopping, unhygienic vagina; heard her emit a soft moan; accidentally looked down, seeing her bespotted and unaesthetically stretched and lined back, on the other side of which was an incongruous layered paunch; smelled all too much of her long-unwashed, sweaty, stale garbage scent again, combined with the also-overpowering one of the biological waste of many. And so, as a result of these combined factors, all being lived and realized within a few seconds, young Stanley—perspiring perspiration high in alcohol, feeling weak, sensing the emptiness of his stomach, feeling a burning in the void of it—vomited; upchucked across the back of the creature he had entered in a reeking downtown honey bucket, startling her, but resulting only in her briefly arching her back before bending a bit again as she had been as the expelled liquid dripped in multiple streams from the sides of her midsection.

It seemed to have been only bile he noted, a trace of it on his lower lip, aware that his nausea had been alleviated and that his manhood remained in the cavernous opening of the bent methhead though was hardly now useful for continued coitus.

At the same time pushing her forward, off of him, he pulled out disappointedly—a bit amazed at the complete grossness of his sexual partner and his lack of dignity, his vision blurry and unbalanced, and unlocked the stall, greatly appreciating the comparatively extraordinary fresh, clean air.

"Hey, you never gave me my six dollars," he heard her caw as she came up behind him.

Never again wanting to see the person a foot behind him and in a sort of foulness- and booze-produced daze Stanley chose not to turn back, yet he felt the bills in his pocket; however, her scabby appendage was next around his neck, she was attempting to choke him, and she had brought a knee up to the small of his back.

He ripped the arm away with substantial force, despite his only minor irritation, without breaking stride. "You're welcome for the dick," he said. Then softer, continuing along the orange-lit street, the establishments—mostly drinking ones—to the right of the sidewalk buzzing with patrons, their median age twenty-three, "You're th' nastiest of all the nassy meth whores," he added.

———◈———

Stanley was feeling pretty good about his insult, all too true insult—not so much about what he had just chosen to *do*, with his penis, which act he hoped more than he had ever hoped for anything that he would soon forget utterly and never remember—but then, loudly, louder than necessary given how near he still was, he heard, behind him, from the mouth of the foul woman; the sick, stupid human, as disgusting as any walking the Earth: "You have an STD now!"

17

Submersed in the sloe of night he staggered back, blacked out— a spectacle, a hiccupping mindless buffoon—to the woman's apartment that not long ago had become his home.

Stanley returned blind drunk, it was about 8:45, and Hope was reclining on the couch in the dark living room. She seemed barely to register her boyfriend's reentry.

"Wow! You'rre on the sofa. What a fuckeen surrprise," he slurred, stumbling to one side just inside the abode.

"Oh my god. Go to bed, you drunk," she said looking up from the TV at him half a second. She seemed on the verge of falling asleep herself. *Family Guy* was on but she appeared to be viewing it with about fifteen percent of her possible attention.

"I'll go t'sleep, you dead-eyed bitch," said Stanley progressing awkwardly through the room toward their bedroom. "Why're you slouchin here in the dark?" he stopped to inquire, standing to the left of her semi-recumbent form, otherworldly blue in the unlit space.

"Because I'm passing out. Because I feel like it."

She glanced over her shoulder at Stanley, who simply stood unsteadily above her, observing Hope with a barely visible expression of disgust. "You know I'm aware you got your feelings hurt because I've been doing things you didn't know about and don't like, but if you keep being a dick to me—I mean if it continues for too long— you're going to end up without a place and without a hot girlfriend. So, you know, don't get too carried away. You've got it good."

Stanley was flooded with indignation, suddenly tingly and hot with ire. He thought of her pretty face, her lovely breasts, her dark peculiarly styled silky hair. Thought of the smart, sensuous, uncommon person she was; yet, despite her propinquity, felt a longing for her, for the false her of the past, that he knew could never now be again fulfilled. He looked down on Hope, who was once more gazing at the television, her mind a locked box, and experienced a deep, intoxicated sorrow. A sadness that engulfed him as a heavy blanket, which he was unable to remove.

The inebriated observer, still in the dark, felt a tear descend his warm right cheek as fully without consciously willing himself to he wrapped each of his hands around each side of her small, smooth neck, thinking, despite himself, *Let's see if I can succeed in ridding the world of you.*

Her surprise at his action made her whole body spasm. She moved defensively toward him, her hands grabbing his, and found his gaze—though focused on her shape, her presence—to be an abstracted one, his eyes to be as veiled, inaccessible though they met hers; then he began applying pressure, as much as he could muster.

Hope's shock remained, but in spite of it she began fighting full-fledgedly, bringing herself chaotically off the couch and toward him only to be kneed in the middle of a flailing frame by the unsteady Stanley, who resultantly fell backward, keeping his tightening grip on his girlfriend's neck.

She therefore fell with and on top of him, bringing her own knee into his groin, which attack failed to phase him as he was nearly incapable of feeling non-excruciating pain due to alcohol anesthetization. Peter Griffin was laughing obnoxiously from the glowing screen behind her as Hope, barely more than a quarter-century old, was being strangled with so much force that both her eyes and those of the berserk booze-fueled man below her were popping out painfully, the pressure seeming to be caused by blood, by thick cords on their unseen side.

Unable to do anything about his grip, in pain, feeling her energy being depleted, and now legitimately fearing for her life, Hope with difficulty brought one then another leg around Stanley's body and over the top of his head; she squeezed them together one on each side of his neck, trying to choke him, while leaning back away from his extended arms with her whole upper body and hips, which—while the leg choke failed to be effective broke her free of the supine homicidal one's grasp, leaving dark red finger-width lines on her neck.

Immediately, weakened but less panicked than a moment earlier, she crawled away from her boyfriend to her feet, unthinking but heading instinctually for the door. Sluggishly though he was, or felt he was, Stanley did a sit-up and grabbed each leg with a hand, pulling himself up to her and bear-hugging her legs to the top half of his body before she had the opportunity to kick free. Her legs writhed in his grasp and he had the impression she was bruising him but he managed to retain the appendages in his tight hold. Then, with all available power, he pulled the legs under him, bringing Hope to the floor on her chest with a thud, her cheek hitting and head bouncing off the beige carpet as the television—a commercial for Taco Bell on, which for a limited time had a new item—minimally illuminated the connected two, both sweating (Hope's snug dark blue jeans and simple white blouse bled through with sweat); as if going through motions (motions that would not be recollected), his attention seeming elsewhere, Stanley pulling his frame up Hope's thin own, forcing her down though she had been propped on her left side—stopping only once his head was above hers, her breath coming from an open mouth fast and hot, Hope's whole body draped with his weight.

"What the fuck are you doing, psychopath?" she managed to utter, breathing raggedly.

"I thought you were the psycho," he said resuming his two-handed choke.

Hope's eyes bugged again in the quiet, barely lit room—the television that was the sole source of luminance giving the presently near soundless struggle an eerie medium blue cast—and she felt so weak as to bring her panic to a new peak. Her legs squirmed, pinned by his; her neck muscles became taut; her arms, pinned too, she managed to pull up and away from her sides but Stanley's exerted pressure and her continued lack of oxygen had rendered them hardly useful, despite her desperate need of them. Her eyes rolled back once more and her diminished and noneffective attempts to escape ceased. The man atop her, eyes bleary, awareness of reality dimmed, kept on strangling, task-accomplishing; and the fight with the body below him—which Stanley had anticipated more of—had reached a conclusion.

⸻ ❖ ⸻

It felt to him anticlimactic, her death—though Hope's demise was not an event, nor the other important ones of the day, he had in a complete way processed. In the case of Hope he thought of her murder only as his ridding himself of a no longer useful object; something he had liked and been fascinated by but come to feel just the opposite about.

What had been discarded though had left behind a body-shaped mass of waste, and he was straddling it still; it was warm (and had discharged a liquid from around the center of its form).

He had said something, in his mind, right after her apparent expiry like *Now the spirit of evil has been released from its earthly captivity*, though how exactly he had expressed the thought, mentally, he couldn't recall. Despite that it wasn't real. There was a heap of prior humanity, a corpse, yes; however, it was not a corpse in any traditional sense: it was merely a byproduct of an episode of a currently unpertinent past, heavy garbage that required disposal. (Not the remains of the *individual* he had loved and dispatched while possessed, regressed by whiskey.)

He remained straddling her body, hardly a thought in his mind. Then, with snail slowness, even given the extremity of his inebriation, something like an awareness of a day spent not eating, constantly imbibing, having unprotected sex with perhaps the most disgusting woman he had ever encountered, and possibly murdering as many as three people—one of whom had been his beloved, or recently beloved, significant other, with whom he lived—began to grow in his clouded and benumbed brain.

Again Stanley sensed a tear rolling down a cheek. It made the quick journey to his lips, where he tasted its salt, but this time others followed it. Coming slowly but steadily, his body producing no sounds just emitting saline drops from his eye corners that were the result of his sadness, his realized mistakes, his resignation—there in a dim TV-lit room, sitting on the yet-warm cadaver that represented the woman who had changed it all, who had brought a young man from unfulfilled wage slave to jobless, happy, and partnered with a stunning woman—until the tide had turned, till the depression had circled back again and the illusion crumbled. Until he saw again that he wasn't special (or was in negative ways) and the desirable state of his life wasn't to last long.

His vision bleary due to the tears he forced himself to look down at the lifeless thing he sat on, a leg on either side. Her fixed unnaturally upwards-looking eyes made her mask of a face appear ghastly. He kept looking though—uncomfortable, a sensation of the liquid contents of his stomach churning—endeavoring by gazing upon the frozen visage of the one hundred-twenty-pound corpse he had created to fully, deeply comprehend the result of his latest and arguably worst unpremeditated and lunatic action.

Finally, after long traumatic seconds, shifting his gaze his eyes went to the glowing screen atop a table in front of the living room window. It was the late-hour news now and a white guy maybe fifty seated next to a perhaps Hispanic thirtysomething woman with a pleasing appearance were in tandem reading off a teleprompter. The current story, which the female newscaster was imparting, was about a home meth lab being discovered in western Oswald, leading to the arrest of a duo, a couple it seemed, whom it flashed mugshots of: the male party a hard-looking thirty-eight, with scabby skin and greasy chin-length dark brown hair and the female a twenty-nine-year-old with orangish hair, sloppily applied makeup, dimples, and an expression of indifference.

He tried to lose himself to the ten o'clock news—stood up and was standing there staring at the screen, trying to focus on, to care about the current story, one about a nursing home fundraiser, the video the other newsperson was narrating over of white-haired women at a card table, smiling as they received visitors—but he couldn't; his mind kept returning to the awful reality of the dead Hope, murdered on a whim by the drunk nobody she'd emotionally fortified and later deconstructed.

Oh well, he thought, sniffing, steeling himself. *No point in torturing yourself. It's a done deed. She's just trash now. Which is what she'd revealed herself to be anyway—even if you still cared about her.*

You killed the only person you cared about.

But you oughtn't have cared about her. That was a mistake. She was a mistake. Trash. She was a cheating bitch. She's just a body now, which needs disposed of.

He looked down at the cadaver, at the horrid lifeless eyes, the look of which if remembered would provide him a lifetime of nightmares; then resolved to get rid of it.

Stanley spontaneously devised a plan, something he had seen in movies. He would pick her—it—up and drape an arm across his shoulders, carry her out as if she were blind drunk and place the corpse in the passenger seat of her car.

He wasn't much of a driver but it was an automatic and he would be able to drive out to the woods or somewhere, probably without attracting attention. He'd just make sure he had a spade with him. And hey, if he got caught, if forensics gave him away in some or a few ways, it was just as well. He was guilty, a fool, and apparently dangerous. And he really didn't have anything to live for anymore. And Hope, sociopathic and terrible significant other as she had been, didn't deserve to die per se. It was not his right to play God.

Realistically though, Stanley thought, if he was to have any chance of success, he was going to at least have to take a nap first. So he went into the kitchen, poured a tall glass of water, took the wheat bread down from a cupboard, practically shoved a piece down his throat, drank the water messily, quickly, and completely, then refilled the glass all the way and drank another round almost as quickly, adding H_2O to his sweat-wet tee.

Wearily, staggering, ol'-time-drunk-like yet, but now likely a spree killer, a murderer of three, he collapsed front first onto the sofa that Hope less than a half hour earlier had been sitting on, quite life-filled. In a few minutes a fitful sleep began; and around two hours later, feeling no longer extremely drunk but very groggy, the whites of his eyes all red, he awoke, for about fifteen seconds disoriented to the extent of actually not recognizing his surroundings.

After forcing himself to a seated position and sitting for a while as the fog somewhat cleared from his mind he flipped the main room's lights on, rooted through her purse to locate her keys, on a keyring adorned with a plastic pizza slice, and, successful, returned to the grim mannequin-like remains of young Hope Brownen, one-time human being.

Bending toward the floor Stanley brought the thing, heavier than her body had been in life due to the weight being completely unsupported, to its limp legs and hanging feet by with a grunt hefting it, a v-shaped hand under each armpit. Then his arms went down to the waist and came together in a firm hug, the corpse's upper half falling backwards a bit. He brought it toward him with a hand on the back then used that arm to place her hanging left arm across his shoulders, turning out so that with effort, with his right arm round her waist, he now held up the slack body with the grip around the pant-line and her one arm—the vacated vessel's one arm—draped around him.

Opening and shutting the front door awkwardly with his free appendage he placed the body as gently as he could on the un-locked passenger side, lifting the legs in, the pretty head slumping immediately in the direction of the driver's seat, and got in on the other side—finding that door also unlocked.

With an exhalation of anxiety and only then recollecting that he was quite intoxicated and so he, a poor and very inexperienced driver, would be drunk driving to the forest late at night with a dead body beside him, he put the car key in the ignition and started up the machine, a twenty-year-old not-well-maintained auto with much mileage that hummed to life emitting exhaust.

"Oh shit." He opened the door, got back out, went back into the apartment and out the rear door, all briskly. He opened the shed to the immediate right and saw at once the shovel he'd forgotten, grabbing it and walking again through the domicile.

Having returned to the driver's seat of Hope's beat-up blue-gray two-door after stowing the implement in the trunk Stanley with trepidation started it up once more, pulling out, turning left, and heading out along the headlights-illuminated dark road, not at the moment thinking about the murder he had just committed (or the probable homicides that preceded it) but only worrying about dumping Hope's body and returning to her apartment without attracting police attention.

⟢ ⟪◉⟫ ⟣

He stayed off the freeways, being primarily uncomfortable with getting on and off them and not even being certain where the entrance to the main interstate was or if it would take him to the spot he had in mind. So, driving cautiously through residential then rural areas, he came via the long route to a stretch of desolate blacktop that soon along either side was tall trees and dense vegetation.

Five or seven minutes later Stanley saw on the right and turned down a narrow dirt drive that tapered slowly into sparse woods. First looking out into the dark forest the narrow deforested length dead-ended in he decided it would work or he would make it work and pulled Hope's body from her car, no longer moving it with care.

He dropped it with a thud at the edge of the trees—high, black-looking, and ever so slightly swaying—then went for the shovel, which he took with him as he journeyed into the woods slowly, feeling sickly but adrenaline-fueled and wishing he had taken a flashlight, branches snapping under his street shoes.

The new young murderer, brain flooded with jolting chemical but extremely tired and as yet very much drunk, could see next to nothing. Tall trees above, but only towering sable versions of them, ominous, seeming in his mind to all be ready to collapse on him, transforming him into a pinned corpse so near another corpse, which bodies would likely be found sometime during the next day given their location. A beautiful strangled woman and a man crushed by a number of giant trees that had simultaneously decided against being rooted and converged on his fragile frame. Both of them in the midst of their third decade, their early deaths semi-tragic, the kind of happening that was often the result of a car wreck, intoxication usually being involved.

He had gone seventy, seventy-five yards—tripping a few times, blood being drawn above the ankle by a shrub's thorny appendage—in a left-veering line and felt he was far enough out into the thick darkness of forest for digging a pit for concealment of the major evidence of his crime. A crime of godlike action that ought not have occurred, a crime of robbery from humanity, even if of a member of it who seemed rather inhuman, at least from sufficiently near vantage.

Cool rain had begun trickling from unseen clouds through the leaved towers of black trunk and branches to land on Stanley's clothing and sweaty head. As it kept up, intensifying, while Stanley dug with effort he had hardly the stamina for the drops made his task slightly easier, though the dirt remained troublesomely hard and the ground abundant with rocks—the aroma of earth and rain becoming that of wet dirt, an organic not-unpleasant smell, a petrichor, that took his mind off the purpose of his digging: to create a space long, wide, and deep that he could dump the damp body of his erstwhile love into, her eyes of death horrifically fixed upon a bleak, middle-of-night, tree-canopied sky.

He was getting wet and was a bit cold but liked it. For a moment he forgot his physical sickness and guilt, the weight of his many major misdeeds was lifted with the shower. Stanley merely was a man digging a hole in earth that was becoming mud. A fellow in the forest in damp clothes, enjoying his exertion, the fragrance of his surroundings, the chill, the sensation of his shirt sticking to his lightly muscled frame. From his hair and forehead the water was bringing sweat to his lips; a creeping organism somewhere made a rustling or the wind did; there was a pacifying stillness, and though the rain had ended the relative silence it contributed to this feeling in him, a feeling of mollification, of nascent peace, bliss in the aloneness of the wilderness.

Then he thought again of the nearby body, and a moment later his eyes were overflowing, saline mixing with the sweaty rain. *But she was just a whore anyway* he thought, crying, drops plopping on his crown through the roof of trees. *And she didn't love me. Only I, perhaps, loved her. To my fucking detriment.* He was fully weeping, dripping, with an upright shovel in his grasp, its point in soggy soil. "Good riddance!" he screamed in the direction of the corpse. *We are just bags of meat; stupid animals walking around, acting the animals we are; born to expire. Sooner or later, doesn't really matter. We're all better off without Hope around. She must've been that person Mary that disfigured guy was talking about. Maybe that was her real name.*

Drenched Stanley sniffled and kept at the mud before him with the wood-handled spade, a killer bathed in darkness who, he thought, deserved to be apprehended but was demonstrably insane.

When, after at least forty-five minutes, he decided the pocket in the earth he had produced would work for his purpose he dropped the utensil and went for Hope's limp carcass, dragging it grunting, hands latched to armpits, over moist dirt to the hole in which he intended for it to decompose undiscovered—Stanley meanwhile going on with his life: probably never drinking again if he could help it; maybe having a girlfriend again someday who, though she likely wouldn't be as good-looking, would have to be more normal; perhaps going to college, pursuing a degree in sociology or anthropology or international studies; being a quiet head in a classroom, an unknown figure who turned in assignments on time and pulled a B average; who got a good enough job, got married in his late thirties perchance, and went gray in freedom; whose drunken acts of one day were never attributed to him.

In a clump the body fell into its earthen home, left arm bent across the chest, right arm running down the length—only a few inches of dirt stratum above, and no room to the sides nor above or below the five-foot-seven frame. A tight fit; eyes the whites of which seemed to glow staring out of the shallow grave with a horrendous expression at the slightly swaying tops of old trees.

Stanley looked down at the human shell a minute, thinking about the person it had been, then pondering whether the pit needed to be deeper. Partly because his body was telling him it had nothing remaining for toilsome labor and desperately desired a long sleep, he concluded its depth would do, given the isolation of the location. But could a long, strong rain wash her nose or more into view? he wondered. Could a hunter, wanderer, explorer see said facial feature and make a call to police about his or her ghastly discovery?

No matter said Stanley in his depleted mind, stomach mewling again. Her disappearance would be noted early and he would be the primary suspect, and even without a body they could possibly pin it on him. His future was likely bleak, would involve prison and little else—if not because of Hope due to the other two, the random duo, badly injured if not dispatched. He sighed with a heavy spirit, resignedly, and began with the shovel to drop soil down onto the corpse, covering the face first—the sight of which, seeing it obscured by the moist dark chunks of ground (grisly, pounding in the reality of her demise), brought him fresh pain—so he wouldn't have to see it anymore.

When the hole had been filled with body and dirt, the rain subsiding, he patted the spot down with the tool borrowed from the dead and moved some organic debris—leaves, moss, lichen—and branches over it with a foot and his hands. Stanley stared at his workmanship a moment as a painter at a perhaps finished canvas and then with a slight nod of approval trudged back to the road and car with the shovel, starting it up, pulling a U-ie, and heading back into town—feeling less un-sober but mentally (and emotionally) exhausted; all-around needing to shut down and to do so for more than eight hours, maybe eleven or twelve.

18

There was a memory, a string of memories very much alike, of road—of blacktop, headlight-lit dotted-white-line-divided pavement. Of looking out the windshield at the street, at many carless streets, and barely staying conscious. Of eyes shutting involuntarily as he watched that he was staying between the lines and forcing them back open with all of his will, the bags under his eyes seeming to be pulling the upper half of his face down; feeling extremely haggard and unhealthy, perhaps the most tired, in a general way, he ever had—and remarkably feeling that way while he was driving, an activity he wasn't comfortable doing even when all of his faculties were operating at a hundred percent.

There was a snippet of memory too of pulling in the parking spot in front of Hope's apartment—the dead woman's, the homicide victim's apartment he resided in, for however long that might continue. Of his sliding the gear down to P with very heavy eyes and sighing with relief that he had made it, had not crashed or been pulled over, had concealed the body without encountering any problems, and that he would now be able to pass out—within the next few minutes, his body aching from yearning for a break.

***

Approximately ten and a half hours from when he pushed open

the front door, barely functioning, Stanley awoke—very groggy, eyes bloodshot and also gluey in the corners with the white excreta that was sometimes produced during sleep—on the floor of the living room (having had a hazily recollected dream in which his view was of, he was apparently within, a sun-bright aesthetically appealing forest, the trees—some seventy-five feet tall or so—spaced out and of a variety not densely leaved. There was a tranquility about the setting, and it seeped into Stanley, bodiless observer, a light wind tickling the leaves, causing a soft whistling as it pushed between the knotted trunks of the hundreds of lofty rooted organisms. But then—evidently causelessly—he was seized by an odd, oppressive terror; a cold, inescapable terror that seemed centered in his incorporeal heart and which tendrilled out from there to be felt in his entire being. This fear was followed shortly by a piercing, shrill, nonanimal sound, from no source but heard at the same drowning volume everywhere: a dreadful, inexplicable clarion—near physically painful and evocative of an intenser dread; an electronic or otherworldly one-tone unremitting noise that coming sourceless, stentorian, and suddenly within the woods was both shutter-inducingly eerie and seemed somehow to herald an apocalyptic or otherwise awful event or impending future).

He had a sensation like emerging from the floor, from just below ground level, and it took him a few moments to understand that he was at home, had had a long weird day, and though he'd just been hibernating awhile could use some more shuteye. What was unclear, other than that it'd involved heavy drinking—maybe unceasing drinking—was what precisely had made the day strange. It seemed like he had been in a dark establishment downtown—must've been a tavern. And that he'd spent some time in someone's house, but a person he didn't know. That he'd gotten into an argument with Hope, or she'd angered him. And that throughout the day he had done vague bad things. Maybe that he'd even had sex, with a woman other than his girlfriend?

But what were the bad things, specifically—that's what bothered him, made him uneasy. There was a weightiness, mental, he was aware of as soon as he'd gained consciousness that he could not explain but that he hated the feeling of. Like he'd forgotten something very important or made an awful sort of mistake.

No matter how plagued he was by the forgotten day—about which he only could be sure that he'd consumed substantial alcohol and that, based on a vague feeling, he'd made myriad poor choices in addition—he failed to call to mind any definite memories other than having gone to a bar; not The Touchstone, another in the same area called Josefina's.

Seated on the couch he put fingers to the corners of his goopy eyes and pulled the stuff out and down his face then activated the TV with the remote on the coffee table. His head had not an ache in a pain sense but a dull, numbing throb, as if many brain cells had in the last twenty-four hours been done away with. *Where is Hope?* he wondered.

⸺⸺ ◉ ⸺⸺

After a few minutes of staring mindlessly at a show of the "Tyrell…you are Not the baby's father!" variety he poured a tall cup of water from the tap and drank half of it quickly, messily, his brain becoming more focused. "Hope!" he yelled, breaking a membrane of phlegm in his esophagus, going to his/their room and peeking inside when he got no response.

He speculated she maybe was at the store or otherwise running errands, then he noticed her keys were on the table in front of him, a fact that made her absence rather peculiar.

Nothing that had transpired the previous day had had anything to do with her being gone, he felt confident of that. Perhaps they had gotten into a fight, a verbal tiff; regardless, no matter how bad it'd been, she obviously wouldn't have left her own house, she would have kicked him out of it. Hope wasn't the type to stay somewhere else to get away from a partner she'd been quarrelling with if the partner in question lived rent-free in her apartment.

<hr>

A half hour turned into an hour turned into two as Stanley's curiosity mounted, as he sat before the television pondering why everything felt different suddenly, speculating about the events he did not remember, making himself some Top Ramen he ate slowly around the time the local evening news came on.

He felt weak, malnourished, hungry but incapable of putting down anything substantive.

The news graphic flashed across the screen. A prerecorded voice said "This is K-O-M-E News at 5."

Cut to two anchors: a late-thirties man in a brown suit and a blonde, late twenties, in a dark gray pantsuit. "Good evening. This is K-O-M-E Channel 12 News at 5. I'm John Terwicker."

"And I'm Shelly Hart," said the female. "Our top story tonight: Two people are found dead in a downtown apartment in an apparent homicide and police are asking the community if they have any information.

"The man and woman were found unresponsive inside their apartment on the 900 block of Bly Street at about 6:35 yesterday evening after a chemical odor emanating from the residence prompted a neighbor to call the police. Paramedics were unable to revive the occupants. Local police said a toxic gas was released in the home and that foul play is suspected. The names and ages of the victims have not yet been released. They ask anyone who might have any information to contact the authorities."

"In other news..." began the male.

"Oh, fuck," Stanley let out, the memory of having gone to a woman's house downtown near Josefina's rushing back to him.

But you didn't fucking kill her. Why the fuck would you have killed her?

Yes, why would you have killed her? But why would you be acting weird about that news story if you didn't think maybe they were talking about her? And why do you have a feeling the other person is the woman's ex-boyfriend she still lived with?

"Fuck, what was her name?" he asked himself.

I can't remember, but I'd know her face if I saw a picture. I'll probably be able to figure out if I actually fucking murdered somebody—two somebodies—yesterday.

A black cloak of guilt, confusion, and dread was heavy over him since he'd woke, and it seemed to him as though whatever were the worst things he might've done while he was roaming the town the previous day those were the things he'd done.

His high-sodium yellow broth had become room temperature while he was ruminating about his inner state—its oppressiveness, inexplicability—and he moved his spoon absentmindedly in the plastic bowl in front of him as his ears received but brain did not consciously process a story about a pit bull that got out of a fenced front yard and attacked an eleven-year-old girl walking home from school. There was a big dangerous blank spot in his recent recollection and it concerned him greatly.

But then one of his pressing questions passed out of his mind when, without even an antecedent sound of keys jangling, Hope—backlit by the shining morning sun—opened the front door, for some reason beaming, uncharacteristically, her smile toothy; as if she had been replaced by a version of her that was new or fake, or perhaps some happy event had happened in her life. (As if she were not present, not in the doorway, framed by natural light, but were a figment of Stanley's psyche, gone in short order the way of derangement; the impressive product of desperate desire combined with an imagination eager for commands.)

Hope! he thought but did not say, his excess of cheer at the sight of her also somewhat surprising to him.

"Hi, lover." She came in, dropping her patchwork purse on the floor beside the table. He noticed she was wearing more makeup than usual, which when she wore it was very little.

"Hello." He sat up on the couch. "Where'd you go?"

"Just out. I needed to get out of the apartment for a while. Are you in a better mood today?"

"...I suppose," he responded, thoroughly perplexed by her demeanor, as he watched her go into her room for something and reemerge.

She joined him on the couch and filled the bong stationed on the living room table out of a plastic canister. "Anything special you feel like doing today, Mister Lots of Time on His Hands?"

"Only recover from an especially alcoholic yesterday I guess," replied Stanley Northrop talking to, on his right, a now non-existing girlfriend, chipper as never.

"Would weed help?" she sweetly inquired, perched to take a hit herself.

"When wouldn't it?" Stanley laughed.

She lit; inhaled deeply; finally exhaled a gray cloud that made its way laggardly to the middle of the room, dispersing; handed the device to the man beside her, a glass green and yellow toad looking up at him.

———————— ⟨⦿⟩ ————————

The smoke session—though he was in actuality the lone person partaking, partaking of a deceased person's supply of marijuana, which was only about half a gram—had made him drowsy, and anymore he didn't do much with himself, so rather than lying across the sofa staring at the TV he opted to go into the bedroom and lay out on the bed; and a few minutes later he was sound asleep.

And he dreamt, deeply, vividly...was at some point plunged into a dream that began with him walking along some railroad tracks. Grass was growing within and on either side of the tracks, grass that was thriving, stark green, three-some inches high. He was mostly looking down at his feet as he walked, his shoes a sort he never wore—wouldn't wear: tattered black Chuck Taylors, low-tops. The light-blue sky above was spotted by fluffy clouds lazily progressing east and the temperature was a pleasant high sixties and Stanley, wearing also a ringer tee and snug faded blue jeans, glanced up at it every few minutes on his way to nowhere, as he followed the tracks away from where he started on a carefree day, another in a years-long string of days of no responsibility.

Ahead thirty or so yards, to the right of the twin iron lines that shone in the sun, was what looked to be a large windowless shack fashioned from dissimilar bits of wood, a rough rectangle of boards of various browns, widths, lengths, grains. This Stanley approached with piqued interest, deciding well in advance of reaching it to investigate the structure for evidence of inhabitance.

There was a makeshift door, some faded graffiti on it, in the front, tracks-facing side of the ramshackle domicile. Hearing no sound from within he pushed it open. It creaked, opened little; so he pushed it a bit more.

Light shone through the many cracks between panels of wood, from which an abundance of nails jutted. At first the place, musty-smelling inside, appeared empty. Then, among various litter on the ground—it had no floor—he saw a human form, supine, its arms cradling its head: a sparsely bearded man, somewhere between thirty and forty probably, asleep; a man whose face had in some way been disfigured. A fly buzzed in the striated darkness inside.

He stared in from the doorway at the slumberer for minutes, until the figure slowly stirred, wiping sweat from its scarred forehead, then repeatedly scrunching the area around its eyes before opening them for good. The man turned his head backward toward the light, toward the ajar door, toward Stanley, looking at his face half-asleep, quizzically, still lying on his back.

"What's going on? I was napping." He maintained eye contact a few moments, then went back to lying with his head on the ground, producing a long loud wide-mouthed yawn.

"I was just wondering who you are, what this place is."

"You like it? I built it myself a couple summers back. ...Gets cold in the winter. We bundle up."

"Yeah. Seems like a good squat pad." He looked around. There was nothing in the way of decoration. There seemed to be little besides strewn trash and a blanket or two, a pair of pillows, some canned food. "Do you live here all year?"

"Sure do."

"You and who else?"

"Girl named Twila. You like pretty girls?"

"Ha. Yep."

"Bet you'd like her. Young. Quiet. Different."

He saw what appeared to be a gray field mouse scurry from one heap of rubbish (part plastic, part cardboard, part paper) on the ground to another. The ground was dirt, and the person he'd been talking to had a layer of dirt on his scar-tissue skin, dirt mixed with dried sweat. He felt certain if he were close enough to the shack's dweller that the aroma of body odor would rise to his nostrils.

"Where is she just now?"

"I'm not sure, man. Out gathering flowers maybe. Soaking up the sun. Pretty nice out there isn't it?"

"It's an ideal day." He became self-conscious. "Am I keeping you awake? I wasn't expecting anyone to be in here."

"No. I've been sleeping a lot. I usually do. I should wake up for a while. All the sleeping I've done has made me tired." A chuckle. "I wasn't expecting anyone to enter," he said, twisting his neck to look again at Stanley in the doorway. "It happens from time to time though. And sometimes they make it out alive." He laughed, revealing teeth that cursorily seemed to be in good shape, contrary to what Stanley would have anticipated.

He laughed too, but Stanley's laugh was false, obviously so.

"Mind if I sit down? That is since I'm aware of the risks?"

"Ha. Yeah, bro—go for it. Mi casa dot dot dot."

Stanley planted himself on the dirt a few feet in front of the door, which he had shut, making the interior of the small simple domicile significantly darker. "So you live here with an attractive young girl and she's not your girlfriend?"

"I can't say nothing has ever transpired. But I don't think of her like that. We're friends. And that was a long time ago. And all we did was kiss. While we were high."

"Has she lived here since the beginning?"

"Close enough. I'd known her before this place, and invited her, when she became unsheltered."

"It was your own homelessness that led to your building it?"

The man sat up and turned to face Stanley. "No actually. It was a choice I made so I could live outside of society, basically. So I could live without a job. Because I didn't want to work anymore. I had, almost continuously, for a dozen years. And all that time I didn't like it, and I didn't save any money, and didn't have enough time for myself. To enjoy life. To appreciate existence." He seemed to reflect, eyes on the dirt carpet. "I wanted to live simply. Without a master. Without an alarm clock. ...I didn't want to be in the system anymore, any more than I had to. I didn't want to play that game. You know what I mean?"

He took a moment absorbing. "Yeah. I believe I do. ...You chose to do the Christopher McCandless thing. *Into the Wild.*"

"Yeah." He smiled. "Yeah, man. Only I stayed right on the outskirts. Within the city technically."

"Mere miles from the heart of the urban zoo."

"Ha. ...Yeah. 'Urban zoo.' I like that."

The conversation hit a lull. Stanley consciously processed the strange man's garb: he was wearing a red and blue flannel shirt that was a bit ragged, a thick shirt, without a visible undershirt—which, in that the temperature within the dwelling was easily eight or ten degrees higher than outside, seemed an overly warm choice; even if it was his only shirt (a likely possibility) shirtlessness made more sense. He wore also a dirty pair of black jeans the knees were almost worn out of. His feet were bare—vascular, tan, with noticeably long nails.

"How do you get food? Food boxes? Panhandling?"

He laughed. "You interested in living like I do?"

"I kind of do. But I live with my parents. They have a house full of food. I have a clean room decorated just the way I want it. I have a cat, a game console, a bass guitar. I spend my days as I please. I don't have to work. No one makes me. I am free too."

"Well...that's not quite the same. But there are similarities, yes." He moved his forefinger around absentmindedly in the dirt. "I steal a lot of food. I don't eat much either. Twila begs on corners and her proceeds buy some food, which she shares with me." His eyes met Stanley's. "We pool our resources. ...Also, I sell bane on occasion."

"Oh. ...Bane?"

"It's a drug. As far as I know I created it."

"You're...a chemist?"

"Of sorts. No formal training. And very limited experience. Kind of a autodidactic one-trick pony chemist—of the homeless drug dealer variety. ...Unless, you know, you wouldn't count a guy who lives in a rinky-dink self-made shack as homeless." The man smiled broadly, sitting in the dirt, thin stripes of sunlight cutting across his form.

"I mean, I guess you're kind of sheltered."

The soiled shack dweller got to his feet, his back turned started apparently rooting around in what looked to be a pile of garbage, no different from any of the many others in the dark domicile. Stanley heard a creaking behind him.

"What...what's it like, the drug you make?"

Bent over he directed his attention at his self-constructed home's other occupant. "Ask her."

Stanley turned his head and saw that the sound he had a moment earlier heard was the sound of the aforementioned young woman coming quietly into the shack. She stood at the door behind Stanley, biting her lower lip in a manner that he judged to be indicative of nervousness, social discomfort, her brown eyes circled with dark eyeshadow meeting his. She was short, maybe five-two; her face held numerous small silver rings: three or more in each lobe, one in an eyebrow, one in a nostril, and also a metal bead between her small mouth and slightly indented chin. Her look was, in Stanley's opinion, goth in a stereotypical way—her hair was messy, some of it in a scrunchie, black; her fingernails had been maybe a week previous painted with black polish; she wore a stretched out, old-looking black sleeveless shirt without a bra; her lower body was clad in shorts the color of everything else over holey pantyhose, her feet in canvas shoes, the left with a hole in the toe.

"Hi."

"Hello," she responded, releasing her lip.

"Pretty flowers," he said, referring to the bouquet of wildflowers held upside-down in one hand she had returned from plucking, as her housemate had supposed she might've been.

She said, reading as timid but continuing to make eye contact: "You want to know how bane makes you feel?"

"Yeah. I'm curious."

The young woman set the flowers on the ground, sat down. Stanley did the same. "It takes about fifteen minutes to come on," began the lady in black, seeming to have become intense, an openness, unabashedness, to her unbroken gaze into the guest's eyes, Stanley growing conscious of coming to find something appealing about the dark deep pools that were her most attractive feature. "Then, in a very short time, you are in the peak—the best part. And it is an ecstasy of about a half hour that's unlike anything you'll ever experience. A kind of hallucinogenic state of overpowering joy. It's amazing. And once that feeling starts to fade—when you exit that world—you still have two hours or so of lethargic tranquility, a bliss that terminates in a long sleep." She looked at him in a way that said *Sounds pretty great, huh?*

"Ha ha. You guys happen to have a batch handy?"

"I'm going to take some with you," Twila was saying sometime later, in her hand a piece of previously crumbled tinfoil atop which was a ragged square of the stuff—its color a kind of beige-gray, its texture rough and look sporadically jagged, the appearance of it not unlike a small thin piece of peanut brittle of a different hue. She sat across from him on her knees, Stanley sitting on his knees as well; they were three feet apart in grass within eyeshot of the shack; the weather was still lovely and it was around three hours till sunset.

"How much of that is a dose?" inquired Stanley, aware of feeling a degree of excited anticipation that had mostly to do with trying the drug before him but somehow something to do with his attraction to the woman in black, whose nonintact hose-sheathed slender legs he kept stealing glances at.

"Not much. If one of us took all of this we'd go into cardiac arrest. A fourth per would still be too much. Tolerance builds slow. We both want to take approximately an eighth of this little piece." She looked down at the stuff a moment contemplatively. "I'll break yours off for you."

She moved her alluring legs out in front of her and crossed them Indian-style, moving a little closer and handing Stanley the piece of stuff that would allegedly transport him mentally to another realm within the present one; then with thumb and forefinger she squeezed off a bit for herself.

"Ready?"

"Yeah. Ready," said Stanley.

He watched her pop the small dun-colored morsel of unheard of drug into her mouth, snapping her head back as she swallowed. Her eyes, when her head returned to its forward position, were upon Stanley—looking into his eyes, with the same frankness as usual but this time as if she were playfully beckoning him, mischievously daring him to perform some action, perhaps to see her with the same freeness and focus as she seemed to see him; with a gaze that hid nothing and was fearful of no revelation.

Twila observed as Stanley consumed his portion similarly, making eye contact, intrigued and entranced.

"This is going to be fun," she said, pupils dilated with glee. "I'm glad you decided to do this with me."

"Do you often?"

"Whenever Shane makes some."

He looked around, thinking more of Twila than his surroundings. "Nice day."

"Soon everything you see is going to be utterly gorgeous. It will be like you never saw the real beauty of the world—it was concealed from you—until you were enabled to see it, by a substance that comes from nature."

Stanley was in his mind. "Why does Shane look like that? Why is his face so rough and ugly, like the skin got peeled off of it a long time ago?"

"Well..." She was no longer staring at him, into him; her head hung, her eyes on the grass at her feet. "This stuff, it's not without potential side effects."

His heart plummeted. "Tell me." In an instant he was flooded with worry, felt small beads of sweat form on his upper forehead.

Her eyes were meeting his again, forehead furrowed somewhat. "After you've done it enough you tend to develop a thin coating over your skin while you're on it—over all or some of it. It's kinda gross and doesn't wash off. You have to scrape it off. Hence his scarring."

"That's a pretty negative potentiality!" he uttered wide-eyed.

"You have to take it a lot of times. Like many more times than I've done it."

"How many times have you done it?"

"Somewhere between seventeen and twenty I'd say."

Twila leaned into him. He could see clearly the texture of her pale skin—the face sheeted with tiny bumps imperceptible from any distance—makeup-less except the eyes, their brown, in which he could a pattern of branchlike buff lines radiating from the pupils, becoming lighter toward the center. They entranced him; the way she used them, her intensity, sincerity, in combination with their aesthetic appeal hypnotized him. The woman said, "Don't worry about it. Soon, you'll have forgotten all about crystal skin."

"Crystal skin?" The term horrified him. Fear competed with the upsurge of sexual preoccupation produced by Twila's proximity.

She smiled a smile communicative of compassionate understanding; it seemed to say *Don't be silly. All is well.* Then, for a fleeting moment, her lips were pressed against his. It was a second, at most two, of concentrated happiness combined in equal measure with the kind of deep exhilaration he didn't think he'd known since he was a teenager. Coming somewhat out of the extremity of this feeling so that he was also aware of his surprise he gained consciousness of the memory of the taste of her, the feel of her soft lips, the natural perfume of her; an awareness of the lingering miniscule amount of her saliva on his lips, which to his mind had instantly become the most precious and erotic of substances, which it was a terrible shame would be gone so soon. He just looked at her, she who was looking at him; the stranger from the shack with the eyes set in darkness.

"You're cute. Hope you don't mind."

"Thanks," he said, near dumbstruck, so alive his body tingled.

Her eyes moved seductively so that she now looked at him almost from the corners of her eyes. "I've always wanted to know what it's like to fuck on this drug," she said.

These words his body processed before his brain, causing a cardiac surge, his groin to come awake. He took in her inherently sexual expression, her slightly parted lips, the twist of her upper body, her somewhat small high-set breasts concealed by a loose black tee, her pale thin arms terminating in weak-looking hands, the right's fingers touching, seeming to lightly pet, the grass below. Drunk on her sensuality, her mystery, Stanley moved in to kiss her, with no discernible volition. She said: "Wait."

<hr />

A matter of minutes later he was writhing supine on grass so saturated with color as to seem simultaneously unreal and realer than grass ever had; like it was grass as grass truly was, and it was a plant brighter and more life-emanating than he had known—an organism exuding vitality and vividness.

Twila, wide-eyed, in the same other realm, was in a similar posture to one side, taking in the cloud-traveled sky with a part of her mind; another piece of it focused on the bed of green on which she lay; another on the magnitudinous ecstasy she felt, an overpowering sensation that made her somehow wholly athrob.

Stanley adjusted his head to look over at her. The young lady with the affinity for ebony-hued garments and accoutrements was radiating light in his perception, as if a body of light was harbored within a suit of human body that was shining through it—and on bane he could see it, the physical shell became transparent or the light-body too luminous for its brightness to be concealed by the other; could see this, could see the actual quality of the grass all around them, and, if he looked up, as Twila, could discern the genuine character of the sky: it was a sentient sheet of cerulean majesty, near, far and nowhere—a planet blanket that was illusion rather than substance but yet very much alive, and ever-changing, always in motion, a heavenly membrane inviting interpretation.

She was the most beautiful of all the surrounding fauna and flora—the most complex, luminance-emanating, animated, enigmatic. Stanley brought his body up and laid it over hers, substantially smaller, one leg on the outside of each hip. Eyes that seared into his soul betrayed delight; she seemed to've not expected but to be relieved by his action. He began to move his hips so that his manhood was being rhythmically rubbed against her womanhood; then he lowered his jeans so that he could feel more, and in turn she lowered her shorts and pantyhose, so that with a rush to his mind, heart and organ Stanley could see her delicate, sparse-haired mound and when he craned his head light-pink prim lips that while the height of pulchritude he at once wanted with the entirety of his being to puncture with the pulsating vascular spear that when he set his weight on her again and he felt his skin, that skin, on hers—that skin of hers, the best skin of hers, the present, corporeal seat of her fertile femininity—seemed on the verge of entering into the best place, the too good place, of its own will.

And then, slowly, at first only the smallest bit of his parting the beginning of hers, it did. He sighed as the head went inside and she made a quiet feminine utterance. But then maybe half of him was within her, soft, wet, tight around his protuberance: the sensation of her around him, him inside her enough to really feel her, to really have entered, a paradise of pleasure, a perfection of organismal inter-connectivity—a sensation of everything being correct in the whole of the universe, of all his life being retroactively justified by the moment of his coming to be within her, Twila, who moaned at a low volume as gently and snail slow Stanley using hips put and pulled, went into and went again an inch or so out; head afire, synapses in wild celebration, nerves exploding, penis and anything physically linked with it in a gradually boiling bath of stupefying contentment.

His right hand went up to lift up her shirt. A bare left breast was revealed, its shape, slight movement, pink nipple and pocked aureole causing an upsurge of lust in him; his eyes in turn on this, her lips, her sometimes shut sometimes open eyes of glassy ataraxia, disarranged dark brown hair, pale dark-haired pubis, snug silken lips on his reddened manhood being pressed forward and partially withdrawn; despite flooding dopamine his mind engaged enough to draw the shirt above the breast's twin beauteous specimen.

"We are one."

"It feels better than anything."

"Being one with you is...the ultimate."

"I want you."

"I want to be inside you forever."

"I don't want this to end."

"I never want to stop... I'm going to go all the way inside you and just stay for a second."

"I want to feel all of you."

Twila outstretched her arms, splayed her fingers, an alabaster and black creature in a bed of otherworldly squat vert stalks that reached up through her fingers and around her frame. Stanley's face was sweaty, his forehead veiny, his head hemorrhaging with pleasure, glossy eyes seemingly unfocused.

Such...fulfillment he cogitated, his brain aroam over the world but concurrently totally present with the source of his joy.

Luxuriating, Twila met his thrusts with her own forward motion.

"Your body makes mine feel more alive than it ever has."

A small still pond topped with trash and toxic algae lay to their north, just beyond the shack. Stanley, in the relative silence, could hear the sound of the suction of her warm vagina on his penis which—as her exposed breasts bounced, as she bit her lower lip—further heightened his arousal, until it felt the tumescence inside the warm center of the focus of his world was a volcano on the brink of ejecting a mass of pressurized lava from its depths.

After some seconds of holding back he screamed as if seriously wounded, his seed being released within her in three or four sapping spurts as he was in to the hilt—her body beneath a light-shot thing of shared ecstasy.

Terminating the visceral apex of their union he groaned as he slid down, laying his head on her breast, her chest rising and falling, causing his head to, as she heavily respirated. One arm crossed her abdomen, his hand resting on her lower stomach and hipbone. He felt at once like a prototypical young lover, spent and reeling from joy, his object of desire's perky pink breasts his pillow and view—both of them shiny with sweat under the sun and emitting bright luminance from every pore. Like a creature that did not know itself, that possibly had been stripped of its internality and was an entity, bodiless, experiencing but unattached to the Earth; a being dizzy and disoriented, whose consciousness had been short-circuited by bliss.

Stanley, aware too of the rhythmic movement of his head, of the way the wind caused the blades of grass to bend with its flow, imagined he could hear insects moving in it, at soil level, imagined those of the same species cryptically gesturing or exchanging scent signals.

He occupied a mental space of complete and total mental-emotional contentment, postcoital, Twila's slim, white legs, a lone tentative freckle here and there—between them a small pink softness that was the origin of the world—in the squinted view of his upper eye.

But, as always, he could not reside there, not in this case beyond the hours of afternoon—which became a blur of peaceful sleepiness under the laggard motion of clouds, among nature's small, shrill, and sudden sounds, and faded into a long blackness, blankness that he awoke from chilly, no longer holding Twila: alone in the grass; stars above; the shack minimally illuminated within by what might have been candlelight.

Stanley didn't talk to her much the next day, nor to Shane, and spent most of the day outside, staring, observing, passing time indolently. He began to spend a lot of time outside, next to the shack, often looking out across the pond, soaking in its forbiddingness, ugliness, acquired repellency.

Its unrippled surface was a sort of dark green-gray, a sickly color, the water murky, everywhere opaque. Nearest where he sat, on what constituted its bank, a denuded patch of claylike light-brown dirt, a diagonally floating—time frozen-seeming—empty wax-coated cardboard pint milk container, white with blue, the lettering faded, hung trapped by the toxic water, almost sludge-esque, as if set in poisonous gelatin. To its right, farther out, more subsurface, was a treadless automobile tire, about a fourth of it visible—which tire theoretically might've still been attached to a car or some part of a car. There were swirls of inexplicable black in the water here and there that he could make out from his vantage, perhaps spirals of lethal muck also suspended in the dark gelatin. Along the same bank on which he sat, to his left, was a smaller than typical shopping cart from a store called Grant's (the handle logo informed him)—on its side; a long piece of apparent ribbon, frayed, dirtied white, twisted about an upper wheel occasionally catching the wind. A beetle walked in the direction of the disused cart, an inch from one of his bare feet, wings encased in a shiny black shell, segmented legs the shape of fallen Ls. Across the pond, eight or nine yards wide, was more grass, then tall weeds, then low hills, long baked by sun, some spread out skeletal trees on the slopes of and atop them, trees that seemed water-deprived, near death. He found himself imagining walking along the bottom of the pond, which at greatest depth was likely no more than four feet—imagined stirred up silt and disturbed near-microscopic creatures there were identical thousands of that had been placidly swimming in a side-to-side motion, foraging; additional assorted refuse, some of it decades old; pieces of glass that would open and infect the soles of his feet.

He heard the shack door creak open behind him and soon Twila was standing over one shoulder, looking out across the expanse of stagnant water long used as a garbage receptacle. "Hi," she said.

The man twisted his head to look at her. The sun was falling and the orb's placement made her expression indiscernible. "Hi. ...Haven't talked to you for a while. What have you been up to?"

"Not much. I tried to get a job yesterday. I think they thought I was a drug addict. I thought I looked presentable."

"Where?"

"An industrial supply company not too far away. They needed a receptionist."

Stanley looked back at her again, shielding his eyes, the star's rays that shone from around her head blinding. "Are you? A drug addict?"

"I don't do it that often. I like it but I don't do it that often. I'm definitely not addicted to it. Any more than I'm addicted to...tacos."

"Ha."

"You liked it, didn't you?" He got the impression she was looking at him in the locked-on, soul-searching way she would sometimes.

He became stone-faced serious. "You know I did."

The foul water filled his vision as he considered that he couldn't say whether or to what extent he would have liked it if not for the experience he had with Twila; as he ruminated on the fact that that had been the single occasion on which she hadn't seemed frustratingly unavailable to him, in his mind; as he thought about the fact that she came into his mind frequently yet perhaps rarely did he enter hers, that she no doubt did not harbor similar feelings.

"Do you ever think about us?"

"Of course," she responded after a moment. Then he heard her begin to slowly walk away, back toward the simple home they spent their nights sleeping quietly and separately in.

Weeks passed. Stanley took bane another two times, on both occasions by himself. He got the impression Twila had been taking it too, also by herself—that she would go off somewhere secluded and trip by herself. Stanley went to the same spot where he'd had his initial experience, never matching its intensity, his fulfillment, despite the fact he increased the dose.

One day a strong wind rose. It grew increasingly more powerful, shaking and slanting everything. The news had said a hurricane was due but he didn't know that since he never watched TV anymore. Hurricanes were not uncommon as they lived in Florida or Georgia or someplace humid and southerly.

Branches began being torn off the scattered trees. The shack— which he was standing near observing, body being bent by the wind, fighting against it to maintain some semblance of a normal posture—started to show signs of distress. Then panels that had been vibrating in place were coming off and flying spinning in midair. Shane and Twila came out, watching next to him.

"Pretty crazy," remarked the former.

"Yeah," said Stanley.

Before their eyes piece after piece of the plywood and random bits of lumber that had been utilized for the roof and more from the walls were torn free by the gale.

"Fuck, dude. It's destroying my long-standing handiwork."

The other man looked at him. "Did you know this was coming?"

"I saw something about it in the newspaper a few days ago, when I was in the city square. I'd forgotten about it."

Twila's animated eyes were locked on the ongoing destruction of their home. She had not looked at him; rarely did. A board flew by perilously near.

"Let's make sure we don't take a wood slat to the mug," said Shane.

Stanley: "I know."

Twila: "We could go sit by the pond of death. Watch from there."

Shane: "I don't want to see any more of my house built of my brow sweat being ripped apart by the cruelty of Nature Mother!"

She laughed. They were walking to 'The Pond of Death.' "I can understand that."

The trio sat with their gaze directed at the dwelling, perhaps a quarter of it gone, the wind-thrown bits everywhere. It was late morning and the agitated surface of the water revealed a lighter semi-translucent body of putrid liquid below. The month was August; possibly early September.

When, after hours, the destruction was over, the hurricane having moved south, nothing was left of the roof—and the walls had been half ripped off. The day became one of forlorn restoration. First they sought out the strewn boards, finding many and piling them up next to the shack until they had acquired nails Shane planned to go into town for.

"If this is all we can find we're going to have to gather more wood," said Shane, his pronouncement turning their mission to collect what had been scattered into a foraging one, the gang of squatters out for whatever they could find that would suffice for the rebuilding of their humble abode on the outskirts of a medium-size city.

Stanley ended up atop a hill, Twila nearby, the two seeking out large branches no longer attached to the trees here and there along the mount. He made a point to move closer to her, eyes on the ground but mind on the quiet lady ebony-clad.

"It surprises me how little we talk, considering we live together."

She looked up at him. "I'm quite a bit of an introvert you know. ...I'm finding some. What about you?"

"I've located a couple big enough ones. I'll only be able to take a couple down at a time."

"Yeah."

"I want you."

She kept moving, didn't respond.

"I loved being inside you. I loved it."

"You loved bane. You don't even know what it's like sober."

"I want to."

Twila continued walking away from him.

"I want to get to know you. To be with you again. Are you only interested in being with me if we're on bane?"

"I prefer to be alone."

"You live in a commune, Greta Garbo."

She chuckled. "You can call it that. I like having a roof over my head." The girl bent, picked up a large branch. "I'm going to take a few down."

Stanley did the same, following a few paces behind her down the hill, two branches nearly as long as him in his arms, watching Twila's slightly protuberant posterior as he descended—vexed, longing.

That evening, the three of them having gathered enough wood, branches and logs mostly, to make it work, Shane and Stanley propped some logs against the shack and the former walked up top of it, being careful not to fall through. Stanley and Twila handed up the assorted wood to him and he formed a sort of steeple with it that he secured with rope. He and Stanley had repaired the walls earlier, after Shane had come back from town with nails. He had also returned with a large dirty blue tarp—a thick, used covering the origins of which he had not spoken of—and now, the steeple top having been tied tight, Stanley lifted the messily folded tarp up to him and he pulled it over the triangular makeshift roof, making it presumably rainproof. Shane came gingerly down along a propped log and he and the motley stood back taking in their home's new appearance.

"We'll have to secure the ends to the ground with some twine later, like a tent. Else a strong wind'll just take that thing offa there," he said referring to the mud-crusted medium-blue cover that fell to about five feet from the grass.

The day's unforecast destruction having exhausted them physically and emotionally both there was a perceivable tentative relief among them that the domicile was seemingly fit for occupancy again already. They ambulated collectively towards its door slowly, the housemate who had once briefly, in an encounter surreal and celestial, been his lover—a sentient palace of overwhelming pleasures open to him only—in all ways distant from him.

Twila was now, Stanley deduced, obtaining bane from Shane and dosing off alone nearly every day, arousing her admirer's impotent concern. As for himself Stanley ingested it of late as a kind of self-medication—which need he felt as a result of his numerous torments related to the young woman he each night laid on a floor of dirt only yards from, sometimes watching her face after she had gone to sleep but he was still trying to: taking in the peacefulness of it, the pulchritude; wondering what had happened to her; wondering if she was more afraid than damaged; wondering whether if he were someone else if she would be more available to him, as open as she had been on day one; wondering what her past had been like (he had previously asked her questions about her childhood, adolescence, time before she'd come to live with Shane. "It was average, normal." "I guess I was a bit awkward. And quieter." "Nothing too interesting. I drank. Partied some. I didn't tend to get too crazy.").

⸻ ⸨◉⸩ ⸻

A man wearing a soiled green tee with sleeves that terminated in yellow rings and a yellow ring at the neck, snug jeans in need of laundering, and black-white Converse low-tops laid under a tree of sparse branches, cogitating, very high, considering the suddenly changing appearance of Twila. He was looking up at the tree's peak, able to still see the sky's tranquil blue past its apex. The grass about him radiated light and color, seemed to vibrate in a way only he could perceive; was as he was inseparable from the whole of the unfathomable universe; the integral living carpet of an integral living biped whose waves of mind were ascending through the dendritic life filling his view, mind-stuff rising and dissipating and able to be tuned to by those of broad enough consciousness (who would likely be unaware of what they'd absorbed and so distant they wouldn't know the data's origin, data that might come to them as fog added to fog).

He hadn't seen the woman his mind was on for five days, but the last time he'd seen her her face didn't look as it had the day before, and the day before he'd noticed it had changed for the worse, and not subtly, in a way that was no doubt the result of crystal skin.

Concerned, he'd asked Shane if he knew anything about her whereabouts.

"I'd have to say she's probably on a bane binge, bro. She got quite a bit from me the last day either of us saw her and then she disappeared. So...yeah: she's likely hidden herself somewhere and is just taking bane all the time."

Stanley had frowned, feeling helpless, wondering why she had taken a downhill turn. Bane was amazing, but moderation was important; and also quitting before it resulted in the side effect that had disfigured Shane and had now altered Twila's appearance. Her previously pleasing visage had within the last week been transformed into something unnatural, her face become rough and perceivably ridged.

"Mind if I join you? I'm tripping too."

She had given him a start—and more than because he'd not known there was another soul nearby.

It was Twila, a new, horrible Twila, standing directly over him, looking down at his face, into his eyes, smiling widely but oddly—creepily.

"God."

"Sorry. Didn't mean to scare you." She sat down next to him.

She was about three times uglier than she had been last time. It was as if the skin had been sandpapered from her face, then unevenly replaced with tree bark of the same tone. Her countenance was now a jarring sight, even for one unfamiliar with how she had once, recently, looked it would've been; for Stanley it was emotionally painful to behold, though he was able only to glance briefly at it.

"I've been thinking more about you. About us. Lately."

"I thought you liked to be alone."

"I do. I do. But..." she turned to him, "that doesn't mean I'm not interested in being intimate from time to time."

He met her eyes for a moment, attempting to conceal the effect of her new face.

"I've thought I loved you before," he said after a moment. "I've thought that many times."

She smiled. "And?"

"And, you rejected me. And now you've destroyed yourself." He made eye contact again, with effort, holding his gaze. "Why? Why have you done this to yourself?" The drug was making him feel as if his heart were beating stentorianly, beating on the outside of his body, on the verge of seizing up.

"It wasn't on purpose," she said after a moment almost guiltily or perhaps regretfully. "I got carried away with it. Uncharacteristically."

"You're young. *Were* beautiful. Why?"

"Depression I guess. It's an escape from it."

"What if the depression stems from within?"

"You don't even know me."

"I just said 'what if.'"

"You're diminishing my high," Twila said turning her head from him.

Slowly, following a moment's deliberation—with far less bodily control than he had sober—he rose to his feet and with a sigh began to amble away. Somewhere distant from the person who was all walls and no interior, who now was no longer even a pleasing package, the image of the luminous grass he looked down at as he sadly walked, probably to the pond, fading gradually.

19

Stanley was haunted. Maybe he would always be haunted now. Traumatized. It was his new reality, thanks to her, the whore, actual whore.

He had dreamt of Hope the previous night—dreamt she was about to leave for Emile's with copious makeup on her face (in contrast to her custom of wearing none), with hoop earrings dangling from her earlobes and her hair back; in high heels, a corduroy miniskirt that barely covered the aesthetic curves of her buttocks, and a low-cut nearly transparent white half-shirt under which were her firm beautiful C-cups and no bra. A dream from which he woke hot with jealousy.

She in fact had gone to meet Emile two evenings earlier but was dressed normally, even, for her, on the conservative side. Regardless of her appearance she had been leaving to have sex with someone else, that was the important part, was what Stanley could not psychologically cope with. And so his mind was making a terrible reality worse. *Why didn't he just get rid of her?* he asked himself. *Regardless of the cost.*

He'd woken from the dream—nightmare, of which he remembered only a fragment—and remembered that Hope had told him in it that Emile sometimes called her "his practically perfect whore." Which had solidified in his psyche a strong need of doing something about the situation, for his own sake, for his mental health. And sitting there in bare feet, mussy-haired, with a brain that felt as if it'd been in a centrifuge awhile, he determined to end the arrangement it'd anguished him to learn of, one way or another, and quickly—and he began to concoct means of doing so, other than leaving Hope (and becoming homeless), killing Hope, or finding and managing to murder her temporary employer, the well-off john.

———※◎※———

Hope was out. He didn't know her whereabouts. He wasn't sure he cared. She often was gone lately.

It was afternoon, about three-thirty. The sunlit living room made him feel (more) depressed—the light contributed to his melancholy, his lethargy, discontentment.

The TV was off. He was on the couch doing nothing. There seemed to be nothing worth doing; anymore he mostly did nothing. Everything seemed dead. The world outside was mean, indifferent, a stream of cows with their heads bent to their phones; and home-less people, lots of homeless people, those who were on the outside looking in. Without a smartphone to focus on observing the scat-tered cattle.

Vaguely horny, he decided to watch some porn on the internet. He hadn't for a while, three weeks maybe. He spent some time—more than a half hour—perusing various sites and the top videos in various categories before he settled on a forty-five-minute one that seemed sufficiently titillating to view beginning to end, a video in which a hot twentysomething brunette came over to some stocky pretend drug slinger's swanky apartment and fellated and copulated with him in exchange for a discount on his wares.

He had ejaculated, powerfully, just after the porno's climax; and a few nights later Stanley found himself imagining as he lay on the bed, looking up at the ceiling with glossy eyes—as often furious, hurt, bewildered, in state near derealization—daydreaming in fact, quite vividly, in great detail, that the male in the movie was Emile and the female Hope, replaying in his mind the content he had masturbated to with the parts recast; daydreaming of Hope going to Emile's place, a loft apartment, after arranging it with the dealer, in order to buy a quantity of cocaine from him.

His absent girlfriend was clad in an outfit flashy and sexy, a tight low-cut and high-slit red-and-green dress, underneath which were neither panties nor brassiere. Glittery crimson large hoop earrings hung from either side of her head and her hair, stylistically uncharacteristic of her, was stiff with hairspray and molded in an anachronistic eighties style. She stood outside his door knocking.

The portal was pulled open and a wide grin greeted her. "Hey girl. Good to see you. You look great. Why're you so dressed up? Going somewhere?"

"I just wanted to get your attention." She smiled as she walked into the spacious dwelling. Framed pop culture posters decorated the walls and black leather couches and glass-top tables were arranged in the living room, at the front of which was a sixty-inch flatscreen television hooked up to a stereo system.

"Here. Before I sell you what you want we can just do some." The peddler plucked a small Ziploc bag from a pocket.

"Awesome."

The two seated themselves on one of the comfortable couches and snorted four thin lines each off a mirror, Hope's hairless crossed legs pointed toward Emile, who like Hope was sniffing as he took in his companion's body with his peripheral vision. Emile felt the mucous containing the stimulant making its way down sluggishly but wasn't yet feeling what he'd just ingested; he was, however, still high from the lines he'd been having throughout the day. He was about forty pounds overweight, had a trimmed van dyke and wore a loose-fitting, new-looking pair of black slacks and a long-sleeved cotton shirt, black too, some logo over the left breast. He'd removed an also new-looking baseball cap, the sort he typically wore, and placed it on the table when he and his prostitute acquaintance had sat down to ingest the quantity of powder he shook onto the square of mirror from the baggie.

"Your stuff is always really good. I'm going to be very high." Her pupils dilated as she looked at him. "And since coke always makes me a lot hornier than usual—which is pretty horny"—she and Emile both laughed—"I'm going to be *extremely* fucking horny."

"You look hotter than ever by the way."

She blushed. "You're always sexy," she responded, meeting his eyes and grinning broadly.

Three uncongenial-looking friends of Emile's sat in the living room at a distance. One on another of the sofas, lost to some mindless unwinnable game on his phone, a dark beanie on his head and scruff on his chin; two on metal chairs playing cards at one of the glass tables, frowning, a ballcap on the bigger of the twain. They seemed oblivious to Hope and their probable boss's presence.

"You feeling it yet?"

"Fuck yeah." The woman beamed, seemed now a bit antsy, her synapses hyperactive in the bright expansive den.

Emile relaxed his posture, turned into her slightly. "Me too." He smiled provocatively, eyes traveling down across her body, a body that on a number of previous occasions had been the cause of an upsurge of lust he'd used it to unrestrainedly indulge.

Then the reclining dealer with the enviable apartment and the tiny squared diamond in one lobe, blood feeling afire due to the dual stimulations of the snuffed anesthetic and his concupiscence—roused by Hope's appearance in the revealing dress—mental and physical state to his liking and eyes locked with his companion's, asked her: "So how 'bout it? You want to suck my dick, bitch?"

Hope sniffed, glancing involuntarily at his crotch, eyes wet and wide.

"You can tell the bitch really wants to," he commented to his nearby pals. "Don't you?"

She smiled lasciviously at him, biting her red-lipstick-coated lower lip, then began to caress his left bicep, staring lustfully at the whole of his image.

Emile, appendage gaining blood, gazed at Hope as one famished would a steaming plate of victuals, while she, still rubbing the muscle, leaned into his side, making a point of pressing her breasts into him.

"Goddamn that's a good dress on you," he said to her compressed cleavage, her dress having slid down slightly, revealing even more of her creamy fair-sized feather-soft mounds.

"I'm glad you like it, stud," she said moving her hand down and up his arm. "I wore it for you."

"I got a fucking boner now, girl. You rubbing your tits on me gave me full wood. You're gonna have to do something about that I think."

"Are you going to make me, sexy?" she said to his eyes in the most sexual voice she was capable of without sounding ridiculous.

"Oh fuck yeah, bitch," responded Emile, starting to exert slight downward pressure on her head with one hand as an indication for her to bring her mouth to the vicinity of his crotch. His member pulsed along one leg of his pants, extending halfway to the knee.

"What's in it for me?" inquired Hope, resisting, though with chosen strengthlessness.

"How 'bout some money off that cocaine?" suggested Emile, anything other than his libido or Hope (her well-formed breasts mostly visible) having ceased to exist.

"If you give me thirty percent off I'll give you a hand job."

"Okay. But only if I get to come on your face. And you don't get to wipe it off before you go either. You have to walk out of here glazed."

"Definite deal." Her hand moved to his thigh, began slowly to caress the appendage within his slacks.

"You're going to be soaked, girl."

Emile watched her a moment. "Yeah, I like that."

"She loves jizz so much she talked me into coming in her mouth the second time we fucked—even though I like to come in a woman's pussy," he informed one of his guys.

"Then she told me how good it tasted and how hot it made her to swallow it. She said she hadn't stopped wondering what it would taste like since the first time. I shit you not: after she swallowed my load for a while she acted like I'd just given her a gold brick or something."

His attention returned to his source of arousal. "Nasty cocksucking hot bitch," he said happily as Hope, with a big smile, having undone his belt, the upper button of his pants and his zipper, tugged down his slacks and boxers simultaneously, her head lowered to inches from his groin.

An unusually large erect penis flopped out, brushing the right side of Hope's makeuped face; she grasped it with her comparatively small hand, her countenance a harlot's in mirthful anticipation of ungentle orgasm-producing coitus with a customer who had satisfied her previously, who she was comfortable with. The uncommon organ she gripped like a trophy was a foot in length or more, with an unusually substantial circumference—a monstrosity the laundromat owner from a bleak sector of Europe likely regarded as a blessing not a curse. A body part the woman holding it had many times shuttered on; coated with saliva; choked on in view of a few of the homies in the main room of the massive bachelor pad of a home on the fourteenth floor of one of Oswald's few high-rises, a building occupied solely by the well-off—feeling degraded and liking it.

Beautiful Hope, heart pounding, on her knees at her sometime john's feet, looked with lust at Emile; then for longer, with greater desire, at his member, extending far beyond her palm, the distance distended between upper and lower lids, mind removed to a plane of ecstasy.

The tableau, as Stanley imagined it: the most physically attractive woman alive partially obscured by an enormous penis her fingers were wrapped around, the better part of her healthy teeth showing as she grinned genuinely and widely, her elation correlated to the prospect of having a near-stranger's gargantuan manhood inside her once again, her breasts of aesthetic excellence nearly popping out of the top of her dress.

A conscientiously garbed and diligently painted twenty-six-year-old female of Stanley's mind, now exclusively of Stanley's mind, who was being utilized as a sexual object by her so choosing by an illiterate indoctrinated in thug culture, who presently released the primed penis for a moment to reach around her back and unzip her dress, sliding it down to about two inches below the bottom of her breasts and doing so releasing them bouncing to full exposure.

The appearance of this flesh prompted Emile to immediately begin caressing one, Hope letting out a coinciding just-audible sigh, then firmly grip the pair as, his organ back in her dwarfed hand, Hope with a look of abject pleasure began to masturbate him, vision monopolized by her sex act. A cheap silver bracelet moved erratically on the wrist in motion.

"I'm really excited to be on my knees jerking you off. It's not only because of the money that I'm happy about our arrangement," communicated the topless fornicator, one breast still squeezed by the luxuriating pleasure-receiver, both her hands now at his genitals, as she gazed adoringly up at him.

"It's also because I love it. I didn't know that I would—but I do. I don't like it, or even thoroughly enjoy it—I love it. And I loved the way your come tastes. I want to taste it again. And I love that your dick has been the cause of many intense orgasms for me."

She continued two-handedly jerking off her customer, the cocaine peddler, who was somewhat in a world of his own; soon she rose, using him as support, saying simultaneously, "I've decided I'm going to do what I've been wanting to do. Which is to give you sex for free. I don't need a discount."

Emile's eyes brightened. "I'm gonna get blown by this fantasy-caliber girl, just 'cause she wants to blow me," he announced, chipper, to his cadre, glancing back with his peripheral vision.

"Oh yeah you are," said Hope, looking expectantly at Emile. "But first I want to do something with you that we haven't done. Make out."

"Hope," began Emile, at once touched, his visage serious, locking eyes, "I've wanted to kiss you since I first saw you. You're a really cool chick. Different. But in a good way. I wish I knew you better."

"Aww. You should try to make up for all those kisses you didn't get to have," she said.

Emile stood and almost immediately engulfed Hope's lips with his own. The half-naked woman kissed back, the bulk of the other's body pressed into hers; in moments their lips, then tongues, were in passionate motion—oral organs briefly dueling, Hope momentarily sucking the desire-frenzied dealer's.

Remaining up against him after some minutes she ran her bare-breasted body down Emile's frame slowly until she was kneeling again and, holding it in her left hand, began kissing his erection. She started with the base, then kissed it randomly everywhere, with a closed mouth; finally with a somewhat open mouth, from which her tongue began issuing quick licks, all over the entire dozen-plus inches.

"This is already so fucking hot," she stopped for a moment to say, her eyes become bleary with arousal, as she gripped Emile's phallus with left and right. "I can still hardly believe your cock...it's by far the biggest, most arousing one I have ever seen." She stared a second admiringly before her eyes ascended to his face. "I am going to suck this thing for you like I am trying to pay you back for all the times I've orgasmed on it. And," Hope added, words running together, "I am going to be intentionally sloppy about it."

Both hands near the base she began to lick the entirety of the shaft—initially with casualness, but gradually, becoming progressively more stimulated, voracious, as if trying to take all the flavor from it. Her body tensed as she continued stimulating the engorged organ in this manner, with increasing intensity, licking and sucking the outermost few inches, until—letting out a quiet, distinctly girlish moan around the member in her warm mouth—she had a subdued orgasm; then, very wet, she commenced fellating him to four inches down, running her open mouth and extended tongue over the protuberance, lust ratcheted up due to her climax; the person to whom the organ was attached on cloud nine on his couch in his climate-controlled loft; having another in a series of trouble-free days, a day of uninterrupted comfort, of plenty, of insulated ataraxia.

Before Hope started taking in the tumescence to the best of her ability, sometimes fitting most of the penis down her throat, her lips spread wide around his wet manhood, their lipstick lost to his mouth and member long ago, she had made a point to produce as much saliva as possible while she ran her mouth along and down his appendage—making it much wetter, what she was doing much messier. And, as she repeatedly buried it in her mouth—Emile's center of pleasure dripping with her copious spit, spit coating the lower portion of her face and dripping from her chin, long strings of gluey spit extending from his glistening genitalia to her gaping mouth each time she pulled away—she had another orgasm, this one dampening the tops of her thighs and causing her to groan animally, while the thin bridges of transparent excreta connected her body to Emile's.

She required some moments to recover, after which she resumed fellating the reclining one, the receiver, the other animal in the pornographic frieze—feverishly, rapt—till ten minutes and a number of increasingly draining orgasms later Emile, who had begun sporadically moaning, showed signs of approaching ejaculation.

Hope—her face smeared with combined makeup and saliva, eyes foggy and unfocused, appearing spiritually unpresent, like a vaguely inhabited puppet of pliable flesh—pulled away from the focus of her effort just long enough to say, breathlessly, "I want to swallow a big mouthful of your come" before plunging her mouth back onto Emile's swollen projection, her many climaxes seeming to have transformed her into something like a lust zombie, capable exclusively of experiencing and producing pleasure in a mostly brainless, blissful, abstracted state.

When the initial jet of hot seed shot into her mouth only a small portion of the erection—which, testicles included, appeared as if it'd been dipped in Hope's expectoration—was in her mouth. The long built up orgasm was loud, the thick sprays that issued from Emile's appendage synced with full body convulsions, and when the spurts ceased her mouth was overflowing with warm semen.

She tilted her head back to avoid spilling any from her mouth; nonetheless a quantity cascaded down her lower lip and chin, a glob becoming cemented to the bottom of her face. Then—sweaty; her face superficially, cosmetically, fairly destroyed; her bare C-cups (the pink nipples of which were firm with arousal) suspended perky above a downward-driven dress; the viscous fluid sloshing slightly in her brimming-full wide-open mouth—Hope in one large gulp swallowed the whole, causing her to momentarily shudder.

"Oh god that was unbelievably sexy, baby," she said to her partner in lechery, esophagus and oral orifice tasting chemically washed, her voice conveying the impression she was on the verge of crying or needed to catch her breath, as she remembered the stalagmite of biological jelly on her chin and wiped it off with her forefinger, from which it was immediately ingested.

"Got-*damn* that was good, girl," said Emile after a considerable exhalation, pulling his pants up leisurely, exuding satisfaction. "You know all my homies that have seen you want to fuck you, right?"

Hope smiled up at him with sparkling eyes.

"Fuck. You're probably the best cocksucker in ten states," he speculated aloud.

"I can't wait to see you and your beautiful tits again," Emile continued, pock-marked visage beaming, as he helped Hope up. His customer and lover had pulled up her outfit, her face reading beatific fulfillment, and was immersed in the residual warmth of expressed carnality; unconsciously experiencing herself as a vessel, sentient receptacle, and a vacant one.

"Good fucking *girl*," added the cocaine merchant, patting her tight-clothed posterior lightly as he trod legs wide, sapped, to the kitchen area.

"I'll get Taytay to give you what you wanted and show you out. And she's getting a sixty percent discount, 'kay, Tay?" said Emile from the other room, displaying a toothsome grin; and the hired hand, who'd nodded assent, lumbered over from the right—where there was a hallway that led to other rooms; one almost as large as the one they were in (Emile's bedroom), within which was the entrance to a significantly smaller room, containing an arsenal, and safe—already holding a thrice-wrapped package meant for her.

And Hope, face yet glossy with the byproduct of unromantic sex with the local entrepreneur whose surname she did not know, took the elevator down to the parking garage, drove home (it was a mostly silent seventeen-minute drive), and shortly after returning showered—Stanley imagining they had doggie-style coitus in bed, in electric blue light (he lasting only a minute and coming much and powerfully), while *Peggy Sue Got Married* played in the background, then fell asleep.

Stanley woke feeling scarred, scooped out, dejected; on the whole negatively different (everything was yet worse, due the cruelty of his own psyche, so deleteriously affected by his companion). He had the image burned in his mind, among many, of Hope, somehow empty-eyed, her mouth and throat as wide as she could force them to be—sensual mouth pouring saliva around a giant penis, the penis of his enemy (whom she had been willingly sexually degraded by), erection almost completely orally engulfed by her.

Some time had passed since Stanley last mentioned her arrangement with Emile or the effects his knowledge of it was having on him, and the night following his vivid mental film of Hope and the businessman libidinously engaged she came back from the grocery store with two cases of beer and they were up till around sunrise snorting blow off the den table using a twenty and drinking cans of domestic.

Just before they laid down Stanley in actuality this time (he thought) mounted Hope, the coke enabling him (he speculated) to last for nearly fifteen minutes. They faced the full-length mirror in her room, Stanley wearing nothing, Hope wearing hair-clips and makeup, breasts swinging with his thrusts.

He'd been especially libidinous and his orgasm was particularly powerful and it was a fun, carefree morning, and he was surprised by how easily he and Hope had gotten along (which was as well as they ever had), by how infrequently he had thought of how their relation-ship, or at least his opinion of her, had changed—that to memory it did not once enter his mind that his so-called girlfriend, the socio-path Hope Brownen, was a prostitute, an unfaithful nymphomaniac; was underneath dirt at the edge of the woods.

————))(((0)) ————

"You know I noticed a few days ago that you came home late, and drunk, wearing heavy makeup, and it was smeared. ...I imagine you were at a party or something. And I don't know what you did—I don't want to know. But, in light of the way you are, the things you do, the way you treat me, I was thinking..."

"Yes?" They were in bed in the dark. Hope had rolled her eyes but Stanley had not seen. His arm was across her midsection but the only warmth she emanated was physical. Her well-formed body, Stanley sometimes thought, seemed merely a vehicle for a nefarious spirit—the kind that devoured, was more insectile than human, that took without giving, that was ultimately self-concerned in its every action (and Stanley was the fly in her web, being sapped of nutrients and strength, destroyed from the inside out; the silk of the trap the silk of her womanhood, of her blemishless skin, the convincing cover of a succubus, succubus by more than one definition).

"How about you bring me home a girl? You must know a few, who are sluts—like you."

She laughed. "That's very doable. I'll call one of my friends."

"How about someone new?"

"I think I can arrange that. Actually I met some hot slutty chicks recently."

"...Can I fuck her in front of you?"

"Of course. And I'll make sure I have coke for us."

He audibly exhaled, eyes on her back. She was wearing a thin sleeveless blouse she often slept in and was nude below the navel.

"Hope. As much as I like the fact that I can have sex with other women in this relationship, I'm not okay with you sleeping with other people in this relationship."

"I know."

"Nor is it acceptable for you to kiss other guys—or anything else of the sort," he said.

"Okay," she said.

"Okay. So you aren't going to keep meeting that one guy?"

"We can discuss this later."

"I want a yes or no."

"I've told you—regardless of how you feel I never specifically agreed to monogamy. If you inferred otherwise I'm sorry, but I don't consider myself responsible."

"Love isn't the sort of emotion you want to play with that way. There's a good chance that, sooner or later, I'll lose my mind and thrust a kitchen knife through your middle when you're least expecting it."

"Are you trying to scare off the woman you love? Because that isn't going to result in my sleeping with fewer others, my kicking you to the curb. Which, of course, I never want to do. I want this thing to last. And I sure don't want you destitute, sleeping outside somewhere. You're my guy."

"I was just communicating."

They lay on their sides, Stanley spooning her, in silence, both pairs of eyes open in a darkness in which little more than silhouettes were discernible. He felt helpless, trapped by his own attachment, but pleased he was utilizing a negative situation to his advantage.

"So are you still going to try to find a girl for me?"

"Yes, baby. How does young, blonde, petite and Brazilian sound?"

"Good. That sounds very good."

"Good. Because that description matches a quite sexy girl who said she wants to hang out sometime. And she's single and very possibly down for some N.S.A. fooling around."

"She sounds sexy."

Hope rotated her body toward him, kissed him wetly on the mouth, tongue parting his lips. "Let's fuck," she said.

"Okay." He slid his boxers down and kicked them off his ankles to the bottom of the mattress.

He gripped her nearer breast firmly, kneading the soft flesh with tensed fingers as his phallus began incrementally to inflate with blood.

"I have come to the disturbing, and for me quite unfortunate, conclusion that you're a mentally ill whore," he said after his probing erection had slipped satisfying into her as they lay on their sides. "I think I probably hate you as much as I love you," added Stanley, hips in motion.

She directed a smile back at him. "You're funny."

————)(()(————

It wasn't long after their nighttime conversation that a striking acquaintance of Hope's came over, a woman who Hope had previously informed him had participated in some internet porn videos earlier in her life.

There would be no Brazilian, as Stanley had initially expected. She was out of town, for weeks, and so Hope had lined up someone else, a friend of a friend, someone she had described as "an almost actual whore. A very sexy one."

The woman introduced herself as Lana as she stood on the porch facing Hope, the doorbell ringing at a few minutes past eight. "Hey, girlie" the latter had said as she motioned for her to enter, Stanley looking over his girlfriend's shoulder at the person he knew he soon would be inside.

It was a faux blonde, E-cups (that he discovered appeared unnatural out of clothes) popping out of a low, formfitting, red satin dress; her large lips shiny with a coating of colorless lip gloss; her look, cultivated over years, that of a classic bimbo—the whole of Lana the ex-porn star's features erotic but exaggerated and evidently artificial (as, though difficult to discern, her cheer was also ersatz, and served to cloak the shallowness, the needs- and sickness-informed drives of what passed for her personality).

"Stanley. Nice to meet you," said the male resident as she came in, glancing around, a locomotive mannequin-person taking in new environs.

"Nice to meet you. You're good-looking. Your girlfriend told me you were."

"So are you," said Stanley, his manhood just perceptibly stirring anticipatorily.

Hope—wearing heels, a salmon-colored miniskirt, transparent sleeveless blouse, and fire-engine red lipstick, uneven hair communicating as always an underlying atypicality—watched, apparently excited, as Lana without ado, as Stanley's eyes bulged, pulled her huge breasts from her dress—her mammaries taut, dark pink areolas sizable and nipples hard in their middle.

"I figure this'll help everyone get in the mood faster, if I let the ladies out." She smiled.

Stanley pulled off his tee, went up to her, penis jutting, at once carnally overcome, and began to kiss her with an open mouth, sloppily, her massive bust pressed against his pectoral muscles, Lana reciprocating while directing them to the couch against the far wall.

She sat next to him, close. For a few minutes Stanley fondled her unsoft surgically enhanced breasts, sand dollar-sized nipple pads centered on them, as they deep-kissed; then Lana leaned toward the tented crotch of Stanley's pants, unzipped his fly, fished out the pulsating part of him, and began to wetly lick and kiss it—head to base, base to head.

A quarter-hour later, under Hope's continued observation, Stanley was rhythmically fornicating with the moaning visitor with substantive force, positioned behind her, when he withdrew his engorged incarnadine hard-on from her vagina and exploded in the mouth of his anticipatory girlfriend—who intuiting, as in a fantasy, that he wanted her to capture his expelled fluid orally dropped to her knees to the right of the blonde.

Lana had been brought to the precipice of orgasm but despite her lack of climax was woozy from pleasure. Instigated by Hope, who stared communicatively at the recovering erstwhile prostitute bent across the couch with an open mouth brimming with warm seed—some of which had sprayed her chin—Lana sighted the pool of Stanley's excreta in the other woman's oral cavity, pushed off the sofa, kneeled in front of Hope, tilted her head back, and when her mouth came open Hope allowed a slow gluey stream of semen to descend into Lana's cavernous orifice.

The practiced trollop, nipples pebble-like on firm fake breasts, swallowed it with a gulp and a smile. "That was good, baby," she said with a glance back at Stanley, watching at her posterior; then to Hope she said, "Your boyfriend's quite the fuck."

"Thank you," replied Hope, looking proudly at the man referenced, then subconsciously wiping sperm from the bottom of her face with a forefinger.

Stanley, who'd ejaculated intensely, was pondering his surprise at discovering that he actually preferred the feeling of Lana's vagina to Hope's (the former substantially looser and very wet from the beginning; in the time they had been connected he'd moved laterally and vertically within her to the sound of moist suctioning as she grew increasingly lubricated, which aroused him greatly), and he was quite certain this was unrelated to his having devaluated Hope (to a conscious degree), with whom his sexual experiences had remained as fulfilling as the first time. He was surprised at his strong desire to be inside her again, a yearning he began experiencing moments after coming. The next time, he thought—and he would be very disappointed if there weren't one—as novel and psychologically appealing as being witness to real-life semen swapping, his own, had been (it had been like a mimicry of porn, and so difficult to process as reality he just-consciously questioned the entire Lana encounter as that), he wanted to ejaculate deep inside the busty blonde bimbo who, stereotypically like a star of X-rated movies in her appearance, had acted like one too.

20

The events of Stanley's largely forgotten drunken night had transpired about a fortnight earlier and he'd found himself getting along easily with Hope once more; but—it was the strangest thing—he kept randomly seeing with his mind's eye, very vividly, the image of her rotting underground: face going blue, skin peeling away, lifeless filmed eyes gaining the progressive appearance of deflated balls of white jelly; lips cracking horribly, fingernails becoming claw-like, still growing hair going brittle, entirety of the epidermis becoming dry and wrinkled like an old woman's and if touched coming off on the fingers like dust; every opening receding, every orifice desiccated. This he could not explain (and did not share with her); Stanley was quite disturbed by it, and wondered whether his hold on sanity was weakening.

Also he sometimes remembered what she had done to him, how she had treated him, the fact that she had slept and was sleeping with another, and murderous impulses rose up in him—even images of his making her a corpse—yet he almost immediately willed this reality, the reality of her noncommitment, from his thoughts. Though he felt his ability to relate to killers—those who committed crimes of passion, those who full of rage repressed kill a great number in a single afternoon—was stronger than it had ever been, and often he would read about serial and spree killers and perhaps to some degree experience a vicarious catharsis from educating himself on their personal histories and crimes.

It was a fact he accepted easily that he couldn't recall the last time he had thought to brush his teeth or tidy up the apartment, or shower. And when it did, on rare occasions, occur to him to do one or all of those activities the will to do so wasn't there, and anyway the idea of engaging in self-care or tending to the condition of his environment soon left his mind—for some reason nothing struck him as all too important anymore, least of all picking up trash or removing the film on his choppers; and besides, Hope didn't seem to care—she could clean up around the place if she wanted to, could tell him he stunk, was gross.

More than before he spent his time aimlessly, in front of the television, semiconscious of a feeling of wasting away, of wasting his life; was spending a lot of time laying around, as if in a haze; a lot of time sleeping, or in a hibernatory state between slumber and normal consciousness, indifferent to the time of day or day of week; a lot of time dreaming, dreaming of a life he did not live and often of experiences he had never had, of imagined existences that were far different from yet not necessarily superior to his own.

As minimally aware as he was lately, slumbering while awake, he had nonetheless realized that not only was he out of marijuana, and had been for at least days, but his food supply was decidedly pretty low, even the canned goods—and that mattered much more than it otherwise would have because the other thing that was running quite low, which in fact he was almost out of (since he had seven-fifty to his name) was money. It was like Hope was no longer buying weed, or food, or doing much of anything anymore.

But the fact that it seemed he was soon to begin to slowly starve, while sober, just made him want to sleep more—as an escape. And so he did, and therefore dreamt more. Dreamt of a Hope that was somehow more present, more real, more alive, than she was in reality; dreamt of other women, sexually appealing women, sexy women who were sometimes interested in him; dreamt a dream that might have been influenced by the story of a young mass murderer he had once, long ago, mentally ingested...

The main character was a boy, a teenager, who went by Louis—a lanky boy of seventeen with stringy, nearly shoulder-length blond hair and a prominent mole on his right cheekbone, a bit pocked from past pimples, who lived in the northwest corner of a nation that had many generations earlier and over the course of many decades, via no small number of wars and deceptions, been effectively stolen from its initial inhabitants—a dark-skinned people—by a light-skinned people motivated by profit, appropriation, accomplishment, and a hunger for adventure. Young Louis was first seen attempting to read his mathematics textbook in the sunlit living room of the family home, his dark brown rather beady eyes flitting from left to right across a page of equations and instructions. To the right of the book on the table he hunched over was his weekend math homework, two pages stapled together, about fifteen problems in total. He was trying to focus but couldn't, would manage to concentrate, or almost concentrate, for as long as thirty seconds and then his attention would turn to the sunny world beyond the window at his back. Out there, whether or not anything was specifically happening, there would not be a math text before him he was forcing himself to try to absorb. And out there he would not be in a room that was negatively affecting his mood in a house that he might as well've been the only occupant of—though his mom was there somewhere, in another room where he couldn't hear her, tending to laundry or working on a sewing project or some other domestic task, perhaps getting an early start on supper.

And so he made the decision, and felt fine about it—after all, he had the remainder of the day and all of the next day to solve the dozen or so equations—to go on out. And—the moment he opened the front door no longer experiencing an oppression, a bodily sensation intensified by his awareness of the present pleasantness of the Saturday afternoon in his tranquil neighborhood—just after he was feeling the sun on his face, beating down on his head, heating up his thick hair; hearing the unseen birds and feeling the breeze, seeing it make the leaves of the trees overhead quiver; watching a squirrel make its way in fits and starts, anxiously, across the warm pavement and disappear between two parked vehicles; no more in an imposed hell of books and figures, varnished furniture and dully adorned walls.

How hard would it be to capture a squirrel? wondered Louis as he absentmindedly, slowly—with his awkward, imposing wide gait—wandered in the direction of the not-so-near city center, where there was a quite small park, Ashland Park, named after city founder Bert Ashland, and a shop-lined avenue split by an oblong concrete-encased divider of trees amid well-maintained grass.

About thirty-five minutes later he was sweaty but happy and stood before the mouth of the avenue, his eyes following a young couple in their mid-twenties as they walked hand-in-hand toward him on the left side of the line of trees, a boutique bag in the female's hand, a similar bag in the male's outside hand.

He was thinking how they too seemed happy, in their peaceful world of sunny Saturday shopping, of being contentedly mated—but his consideration of their felicity, whether or not imaged, soured or darkened Louis's mood instead of elevating it, and the next moment he was envisioning himself engaged in coitus with, beneath him, the female with the healthy body and long brown hair, divested of all her fashionable form-fitting clothes.

Ramming it into her hard she wasn't saying *Fuck me, Louis* or *Yeah, like that* however; rather she was urinating out of fear around his engorgement, tears coming from the corners of her eyes, her face wet with them, slimy with snot from weeping as she pleaded for mercy. He was raping her, in a dim lit void, with an expression of malevolent glee, focused on her tortured expression while his sadism was on full display, eyebrows arched, eyes icy, closed mouth smile high, forehead beaded with sweat, torso shirtless, the force of his thrusts increasing his arousal. He had ripped her shirt open, her blemishless C breasts bouncing, and now his manhood throbbed within the orifice he had penetrated so violently he had probably injured her.

Louis was walking, absorbed. The pair passed him. He smiled evilly at the female, who seemed momentarily chilled by his visage. Glancing back he got a look at her small buttocks, clad in shape-displaying black nylon.

Then, as he passed a store that sold minerals, crystals, incense, New Age accoutrement, he became a Roman tyrant, plunging himself as was his right into the pristine flower of the newly married woman, now wearing a thin white dress bunched at her waist, as she whimpered with an averted face, her cheeks blushed, pain branching through her body, Louis the toga-garbed ruler's each mechanical forward movement swaying the whole of her firm corpus on the table for feasts on which he had taken her; as he approached orgasm a tear, perhaps from pain, perhaps from sadness, rolling down her face—the sight of it bringing him a thrill, widening his smile, the aflame soft womanhood of a commoner's comely new wife tight around his swollen red veined protuberance.

His stride slowed; he came to a stop, came out of his fantasy to notice he stood below a rounded multicolored awning with bubble lettering on it that read Vito's Video. Opening the heavy glass door with a bell tied on the opposite side of it the flaxen-haired young man entered the small rental store he frequented, had gotten at least a movie a week from for almost two years. Vito, a thin, high-strung bald man in his mid-forties, was no doubt behind the counter where the cash register and pornographic offerings were but Louis did not see him. He went by rote to the left, to the action section—considering renting *Bayou Bill 2* (poorly reviewed sequel to *Bayou Bill*, about a kung fu-trained Louisianan battling an organized crime syndicate) or *Crimson Justice* again after noticing nothing he'd never seen that appealed to him. As he scanned the shelves, thin plastic over cheap wood eight rows high, it occurred to him to check the new releases, that the latest film in the Jim Hodges series had recently been released on home video; and there he discovered that there was one copy available: *Vindication by Violence*, starring as always British-American actor Benjamin Lonington as the franchise's hypermasculine intelligence agent. Three-day rental only, $2.99. Encased tape in hand he ambled up the center aisle toward the unmanned cash register.

"Vito," he called out at the counter, able to see a piece of the man's moving flannel-clad back in a room off to the left he used as an office.

The summoned shop owner came out hurriedly, holding in one palm a steaming meal he was in the midst of consuming while conducting business on a computer. His sleeves were rolled up, revealing forearms black with thick hair. The food was in a transparent plastic container and appeared to be reddish orange globs in a steaming toxic-looking olive green sauce, a slice of white bread to the side.

"Louis!" he exclaimed, taking the case; he was always happy to see the teen, who was one of his best customers. The wiry fellow in casual cowboy attire looked quickly down at the boy's selection. "The new Hodges, huh? It's good. Yellow movie today from my special stock?"

"Got any new offerings?"

"Hmm..." he looked over his shoulder at the shelf of tapes in clear unmarked cases, the titles printed on labels on the spines of the videos themselves. "I recently acquired a British production called *Shagged By Juggernauts in Outer Space*. Another one called *Small Whores v. Big Dicks*. That's a newer movie."

"*Juggernauts* is busty babes?" inquired the young man in the same way someone might ask whether the word *definite* has two Is.

"Oh yeah," responded Vito with wide, glossed eyes, taking a bite with a silver spoon from his container of unappetizing sustenance, the stuff's steam dampening his face, the bit of vermilion blob he had put in his mouth being swallowed unchewed.

"Hm. I'll take that one then. English babes with large hooters sounds good to me!" He laughed.

"Great choice," Vito said smiling, as he found the video and placed it atop the other, then put both in a plastic bag. "That'll bring your total to four ninety-eight."

Louis was fishing through his billfold, a length of hair in front of one eye. "Got any fun plans for this weekend, youngster? That is, besides waxing your pole? Har har."

"Ha. No, Vito. I got some homework to do. Math."

"Oh. Poor guy. Well, enjoy the sun while you can."

"Looks like you could do with some," Louis remarked, handing the man, whose face and visible hirsute patches of flesh were pallid, the face spotted with unsightly raised moles, five ones.

Vito emitted an insincere 'ha.' "You can be a mean boy sometimes, Louis."

"I can be mean all the time. I just choose not to be," retorted Louis as he took the bag and turned toward the exit. "Thanks, Vito. See you in a few days."

"Alright, young man," he called.

⇒«(»⇐

In the next scene Louis was in the woods. It might've been the same Saturday or a different day, but the sun had mostly gone down or was just coming up; the teen was bent among trees, silently watching a crude trap he had set in a clearing he watched seven or eight yards in front of him. In one hand he held a string attached to a branch that held up a light crate fashioned of small pieces of wood. He had an intent expression and had been standing waiting for his quarry to approach, lured by a bit of hamburger within, for some time.

The blond, thin-framed teen, stringy hair in his eyes as often, did not know what might come along, if anything did, but knew if he were to capture a small animal it would have the worst and the final day of its short life: for his goal was neither to practice trapmaking, trapping, or to take from the creature its meat, pelt or any part of its body—his goal was torment, the practice and the thrill of the infliction of misery; physical, immediate, unescapable, excruciating;

the same sort of pain he ultimately, someday, wanted to subject a captured human to.

Though he had no expectation what he did manage to lure and confine was a surprise to him. From the thick of the woods emerged slowly, perhaps cautiously, a black and white low thing with a wide bushy tail and lush coat, a face that Louis regarded as weasel-like: *Mephitis mephitis*, a skunk.

And soon it was under Louis's box of branches, its nose having demanded an investigation; and he pulled the string, and the animal hissed and squealed, attempting to turn in the too-small space. *But how the fuck do I torture or even kill a skunk?* the boy, the captor, asked himself, observing absently the panicked badger relative.

He was hesitant even to approach, but he did walk towards it a few feet, which was when the frightened musteloid's infamous spray was emitted from its posterior.

"Fuck," said Louis.

The extreme musk of the scent filled the air, and enough molecules of it found their way, with the direction of the wind, onto the teenager's clothing—a light jacket over a solid-color tee, a pair of beige cargo shorts—that the creature's primary defense, despite Louis's wariness, was not without effect.

"Shit, fuck," the expletives continued as he smelled the torso portion of his jacket, an item he was fond of. "You're going to really get it now, skunk," he said, closing in, thinking the worst-case scenario had already occurred. He could hardly see his quarry through the trap and was behind it when the tail went up again and malodorous pungent chemical was released from its anus, almost directly on Louis, on the lower half of his lower body—his unclothed knees and calves, his socks.

"AHHH!" He felt the fluid running down his legs, the overbearing aroma burning his nostrils, the appearance of it a toxic green that quickly became clear. His socks and legs below the knees were soaked. The smell, a bit like burning rubber combined with a woodsy aroma, but concentrated, intensified, was almost choking him. He gagged, astonished at the power of it, a defense more repellent that he had imagined.

Taking from a back belt loop the long sharp kitchen knife held by it he dropped and plunged forward with the weapon, between the tied together branches at the cacophonously vocalizing animal, which now indeed was without protection—its mouth pointed away and sharp paws useless, its supply of bodily chemical depleted.

The tip of the blade penetrated the creature's posterior just above the tail, a half-inch only. But blood began to flow sluggishly from the wound and Louis withdrew the knife to stab again with greater accuracy and less emotion, the tool puncturing the back higher up and getting stuck there, going through to crucial organs and causing the skunk to emit an unceasing horrendous death mewl unlike anything the teen had heard—the creature spasming helplessly within the snug wooden box of its demise, its erratic movements serving only to further diminish its energy and cause the crimson river gushing out around the knife to pour more rapidly across its reddened coat, down onto the blood-wet dirt being kicked up below—the small speared dichromatic biote's life force dissipating with some speed.

Fuming internally, Louis watched it die in a coffin fashioned of branches—painstakingly, by him—with eyes devoid of light, which between strands of unruly hair that fell to about the middle of his nose shone not with soul but with malice. A hate that had been focused and for which he had just succeeded in finding an outlet, albeit at the cost of being baptized by an uncommon stench that burned his sinuses while he watched the desperate culprit expire pitifully and that he knew too well he'd not easily be rid of.

Strangely though to Louis he felt little to nothing, outside of ire due to having been sprayed. He felt little release. As expected there was no discernible empathy or regret, but there was a perceptible absence of catharsis also, a lack of emotional impact altogether. He felt more a deadness, a deep chasm within that his killing of the animal had done nothing to fill but had only made him aware or increased his awareness of. Perhaps he thought, and the thought crystallized into a conviction, the murder of the woodland creature hadn't had any real effect because his prey had been too inconsequential, too disparate. Perhaps—and over passing days, weeks, and then months of rumination, planning, his speculation became a certainty—if his victim or plural were human he would feel a great deal: power, excitement, accomplishment; glee.

———

The subsequent scene opened with Louis following a young female, Gillie, as she walked to school. Gillie was the little sister of a girl he had gone to school and was neighbors with named Minnie. He had had a crush on Minnie in grade school but nothing ever came of it and he had just about completely gotten over her by halfway through middle school. Minnie had grown rather tall and boyish. Gillie, on the other hand, who was Minnie's half-sister, had developed early and was fairly curvaceous, especially for a high school sophomore. She was the sort of maiden—Louis's private word for girls in her age range—that he fantasized about often, sometimes while self-pleasuring in his poster-adorned bedroom with the music turned up (the posters mainly for seventies- and eighties-era rock bands).

He stayed a good twelve yards behind her and knew if she were to turn and notice him there was no reason to think he didn't just happen to be walking the same direction on the sidewalk at the same time. Louis kept looking at her butt as she walked, clad in contour-gripping jeans, a packed purple Eastsport backpack on her shoulders—but what he especially liked were her breasts, easily D-cups, just now thinly covered by a striped tight tee, the outline of her bra visible. In truth he liked everything about her appearance: she was five-four, had shoulder-length medium brown hair, an unusually pretty face, and full lips she typically applied a liberal amount of glistening lip gloss to.

Gillie (short for Gillian) had caught Louis's attention shortly after she had gone through puberty and, as she blossomed, had been on his radar ever since. One of his most common fantasies about her cast her as a precocious student clad in somewhat too small clothes and Louis as her tutor in some subject or the other, whom she invariably seduced via much inward leaning and innuendo—ending in Louis happily becoming her supposed first lover and cutting off at some point after he had her shirt and bra off and had entered her snug wet womanhood but before, plowing with an exposed posterior, he climaxed in that wondrous place, there in an otherwise unoccupied classroom, with an extended grunt capped by a sigh.

Another fantasy he occasionally had in which she figured prominently was darker and less typical in its content. It involved his entering a classroom clad in blue jeans and a long leather coat, black, his hair slicked back, and finding there a collection of maidens of his liking—real and imagined ones—about a dozen or so of them, all immobile, unmoving as if dead; but not cold or pale, instead apparently, unexplainably, frozen in time. All quiet, motionless, and seated at desks. And he would slowly walk through the rows, looking closely at these girls in their skirts and tight pants, taking in the curves revealed by their clothes, reveling in their accessibility. And then, having selected someone to disrobe first, just as he was about to shimmy the pants off the imagined student's hips, he would wake, disappointed but pulsating hard.

This was the specific dream, by an exercise of force, he wanted to make a reality, somehow. It was a Thursday morning about 7:35 and the reason he was stalking Gillie, object of his erotic attention, was because he wanted to end up in the same classroom as her—and then make her sit totally still and unprotesting at a desk while he leisurely had his way with her. Ideally others would be there too who he could do the same to, and the classroom would only be occupied by girls he had selected based on their desirability.

He wasn't quite sure how he would achieve this, but he had a handgun tucked into the waist of his jeans—9mm, taken from his dad's room the moment he left for work—and with this tool Louis hoped to make his licentious vision a visceral reality; even if it meant ending a few teachers, which was a possibility he welcomed.

The school, the same high school Louis was attending and getting low marks at, William Frenckel H.S., was a broad rectangular beige building that stretched back three blocks. It had long sectioned windows in front and past the main hall three long wings were broken by bench- and grass-lined courtyards of smooth concrete strips, which wings—each being primarily utilized for a single grade— were joined at the complex's terminus by a hall called Worthington that was home to many storage rooms; beyond Worthington were a gym, track, a basketball half-court and a tennis court.

Louis followed Gillie seconds after her up a few oblong stairs past the mounted wooden Frenckel High sign across a spacious concrete forecourt spotted by forward ambulating students and through the brass-handled heavy double doors of the front building. It was cool inside and bustling. The school was located about fifteen minutes on foot from where Louis and Gillie resided and they had arrived about the same amount of time before first period would begin. The now adult stalker watched his oblivious focus stop a minute and converse with a group of similarly attired friends, one of whom the young man, who looked as if he'd recently rolled out of bed, also appreciated the appearance of. They laughed, their healthy teeth showing, Louis—trying to seem busy tying a shoe that was well-tied while observing Gillie and the group with the peripheral vision of one eye—too distant to hear what they were communicating. Then the girl waved and moved on, accompanied now by one from the trio she'd briefly socialized with—unfortunately, noted Louis, not the tanned teen he thought good-looking.

To her locker and then to the location of her first class, her and her friend's first, she went—the class being based on the equations on the blackboard a math class, so far about a dozen students inside, the stringy-haired acne-scarred man feeling odd, odder than usual, going inside and choosing a desk, though no one seemed to notice his not belonging.

As inconspicuously as he could he tried to glance at the other students in the room, noting that seven were female but only three (including Gillie) were attractive—though the one who already occupied the classroom had particularly caused him to perk up, a slender, tallish girl with her straight brown hair parted down the middle who wore a fashionable blouse over perky breasts and whose long, smooth legs capped by white ankle socks and canvas shoes were displayed by her skirt of mid-thigh length.

Feeling the body-warmed butt of his gun under his shirt to reassure himself it was really there and ready for use he waited anxiously, as additional peers of Gillie's trickled in (including another who caught his eye), for the arrival of the instructor—and for the clock to hit 8:05, having decided not to spring into action (though what action exactly he couldn't say) until after class had begun, after everyone who was going to show up presumably had.

Then in walked—with a waddle none too complimentary—thirty-four-year-old Mrs. Alvina Halsbert, forty pounds overweight, her expression conveying an internal state between vacant and serious, her hair and attire choices contributing to a certain frumpishness of aspect. She erased the problems on the board with the chalky pad, writing new ones from a notebook held in one hand, then turning and without looking before her said "Good morning, class."

Louis was sitting near the front, trying not to nibble at his nails, feeling a sweat break on his face, his gaze going from preoccupied Mrs. Halsbert to the clock, which indicated it was seconds before five past.

By his count there were twenty-one students inside, five of whom he had a sexual interest in. His plan, the details developed in the previous anxious minutes, was to kneecap the woman, threaten the others with the same if they didn't keep quiet and obey his instructions, and make the five that piqued his lust disrobe in their seats—and the thought of what he was about to attempt to do, to force himself to do, envisioning the fulfillment of his fantasy, his dream of illicit sex, unjust violence, and demonstrated power, was making his head swim as if he were under the influence; his gut and manhood to be stirred also.

The bell rang. "Did anyone have problems with their fractions homework?" the woman in front asked and waited, looking out at the class, her mouth slightly open.

There was no response. "Well, everyone go ahead and hand up your assignment and then we'll go over each answer on the board after I call roll."

"Wait!" cried Louis from his desk, almost surprising himself.

"Can I help you? Are you in the right class?" Mrs. Halsbert was visibly flummoxed, the young man's outburst having generated a widening of her eyes, fixed on him with a piercing focus.

"I don't want anyone to move from their seat," he said in a voice deeper than normal.

"You have no right to be giving orders here," proclaimed the teacher, indignancy immediate, her eyes swollen to full orbs of eerie white.

"Oh, don't I, bitch?" Louis retorted, standing and withdrawing the weapon from the waistband of his jeans; pointing it at Mrs. Halsbert's skull, the eyes at once seeming to nearly explode outward, her pudgy cheeks grown rosy.

"Yeah, that's right: you're not in charge anymore. This is," he gestured with his head to the gun. "I'm going to make sure I put you down if I use it too," added the class's captor, looking down the sight and lining up Halsbert's glossy forehead.

A hush had fallen over the students behind and around him and the firearm's appearance had petrified the teacher. Louis quickly looked back to see ovals of mouths frozen in shock, eyes teary with fear—rigid postures and the full attention of nearly two dozen people, all of whom he got the impression were looking at him not as a person but as an object, a danger, a possibly lethal impediment, or were looking rather than at him at his hand, the gun.

All it takes is this little projectile-propelling device and I can do anything thought Louis, continue to train the mechanism at the doe-eyed woman in the long dowdy skirt and frilly lavender shirt stretched by large hanging mammary glands a yard and a half in front of him as he shot a lascivious glance at a female he was soon to molest, in front of everyone—saving Gillie for last, the best for last.

"Now..." He stared with wide lightless eyes, gun a bit lowered, at the slightly quivering grown woman before him, adrenaline pumping through his body, causing an alike sensation to having recently drunk six shots of espresso. "Lay down flat on the floor slowly, staying very still, and don't make a fucking sound." Louis motioned impatiently with the handheld tool. "Go on."

The married mother of two obeyed, looking to be on the verge of crying. Once on her belly she stretched her arms in front of her and cast her eyes up at Louis as if seeking approval or further instructions.

"Don't hurt Mrs. Halsbert," he heard behind him, from a high tender voice.

Louis swiveled toward the spot the sound had emanated from, seeing a small meek-looking girl with a red clamp in her shower-damp hair and lips downturned into an exaggerated-looking frown, slouching in her desk but watching the teen villain carefully.

"Let me explain the conditions in this classroom currently, to you, the courageous youngster in the third row," he said approaching, 9-millimeter at his side, fuming with indignance. "Mrs. Halsbert, and all your pals in here also, are my prisoners, my puppets—that is where things stand. The reason why, in case you couldn't tell," he was standing before her desk, her watery eyes now looking down at it, "is because if you any of you decide against doing precisely what I tell you to, and when, I will goddamn murder you."

"Fuck you, loser!" screamed a boy to his left, standing suddenly and jerkily making a move to rush Louis.

He cocked and across his body thoughtlessly fired the handgun, the position of the gun directing the bullet at the student's upper chest.

The projectile went through the right side of the teen's neck at seemingly the same second as the trigger pull and the resounding noise, the room gaining a distinct aroma of gun smoke. There was no blood for a few moments, only a wet maroon-colored hole, the mouth of the student—who looked to be falling slowly backwards, to be crumpling in slow motion—agape, his eyes changed to convey mixed fear and surprise, as if he'd woke to find himself staring into a pit of vipers into which he was inexorably being lowered headlong. The student Louis had been addressing had screamed, as had a few others. Someone somewhere in the room was now crying, a female judging from the sobs. Then, the boy's descent at its midpoint, blood began to gush from the wound—out of the clean hole bored through the cords and veins of the nonresistant material of the neck through which the ammo had passed fully, being halted in its travel by the thick plaster wall behind him, the bullet nestled it in warm and shell-less, its previous form permanently altered (as the boy's, from whose eyes the life had drained and who now—a mere body—was collapsed upon himself, legs bent behind the back, on the off-white and pale-green checker-pattern linoleum at feet level, his heroic or anger-fueled effort checked by his sudden death, a death that had made young Louis an official murderer, its cause having been loud enough to bring outside faces to the door's small window with the inner chicken wire; meaning that just after the discharge the administration and then the drowsy average-sized city's police force became apprised of the classroom gunman, that a number of trained individuals with bigger guns, with body armor, were soon to attempt to foreshorten the killer's period of power over the twenty or so people still alive in the air conditioned room with the walls lined with textbook-filled shelves and adorned with colorful math-pertinent posters at the front of which a spread-out thirtysomething-year-old woman with moist squeezed-shut eyes and flushed cheeks was pressing her nose to the floor praying silently for her survival while largely overcome by mind-clouding primal emotion).

The teen murderer felt little about his kill, other than a suppressed sensation of glee that he had exercised such a level of control as to bring about another person's demise. A happiness resultant from causing the finality of the end of life in response to another's attempt to alter a situation he, Louis, was engineering. He felt as a consequence of his ultimate manifestation of dominance a high that, while not intense, was nonetheless rather satisfying—that he could imagine was addictive.

As the corpse bled he turned back to the front of the class, to the prostrate teacher, distraught visage squished to the checker floor. "You see, bitch: I'm in control. I take life, or permit its continuance."

He watched her contorted face a moment, watched her being too fearful to look at him, to do more than squint at his sneakers; then spun and immediately focused in on one of the girls who he had it in his mind to assault sexually—a brown-rooted blonde with a promising looking pair of perky C-cups hidden in a bra and thin white blouse, with a less than ideal complexion but a set of sensual lips, whose well-sunned legs below mid-thigh shorts had a pleasing shape to them.

"What's your name?" he asked brusquely, approaching her.

"Veronica," she said making brief, timid eye contact.

"Take those shorts of yours off, Veronica. And your panties. I want to get a look at your pussy," he commanded, gun lazily pointed at her thorax. "Don't let your fellow students make you shy. They won't look. ...They might want to though." He laughed. "I know one guy who won't be looking," he added, indicating with his head his victim, as Veronica with reddened cheeks and hurt eyes began slowly to comply.

The girl seemed to move in turned down time. But Louis liked this, liked watching her—seeing her dread and seeing her revealed under duress—and felt no sense of anxiety about impending armed opposition, no urgency.

He felt certain her vagina would be very beautiful, and lost in a fantasy that combined an image of her exposed femininity in the brightness of the public space and the young man's joy at his microcosmic dominance Louis saw himself spinning arms outstretched amid the terror-stricken seated hostages of the room, eyes closed in his immersion in fulfillment. And near enough to be graspable, his to draw pleasure from despite her own wants—because he had handicapped her will—was loot, a prize, in the form of a person whose physical facts placed her high on his desirability index.

And then he snapped again into the mind-mimicked present of the girl, gun, white bathing overheads; the female's now-nude genitalia was nonetheless compressed between tight thighs, and the empowered one commanded "Open your legs" and the half-naked prisoner showed herself fully, extracting a leg from her lowered panties, Louis making a mental appraisal that his expectations of her loveliness had been met in vivid tangibility.

Meanwhile two well-equipped SWAT team members, arrived moments previous, were looking in via the small oblong window—able to see bleary-eyed Missus Halsbert but not, where he stood, Louis the captor, leering, the girl's underwear down at the ankle of one smooth tan leg and her wet-eyed visage a pained mix of discomfort and communicated violation.

He went to his knees and positioned his face exactly before the aesthetic slit at the culmination of Veronica's warm thick haunches, with care inserting the index finger of his left hand—gun in his other hand at his side—between her kissable lips, discovering that despite the subjectively unerotic circumstances including her lack of attraction she was very moist. As the door to the room was being cracked open and one scowling, wary policeman was ascertaining Louis's position in it, a fact many of the students silently noticed, the young man—back to the entrance—was sucking the tanginess of Veronica from his finger, penis pulsing in his jeans; then reinserting his saliva-wet digit, feverish with a desire to enter her with the throbbing lower appendage that he expected to within seconds be acting upon.

"GET DOWN! GET THE FUCK DOWN!" the man yelled behind him, half crouched, assault rifle trained on the middle of his startled target's spine as Veronica, mortified but relieved and generally overflowing with a plethora of sensations, her face—pretty though with rife tiny pimples—tomato red, immediately began to pull her panties up, visually locked on the shielded face of the forwardmost law enforcement officer, behind whom the other's knees were similarly bent, same weapon similarly pointed.

"I'm already down!" said Louis, disappointed and already picturing a lifetime in a penitentiary, assuming a posture like the berated Mrs. Halsbert's, which person started gradually to come up from the floor.

"Get the fuck down there," the man in the helmet and Kevlar said smashing Louis's gun-gripping hand with his heavy polished black boot.

"Oww."

"Shut the fuck up, scumbag." He addressed the students around him over both shoulders: "Alright. You kids are going to be fine. It's all over."

The other SWAT member came and stood inches from Louis's head. "Don't even fucking twitch if you don't want to lose half your teeth to the stock of my rifle," he advised, self-satisfied and adrenaline-high. And then the captive's spinal cord was being crushed by the knee of the other police officer as he was immobilized to be cuffed, the man cuffing not just his hands but his ankles also, the sets of cuffs attached by a short length of chain so that when the pressure of the knee went away he found himself hog-tied with steel in the middle of a high school classroom—two cops, a dead body, and a sexual assault victim nearest him, and beyond the malice-brimming faces of about a score of primarily still-seated individuals, some of whom had minutes ago been sobbing, thinking their lives might soon be ending.

His dream of the molestation of many in one morning would not transpire. He would perhaps never again be free. This was it for him, end of the line, the terminus of decisions and liberty. A nonlife of gray impenetrable walls was his future—and it would be a long future. Why had he not foreseen that inevitability? Was he an idiot?

Did he actually possess no self-concern?

Sweaty strand of hair stuck to his scarred face, face pressed to the shoe-scuffed floor, a police officer above him talking into a walkie-talkie, he was here on out no better off than he was at present; as a prisoner belly down on the ground with his legs ceiling-ward and chained to his wrists, everyone in the outside world indifferent to or full of spite for him, a maladapted psychopath not yet of drinking age though permanently a murderer.

21

Approximately six weeks had passed since the day that Hope—who he saw increasingly little of and recently almost never had sex with—had told him about her sexual services arrangement and everything had changed; the day his heart plummeted, the day he'd been broken the worst he ever had been, since the revelation he would never recover from.

Stanley had fallen asleep the night before on the living room sofa and woke with a start, his head pounding, wearing mismatched socks and a pair of boxers.

Rising awkwardly he banged a knee on the coffee table.

"Fuck."

He noticed an empty bottle of red wine on it, merlot. It took him a moment to recollect how he had obtained the bottle he'd consumed happily and quickly the previous evening, given his total lack of money, given that Hope no longer provided him anything—remembering after some searching through a mental fog a hangover and his grogginess were responsible for that he'd stolen it from a downtown store, one of the stores he had sometimes been stealing snacks from.

The half-asleep man went to open the front door, fairly certain a loud knock had been what'd woken him from a deep dark slumber. On its outside face a piece of paper had been tacked, a notice, a notice of the eviction kind. Rent had not been paid for over thirty days and all occupants had seventy-two hours to vacate, with the whole of their possessions.

Huh thought Stanley. *That's a bit surprising. I wonder why she stopped paying rent.*

"Hope!" he called out, having no idea whether or not she was even home. "Hope!"

He heard her moving around in the bedroom, heard a cough. "Yes?" she said with a scratchy voice, slowly emerging, her eyes bleary and wearing a plain tee and cotton panties.

"We're getting kicked out." He held the paper out to her. "Why the fuck are we getting kicked out?"

"What? I don't know anything about it. ...Are you sure?" She came over to him.

"This is a fucking eviction notice. Take it."

She looked the notice over a minute. "No. This is wrong. I paid. I'll walk to the office and talk to the manager in a second, after I've had my coffee."

"It better be wrong."

Hope was walking toward the kitchen, yawning.

"Hey," he said, looking at her thinly clothed buttocks.

"Yeah?"

"I want a cup."

———◦((◦))◦———

The notice had not been a mistake. They were getting evicted. Hope had not paid. The reason for this, in actuality, was that she had been murdered. But Stanley did a good job of ensuring that this fact did not enter his consciousness. For it was too painful, too disturbing, too concerning a fact, considering Stanley was her murderer. Even the reality of the eviction he pushed from his mind. And when he found himself homeless perhaps he would continue to imagine himself at home, with Hope, in the apartment she had allowed him to move into. And if he failed to conjure, in his mind, the continued presence of Hope Brownen he would invent some story in which she left him or moved away.

"I can form deep attachments to people, be lonely, value friend-ships," she would tell him, "but I cannot be in love with someone, certainly not for an extended period, and perhaps never with you.

"It's really nothing personal," she would say. "Perhaps you, too, can never *truly* be in love with someone, but merely allay loneli-ness—the accurate feeling of being alone while alive—have reprieves from an inner feeling of emptiness, become addicted to someone, at-tached, codependent.

"Like most people," she might say, "I can temporarily stop feel-ing and don't like feeling lonely. I like being wanted, being adored, appreciated despite my many faults. And in the long run I'm sure you couldn't be happy with me, if for no other reason because I could not in the long run be happy with you, except as a friend and/or sometime/temporary fuck buddy."

She might explain to him that she was easily bored; could not stay satisfied or was anyway wary of and highly allergic to what she sensed as stagnancy; in fact perhaps had a problem with the feeling of contentment. And, the next day, would skip town, the nation, the hemisphere—leaving him a brief note telling him of her expatria-tion to Southern Europe, Bulgaria maybe.

Fucking Bulgaria he would think. *That bitch.* Then it would occur to him that, if he wasn't being naïve, he didn't really have any reason to believe the note. That she had no doubt left town but as to where she'd gone, was going, he had no means of saying.

22

Hope and some societally good-looking guy, around her age probably, were standing completely nude (Hope holding him loosely, a hand on each arm), in the middle of her living room—her and Stanley's living room.

"I took some E earlier that I'm starting to feel too, so I'm probably going to have a lot of orgasms," she was telling him, oblivious as was the other to Stanley's entry.

The guy led her by the hand to the couch, pushed her down on it and almost immediately entered her.

"Yeah. I want you to bang the fuck out of me," she said making eye contact.

Stanley—frozen in front of the door, feeling literally unable to move—watched them work up a sweat, Hope's mascara begin to run, heard their bodies slapping together in the otherwise quiet sunlit room; their flesh pink and warm, nakedness unusually visceral. Then, some searing minutes later, minutes that occurred outside of time, he observed Hope climaxing loudly, her pink nipples hard, her ideal breasts bouncing violently.

"Yesss," came her synchronized vocalization, in Stanley's infiltrated psyche a transfixed, libidinous serpent of another form. A leg on either side of his lightly muscled body the person inside her followed by spasming—as he moaned, arched his back, removed via pleasure just as Stanley was self-severed due to pain.

"I just gushed all over your cock," said Hope grinning, a mocking dream-demon—a demon mocking the whole of life—the young stranger's eyes cloudy, her brown bangs glued to her forehead with perspiration and her whole body sheeny with it. She sat up still smiling toothily and kissed him on the mouth, her tongue going inside. "Thank you," she said. "Bringing you over was a good idea."

His sensation of bodilessness—as he observed Hope and the man she had just had intercourse with, both of them breathing heavily, unclothed beasts panting and contented, ataractic, at their biological peaks—then morphed abruptly into physical inhabitance and nausea and Stanley walked briskly past them into the bathroom, his presence visibly surprising the sofa-situated lovers. There, bracing himself against the wall, he violently vomited.

As he propped himself against wallpaper-covered plaster, looking down at wet fresh orangish expelled stomach contents, probably traumatized, a cold sweat broke out across his epidermis, and something clicked in his mind. At once he collapsed to his knees with a force that might have been painful had Stanley's consciousness been less internalized.

Slapping his hands to his ears in front of the excreta-sprayed toilet his body began moderately convulsing, despite the blankness of his mind possessed fully by anguish. And, when the convulsions—which caused his eyes to water and left his hands trembling—had subsided, still thinking consciously of nothing and still without physical pain (discomfort of the organism had been overridden), he began to gouge his own eyes.

Gelatinous gore went under his fingernails, accompanied by a sound of released suction. Copious viscous blood covered his hands and flowed down his forearms, ran down his cheeks. At the same moment he experienced a feeling of freedom and astonishment, and was deeply horrified, in a way beyond known comparison. He thought *20/20 vision is a curse to those who don't want to see.* But the next moment he questioned why he was destroying himself, violently, irreparably. And then he was puking again, all over himself, as blood in a rivulet traveled down his chin and combined with the vomit on his shirt. Next, hearing himself but not feeling himself acting, was screaming—the world already forever black, his former sensitive sight-giving globules useless mush in his skull; his existence an empty, bleak one that the deprivation of vision would make less cruel, more manageable.

And the scream of a self-made ruin broke into the actual—for in the true present he wore a pair of boxers, was partly covered by a sheet, and was lying in bed at home at a little past two, the room flooded with afternoon light—and as it did caused him to begin to wake up.

He swung his legs to the side of the bed and lowered his feet to the floor. The instant they touched a jolt of mixed alarm and confusion caused him to jerk them from what should have been the floor's carpeted surface and look down with a knitted brow. His toes and soles had told him there was water, or some liquid, instead of rug; and when he peered toward the former ground, to verify the room was inexplicably flooded, what he saw was odder by no small degree. Bright orange fish with yellow gills—some tropical variety unfamiliar to him, mouths open and toothlessly chomping; fat and compact, maybe four inches in length—were spread out across the space, and there appeared to no longer be carpet, a floor; they bobbed in cyan-hued water of indeterminate depth, water the bed apparently floated upon, that judging from the view the open bedroom door allowed had replaced the flooring of the entire domicile.

"What the *fuck*?" he said watching the seemingly identical marine animals open and snap shut their large-lipped mouths, wide filmed eyes appearing to look at nothing, as he considered that there was no rational explanation, as he wondered whether having a toe in one's mouth when it closed would do harm, as he speculated as to whether they were all hungry (if the jaw movement was due to that or just typical fish behavior), as he reasoned that the least far-fetched hypothesis was that they weren't even truly there—and since he was seeing them and had had a tactile experience of the liquid how, he asked, would he be able to determine if the creatures, the greenish water, were consciousness-created or existent independent of it? (For that matter how could he know with certainty that anything he'd taken in with his mind was externally extent? Perhaps even those phenomena that fell under 'consensus reality' would not exist if there was no consciousness to perceive them—would exist exclusively as a mass hallucination.)

How the hell do I...get off the bed? Seriously—what is happening?

He let his feet make contact with the surface of the water. None of the creatures were below them. A few moments' deliberation culminated in his decision to lower himself into the water, which proved to be more than deep enough not to feel a bottom of any sort. Before him, and very near, was one of the dead-eyed constantly snapping fish. Seeing them so close up they seemed even more non-threatening than they had. They did not move from what he could judge, their most peculiar quality. He flicked one, finding its bright skin slimy, just to know how they'd respond. The thing was sent back an inch by the force but otherwise was without response. Its jaws like clockwork continued to open and clench its mouth. They behaved like uncomplex mechanisms with organic exteriors.

Dog paddling, he began to move at a laggard pace through the scattered machinelike ichthyoids toward the door, occasionally submerging his head and seeing only the lowest portions of the domicile's walls and below merely water, water that he'd formed the impression went to a substantial depth—the genesis of which (as the cause of the apartment floor's disappearance) remained wholly mysterious.

Swimming through the boudoir's doorway he swiveled himself left for the living room and found, like with the bedroom, only the largest item on the room's floor remained: in this case the couch, floating motionlessly (as though set on a solid surface) where it had always been situated.

Stanley treaded water, taking in the strangeness, nearly convinced the environment was a psychological concoction, trying to devise a plan for waking himself from what he felt had or that he wanted to be the nonsense invention of a slumbering man.

Deciding to exit the dwelling, to see if the rest of the observable world was also flooded, he swam toward the front door—encountering a hitch when he could not reach the doorknob from the water. Leaping he managed to grab hold of the brass protuberance with his right hand and twisted it left, the door coming forward slightly out of the frame. Releasing the knob and splashing back down he got his fingers round the edge of the door and with effort pulled it farther forward against the pressure of the water. As the door opened into the room one then two feet the water inside began to flow from the space, and Stanley was able to see that beyond, in the out-of-doors, everything appeared normal and the volume of water was not joining more of the same but instead pouring out across concrete, across a parking lot, that it rendered a darker hue of gray.

The sun was out—it was a bright and ideal day, the kind of day that initially revealed nothing of the world's turmoil. Stanley was swept upon the rush of water out onto the pavement, where once no longer borne on a liquid cushion he sat wet, squinting, totally perplexed, noticing that before him some of the odd fish were dying as they flopped helplessly in a parking space, evidently biological in nature.

A man was walking past. "What was that about? Spring a leak in there?" he asked, stopping in his tracks, Stanley's lower body stretched across the walkway anyway. The addressed looked up at him. He was wearing an earlier era's straw hat, a hat like a poor, rural, circa-1800s Southerner's; faded jeans transformed to cutoff shorts; a white shirt with black stripes; held a small backpack that seemed empty. He had a trimmed beard medium brown in color.

"I don't know, man. I woke up just now to a house full of water."

"Isn't that where that girl who died lived?"

His body became cold, or so it felt, from the inside out. "What did you just say?"

"The girl who died. Didn't she live there?"

At that moment, Hope—her mouth a confused smile—wearing pajama pants and sunglasses with overlarge lenses, her oddly cut hair messy and a portion of it bunched in a scrunchie, patchwork bag over a shoulder, came walking toward him. "Um...? What happened? Why is everything wet? Did the apartment...get flooded?"

"This is my girlfriend right here. Well and fine. What are you talking about? Did someone tell you to say that?"

"Sorry, bro." He continued on.

"Hey," Stanley yelled after him. "Hey! Why did you say that?"

"Why did he say what? What the shit's going on? I was gone for like thirty minutes."

"He thought you were dead. Or he was talking about somebody else."

"I've never seen that guy before."

"Where were you?"

"At the store."

"Why didn't you drive?"

"It's nice out. I felt like walking."

"You don't have a shopping bag."

"All I bought is tampons. They're in my purse. Stanley: What the fuck happened to the house?" She walked past him into the apartment.

"I woke up and it was fucking filled with water!" he called after her, remaining on the concrete, legs splayed before him.

Behind him he heard a horrifying scream, an hellish guttural utterance like none he'd ever heard emanate from her, and twisted his head to see her braced in the doorway, turn around nearly purple with anger, and begin to stomp back over to where he sat—his perplexed, weary expression growing more consternated as she saw her frighteningly ireful countenance clearer, the intensity of her reaction totally out of character, out of all proportion, mucus seeping from her nostrils as if she'd started sobbing, a generally murderous mien to her.

"Good god." He came to his feet and was backing away from her slowly. "Is it because of your stuff? Is something missing, did something get destroyed? I don't know what the fuck happened! What's wrong?"

"Something did happen, you fuck-up! And you well know what." Hope's fiery face and visible flesh were transforming into that of a decaying corpse, gradually, as he watched—the skin going zombie green to deathly gray, beginning to flake away. "That guy knew! That guy knew because he's you."

He was being addressed now by a verbalizing cadaver that could stand and pose and the sight was so awful he could not hold his gaze on it.

"You killed me!" Stanley shuddered, eyes tight shut. "Why did you end my life? What did I do to deserve that? You aren't god. Look at me!"

For a moment he did, and retched, could've vomited had his stomach contained anything. She had a hand on either shoulder, was beyond any feat a makeup artist might achieve—even her eyes were now deflated, exsiccating white-sepia orbs set in the skeletal head, atop which her varying lengths of smooth brunette hair was the same as ever.

"I can't." He bent his head toward the ground, clamping his eyes closed so forcefully deep furrows resulted at their corners. "I didn't mean to, Hope! I killed a lot of people that day. I fucking lost it! And now you're rotting under dirt. I'm aware of that—but I can't think about it. I can't be conscious of what I've done and go on. Even the anxiety would render me unfunctional."

He was shaking, on the edge of crying, held by an animate corpse in an apartment complex parking lot on a sunny afternoon, but his breakthrough—remembering his recent actions resulting in his girlfriend's demise and others' and realizing his pathological and near impermeable denial—had caused also the realization to emerge that he was still dreaming. All the signs were present, and he ought've known; however, he was overly immersed. His seeing the illusion for what it was though had made Hope—the thoroughly decayed but sentient impossible version of her—and the entirety of the surroundings disappear in an instant. All that remained was blackness, and the sound and feeling of Stanley yawning wide, his spatial placement utterly unknown to him.

Then there was wind on his cheek, cold and brisk, wind whistling in through the window to his right, which was down about an inch. It was just past sunset and he had apparently been so exhausted as to doze off in the passenger seat—Hope behind the wheel of her car with character, the two-decade-old two-door, spotted with dents of various depths, its flaking blue-gray paint revealing a dull brown; a vehicle she had purchased used and cheap many years prior.

They were on a winding road that skirted a long, wide drop to a floor of forest-carpeted uneven land. Beyond this woods-bottomed valley were receding mountains, gray scarred and tree-bearded. Beyond that, somewhere unseen but near, was ocean, dark, raging, immense; the same ocean that touched Japan and Russia; which as the stars made the scurrying humans with their petty problems and successes all seem akin to bacteria on a floating cosmic rock.

Hope was headed south at exactly the speed limit, air rushing in playing with her hair, just now going around an outside curve drivers had to navigate precisely at forty mph. "Wanna do it?" she said looking at him a split-second as she steered, something he didn't like in the flash of her eyes, beautiful, a dark not-quite-discernible hue, her words and her momentary shift of focus from the road producing in groggy Stanley an uneasiness the source of which was no surprise to him.

"I hope you're talking about getting married," he replied—looking at her but hoping she didn't again make eye contact, his own eyes a bit wild—and fake-laughed nervously, then tuned his attention to the small metal machine they were strapped into going around the bend and to their left the precipice, a craggy wall of land that descended ninety feet or more into the unilluminated wilderness that separated the granite ridge from the elevated roadway.

"Well, Stanley," she said without looking at him and laughed sincerely, her voice with a quality to it to now that (along with the content of what she said and the circumstances) caused an unpleasant visceral reaction in her trapped partner, "I was talking about taking the big plunge"—his eyes went wide, he saw the chasm before them—"but," she looked at him, a full second, two, "I wasn't talking about getting hitched."

As Stanley's eyes bugged fully she laughed again, at length, heartily, simultaneously maniacal and carefree, and ceased to turn the wheel, so that the old car with the nonengaged operator went straight, a forest-launched projectile, smashing through the flimsy guardrail and only minimally slowed beginning a plunge toward the woodland and for the passengers the hereafter or lack thereof—as Stanley began to scream ear-piercingly, the sound that of a desperate doomed animal, and Hope put her arms in the air, smiling ear-to-ear, as if on a roller coaster (which in a manner of speaking she was and had been, this ride, their rides, about over).

And Stanley awoke, terror-filled, sweat-drenched, on the mattress's perspiration-wet fitted sheet; propped himself with one arm, hair glued to his forehead, breathing heavily. "Fuck," he said quietly, wiping body fluid from below his hairline with his unassigned arm; then swinging his lower body off the bed, his feet making contact with the soft carpet—aware at once that this time he was truly conscious (but again not consciously cognizant of the fact that Hope was long dead and wondering where she was).

23

"I'm fairly lucky genetically," Hope was saying, sometime later, some other day, in Stanley's mind, which of late was a bit like a rubble-filled war zone. "And I try to take care of myself—and aside from the occasional scrape or bruise have done a pretty good job of protecting the outside of my body—though admittedly maybe not so much the inside, including my mind. I'm pretty active too."

"But now you're dead," said Stanley matter-of-factly, looking into her eyes. "So what good did it do?"

"I'm not dead! Silly. I'm alive, clearly. I'm sitting right here."

"No. You're only alive in this dream. In reality you're dead. Buried in the woods. In a shallow grave. Maybe you oughtn't have done what you did to me, emotionally. It's what killed you. A drunk, damaged Stanley Northrop."

"You would never kill me. You don't have anything close to the right temperament, intoxicated or otherwise."

"But that's where you're wrong. I was temporarily insane. ...I mean I guess since then I've been consistently insane, increasingly insane." He watched her face for a reaction. "Just goes to show you don't know me as well as you thought. I discovered I don't even know myself as well as I thought. Because let me tell you: I certainly never would've thought I'd strangle you in the living room while blackout drunk. That's how it occurred though."

She stared blankly. "I'm always running around town. I occasionally jog. I practice with the band now and then. Get together with

friends," she countered. "Read. Paint. ...I have a life. I am *full* of life."
Hope, vexed, was trying to coax an explanation for his behavior from
her psyche. "I don't think this is a funny joke. Why would you be saying this? I'm not getting it."

Stanley regarded the pathetic figure, figment, with eyes of compassion—eyes of luminosity that regarded nothing and were in fact
closed tightly. "You, Hope—don't you see? You want so badly to be
alive because you—I—can't accept that you aren't. You thought you
were invincible, at least for decades to come. You thought you'd die
of old age, because you were smarter, better than everyone. You could
just do whatever you liked, without any significant physical or emotional repercussions. However you were proven wrong; by some guy,
by me. Unassuming, unemployed Stanley Northrop—possessor of
no unusual strength or abilities. Stanley Northrop, the man you just
didn't really care about or think much of. The man I don't think
much of." He chuckled. "The man who is possibly living under a
bridge somewhere already, having been evicted from the apartment
he moved into with you due to rent nonpayment. Mister Stanley
Northrop—a deranged killer, homeless on the streets of America,
able no longer to financially support himself."

<hr />

He heard footsteps on concrete. They were his own. He was still
dreaming; this he was vaguely aware of. The street was wet. It had
been raining, no more than ten minutes earlier, and it had rained
for hours. Puddles were ubiquitous; they were below curbs painted
yellow, at the ends of crosswalks, shone iridescent under fluorescent
lights of businesses still open at nine P.M.: a nudie bar named (due
to its location on Harrison Street) The Harrison Hothouse, a diner called Tasty Dish Café, a small laundromat (Coin-Op Laundry,
QUARTERS ONLY read a window-hung neon sign), a hole-in-the-
wall cinema that played only independent films (Oswald Arthouse)

managed by a stocky fortysomething man with a trimmed beard and a pierced septum who responded to Chaz.

Presently, more conscious than usual of the world around him, which ironically seemed more tangible than it did typically, Stanley was crossing the street at a designated crossing—cars waiting in two lanes to his left. Some guy was crossing simultaneously, from the other side, a youngish guy, cocky scowl on his mug: a posturing sort of guy—a thug image fostering guy, who was wearing tan Timberlands; a two sizes too large black tee; sagging work pants of a material coarse and blue, overly big also; and a black and white paisley bandana under a black L.A. cap worn askew. As their paths crossed, the person making unnecessary eye contact with the dreamer, he stepped directly onto Stanley's left foot—in a tennis shoe—with one of his boots, a fact he was certainly aware of though he neither apologized nor gave any indication he knew what he'd done, merely continuing on at the same casual pace.

Stanley, foot dully throbbing as he walked onward, turned his head to watch the young man in the baggy clothes step up on the opposite curb and progress along the sidewalk, his head hot with ire and antipathy focused on the back of the pedestrian's receding skull.

Fuckin' monkey he detected himself thinking. *That's basically a fucking assault, man. The world is full of guys like this, and they just act like they can treat people however they want. Or they take a look at me and think "He's no threat."*

He was walking back in the other direction without even realizing it and gaining on the guy, the back of the overlarge black shirt growing larger in his vision, his focus's stupid swagger augmenting his rage. *Motherfuckin' fuckhead. Fucking thinks he owns the world. Has all of the confidence and none of the justification.*

...Guy's feet splashing on the wet pavement. Noticing he's about three inches shorter. Tapping the guy on the back. He looked over his shoulder quick. "...the shit?" Eyes widening briefly as he sees Stanley's visage discolored with volcanic emotion, his arm cocked back and hand in a tight fist.

The punch was more than sufficiently forceful and its trajectory terminated eight or ten inches behind the thug character's head, which along with the rest of his body was sent back, the receiver of the blow stunned but within a few moments instinctively putting up two balled hands, swinging the left widely without aim and while off-balance, missing smiling Stanley by some distance. Just then the one who'd been stepped on swung again, other hand, hitting the baggy-clothed one, hard, in the right side of the head, hurting his own mitt.

"Oww," he uttered but upper-cutted him anyway while he was still processing the hurt hand, strike lifting the man's chin and sending him to his buttocks on the rainwater-coated concrete. Stanley looked down upon him with a degree of glee that was readily apparent, as he felt the gazes of more than one individual watching the event from nearby.

Straddling him he hit him in the face with his right, then left; right again left again in rapid succession, seeing the blood begin to ooze, the eyes start to swell. Right, left, enjoying it, the guy powerless, unresisting, barely conscious, eyelids fluttering, his face coming to resemble a red-pink leaking melon, overripe and unappealing. He was spitting blood from his mouth now, weakly, bottom lip badly split as Stanley continued to deliver punches with alternating arms, overcome by the happiness his destruction of the person's currently hardly recognizable countenance had caused to well up in him. He was thinking *Good, healthy ways of achieving states of ecstasy that don't involve drugs* as he pummeled, and pummeled more, the head below him now looking like a maroon mash between a wet dark shirt and a street-situated ball cap—appearing grotesque, severely deformed, blood issuing in steady stream, from numerous scattered exit points.

"Get off that guy, crazy shit!" someone, some bulky fellow with a concern-wrinkled expression, said tugging on his shoulder and bringing Stanley to his feet.

The dreamer was experiencing a diminished awareness, as if on a different plane, senses altered by endogenous chemicals and his ferocious spontaneity.

"I'm calling the police," someone different, a woman somewhere, said as he stood beside the man who had pulled him off the supine unmoving one, vaguely looking at the mess of a person he was responsible for but not truly taking in the sight except subconsciously.

And then he was walking away, at a leisurely clip, mind somewhere beyond, above it all, the street scene, the beaten lifeless person and the stunned small group whose attention shifted between Stanley and the other stranger, who they were uncertain was alive— Stanley noncognizant as before of his destination (if he had one); unconcerned about his victim's prognosis or legal consequences; thinking about neither where he was headed nor about the receiver of the savage attack he had just inflicted as an actual human being instead of an object, a receptacle for his voluminous violence, a deserving one.

24

"How would you like to make as much as you would working eight-hour shifts for a couple months in a few minutes?"

Across from him, wild look in her eyes, young Hope Brownen—force of nature, child of God, immortal soul in a stardust body, the punk rock chick with weird hair and a personal history that induced her boyfriend to believe her to be either a sociopath, a liar, or both—was posing the question. She was high on Adderall and though Stanley was of course high also the proposal sounded too good to be true to true.

"Of course. I mean, it would depend on what I had to do. Why?"

"Well...I know a guy who works at The Satyr's Grove. And he says there's up to like twenty thousand dollars in the safe in back every Thursday before they make a deposit. I've talked to him and, as long as we make it look realistic, he said he'd open the safe for us and we could split the contents three ways."

"Make what look realistic?"

"A burglary."

They were in her car, headed up Broad Street downtown en route to a liquor store, and had just driven by the establishment in question.

"That's a pretty nutty idea. ...Twenty grand, huh? Not sure that even sounds worth it, split three ways anyway."

"But there's really no risk. Because even though he'd have to call the cops they're not going to find us. They just wouldn't have enough to go on. He'd obviously tell them as little as he could without drawing suspicion and no one would get hurt. Even the business could absorb the loss rather easily."

He was processing the pros and cons of such an endeavor, eyes locked on his partner's face, as she pulled into the small parking lot of the shop, which was situated around back. What he was thinking was something along the lines of *This woman's got a screw loose and I probably oughtn't rob a strip club with her, no matter what the plan.*

"I want you to be the trigger man though. It'd be good for you. We don't even have to load the gun." She opened the door of her worse for wear sedan, Stanley doing the same. "It'll be fun. And profitable," Hope continued as the bell hung on the front door jingled and the duo veered left to peruse the whiskeys.

"I'm not convinced participating in an armed robbery, staged or not, is exactly the sort of activity I should be engaging in, at this juncture in my life, Hope." They stood before a row of Wild Turkey. "As it is everything's changed a lot for me since meeting you, and not all of those changes have been positive."

"Is that a reference to your being unemployed?"

"It was more of a reference to the damage you've done, emotionally."

She sighed exaggeratedly. "I may not be perfect. I might not be the typical girlfriend, or person. But I'm exciting. I expand your horizons. And I provide." Picking out a bottle of Jim Beam she chuckled.

"I want to make sure we never run out of things like weed after all. We do smoke a lot of it."

"Don't we all," contributed the guy at the counter, bearded and tattooed, ringing up the bottle and brown-bagging it.

⊰⊱

Back in the battered automobile Hope's campaign of persuasion went on.

"So are you saying 'no'? Because I think you ought to give Hope's idea a shot. She's got some good ones. And this one'll be good for us."

"Why are you referring to yourself in the third person?"

"You haven't answered."

"I don't know. How low risk are we talking? I'm awfully disinterested in spending the next seven years or something in a penitentiary."

"The guy I know, the guy I've spoken with will be there. Will be the manager on shift. Like every week. He wants some of that money too. And he'd have nothing to gain from fucking us over. So we won't have anything to lose. All it'll take is a little confidence."

He looked over at her, smiling Hope, driving through a residential neighborhood mere blocks now from their abode. "Fine," he said, expelling air in exasperated fashion. "Just give me the specifics. Let me know when we're doing this so I'm mentally prepared. ...Make sure I have whatever I'm going to need."

Hope's smile widened. She met his eyes with large, glistening, dark-centered orbs that seemed to smile too. And four days after he'd consented the young man, rootless now aside from Hope, the best friend who was his worst enemy, was stuffing a snub-nosed pistol into the pocket of a light olive-green jacket he wore over a black tee—feeling approximately as anxious as he felt was appropriate, even if the burglary was an inside job, with little to no element of danger; according to Hope.

She drove to the site calmly. It was around two P.M. The traffic was lazy and the sun was enshrouded by cumulus clouds. The dark interior of the establishment contained no more than three patrons. At the distant bar a woman in a tank top with her back to the door was checking her stock. A lone dancer gyrated on stage, clad in pink bikini bottoms. Her breasts were natural but small, the makeup she wore heavily applied.

Stanley kept his hand on the gun in his jacket as he waited for the stocky man to extract the totality of the cash from the small, modern-looking wall safe. Being out of public view in the back he was no longer feigning fear, but Stanley kept up some degree of a façade.

"You're fucked, idiots," yelled someone behind them.

"Oh fuck! The owner!" said Hope.

The man of whom she spoke approached the trio rapidly. He was bulky, middleaged, jogging, red-faced, held a raised baseball bat, was quickly closing the distance to Stanley—who mostly instinctually withdrew from his pocket the hand holding the stubby firearm and fired it once at the proprietor, hitting his left shoulder.

His arm jerked back from the kick and his mouth came open. "I didn't even know you loaded it."

The owner, shocked, dropped his Louisville Slugger and grabbed the point of injury, grimacing. Then, remarkably, he continued, slowly, to advance.

Deliberating momentarily, the criminals watching his slackened progress, Stanley opted to shoot him in the right kneecap. Again the weapon's pop filled the space and convulsed its operator's firing arm. The man ululated in pain, dropping, dark red soaking his pants around the entry point. Grabbing the legal tender that had been accumulated in a sack with his free hand Stanley returned the gun to his pocket and he and Hope stepped over the moaning floor-situated wounded proprietor.

"He wasn't supposed to be here," Hope explained as they hurried through the place of business, bartender woman staring aghast at them, toward the front door. "He never comes in."

"Honestly I wanted to do that just for the thrill," she told adrenaline-flooded Stanley, practically in a state of derealization, on the way home. "I can tell you got a good one."

"I shot a man, a stranger. Twice."

"Non-life-threateningly."

He just stared at her. There were beads of sweat below her hairline.

"Well, I enjoyed myself anyway. And I bet we probably ended up with about twenty thousand, as anticipated. Two-thirds of which, thirteen grand, is ours."

———— ((O)) ————

At the apartment they sat on the mattress counting the loot, which was poured out on the bedspread, the bulk of it smelling like something frequently used and well-traveled. Hope's face again displayed a wide, cat-that-ate-the-canary smile.

"That's it. Nineteen thousand, eight hundred thirty. Not bad. A not shabby haul." Hope beamed at her partner/partner in crime.

A calculator was on the bed beside the pile of ill-got cash, some bills crinkly, some crisp; some in bundles with thin paper bands that told the amount.

"Comes to sixty-six ten each. Six thousand six hundred dollars in a few minutes."

"Do you think it was worth it?" Stanley asked, furrow-browed.

"Yes. Of course." Her look was quizzical.

"I put two bullets into the owner of The Satyr's Grove. I think it's fair to say the police are going to be seeking us, and especially me, pretty aggressively. And the consequences, for me, of my being located are going to be—needless to state—rather hefty. Are going to distinctly not be worth it for a measly six grand; which if I get arrested within the next week I won't have done much with anyway."

"But you're practically certain *not* to get found. They just don't have enough to go on. Not without Harry telling them who we are. And he won't. You weren't picked up on any camera. They have, like, one. And it's over on the far side of the bar."

"I would rather have robbed that Emile guy. The drug dealer with the laundromats. The rich guy. In fact, I'd like to more than just rob him."

"I guess he's got a good amount of money. But, you know, I never even told him I was in a relationship. As far as all that goes he really didn't do anything wrong."

"I don't care honestly. Irrational or not, I want to kill that motherfucker."

"What if we were to extort money from him?" Stanley proposed that night, brooding. They were sitting on stools in the kitchen drinking cans of domestic beer. "He sells illegal drugs. Sounds like leverage to me."

"I'm not going to do something like that. I can't see it working anyway."

"Do you know anything about where he keeps his money? Does he have a safe too?"

"I think there's a good chance if you try to do anything you're going to get yourself killed or beaten to an inch from dead." Hope was looking at him with stone seriousness. "You might as well just shoot yourself in the head if you plan to do that. Same thing. You know, you also might want to consider that the actions you take with Emile could theoretically endanger me too. If he found out we're connected. And I probably don't need to tell you there are people above him far worse," she added.

"I can't shoot myself. Because I don't have a gun."

"There's mine," said Hope.

"I wouldn't shoot myself with it."

"I didn't think so," she said.

"Why do you have a gun anyway?"

"Why not," said Hope, taking a swig and adjusting her body on the cushion-less uncomfortable stool. "Protection."

"Have you ever fired it?"

"Yes."

He was looking at and thinking subconsciously about the beauty of her face, about the still unsolved enigma that was Hope Brownen, catalyst of his life's transformation. "Do you have much experience with guns?"

"Oh, I've taken a gun safety class, owned guns for years. I know the basics." She was intermittently looking down at the linoleum, gaze fluctuating between Stanley and the floor; absently she traced the same pattern on the kitchen counter with the nail of an index finger again and again. "I bought my first one over five years ago. I have two handguns. The one you used today and a Magnum. Long-barreled. A lot of kick."

Who are you? he asked internally. But he feared, was convinced, there was no real answer; that Hope was essentially an empty vessel he had erroneously poured his life into, a husk with which he was inexplicably entwined. And whatever the future held, whatever had occurred that he dreaded to acknowledge, he was doomed to endure the costs of both—unable to alter even the sequence of events that had not yet transpired. For it was obvious to him a penance was being paid (that Hope, of late, was a major part of). And maybe all his life had been an elaborate punishment; though for what acts, what sins, he might only futilely speculate.

25

I'm going to kill two birds with one stone thought Stanley.

A drug dealer and pimp's not going to put all his money in the bank. There's probably a bunch at his house. So...I'm going to gain entry to Emile's residence, take whatever cash I can get my hands on, and put some holes in him. Fuck, I've already shot a guy.

He knew using one of Hope's guns without her knowledge was a potential option, but then the crime could theoretically be linked to her down the line, and anyway something with more firepower sounded preferable when it came to raiding the den of a guy the likes of Emile, who no doubt had protection in the form of weapons or people (or possibly dogs).

And based on this supposition he hatched a plan to ask a former housemate who was a criminal sort if he could briefly borrow the illegally obtained assault rifle that was last he knew in the guy's possession, a guy with the given name of Baker who, humorously, had been and he was sure still was employed as a cook at a locally famous eatery downtown on Franklin called Susan's Spot (Susan being the business's deceased cofounder, her wizened widower Daniel the surviving owner—a taciturn, hunched, stocky fellow who shied from even the communication of eye contact; a fellow the public felt was either autistic, sociopathic, or in a state of permanent bereavement).

Stanley was fairly certain he could talk Baker into letting him have the AR-15; however, Hope wasn't going to give him Emile's address, especially since she suspected him of wanting to do precisely the sort of thing he was planning to. So the means wasn't a problem (Stanley couldn't imagine his target would be able to successfully defend himself against a surprise attack by a crazy person with the kind of weapon they gave police/military tactical units), he just didn't know how he'd find the guy. But there were only so many prostitutes loitering on the streets of Oswald, which meant that twisting the arm of two or three might yield an address for the right pimp.

A few nights later he was walking the sidewalks of a neighborhood known as the Glenn District, the seedy part of town—three square blocks of vagrants, drug addicts, and whores on the prowl— stepping over shattered brown bottles and politely responding in the negative to requests for change. A prostitute in scuffed knee-high boots, fishnets, a red pleather short skirt, a similarly hued halter top, with a black purse strung over a shoulder, a maybe half-black woman with a cynical smirk asked him if he was looking for a date.

"Maybe. You know a guy named Emile? Is that your pimp?"

"Baby, I don't have a pimp. I work alone. I don't need that," she answered with apparent irritation. "You want a date or not? Fifty for a half hour. Hundred for the hour or if you want to fuck my ass."

"Next time perhaps."

Her lips twisted in a manner that indicated disgust. Less than a block later he approached another girl, younger, semi-attractive; she was pale with long medium brown hair; she wore a jacket but was shivering, her eyes occupying the center of gray rings.

"What's your name?"

"My name? Shara."

"Cold?"

"Yeah. It's the skirt. Got any blow?"

"Not right now."

"Oh. ...So you want me?"

"Well, I've got a girlfriend."

"Oh. Okay." She seemed confused.

"Do you know a guy named Emile?"

"Uh, I don't think so. What's he look like?"

"I don't know exactly. Bigger dude I guess. Five-nine or so. In his thirties."

"No one comes to mind."

"He's a pimp. A lot of the girls around here have a pimp, right?"

"No. I'd say...most don't."

He looked at the abstracted eyes of the sickly, pained-looking young woman. "...Do you know where I might find prostitutes that do?"

The streetwalker regarded him queerly. "Yes. Escorts. Plenty of the escorts that advertise on the back page of the weekly have pimps."

"I see. Alright. Thanks."

A cold glance went his way.

"Hope you find some coke," Stanley said as he continued on, the girl's thin body shaking in the night air, his new mission to locate one of the green plastic boxes with the plexiglass windows that opened out to which Oswald's free weeklies were distributed.

Finding one between the walkway and the curb a block on, among such boxes for other free local publications, he grabbed a paper, flipped it over and perused the small square ads, each with an airbrushed photo of a seductively posturing lady, that comprised a significant portion of the Oswald Outlook's (est. 1980) rear cover. The first such that his gaze locked on, featuring a blonde of thirty or thirty-five whose mouth was coated in shiny dark red lipstick, read

♥ DARIA ♥

MAKE YOUR DREAMS COME TRUE

NATURAL DOUBLE D'S AND GUARANTEED

TO PLEASE

IN OR OUT CALL

555-918-4556

His cell phone came out and he entered the number sequence. *Alright, Daria, guaranteed to please, let's see if you know this Emile douche.*

"This is Daria," said an affectedly sensual voice.

"Hi, Daria. How are you? I was maybe in the market for a date, but I have a question or two."

"Shoot, honey."

"Well, this may sound odd, but, if you have one, is your...handler's, the guy who runs the show, your behind the scenes guy—is his name Emile?"

"I'm not going to discuss that with you." She sounded unpleasant now. "Where'd you get that name?"

"He's an old friend."

"Well then ask him yourself." Click.

Bingo, thought Stanley, putting the device back in his pocket. And so he purchased a burner phone from Walmart and recontacted Daria, asking about her rate. She was a bit pricey, five hundred for an hour, but it would be okay that he didn't have the money—any part of it—because he only needed to get in the same room with her. The room in this case being apartment number 51 in the Mossy Brook apartment complex on the west side of town, where he had arranged to meet Daria of the oldest profession at seven o'clock in the evening on a Monday night.

"Hiii," she answered moments after his knock, smiling wide and brimming with put-on happiness, attired in a v-cut thin cheap floral-print dress and discount shoes with raised heels, her bountiful bosom tan, pushed up, and sparkling with glitter body gel. "Nice to meet you, Stanley. I'm Daria." He entered.

The place was a little chilly but clean and staged across from the door was an oblong polyester sofa an abundance of variously sized pillows had been placed atop. The carpeted floor featured a multicolored tasseled rug, beyond the sofa was a circular wooden table, and in the left corner was a many-tiered cat tree at the top of which was a sort of shag-upholstered cave with an oval entrance, though no feline was anywhere in sight.

"Make yourself at home," Daria said, indicating he seat himself on the couch (he obliged, moving pillows to make space for his posterior), as she moved past it to a shelf, taking a condom from a box on it and coming over to where he sat. "What's in that big bag that you need?" she asked, wary, referring to the black duffel bag had brought in with him, slung over one shoulder.

"Oh, I just got back from the gym and I'm on foot, so..."

"I see." Daria regarded the bag with a confused expression. "Well, I have one of these, in case you didn't," she said, prophylactic in glossy colorful wrapper between her thumb and index finger.

"Thanks, whore."

Her face changed at once into a defensively contorted mask, radiating anger. "What did you just say?"

Stanley was reaching into the zippered sack he had placed beside him; out came a long heavy gun, the sort of gun some would never see in real life but only in action films. Daria gasped at the sight of it, her mouth remaining open for long seconds, during which her brain—gone into bestial fright mode—weighed her survival possibilities and selected the option of sprinting for the door.

The safety wasn't on and a clip was snapped in. Already familiar with the weapon Stanley quickly chambered a round and aimed at the lower half of the fleeing frame of the young woman, who was at the threshold. "STOP RIGHT THERE IF YOU DON'T WANT A FIFTY-SEVEN-MILLIMETER FUCKING BULLET IN YOUR THIGH!"

She froze, back to him, shoulders and scapulae dropping with a tension release, her whole body though quivering just perceptibly.

"Now: Turn toward me." The woman obeyed, watery eyes a scared child's. "You seem to know Emile. He is obviously your confederate. So—all I want to know, in order for me to get the fuck out of here, leaving you unharmed, and for you to never see me again, is what the guy's address is. And don't lie, or I'll come back over with this thing."

"Uh...I'll have to look through my phone. It's in there." She walked slowly across the front room—shaking, her nose running, mascara becoming diluted—to the table where she'd set her purse, pulling the device from its interior and tapping buttons, unbeknownst to the criminal behind her dialing 911 and leaving the line open while she located the requested information in her digital address book.

"Okay," she said, walking back to where the man with the rifle in his lap was tensely seated. "513 Terrace Lane, number nine. Oswald. It's not far from downtown."

"Thank you, Daria," Stanley said, rising, returning the firearm to the gym bag. "You've been most helpful." He headed to the door.

"What did he do to you?" she inquired, wiping her eyes with the back of a hand.

"Participated in the ruination of my dream."

Five minutes after Stanley departed a cruiser black and white drove into the apartment complex parking lot.

⸺◈⸺

The following evening, having already taken a look at the outside of the place, a new building comprised of ten high-end apartments, the individual with a powerful gun in a duffel across his back returned to make entry to the apartment identified to him. This unfortunately involved waiting twenty minutes for a resident to enter and then walking in behind them, though fortunately the resident ended up being a decrepit lady who trailed a musty scent and who was apparently quite unaware of Stanley's having quietly followed her inside.

He rang the doorbell for unit nine, nervous, and heard its chime, over the noise of a television, within. A large black man in a black sleeveless shirt and black shorts answered following a brief wait. "Yes?"

"I'm here to talk to Emile."

"Is he expecting you?"

"No, but I'm familiar with his business and I know a girl looking for work—very beautiful—who I'm sure he'd be interested in."

"I don't think he's going to want to talk to you just showing up at his door but I'll go tell him." The guy lumbered off, leaving the door an inch ajar.

Emile himself was the next person at the door. Dressed in FUBU casualwear and sporting a brand new pair of basketball shoes, a gold stud in each earlobe, the fabled upper middle class businessman, the entrepreneur who dealt in illicit drugs, illicit sex, and laundromats— who according to Hope had five escorts working for him and owned a two-location chain of oblong rooms where poor people went to wash their clothes, who (told the same source) had a dream of also opening a Korean restaurant in the city—reeked somehow of arrogance. He had a wide nose and acne scarring on his cheeks, a sporadically freckled face light brown in complexion, hair black and cut so close to the scalp his skull appeared merely dusted with hair.

He looked at Stanley for half a second, then addressed him with a gaze directed below and to the left of his face. "Taye said you wanted to talk to me about a girl."

"Yes. She's gorgeous, and young—only nineteen. But she's not naïve. She's ready to go and a great fuck. I know from firsthand experience. Can I come in to talk to you about her?"

He ignored the question, his demeanor a man's in the grip of intolerable ennui. "That's great, but I really have all the women I need. Too many if anything. It can be a hassle. You got a picture though? Like to know what I'm passing up."

"Yeah, I'll find one. I'd like to get some coke from you too. I've got a bunch of money in my sack here." Stanley had lowered the bag to the ground and was unzipping it.

"Whoa. I don't sell cocaine in bulk to guys I've never seen before in the fucking hallway. How the fuck did you ever hear about me?"

In a flash the AR was out and its barrel nearly touching Emile's forehead. "Do not fucking move."

The other's eyes had in a moment expanded with the same dumb animal fear he had seen in many recently, his expression the one that said *I only care about my own preservation and I am now thinking exclusively of what to do to maximize my chances of survival.*

"Walk backwards into the apartment and as you do tell Taye and whoever else is in there that they better not so much as think about a weapon if they care about your brain remaining in that thick case you call your skull."

Emile complied. "Taye man—don't take out your piece. Just don't do anything. This fucker at the door's out of his goddamn mind and he has a fucking tactical rifle and it's pointed right at my forehead."

Stanley followed his hostage into the latter's apartment, impressed by its interior—it was spacious, had a high ceiling, all the furnishings appeared new, and the place was conspicuously antiseptic, suggesting a tenant with a penchant for cleanliness or who had just moved in. To his left as he entered was a now anxious-looking Taye, standing statue still, his arms at his sides and his lips quivering just perceptibly.

"Sit down," Emile was commanded. "On that couch directly behind you." He gestured at the bulky other with the weapon. "You sit beside him. No movements that might make me nervous."

After Taye had joined his employer on the sofa, the attention of the two undividedly on the well-armed intruder, the stranger with mysterious motives said, "I know you have a gun. Slowly and carefully take it out and, holding it by the barrel, throw it across the floor in my direction."

Emile's bodyguard did this, removing the item from a shoulder holster worn under his tee, his pace a seeming indication that he was appropriately concerned about being shot by the crazy entrant with the rifle aimed at his fat torso.

The gun, a Glock, came to a stop ten inches or so from and just to the right of Stanley's lead foot. He took notice of where it came to rest without his view shifting from the duo before him, Emile's hands clasped and spine perpendicular on the leather sofa, Taye's posture and general mien a seated version of what it had been a minute earlier (he was a giant ill at ease, but disconcertingly Stanley got the impression he could spring into action at any moment; although he felt reasonably confident—the safety off, the gun primed—that if he should the aggressor's severe injury or death would follow).

"I don't know for sure," he addressed Emile, "whether you have a weapon on you or not. I don't think you do. But if I get the impression you're going for one because of a too quick motion or your reaching somewhere one could be you're probably going to wind up getting shot dead in your own very nice fucking home. So, you know...don't test the waters."

The group's eyes remained unhappily locked on Stanley's face.

"Don't hurt me. Don't hurt me," came a high, whiny, somewhat quiet voice from the corridor to the left, off of which opened many rooms. Barefoot, head down, wearing a pair of simple panties and a medium green tank top, an obviously terrified young woman of Asian descent was headed into the main room hugging herself, nearly on tiptoe—having merely heard but chosen not to look at the man who had forced his way in. Unasked, watched with aquiline attention by Stanley—who nevertheless consciously kept the furniture-situated two in his peripheral view—the half-clothed lady sat down beside Emile, who moved a few inches over to make room.

"One of your ladies of the night?" inquired the caught off guard gun wielder.

Emile nodded in the affirmative, not having shifted his focus from his captor.

"Sample your wares, huh? Not surprising." Stanley dropped the barrel of the killing machine to about the level of the trio's knees. "Alright everybody—here's what's going to happen. Everybody's friend Emile here is going to give me any and all money and light valuables he has on hand. Then I'm going to decide—likely without anybody's input—how I feel about allowing you, or some of you, to live." The woman began to sob pathetically, head drooping and face hidden by hanging shoulder-length black hair, ignored by both men to her left. "And, if all goes well, I'm going to be leaving here shortly with a big smile on my face and the fair amount of cash that I know

Mister Drug Dealer slash Entrepreneur must have setting around somewhere."

Presumably he had everyone's attention, yet the woman continued to be in a world of pain that involved her teary eyes being directed at her lap. Soft sad sounds issued from her at a regular interval.

"So where's your cash, Emile?"

The man looked at Stanley, wide-eyed, almost questioningly, but did not respond.

The out-of-work gunman trained the weapon's business end at Emile's midsection. "Shall I repeat myself?"

"I...I have a safe. It's in the bedroom, my bedroom." His eyes glanced right indicatively.

"Lead on," he said, gesturing with the AR for the person he was holding hostage in his own home to come to his feet. "I don't want to have to worry about you while we're over there though," Stanley said to visibly anxious Taye and lightly squeezed the trigger of the gun he held pointed at the upper portion of his chest twice, hitting him between the clavicles and with the second bullet at the top of the right lung, both wounds appearing as dark red circles that immediately poured blood—Taye, in shock, gasping terribly and pointlessly flailing one arm as he gradually expired on the sofa, which the lead had exited the back of, mouth agape, eyes comically bulging.

Emile witnessed this damage and his friend's demise but reacted little, merely becoming discernibly doleful; his lady acquaintance alternatively went into hysterics, as Stanley might have forecast, her uncontrolled girlish screams piercing, vexatious.

"What's the female's name?" She acted as though she were being tortured but was unable to rise from her seat.

"Trini," answered Emile, monotone, standing by his dying friend, shirt drenched in life fluid, open mouth now crooked and body slumped toward the unhinged escort in panties.

"Trini! ...TRINI!"

"Yes." Her voice shook, she made hesitant eye contact. "What?"

"I need you to shut the fuck up. I can't harbor a thought with that racket."

"Ye-e-s." Her gaze descended to her pale thighs again as she began to spasmodically catch her breath in the manner of a child following a tantrum.

"Thank you," he told the top of her head, and—deeming her a non-threat likely to go on being lost to her emotions on the couch—added "Stay."

His focus switched to Emile. "C'mon." Again he gestured with the rifle. "No time for a eulogy."

Stanley trod behind Emile, barrel nearly making contact with his dark t-shirt, as he walked slowly to his room down the corridor distraught Trini had emerged from, the husky captive giving the impression of having been rendered an animate but internally lifeless quantity.

Within his unsurprisingly ample room, which was furnished with all the usual items including a king-size bed and included a wall-length closet, Stanley's guide veered to the east side of the rectangle of the boudoir and approached a small black steel door flush with the wall about five feet above the baseboard.

"Good. Open it," was the command behind him.

Emile spun the safe's dial, right-left-right, its deep interior revealing rubber-banded stack upon stack, stretching a foot back, of hundred-dollar bills.

"I like the look of that," said Stanley, bright-eyed. "Go ahead and remove it all. You can just toss it behind you onto the bed."

The task of relocating the many bundles took a few minutes, Stanley's serotonin progressively increasing as the packs of unutilized treasury notes landed on the mattress to his rear. When the apartment's tenant had emptied the clandestine recess the man with the gun to his back inquired as to the quantity.

"It's a hundred and thirty thousand. I think."

He heard a quick patter of feet on the living room floor.

Almost sprinting Stanley came down the corridor to the sound's source, finding the woman at the door about to turn the knob, Baker's rifle already aimed at her head.

"Stop right fucking there! You wanna get murdered?"

Pathetically, frustratedly, she answered "No," near tears, her nose and eyes inflamed from her recent weeping.

Just then the *nouveau criminel* spun around on instinct, squeezing the trigger blindly as his body swiveled, alerted by another noise, his anxiety at a peak due to the dangerous and likely desperate person he'd left standing in the bedroom.

Stanley saw, in the next moment, that it had indeed been the sound of Emile ambulating toward him along the hall, sawed-off shotgun in his hands. In the same instant the shotgun was fired, missing Stanley—as a result of distance and the shooter having received a bullet to the abdomen—by a foot or more; sending plaster from the edge of the wall to his left spraying across him, the hardwood floor, in an explosion of off-white building material.

Emile doubled, toward his central wound, a clean immediately maroon-gushing hole, the hot blood spreading rapidly down his shirt to the top of his pants. As, groaning, back against the wall, he crumbled to the floor—losing the power to maintain the weapon, which clattered before his sapped corpus—a new degree of resignation seemed to take him over; yet both suspected, the dying and the watcher, that the injury itself might require excruciating hours to end his life.

Trini stood at the door shaking, one hundred five pounds of fear-petrified human, her gaze on the bleeding mortally wounded person slumped in the corridor—her lover and employer and possibly friend.

"Follow me into the bedroom," Stanley told her. "I'm not letting anybody out of my sight anymore."

As they approached the fallen Emile Stanley lowered his rifle so that its warm barrel touched the man's perspiration-beaded forehead; he was breathing heavily with his head down, sitting now in a small puddle of dark sticky fluid and intermittently wincing.

"That wound will in all probability take many hours to finish you and the pain will intensify. You're going to be in agony."

Emile looked up at him, his expression communicating contempt for the enigmatic angel of death above, that in a fair contest he'd have easily triumphed—then Stanley squeezed the trigger. With a space-filling pop an oblong projectile went through the middle of his brain, turning his scowl into a look of placid emptiness, gray matter and blood being ejected onto the barrier behind the corpse, the gore centered around a bullet hole. The decommissioned body slumped over to one side along the wall.

The fully distraught woman at the killer's tail seemed to react less than to merely remain in a condition of function-limiting horror, her delicate body still quaking, giving her thin tank top the appearance of a garment exposed to a spring breeze—her face that of a person who'd just had their limbs blown off but could not fully process the nightmare of their reality.

Stanley grabbed the sawn-off and back inside the bedroom went rooting around, finding in the drawer of the late Emile's bedside table a loaded handgun and above his wardrobe in the long closet a pistol and putting these and the cash in the gym bag he had left in the living room, making the load uncomfortably heavy and leaving no room for the rifle. He ripped the bedsheet off the bed and quickly wrapped the item in it, but a notion crossed his mind that caused his lips to bend into a sick smile and he looked back at wide-eyed Trini, absentmindedly playing with her fingers and staring at a point three feet off the ground, then placed the sheet-camouflaged AR on the hardwood next to the bed.

"Are you clean?"

She stared at nothing, to all indication unaware of him.

"Are you clean?" he screamed in her face.

"Yes!" she replied quivering-voiced, without looking at him, and teared up once more, for a moment unconsciously curling her toes in a childish way.

"I find you very attractive," he said, eyes locked on her face. "And it occurred to me: why leave home without you?"

Her sobbing became full-fledged crying.

"You're what—five-one? Twenty-four or so. Beautiful. With sleek hair, smooth legs." He lifted her chin with the bent fingers of one hand, a conqueror or slave trader's scrutinatory motion. "Pretty eyes. ...A slim little soft body."

With a thumb Stanley wiped a salty drop from her white cheek that was descending to the small slightly cleft chin. "Come lay down on the bed," he said. "Take your clothes off first."

With little hesitation the prostitute, one of the dead loft occupant's lovers, climbed up on the bed and removed her thin top—under which she wore no bra—and shimmied off her white panties. Her breasts were small, mere palmfuls, the areolas brown, the nipples firm; her sticks of legs were smooth and goose pimpled, the vagina they led to a slit of simple beauty topped by a sparse patch of dark hair neatly shaven into an upside-down triangle. Stanley joined her on the bed, the comfort of the thick mattress surprising him.

He removed his own shirt. "I want to feel your skin with my skin," he said and leaned toward her, pressing his lips into hers, unresponsive and meatless.

"I know you're probably not feeling great, emotionally, that you might even have been fond of Emile out there, but I wish you'd be a little more receptive—that you'd fake it for me. You are, after all, a prostitute." He kissed her neck, just above one of her breasts, causing her to shudder slightly, which Stanley noticed. "I mean I know you're not on the clock, but you have the experience, the skills, to at least make it seem like you don't mind my having my way with you."

"No kissing," she said after a moment, avoiding his eyes.

"I guess that is generally a rule isn't it. No kissing on the lips. ...But I don't care about your whore stipulations." He gripped her wrist with pressure. "I'll do what I want. And if you don't act for me I'm going to be meaner. ...I have the power," the hostage taker added as he threw her arm from his grasp.

Stanley planted his mouth fully on hers, roughly, feeling a miniscule amount of her saliva on his, along with the sensation of her bare breasts against the epidermis of his chest precipitating physiological arousal. Then he looked quickly around him, locking on a chest of drawers, its dark wood shiny, handles brass.

Keeping in his peripheral vision the nude Asian probably Japanese American kneeling on the newly deceased local businessman's bed the of late murderous Stanley went to the piece of furniture he eyed and, opening the top drawer, discovered inside what he had hoped to: socks, some dozen and a half pairs. He removed two pair and went back to where the woman was, Trini watching his movements but without looking directly at him, the area around her eyes wet but her tears abated.

"Lie down. On your back."

The call girl complied and, bending over her, starting with her right arm, Stanley tied her little wrist to one of the bedposts; Trini emitting a slight involuntary squeak, due primarily to surprise, but not resisting.

Unhassled, the man restrained her skinny legs and other arm to the corners of the bed using the remaining three socks; then he stood staring at the supine, helpless form of the weak, small specimen splayed on the expensive king-size. He knew he was going to enter her but he didn't know what else. He didn't know why he had chosen to tie her. He was consciously alarmed. It was as if since he had killed a few people (something he did not think about, that he had definitely decided wasn't real, hadn't happened)—since Hope had informed him of her infidelity with dead Emile, really—he had become a deranged, increasingly dangerous individual, whose own acts he could not forecast nor necessarily fathom; become a shadow version of himself, unrestrained, unknown, and unceasingly havoc-creating.

Stanley removed his shoes and socks and got back onto the bed in the just-right seventy-some-degree room, laying shirtless on his side next to her. He draped an arm across her bare stomach, burying his face in the side of her own. Though she occupied quite a different mental-emotional space, though beyond the room were two dead people that Stanley was responsible for the demise of, he felt a placidness come over him, warm and blanketing.

"I hate you for the power you have over me you know." He spoke quietly into her ear. "I mean, I don't even know you and I feel like a baby—like I've reentered the womb; within which, and only within which, I can be blissful, in a peaceful state."

He began slowly to stroke her smooth black hair and at the same time to softly sob. The tears wetted her face and he pressed his body even tighter against hers—Trini's fear mixed with aversion having yielded to confusion and guardedness.

Crying, snuggling her restrained body, he said: "I thought, again—I fooled myself into thinking I could have her, that it would work, that I would not be left emotionally destitute. That I could have a woman who turned me on, could have what other people can have; without the price being so high it wouldn't be worth the time I had with her, the brief period of perceived happiness, of contentment."

Over the previous minutes his penis had grown firm and Stanley in his silence became aware of its condition, an awareness that prompted him to prop himself over the splayed prisoner preparatory to penetrating her feminine nexus, the outermost part of his organ finding it to be helpfully moist.

Trini was, discernibly, resigned to her helplessness. Her observer interpreted her face as communicating that she felt herself the rag doll of fate's insensate vagaries.

"You're a hot bitch. But—maybe I have a problem with you, for reasons that have nothing to do with you. Maybe I am embittered and want to make you the receiver of a pain that has to do with other women. Who I wanted but couldn't have. Or had but couldn't keep. Maybe didn't want to keep."

He sighed with pleasure as an inch of him slid inside, feeling her snugness and warmth, somehow relieved as he had been many times by the initial sensation of oneness with a new partner.

"Maybe I want to treat you like a thing because that's all your body is—and if your body were not as it is perhaps there would be nothing about you that interested me." He was, quite slowly, using his hips, causing his blood-filled appendage, extending from the fly of his pants, to go forward into and be partially withdrawn from— having yet not fully entered the idealness of—the membranous interior of her flower of flesh.

"Maybe...I want to rape a baby into you. Want you to either deliver or be forced to abort a baby that resulted from a stranger violating you." He was thrusting now, ecstasy rising in him, his member wet with her juice, her breasts vibrating with his movement. "A self-revealing murderous stranger. A stranger that dispatched the boss and used his merchandise as his own sperm depository. Ha ha."

26

Stanley didn't untie the woman after he climaxed, knowing the longer it took the restrained Trini to inform the authorities of what had happened in Emile's apartment the longer it would be before an investigation was mounted. He wasn't particularly concerned she, too, might die—figuring she would either free herself or be discovered before the days it would take her to expire, to die of thirst on the dead man's mattress.

Hope was in bed when he came in though not yet asleep. He wanted to resist the urge to inform her in part, leaving out anything about Trini, of what he had done, but seeing her eyes sparkling in the dark found himself unable not to boast of having plucked her john from the land of the living.

"What the fuck is wrong with you?" She had sat up immediately. "Have you lost your mind, Stanley? Have you?" Hope was fully roused.

"I formed a plan and I executed it." He looked at her, staring at him deadly serious, all contours in the dimness. "Maybe. To answer your question. Maybe I've lost my mind. And you would be responsible."

"His suppliers will be out to kill the person responsible. If they have any way of determining it was you they'll find you, and there won't be anything either of us can do to save you."

Stanley's mind flashed the image of bed-tied Trini, of a moaning Trini being discovered perhaps a day after he'd left her by an authority figure or possibly one of the suppliers Hope spoke of, imagined Trini giving a detailed description of the person who had raped her, killed the others, cried on her cheek—a blanket around her pale nude body, a glass of water in her hands.

"Don't you care? Don't you even care what you've done to me—internally, emotionally, mentally? You're a goddamn whore and now I've killed the guy you were sleeping with, because of you."

"And because you wanted his money," she said, ignoring the outburst. "Did you get any by the way?"

"A lot. A whole hell of a lot." The gym bag was on the floor behind him, along with Baker's still wrapped AR-15. His mind switched gears. "I wish you cared about me. Had cared about me I mean. It some time ago became obvious you don't and never did. But I wish you had." He imagined pouring the hundred and thirty grand onto the bed and wallowing in it. "Anyway, it'll make a nice addition to the comparatively meager six thousand-some I already have."

"How much did you get?"

"Enough so that neither of us will have to work anytime soon. That is if I decide to share, if I elect to stay with you."

"I've been supporting you for months. Besides, you can't leave me. You're much too into me."

He wanted to lean in and scream in her face, saliva flying from his mouth. Scream "FUCK YOU!" Because she was right. Under the circumstances the fact of his attachment, only emotional now, infuriated him.

But he didn't scream, or speak, and he never poured any money out onto a bed, including earlier with Hope, following the robbery. He had no money, and—relatedly—his actions in reality, in the present, had no more to do with stacks of bills of green and white than with a beautiful young woman in a dark apartment room. Reality was sunlight, a candy bar wrapper fluttering in the wind, glued by mud to an area four inches from supine Stanley's head: an unkempt and unshowered man under a blanket in a state of semiconsciousness who was laying on his back near a walkway that wound through a city park downtown—the time, thirty-two minutes past eleven; the date, June 2nd, mid-second decade of the millennium.

This though was a state of things that Stanley preferred not to check in with, that he had difficulty being present in—just as he preferred, basically forced himself not to recollect the fact that Hope wasn't even alive, and a few other people had been murdered by his hand in the not-distant past as well. And so he habitually entered, in fact nearly always inhabited, a realm of imagined life—one in which the malevolent girlfriend was yet well and near, in which he still had a roof over his head and he had never terminated a human being—in which, ironically, he devised mind-stories of his killing others, a drug dealer and his henchman; of thieving and raping; of people who did not exist, which fictional personae were sometimes murderers or existed on the periphery of society.

In which he was being hunted by shadowy figures avenging the death of the intermediate dealer who obtained cocaine in bulk from them. Who drove a long, refurbished seventies-era iridescent turquoise Cadillac, the two of them, and who—though Stanley had both of Emile's handguns with him as he was driven by Hope across town—were far better armed than their quarry, a weak man with two pocket-size weapons in a car that was barely in one piece.

Those who hunted him were presently two cars behind them, and he and Hope already had their suspicions about the twain in the perfect-condition vehicle that shone in the night, having noticed it'd been behind them for a number of miles.

They were approaching the bridge that split off the center of Oswald from its northern section—the rundown Yasheva neighborhood, which was primarily industrial with some one-story apartment complexes and motels in need of repair, leading into the rather upscale neighborhood of Granger Bluffs. Stopped at an octagonal sign just south of the old iron bridge over the O'Healy river the operator of the Cadillac, now only one car between theirs and it, flashed its brights repeatedly.

"It's that car," said Hope, profile illuminated by the lights of both cars to their rear as she looked back and hair glowing unnaturally. "I think they have been following us."

Stanley looked over his shoulder too. The driver of the car directly behind them honked and Hope let her foot off the brake. She started out across the rusting emerald-green bridge, river frigid and foamy below, the bridge over it eighty feet in length. No more than seconds after she began crossing it, as Hope watched in the rearview mirror above her head, the car of their focus accelerated to aggressively pass in front of the vehicle between the two and, swinging back into the right lane, rammed into the left back bumper of Hope's dilapidated auto. Both operator's and passenger's heads whipped back as the car, being pushed at the same edge by the Cadillac, went forward and right—Hope helpless to halt its progression—into the point-six-meter flaking metal wall of the structure, beyond which were cables of braided steel at four-foot intervals. The long gleaming gangsters' car kept at the back of Hope's car with character until from the fender it began to crumple inward as it was crushed by the side of the bridge.

"Oh fuck," uttered Hope, observing this, gelatinous orbs wide in the nighttime urban dimness, the reflection of moonlight and other luminance off the water casting some illumination on her adrenaline-roused visage.

The back of the car was beginning to be pushed up onto the hood of the other automobile.

"Should we bail?" proffered Stanley, Hope's beater being gradually upended, its front bumper ground into the pavement where it met the bridge wall.

"I think they're trying to make it go over the edge!"

"Fuck this," uttered Stanley, pulling the door handle.

"No, wait." Hope lifted the cover of the compartment between the two front seats, bringing out a long, gleaming, almost cartoonish silver pistol about the size of her forearm.

"Jesus," her companion said staring. "Is that where you always keep it?"

"No. I just knew people like these guys would be after you and wanted to be prepared, in case I was with you when and if they tracked you down."

Magnum in hand Hope extended her arm and sighted in the direction of the Cadillac's driver but found she could barely see the top of his forehead over the compacted trunk. She pulled at the door handle but the also-crumpled section of steel wouldn't budge, even when she utilized her legs to push it free. Finally she turned her attention instead to the spider-webbed windshield, swinging her legs front to kick it out, which she succeeded in—the broken rectangle of glass sliding down the hood in one piece, Hope thrusting herself forward by pushing off of the upper edge of the frame and sliding after it on her posterior out of the vehicle.

Gun in her again outstretched right arm Hope closed in on the driver's side of the Cadillac, the front of it partly pinned under the rear of Hope's ancient destroyed auto, and fired two rounds through the front window at the man behind the wheel's upper body— Stanley seeing her fire but unable to see the target. One bullet entered the body of the Slavic short-haired thirtysomething fellow via the bridge of the nose, snapping his head back and killing him immediately, and the second entered between the Adam's apple and the clavicle, which wound blood gushed from briskly, dark red shiny in the limited light. The person in the passenger seat did his best, simultaneously, to exit the machine and run down the bridge to the street; however, with the car's starboard up against the wall of the bridge his door would open no more than four or five inches, and as he attempted to climb to the back of the now far from pristine blue-green classic two more close-together blasts issued from Hope's long handgun—the bullets as before both gaining entry into the body of the human they were meant to: via the middle of the back, at an angle; and through the right deltoid, the side of the ribcage, and continuing in a trajectory that passed and exited into seat cushion just under the heart, a wound that was not immediately fatal but served the function of being fully incapacitating.

The man released a final-sounding expulsion of air, a substantial exhalation synchronized with his collapsing across the middle of the car's interior, between the front seats and at a 135-degree angle onto the center of the rectangular rear one, the crimson of his life-fluid splashing and then gushing over and into the dark soft upholstery.

A visible half-smile serving as the only contrast to a somewhat robotic demeanor, Hope returned leisurely and crawled back into the totaled accordion of a vehicle, the object that had long been her means of long-distance locomotion having been reduced to approximately one and a half tons of scrap, Stanley staring at her rapt, transfixed by her power and strangeness, her danger and foreignness, her emotion-free efficiency and general competency.

The steely executioner settled into the driver's seat once more as her boyfriend-in-title regarded her with laser focus, slightly parted lips, and little self-awareness. After she had stowed the Magnum in its plastic home adjacent the gear selector Hope directed her abstracted gaze to the face locked on hers and said, near inflectionless, "Let's fuck."

"What?" asked Stanley, automatically, having heard but hardly processed her sentence. There were at least four cars stopped behind the ruined automobile crushed against the bridge and the one with the respectively dead and fast expiring unconscious person in it.

"Fuck me. Insert your hot erection into my silken pussy. It's wet."

"That's..."—his eyes seemed to search her face for the answer to an unformed question—"kind of an odd way to phrase it. And particularly peculiar timing. ...I think we should get out of here."

"Here. Now. I know you're hardening. Unzip and ram yourself into me," she said, unfastening and sliding her frayed-hole-spotted jeans down her legs to the middle of her calves. Stanley's penis formed a tent at the front of his cotton slacks as he saw she had not been wearing underwear, his member fully awake as Hope slid half of two digits into the moist warm underside of the minimally lit hairless V between her thighs.

She inserted the fingers with which she'd been stimulating

herself into Stanley's mouth. Surprised, he nonetheless unhesitatingly sucked the taste from them. For him the familiar tanginess had the kind of deliciousness of a rare delicacy, hers the tart sweet biological taste of an uncommon woman—unusual in beauty and interiorly.

A man in his fifties, short, with a bald crown and a thick black and silver moustache, had exited his car—stuck behind the damaged one in which the couple sat and the other—timidly approaching the window of Hope's wreck of a motor vehicle. Looking in he was aghast to see the tableau of a woman thirty years younger with her hand wrapped around the freed blood-pulsating phallus of another twentysomething—both indifferent to their surroundings due to respective apathy, sexual ecstasy. And, before he had torn his attention from the moonlit display of licentiousness, the bewildered husband and father, whose mind had been primed for danger, witnessed Stanley positioning himself over Hope, who he immediately entered the damp snugness of—the receiving party emitting a girlish sigh that seemed to indicate the relief of assuaged expectation.

The old bridge, its decades-old green paint peeling, iron rusting below, became the site of Stanley's last orgasm inside Hope—the end of three minutes of copulation with abandon, Hope coming too, in a crescendo enhanced by the foolishness of their decision; luckily, unexplainably, no police cars arriving while the paired animals moaned and moved connected in the steel and plastic jagged aggregation that recently was a functioning machine; the churn of the water and craggy lunar half-face in an unclear way related in the subconscious mind of the male fornicator to the libidinous female's implicit fertility, on symmetrical pads of dotted flesh her pink nipples rigid under her shirt, her exemplary vagina lubricative and hot, well-shaped lips below a nose of unremarkable slopes imperceptibly engorged.

PART II

27

Outside, on a day the sky's blue was hidden for the most part by clouds laggard and swollen, a man with something of a beard, of an indeterminate age but young—Stanley Northrop—was digging in a packed trash can in a city park, children biking along the path the receptacle stood on the edge of, to the left of a bench iron and wood. Somewhere on the grass behind him was a soiled blanket that constituted his only possession. Usually, it being summer, he only used it when it was windy or sometimes at night. It had been nearly a month since he had showered and he could smell himself; for this reason he avoided propinquity to others when manageable, which given his life of late it almost always was (for there was never anymore standing in lines or sitting in restaurants or cinemas for young Stanley, denizen of the world, free among the free, dweller in the whole of the out-of-doors—and there certainly was never sex, no kissing, no frolicking in the glade hand-in-hand with a fresh-faced lass, smiles on their unwrinkled visages. For he had moved on, moved away, abandoned or lost that life, that world, those activities).

He was looking for cans or bottles he could redeem for the deposit, but was also keeping his eyes open for food judged likely edible; for he was hungry, and discovering discarded sustenance was one of his few available avenues of obtaining the energy his body required (another being shoplifting, which activity he generally shied from).

The young man, garbed in clothing he had sweat in for weeks

without washing, pulled a soggy brown paper bag from the black plastic bag hung in the vented metal bin. Opening the balled amorphous mass he found inside four empty thirty-two-ounce malt liquor containers—a fortunate forty-cent score.

Espying and leveling at him a conspicuous but unseen expression of contempt as she passed a thin woman in her late thirties, small high-energy dog on a leash at her feet, made her way home at lunchtime—she and her canine companion on the return portion of their short daily late-morning walk. Behind her some two score paces came a couple a decade and a half younger, oblivious to Stanley, to appearances quite in love, their love new and untested, a mutually accepted fallacy—their fingers intertwined between them, hale faces jolly and cheeks ruddy, casual strides effortlessly matched.

A man who wanted to get away from himself, Stanley was thinking. *A man who wasn't himself.*

David. David Darian. David Darian—couch potato and secret misanthrope. Middleaged David Darian, his medium brown hair thinning; inheritor of a two-story four-bedroom house and a quarter million dollars from his late father, who had died of cancer at seventy-three eleven years earlier. David Darian, his mother dead too, who was the only occupant of his home. Mister David Darian, unattached loner, who hadn't had a significant other for fourteen years; last held a job ten prior.

Sitting in his spacious domicile, usually on the sunken middle of the sofa in front of the living room TV, he ate—far more than necessary and much too often; for food was his one vice (and gluttony, along with laziness, was among his bad habits).

Popcorn, potato chips (cheese-flavored ones he liked particularly), pizza, quesadillas, chili cheese dogs, grilled cheese sandwiches, tacos and burritos, all manner of candy and pastries, cakes, pies, tuna melts and french fries, pork rinds and taco salads, topping-drenched nachos. Washed down with soda or Kool-Aid—while he watched courtroom reality shows, cancelled sitcoms, talk shows hosted by doctors and erstwhile actors and anchorpeople (some of the every episode a paternity dispute variety), detective dramas and newsmag-azines, game shows, local and entertainment/celebrity news: such was his life in the empty house, well-furnished and well-stocked. And as a result—over the last half-decade especially—David had become, for the first time, a rather corpulent fellow. He admitted to himself that he was disgusted; both by his physical appearance, how it'd transformed, and by his caloric overconsumption—yet positive change wasn't an option he felt he was even on the brink of really putting his mind to.

David Darian, who had spent a dozen years pretending to be a people person, to enjoy people's lousy anecdotes, to care about their emotional states, impressions, opinions, when in fact all he had cared about—perhaps even as far back as college—had been getting away from them, holing up somewhere alone. It was not surprising therefore, to Mister Darian, both in retrospect and at the time, that his few relationships had not lasted long. He'd appreciated the sex, and been primarily interested in only that. And, without it, he often wished he had a woman—but knew all he needed to do to tempo-rarily quench his libido was to self-pleasure to climax; which act he typically engaged in while viewing online pornography, of which he mentally ingested a medley, watching such videos often, spending on average four or five hours a week absorbed by the carnal connections of unselfconscious strangers, their unattached coitus usually having been digitally or videographically captured in Southern California, in the land of the shallow and hollow, the uglified desert of the cos-metically or surgically altered.

...A man of middle age who led a double life; who came gradual-ly to lead such a life, despite the fact he was certain such an existence, sometimes being one person, sometimes a disparate other, would eventually cause his downfall. Ronald Royce: family man, success-ful businessman, a reasonably fit and active fellow, a man who often fantasized about young flesh. Oftentimes, out alone, he could hardly help or couldn't stop himself from looking lasciviously—with lust veiled or unveiled—at buxom college-aged women who came within his field of vision. Not infrequently he thought about such women when he had (occasional) intercourse with his wife—Nancy, twenty-one years his spouse, herself a good-looking woman, an individual for whom ideal health and self-maintenance were important—and when he masturbated, which he thought he did more than usual for someone his age (recently having celebrated his forty-third). He also pictured them at random, sometimes voluntarily, sometimes in public, inopportunely, in some cases beginning to become erect but quickly willing his penis back to flaccidity—thinking of nothing or something or someone else.

He was adept at thinking about nothing; he had for a long time been able to do so without forcing or asking himself to. It had a calming effect, that mode of being. It was meditative. Ronald even fancied himself a sort of Buddha at moments, one though who was sexually dissatisfied and most likely dissatisfied in other ways, and whose mind habitually wandered to thoughts of *femmes séduisantes* seen or imagined, imagined or recollected pornography, went to a facet of what might have accurately been called his dark side.

He was, externally, a fairly average man, albeit a man who was perhaps envied by some in the community. But, below the surface, he secretly prided himself on the number of women he had slept with (sixty-six by his tally, more than twenty prostitutes), and thought it a shame if any male over thirty had had sex with fewer people than averaged to one per year of life. Prided himself on the fact that two years earlier, at a bar drunk following the annual office Christmas party, he had managed to talk his way into the apartment of a twen-ty-two-year-old named Shay, or Shayla—he couldn't remember ex-actly what—whose body was firm and curvy and generally like from a dream. Whose face and figure were approximately perfect (who had, for a few hours, existed for him as an object via which to experi-ence pleasure, such as a jacuzzi or yacht); a gorgeous young woman who he took vigorously, the alcohol having no noticeable effect on his potency; who he phoned a few days later, full of hope to briefly, corporeally, possess again (but who declined to see him, saying she had been drunk too, that he was too old and their seemingly mutually enjoyed encounter had been a mistake).

Ronald Royce, who secretly pined for seen or merely fantasized women daily, women who every so often his pursuit of precipitated their being added to his mental list of sexual conquests. Ronald Royce, who felt he loved his wife but nonetheless couldn't help himself; his appetite prevailed over his better judgment. Who worried—was convinced—that one day his infidelity would be discovered. Ronald Royce—whose carnal longings were for what he did not, but every so often could, have.

Or...Calvin Chaulk...a man named Calvin Chaulk. Calvin Chaulk who was forty-six years old; who lived in a medium-sized city; who had a wife four years his junior and two sons, fourteen and twelve, and a daughter, nine. Who had a good job, was secure in his job, as an installation and maintenance technician for a national sense center company—a job he had held for seventeen years in January. Calvin Chaulk, who just now was waking up on the first of his two weekly days off, the personal assistant on his beside table both vibrating and emitting a loud but jolly tune—his alarm; which, as was typically the case on his days off, had been set for eight-thirty A.M.

The husky man, half his hair gone on top and prematurely gray, opened his bleary eyes to the dimness of the room and set a hand upon the p.a., taking it to before his face and hitting the 'dismiss' button with his other hand. He widened his eyes to accustom them to being open for the day and rubbed them, removing some gound from the corners when he did. Beside him, though he had not looked over at her, was—at a distance of approximately eighteen inches—his still slumbering wife of nearly twenty years, her hair yet the medium brown it was on their day of marriage (April, 2017); her face, forehead shallowly wrinkled, placid in her unconsciousness.

It had been a good rest, about eight hours—rarely did he get more than eight and a quarter hours—and his plans for the day, plans he was running through in his mind, included washing his vehicle and, in the evening, viewing his eldest child's soccer game. Beyond that he had few plans—perhaps stocking up on groceries, doing a little reading, likely watching a movie with Michela late, after the game, which they both would attend.

Michela was usually up at six or so, like Calvin, but Saturday in particular she tended to sleep in—though he expected her to awake soon, before nine, and to have started breakfast by nine (for Calvin these days woke a bit hungry, and their youngest always wanted to eat right after she got out of bed, which she would before ten).

He came to his feet creakily, after first sitting on the edge of the bed for a few minutes, not thinking so much as acclimatizing himself to consciousness. Going to the window he pressed 'open full' on the flat panel to the right of the broad pane and the auto-curtains whooshed apart, revealing an artificially lovely day a week and a half into May.

Tomorrow he would stop by The Cellar, as usual, as he had every Sunday for many years—since he had locked his first personal pet in it. He knew this but he made a mental note of it anyway. He would stop by The Cellar, briefly, not because he needed to (for the sake of the pets, their health, secureness) but because he wanted to. Maybe tomorrow, during the same rough time frame he would do some leisure traveling too; but not this weekend any mischief, for-fun chaos-causing—fun with faces as he oft times internally referred to it. A stop by The Cellar and, perhaps, some leisure jumps were fun enough for him for one weekend. After all, he only had so much time, and appearances to keep up. Which consideration was really always item one on his priority list. The thought of which— his thinking of the importance of preserving the falsity that was his known life—reminded him of the old film *The Stepfather*. A classic, a relatable minor cinematic pleasure, that Mister Calvin Chaulk had seen more than twice.

What would they watch tonight? He wouldn't mind watching the just-released picture with Hume Armstrong (action, about an off-world extraterrestrial tracker), but Michela had been wanting to see that new movie with Catee Grange—which, based on the trailer, was about a bighearted billionairess with a loose screw who takes in hundreds of homeless people only to be variously victimized by a number of them—so they would probably view the latter film; an entertainment that, in Calvin's mind, seemed to at least have some comic potential.

He gripped Michela's shoulder and gently shook it, saying "Time to wake up, honey," before heading down the stairs. She had moved a bit, turning her head toward him as if to look at him, a wide grin on her face but her eyes shut.

As he went down the stairs, carpeted with a comfortable beige material, he was thinking, unnecessarily, for the nth time, *Keimut. Never say 'Keimut.' Calvin, always Calvin. ...Calvin. Calvin sounds just about nothing like Keimut.*

Eh. But what's in a name? he was saying on the inside as he reached the final step, before him a sun-flooded foyer opening into a spacious, well-equipped living room.

28

"Keimut the Fiftieth. Please step forward."

The high chancellor of Lower Volfokia wore an elaborate headpiece and a flowing robe of a velvet-comparable material; he stood at a podium looking down upon the convicted prisoner, the man he was about to sentence.

Keimut was stone-faced, in the simple garb of all Volfokian penitentiary inmates, his hands restrained behind his back—the law stated all captives were to be restrained outside prison boundaries, though this was from a practical standpoint totally needless, arena escape being an impossibility—a silent crowd in the dimness seated throughout an ascending circle he and the official occupied the center of, a multitude that watched the proceedings, observed the man of the moment, with uninterrupted focus.

"Keimut L," the elevated one began, "you were meant to be a great man. The history of your line was enough to assure your community that you would be another giant, a stoic upholder of tradition who gave to society all he might. Instead—as we have all come to know in no little detail—you made your story a tragedy, fleeing from your destiny at every turn and in every conceivable manner; becoming a heinous criminal who has doubtless sullied for millennia the Keimut name by his many acts of homicide and sexual violence. A black mark in the record of 33rd century Volfokia.

"And so," he made his posture rigid, an idiosyncrasy he'd developed in a long career of informing those who had committed serious transgressions of their fates, "in consequence of the nature and number of your misdeeds, I banish you—the fiftieth of the Keimut name, resident of the nation of Lower Volfokia—to the distant Milky Way's world Earth, which planet's atmosphere you will be unable to teleport beyond. This punishment will have the effect of imprisoning you among the primitives of that orb, accessible only via special transfer, for the remainder of your days; likely some two hundred of their sun cycles. As a courtesy to you, prior to your relocation you will receive all the information you need to adapt quickly to your environs. You may even learn to find contentment in your new home, though the dominant species—while similar in many respects—is developmentally at a very primitive stage."

Special transfer. Moving a large yellow sponge exuding soap bubbles left and right over a section of his family-size green-blue electric vehicle, Calvin laughed to himself as he recollected the punitive proceedings of another time in a place at a removal of more than a billion light-years. *Meaning you are jammed through a fold in the fabric of space and come out the other side trying to vomit your organs out. Makes your most horrible hangover seem like a memory of licking an ice cream cone walking along the beach.*

The man, clad in shorts and a tee, looked briefly up at the sky as he moved slowly toward the rectangular vehicle's back end. The fifteen-hundred-foot-high bubble that enclosed the county, protecting its inhabitants and infrastructure from the blistering weather exterior to it, was indiscernible above. Within the bubble, as it had been programmed to be, it was seventy-four degrees; outside the shell—one of which covered each American county or major metropolitan area—it was likely, in mid-May, about a hundred and five.

Belinda, his nine-year-old, came running out of the house, the screen door slamming behind her. She fell onto her back on the front lawn and screamed upward at nothing for no apparent reason—happy, carefree, and brimming with energy. "Hello, daddy," she said, directing her attention to Calvin as she lay on the short soft grass.

"Hello, sweetie," he responded. "Having fun?"

"Yes." She looked up again to the sky, at the imperceivable underside of an enormous curved barrier comprised of thick polymer. "The dog's sick," she said.

"Oh." A gripping hand and porous tool wiped soapy water two ways over painted steel.

"He puked on the floor in the kitchen."

"He must've eaten something bad. Dogs'll eat anything." The father, eyes focused on the task at hand, his feet encased in battered tennis shoes that were his most comfortable pair of footwear, had reached the back bumper and was about to begin working his way to the far side of the van-like machine. "Is your mother cleaning it up?"

"She did already."

Calvin wasn't thinking about dog vomit or dog illness. He was suddenly—perhaps due to the presence of his daughter combined with his having been recollecting his banishment to Earth—thinking back on the first child he had killed, also a young girl, his first child murder occurring not on Volfokia but on Earth, and not long after he'd arrived in a burst of blinding light (nude, initially incapacitated by wrenching nausea for more than twenty-four hours, spending three times as long just hunched in an alley so disoriented the bewilderment felt as if it was causing his head to split open from the inside; three sluggish days with his head between his palms, ignoring the many parasitic homeless, ignoring employees taking out bags of garbage, drivers unloading various wrapped masses to be sold or utilized).

He had been on world for about two months, was hardly even established yet, as a regular citizen, and had as of then only killed two other humans. But somehow his bloodlust and aimlessness had coalesced into an urge to take the life of a youngster, a not-yet—that was what, he decided, sounded particularly fun to him.

Opting pointlessly to disguise himself, his body, via one of his handful of by Earth standards supernatural abilities he had taken the form of a withered and bent old codger; a man nearing eight decades who was toothless and behatted; who wore an old brimmed plaid cap from another era, used a simple black cane, and in glasses and thin button-up sweater and baggy tan slacks seemed generally as harmless as anybody might.

Calvin in the elderly fellow guise—which included an automatic vocal cord modification constituting an important aspect of the willed mimicry—had identified a person of interest, a potential victim, walking hand-in-hand with her presumed mother and was following at a somewhat out-of-character pace behind them, neither noticing him block after block. It was an urban area, a store-lined section of the downtown part of the city he occupied, and he didn't have much in the way of a plan but had expected them to stop in somewhere sooner than they did.

The girl must've been approximately Belinda's age, ten at most. Both she and her mother/maternal figure were well-dressed, their clothing new-looking, fashionable, formal—as if rather than being downtown to shop for nonessential items, as Calvin assumed, they were two members of an upper middle class family on their way to church.

Finally, after maybe fifteen minutes of stalking, the duo swung right into an upscale pastry shop, not long after he had heard the girl plaintively announce "I'm hungry."

Within, mother at the front counter—after the two had spent some time looking past inward curved glass at various carefully laid out desserts and assorted sweet baked goods—ordered a piece of double chocolate cake and a mocha from an amicable fortysomething man in a half-apron who stood beside a cash register, chest hair sprouting from the top of his shirt.

These were soon presented to mother figure, who handed to her junior the brown frosted bit of cake on a white disposable plate, and mom and daughter, or whatever they were, chose a small round table to sit at—the girl wasting no time in digging with a plastic fork into the food before her.

"Excuse me," said Calvin after a time in a quavering voice, getting up from the near table he had been sitting at slyly observing his prey and, back hunched, coming over to theirs.

"Yes?" responded the puzzled matriarch.

"I couldn't help but notice that you're the spitting image of my daughter. She passed away from ovarian cancer five years ago. It was very sad."

"Oh, my." The woman's eyes seemed to fill with compassion.

He grabbed a napkin from the dispenser in the middle of the table, unfolding it and placing it over his face. While it was so situated he instantaneously caused his face to morph from that of the old man to the face of the woman who sat watching him, evidently perplexed by his behavior—then, with a flourish, he whipped off the napkin, revealing the inexplicable alteration meant to elicit from the seated patron a sensation of deepest horror. "She looked like this!" he said, creepily, simultaneous to his presenting this appearance to the copied watcher.

Looking into a weird-eyed precise duplication of her visage atop an old man's body and topped by gray hair and a plaid cap the woman emitted a terrified gasp, shock, fright and incomprehension precipitating an involuntary backward movement in her chair, away from the entity instinctually, precognitively, perceived as a monster—her heart feeling as if punched by a heavyweight through her thorax and out past her spine.

The girl also reacted strongly, mouth becoming a locked open oval in which moist partially masticated brown cake was viewable.

"Don't be scared, young one," lilted Calvin in the mother's voice. "I'm your mom's twin sister. Didn't she ever mention me?" His eyes went from her back to the guardian, who he saw had been unable to cope with the cognitive blow of the alien's doppelganger act and accordingly was in the midst of a lapse of consciousness, slumped to one side of her hard-backed chair, on her face frozen the exceedingly unattractive expression of a deeply sleeping imbecile.

"No," the girl managed upon swallowing the contents of her oral cavity with a gulp.

"I can't believe she never even told you about me! That is so strange, and hurts my feelings."

"You look just like her—except for your hair." She looked over with a scrunched forehead, too much stimuli for her brain to rightly process. "Is my mommy okay?"

"She's gone and passed out. She didn't expect me to be here and hasn't seen me for many years. I guess it was too big a surprise!"

"Mommy? Mommy!" She was leaning over toward her stuporous protector, pulling vainly on her sleeve.

"We'd better let her sleep, dear. Your mother has a heart condition that she likely never mentioned to you either. If we don't allow her to come to naturally it could be bad for her." He tried to judge from the child's face whether his prevarication was working. "Meanwhile, let's go wait where I'm staying. I'll phone my sister in a few minutes to let her know where to find us."

"But if she wakes up and I'm not there she'll be worried."

"Honey, I'm sure she knows I'm not going to kidnap my own niece—no matter how long it's been since I've seen her." Calvin had taken the small hand of the intended victim and was leading her gradually away from the table, the lone employee in the back, a customer who sat at some distance evidently paying them no attention.

"Why is your face exactly the same as hers?" inquired the younger individual, looking queerly at the adult leading her toward the door. "It's really weird."

"Because I'm her *identical* twin, child," responded the entity with the face of a thirty-year-old woman while pulling open the door.

"Why do you have gray hair? And why are you wearing old people clothes?"

"I'm prematurely gray and not an adherent to gender norms."

"What?"

"Not everyone must dress the same, sweetie," said Calvin Chaulk, walking along the sidewalk hand-in-hand with the girl he had minutes earlier been following as they tread the same sidewalk, pictures in his psyche of an assortment of her possible demises at his hands—strangulation; a long knife to her belly as warm blood poured out over the top of his hand; in some corner of the two-star hotel he was living in dislocating crucial spine bones with a forceful twist.

The Marchand, the cheap spot he was paying a weekly rate for a room in, was about ten blocks to the west, and the man—the humanoid—was leading the girl toward it.

"For the life of me I can't remember your name, love," said the captor as they walked along on the gray, cracked sidewalk in a voice the same as that of the woman they'd left unconscious in the small eatery at their backs.

"That's odd. Do you have a very poor memory?" asked the child. "It's Miranda."

"Oh, I'm sorry. So embarrassing. It has been awhile since your mother last brought you up. I apologize for having to be reminded!" Calvin quickened his pace, nearly dragging her, anxious to be off the street and to bring about the girl's end; his motive merely cruelty, a desire to observe young Miranda's reaction to dying, alone, unexpectedly, via the misdeed of an anonymous entity whose true nature would never be known.

⇒·«◉»·⇐

Inside his room the creature from Volfokia eyed his soon-to-be victim from behind with unconcealed predatoriness as she took in the room, what little there was to take in, the space being fairly unadorned and dull in its furnishings, layout and design. He considered switching back to his typical, Calvin Chaulk form but decided against it, not wanting to unnecessary frighten the child before he had her subdued.

"How long have you lived here?" Miranda inquired, turning around. "There's nothing on the walls."

This wasn't strictly true; a poorly done landscape painting, large but uninteresting, in bland colors, hung on the off-white plaster wall behind the smallish television.

"Not long. I've just gotten into town. I wanted to renew my relationship with your mother. Apparently I shocked her more than I meant to." Calvin's eyes were wide with anticipation.

"Why are you looking at me like that? You're scaring me."

"I've never taken a young life before. A life as new as yours. ...It seems like a worse crime, than, say, killing a man of twenty-five, bashing an adult over the head in a back alley."

"What are you talking about?" The girl's lower lip began to tremble; she sensed, but would not have been able to express, her isolation and helplessness, trapped with a being that was not her mother's sister after all, was dangerous, and was possibly not humankind.

"Only thinking aloud, sweet one," responded the maliceful other, closing the distance between them. But just then an irksome thought entered his mind: he didn't know what he would do with her body. There were both pros and cons to killing a child—one of the most obvious positives being that it would be quite easy, physically, to accomplish his task. What though would he do with her corpse, to amuse himself? With a woman, or teen, he would have sexual intercourse with the body, assuming rape had not already transpired just prior to the murder. With a man he would take a trophy of some kind, in the fashion of a warrior; perhaps use pliers on the mouth and remove enough teeth to create a nice necklace (a necklace he would, of course, never wear but would keep well-hidden somewhere, among other such items).

Perhaps I'll try cooking some piece or bits of her thought Calvin with a certain degree of excitement at the notion. *I've never tried human flesh before.*

"What will you taste like, Miranda?" he asked the child who was looking at him with eyes that seemed to appeal for mercy, though she as yet did not truly understand her situation. As he spoke he gently laid a hand on her upper chest.

"What, aunt? What did you say? ...You frighten me." She broke eye contact, locking her gaze on the door behind the shapeshifter with the young woman's face and the old man's coiffure and garb. "I'd like to go. I don't like it here. I don't know why I'm here and I don't want to be anymore."

"Don't worry. You won't have to be anymore," said Calvin, eyes becoming those of a psychotic, the hand resting on her chest going up to one side of her small, smooth neck and beginning to squeeze.

"What're you doing?! Mom!" The girl's eyes bugged. "Mommy!" She tried to move forward, past the stranger, the liar, the immigrant to Earth to the entryway; however, she was unable to do more than kick the shins of the man before her, which hurt him minimally, as his other hand came to the right side of her neck and her power to verbalize was lost. He gradually increased his force, lifting her as he strangled—his fingers going deep into tissue made red and her eyes expanding from their sockets, her legs finally ceasing to flail below the pink taffeta dress she wore.

Shortly after her breathing had been stopped and her struggle ended Calvin released the girl (who theoretically would yet have been revivable via CPR), her limp insubstantial body landing on the carpet with a thud, legs bent, one beneath her, and arms awkwardly outstretched. Her frozen eyes communicated her sudden violent ending—the glassy centered pupils seeming to look past the material world, beyond an unseen curtain, into an other-dimensional hell entered moments earlier.

Her silent, tranquil killer stood over the corpse, taking in the tableau, the oddly postured shell of a recent, random girl, almost thoughtlessly, or with thoughts barely conscious. He knew he would be cooking (attempting to cook) part of the child, the child's body, but for the moment felt peculiarly empty—for some reason hollowed out by the anticlimactic quality of the act that had been too easy and somehow for his tastes not heinous enough.

He had reasoned that to take the young girl's life, on a whim and in no way due to any action of the victim's, would be a supremely evil act—more so than his many previous murders of older people.

Yet the state he experienced was simple dissatisfaction, as if he had removed from the world not so much a person as a person to be.

But then, hovering above a dress-clothed warm cadaver, it occurred to him that there were those who cared a great deal for this now-deceased child—the mother (likely currently in the midst of a great panic) if none other—and that by kidnapping and murdering this person, who would soon be discovered, he had done something as nefarious as imagined, due to the emotional pain wrought.

Lips a faint smile Calvin slowly, aimlessly, walked away from the lifeless form, farther into the domicile's main room, coming to a stop positioned before the unremarkable painting of a meadow of tall dead stalks of grass in which two forlorn-looking bovines stood looking out toward the viewer, barren hills of beige the field's backdrop and above them an overcast sky.

Perhaps he had been too hasty, he was considering, in his judgment of the artwork. There was, after all, something compelling about the cows' expression, conveying a resigned melancholy. Something in an unplaceable way captivating about the piece as a whole; it had a unique, dismal, living quality. It seemed to portray a place Earth-like but foreign; a fearsome place where one might find desolation or pain without alleviation. This was the impression he came to, examining the painting, but could not explain—just as he could not explain why his focus had abandoned the dead child in favor of a painting he had initially cursorily dismissed as commonplace.

Soon, having switched to his typical unattractive Calvin Chaulk form—form of unassuming American patriarch—he went down to the lobby in the elevator, then out to a department store the location of which he'd acquired before setting forth. As the site was too distant for a trek on foot he took a taxi.

All he purchased was a handsaw, paying in cash, considering immediately afterward the fact his supply of currency was dwindling. This though was no serious problem. He had a job, which was unpleasant (due to its involving working with the public) and not particularly lucrative, but he didn't really require one; for it was neither difficult nor risky to steal from people, or to steal items to sell, when one had the capabilities both of at-will physical alteration and spatial relocation.

Back in his hotel room Calvin with ease lifted the compact cadaver into the tub and set to work sectioning it with the newly acquired saw. This though was a task of no little tediousness and after disjoining the head and both arms he made the decision to attempt to cook one of the sawed off appendages, taking the right arm in his own into the main room as well as, under his left armpit, the small, ghastly severed head, a length of soft light brown hair descending between his ribcage and arm, thick drops of blood laggardly dripping from the gore and bone at one end of the skull.

As, seated, he looked from the head in his lap that he'd been lost in contemplation of to the oven—the arm to be prepared beside him leaking crimson life fluid on the girl's dress, which he'd laid on the carpet—it occurred to him that he wasn't quite sure how to cook the limb, as he'd never cooked anything like it, anything so sizeable, in the past. And so he figured he'd turn to the internet; inputting not, of course, "how to prepare human flesh" but rather how to prepare a similar large quantity of meat on a bone—the idea of searching for "how to cook leg of lamb" entering his mind.

Hm... Trim excess fat. Pull skin off leg. He was reading, black mirror in his palm that even the poorest citizens generally possessed. *...Tie leg to compact roast.*

"Fuck," he exclaimed, rattling the head yet looking up at him from the tops of his thighs. *I don't have a goddamn pan, much less twine.*

Guess I'll have to go out again he thought, placing the piece of dead child on the dress and rising. *Suppose I'll buy some of these fucking seasonings while I'm there.*

Once he was back out on the street, however, Calvin decided he had had enough of the taxi business and that he would make use of his other (on Earth) supernatural ability; he rounded a corner and headed briskly down an alley. The trouble with split-second dematerialization was that if anyone saw it occur the result tended to be negative, especially if more than one person saw the event (what would that be then? Group psychosis?), and so oftentimes—as a rule in urban settings during daylight hours—the alien was forced to climb into a dumpster or duck into some dark cubby. [There was also the issue of cameras—by the time he'd arrived on world already practically omnipresent—which were a problem when it came to teleporting as well as morphing. You didn't want to do anything magical on camera, nor did it help to be in disguise if you were caught on camera donning the disguise, via a process also supernatural (from the perspective of the humans) and instantaneous. The fact of the matter was that he might have failed, perhaps numerous times, to avoid utilizing one or both of these abilities in front of an electric eye, and one night sometime in the mid twenties he discovered an immaculate stranger in a black suit apparently waiting for his appearance in the backyard of the family home. The identified individual had said, "There are cameras everywhere. We know about you, Calvin. We have an idea of what you are, though we don't know from where. For now, we watch from a distance. But there will come a day eventually when we run tests, take a bit of skin. You will be in a room and you be will unconscious, and we suspect you can't escape if you're asleep." And then the imposter, prisoner, had observed as he sauntered off casually, not waiting for any affirmation or inquiry.] The fleet middleaged man, eyeing a large green receptacle on the left side of the lane, did the former, as typically a rancid aroma assaulting his olfactory epithelium as he raised one half of the container's ridged black plastic lid and, with a hop, bent himself over the edge, pulling himself gently onto a bed of lumps of white-bagged refuse. The lid fell with a thud; then, seeing first with his variety of clairvoyance an appropriate arrival point, he teleported from the darkness, stench, and multi-textured trash.

Rematerializing with the sun in his face against the back wall of the selected store, Calvin Chaulk looked quickly about to reassure himself that he hadn't somehow missed the presence of a human being before heading right to circle to the public entrance of the business—the same one he'd very recently journeyed to.

The automatic double doors in front were about to slide open for him and an old couple behind him when he realized that he probably didn't have the funds for everything he was planning to pick up.

"Goddammit," he cursed under his breath as, head down, he turned around and headed angrily through the parking lot—knowing he needed to find another target, one who ideally had a decent amount of cash, but again having no thoroughly considered plan of attack.

Weaponless, as before, he chose despite the risks (such as eliciting a shriek) to try out the same strategy he had utilized last: the trusty tactic of surprising someone with their own face. Espying an octogenarian woman loading groceries into the trunk of her automobile Calvin, coming in hot, went up to her and—unseen by anyone in the lot—altered just his head to match hers, skin Caucasoid, pale, and prune-like, topped by a curly quantity of fleece-white brittle hair. She had been fully absorbed in her task—small eyes behind thin-rimmed spectacles expressive of exhaustion, the bags below them many-layered—but, with a start, sensing his proximity, her attention locked on to the man of ill intent, mere inches from her. The moment it did she was confronted by a duplicate of herself above the neck atop a dissimilar body; an unnatural and inexplicable smile on the countenance in common, which expression heightened the horror that washed over her warmly following a shiver that'd traveled spinally to the terminus of the tailbone.

Her eyes went wider than they had in a decade and became locked that way as she lost consciousness and fell backward, board stiff, in response—an inability to cope with the alien's mirroring guise again resulting again in sudden system shutdown.

The predator attempted to grasp the geriatric lady as she fell but moved too laggardly, instead watching her head bounce off the concrete on contact. "Oh shit," whispered Calvin hoping no one had seen, considering the possibility of the impact having killed her.

Switching his face back he rapidly bent, lifted the dead weight—maybe a hundred and forty pounds—and propped the body against the side of her vehicle, searching the purse that yet hung from her as inconspicuously and briskly as he could for car keys, then seeing that her key ring remained in the trunk's keyhole.

Shutting the back hatch and withdrawing the keys he opened the door behind the passenger seat and shoved the responseless senescent one in, ripping the handbag from her shoulder and rooting through the stuffed accessory—finding within a clasped rectangular wallet twenty-two dollars cash and another three-plus dollars in quarters and other coins.

"Fuck" uttered disappointed Calvin just as the crepe-skinned woman he'd been laying across as he dug in her purse awakened, every nerve in her frail body at once on red alert.

"Ahhh!" screamed the pitiful being below him, striking weakly—simultaneously, awkwardly, with both arms—at the frame pinning her. At the crotch her pants grew wet, warm, informing Calvin, who jerked up from her as much as he might, of the occurrence he was occasionally responsible for of distress-induced urination.

"Christ," he vocalized and began to strangle the woman, disgusted but also irritated that she had woken, irritated that she had micturated and the excreta had soaked through to his garment. For the second time in a day he choked the life from a human with little exertion, powerfully, his force fueled by his ire, and as he did heard flatulence, followed by an oddly pungent aroma of waste. The woman, in dying, had emitted a quantity of liquid fecal matter, which covered her buttocks and was forced up to the sides of her posterior—nearly seeping into Calvin's clothes as her urine had.

Releasing her compressed neck, knowing his task accomplished, the human imposter vocalized repugnancy as he pushed himself off the fresh, byproduct-befouled corpse and backed out of the automobile, remembering at the same time—the lines of his frown deepening—that all the woman's murder had yielded was a meager twenty-five dollars.

Calvin, a mild urine smell coming from the upper thigh of both of his pant legs, began a defeated peregrination to the front of the store, worried he mightn't have enough money for the few things he wanted, but confident he had at least adequate funds for the pan—so that he would be able finally to make the meal he intended, though perhaps not to make it as tasty as he'd have liked.

Inside the bright-lit building, brimming with brisk fellow patrons, the serial killer from another world found a container of suitable length and depth and a ball of twine, and also (estimating he'd have the cash for it) a little plastic bottle of dried rosemary; then he made his way to the row of checkers, each stationed at one end of a black conveyor, situated three feet above each a glowing numbered square atop a steel pole. Of twelve eight were robots.

Sighting the human checker with whom he'd interacted less than an hour earlier—a voluptuous lady maybe twenty-eight or so with a ponytail of straight dark hair—and not wanting to be seen a suspicious character he opted to get rung up by a robotic helper, all of which were essentially identical: a pointed metal particolored head of black and white with vaguely humanoid features; a narrow thorax like a tin man's, in the same color scheme; a metallic apron that gave off a distracting sheen; complex hands with interiors of wires that appeared able to crush bones to powder.

After he'd grabbed his meager change from the bottom of a rectangular money dispenser at the far end of the checkout counter and the swiveling object had thanked him for his visit in an amiable faux person voice, vaguely masculine, while with one articulated machine hand pressing a button that moved forward the belt and another's items Calvin went with his white plastic bag of purchases around to the edifice's posterior again and, seeing there was no one about, dematerialized with his cooking accessory, ball of thin rope, and container of spice.

But he chose not to at once recombine in the Calvin Chaulk shape inside the chamber in the squatter's hotel—for a desire had entered his mind, of hazy origin (perhaps though it had something to do with the painting, somehow, speculated Calvin, the painting on the wall of his temporary dwelling that he'd initially foolishly been dismissive of); and since the sense center company he was employed by would only test his blood for intoxicants if he made an major error, and even then he would have to be proven to have been under the influence of such a drug when the error was made, his job situation was no obstacle to acting on his whim.

In a fraction of a second his nonphysical eyes had gone searching, regardless of his having hardly known where to look—but in that brief time he had nonetheless located the substance sought: a plant, the particular green one that so many still liked so well—that while being legal in Maryland it was less problematic to acquire by stealing from a consumer than a place of business. He had decided to find marijuana, and—mind-sight of near-light speed roaming the vicinity, both the urban parts of town and the residential areas—had succeeded while being in the ether for less than the blink of an eye, reconstituting himself within a corridor of a home of average size in a neighborhood about fifteen minutes' drive from the downtown hotel he resided in.

The hallway was unlit and Calvin crept along its carpet with a focus on silence, despite his knowledge that he was about to burst into the room on the right at the end disguised as a fiftysomething-year-old with the appearance of an ex-rocker with a lingering heroin problem. On the other side of the room's door, as he knew, three boys approximately seventeen years of age sat cross-legged on the floor, one of them holding a three-foot bong that smoke wafted up from, the others waiting their turn for it—a half-ounce of premium cannabis in a transparent plastic bag on the ground in the center of the circle they formed.

I need to make a habit of carrying a weapon thought Calvin as he approached the door. Though confident a tool wouldn't be necessary to overpower and rob the trio of young men he knew eventually there would be a situation where it benefitted him, and anything other than complex organisms he could teleport with him; and items like simple accessories he could render from thin air.

The door flew open, knob banging into the wall, the boys' eyes all locking preconsciously on to the face of a crazed-, hippie-looking over-the-hill fellow who stood legs wide, shoulders splayed in the doorway, his pose akin to a gunfighter who'd just split an Old West saloon's double doors and stood at the threshold, midbody-level shutters swinging behind him, waiting for an actor to make a lethal motion. "Gimme the weed, shit pieces," said Calvin in the voice of someone who'd been sucking down a pack a day for thirty years.

One of them without rising pinched the corner of the bag of drugs with a fore- and middle finger and lifted it toward the commanding stranger; another however stood fast and rushed at the figure with an arm that became cocked as he moved. Calvin clocked him with a full-force upper cut from his nondominant hand, sending the teen backward unconscious yet flailing, long-sleeved check shirt aflutter, into a pricey sound system out of which a music loud but not obnoxious had been emanating until his body caused its many components to crash to the floor. The individual, beanie- and Vandyke-sporting, who had been neither cooperative nor offensive merely sat and observed, statuesque, the intruder reading consternation rather than fear in his expression.

Back in his simple room Calvin—who had reassumed his standard appearance, who had taken too some papers for creating joints from the blindsided young people—sat in the manner of those from whom he'd obtained narcotics before the painting he admired, a packed ganja cigarette in his lips not yet ignited. He had prepared Miranda's leg (which took longer than two hours) and, after taking a few timid bites, found that he was pleased with the outcome of his efforts—with the foray into cannibalism that had resulted in his lightly seasoning and attentively roasting a child's leg.

Minutes on he was stoned for the first time in months and rapt by the painting, a plate balanced on his lap with pieces of Miranda on it that he had cut from the bone. He found himself imagining, quite intentionally yet vividly, that he stood among the high brittle grass, dry, scratchy and sand-colored from days or weeks of lifelessness—grass that was actually some weed, that when alive would have served little purpose other than as a source of fuel for the cows some ways beyond where he stood chilled, a wind up that caused Calvin, wearing a mere white tee, to become goose-pimpled.

Beyond the stationary animals the squat mountains devoid of trees, appearing more distant than they were, the man for unknown reason present in this barren place found foreboding—perhaps because of the purple-gray sky behind them and blanketing the landscape, rendering all otherworldly, seeming to grow darker, possibly threatening thunder and its sister, shots of electricity that might set the whole of the brown weeds he stood within ablaze.

It wasn't only the hills though that Chaulk was discomforted by. There was, here, an overall effect of the atmosphere that roused in him a mysterious, primal dread—as if he expected at any instant an insectoid monstrosity to approach, incapacitate, and exsanguinate him; or for the earth to crack below his feet wide enough for him to descend, screaming, into its hot bowels—not dying until a thousand feet down he was crushed between jaws of rock.

His trepidation proved in a short time to be justified when, as he approached the large languid-eyed grazing beasts, and the mountains set against the agitated sky, the displaced and undergarbed experiencer spotted a bare spot in the sea of nonliving flora swaying around him that turned out to be a circle some three feet wide—within which were steps formed from hardened mud that descended deep, into blackness.

This discovery, his mind informed him, was doubtless the most forbidding facet of the setting—and yet despite his strong aversion to the pit with stairs he was compelled just as intensely to follow them down into the subterranean unknown; and in no time he was seeing his feet, his legs, as if of their own power, doing precisely what he so feared to do: journeying to the damp, lightless depths.

Soon there was only a slight slapping sound with each footfall; no light, no sense of himself. Like he was mere consciousness in a possibly endless vertical cave, an earthen cylinder that could any minute open unto a profusion of possible horrors.

What instead he was met with following a few long minutes was an unfathomable red light, similar in hue to a darkroom's, the mild cerise luminance showing the contours of a now wide but low, about fifty-five inches high, below-ground hollow—the cave's walls striated and adobe-like, at the far range of his vision what appeared to be a squatting man the same color as the material of the spacious cavity, the aroma of its trapped air akin to that of wet pennies.

Suddenly, though he believed himself to have been soundless, had been motionless, the creature or person he could make out across some distance with a quick jerk of its neck looked right at him. What it'd been doing wasn't clear but it straightened up a little; regardless the manlike entity was short, its head not quite reaching the roof of the cavern. The thing was advancing toward him. It was nude, but while seeming masculine it did not possess the usual genitalia; none was visible. Its eyes were as hollows and at first considerably unsettling. There was conversely a gentleness about its movements and demeanor and when the anthropomorphic being had drawn near enough that he had a full picture of its physical aspect he decided that while it defied logical explanation the he or the it was, to appearances, comprised of solidified mud, of a scaly quality—that it was something like an animate tar baby. As Calvin stared, perplexed, as they stared at one another—the organism's face mere inches from his own, who knew what occurring in whatever it had for a cerebrum, its entire life (of unknown length) likely having transpired in this large, perhaps enormous, cave—ten or twelve yards behind the thing three similar others appeared, the additional creatures standing staring at the stranger also.

Then more joined the curious trio, crowding to their posterior, some score or so, all with a rather blank expression, all practically stock-still. It was, however, a short-lived motionlessness, for as Calvin took the family or species members in as they did the same with him one toward the back—with no accompanying vocalization—made some jerky gesture toward one near and afterward that one made a similar gesture to another and so forth, until some message, some command or idea, had apparently been communicated to all present. Following this from among them another male-seeming individual—who had been handed a small curved-bladed weapon, karambit-like—segregated itself and, stepping into an area of brighter red light, with no visible hesitation but with perceptible (yet not verbally expressed) pain, began to self-inflict numerous broad, fatally penetrative cuts, the out-of-place human(oid) watching with amplified perplexity.

A viscous silver fluid oozed from the long wounds, injuries that caused the mud-person to gradually double over, finally falling to its or his knees in an expanding puddle of this mercury-tone discharge. Within a few minutes the performer of the act, reminiscent of seppuku, had induced his expiry and Calvin found that he was unanticipatedly being pushing gently, by but the multitude, toward the pool of silver blood from which the husk of the sacrificed mudperson had already been dragged.

"Wha...what are you doing?" he couldn't stop himself from inquiring, despite knowing his words would be incomprehensible.

And then he stood in, held fast by, the puddle of fresh excreta, the liquid a texture like molasses, hot, and reaching to his ankles; and the cave residents—all essentially alike, every of a brown layered goo, a number more feminine than masculine—were continuing to stare at him, vacant-eyed but steady of focus. And as they did the stuff in which he stood, being slowly scalded, began to creep up his legs, these correspondingly out of terror beginning to shiver—the temperature of he who suicided's life-juice increasing, becoming unbearable as inexorably it coated his body feet to peak, the man's screams as those of one burning alive bouncing from the dirt walls, to no degree altering the stony expressions of the observing horde.

The ascending substance, lifelike though possibly merely loco-motive, drowned his cries of agony as it encompassed (while not seeping into) his mouth. Inside the suit of soup-like, quicksilver-hued mudman excretion the extraterrestrial—lost mentally to a cheap painting in a motel with a cockroach problem—continued to sonically externalize his pain and fear, the sounds however never leaving his new cocoon, which clinging, irremovable fluid before it could suffocate him commenced a descent, as before at a steady, un-hurried rate.

Cave-dweller blood seemingly sentient made its way down his body and it revealed in so doing a changed underworld explorer. Calvin Chaulk, disguise master, had been rendered by the uncom-mon body product—during the few seconds of his having been blanketed—a, to appearance, mudman like those nearly thirty that stared ceaselessly at him. And with this metamorphosis there was an accompanying transformation of the mind; for he could hear the thoughts of the two dozen-plus placid observers, in addition to others, a great many others—three hundred maybe. Yet, though he knew their approximate number, the number of those spread out across what he immediately became aware was an extensive subter-ranean labyrinth, the creatures—one of which he had perhaps just been converted to via a unit's martyrdom—all had the same simulta-neous thought, and when a new thought came it was in each's mind at the same moment, for the same period. Their community was a hive, their brains in toto of a network; they were akin to ants, only trivially individuated. And while at once Calvin realized all this his psyche was yet occupied exclusively by what the mass was cogitat-ing—not so much a statement or question as an imperative, one that could best be expressed as: copulate with queen.

She was far off, hidden—back the direction the score and a half had come from but in a large chamber that split off from a long tunnel to the right. Calvin, though he followed the multitude, the crowd growing as they progressed—mudpeople joining from every side, from numerous mouths to earthen corridors that led to other areas where they dwelled or worked at the walls of the cave system, expanding it—knew the way to the rotund matriarch via the same mind link. It was a slow fifteen-minute trek through the maze, among the snake of creatures he was now one with—the path sometimes red-lit sometimes unlit completely.

Finally, over the hairless heads of many, darkness gave way to a room entrance, its ceiling high, the eerie crimson light of unknown source sufficient to render the queen they had made their pilgrimage to a well-beheld behemoth.

She luxuriated, something like a gigantic tapered mound of semisoft mud, with a look of frank complacency—to all appearance utterly unroused by the sudden entrance of many hundreds of her hierarchical inferiors, those who were a mere twentieth of her size.

They were all, every one of the mudpeople crowded into the queen's spacious chamber and spilling into the tunnel behind him, masculine members of the species Calvin for the first time noted; which fact, given their/his operative, stood to reason. Those at the front kept a respectful or cautious distance from the slothful giant at first approach but within seconds ten or more rushed at her, climbing up onto her pliant bulk—attaching themselves at the midsection, via what in probability were penises the assimilated humanoid had not before noticed, seemingly nondiscriminatory about the spot along her mass they elected to connect to. The attached ones began immediately to convulse and moan, their previously blank faces now diametrically animated; the expression of each, rather than pleasure, indicative of great pain or strenuous effort. Soon, more had joined—twenty, then thirty; all engaging in the same presumably unpleasant endeavor, minds empty but bodies wild, the comparatively tiny bodies jerking instinctually in their union with the unresponsive queen.

And then Calvin, body propelled as if by some external mechanism he did not control, was among his new family, in the world below the windswept plain—pulling himself to a place that must have been equivalent to or near the amorphous neck of the unperturbed beast and, with a kind of prod (phallic though not a human penis) that had come to extend out from his frame, thrusting inward with his new protuberance, his extension going through a harder outer skin into a softness that was for half a moment pleasing but then gripping and suctioning, in a purely animal state experiencing a paroxysm that too was excruciating, partly due to his total absence of volition.

Emitting a primal expression of distress, mouth an involuntary 'o,' he epileptically writhed on the expanse of the queen's bulbous form. Around him others that had joined with her earlier began to fall to the ground, either releasing themselves or being expelled. Soon, after what must have been an orgasm—there was a sensation of heat in the prod and then a syrup or some thick chemical sprayed into her and following this there was no more pull on him—he fell as well, sliding down the object of attention and landing with a plop, ungently yet noninjuriously, on his back.

Calvin, new mudman, looked up to see hundreds of his counterparts having seizures spread across the enormity of the flippant cavern community's head, her face a huge, swollen, self-satisfied version of the species members' a fraction of her size; others were hoisting their tuckered bodies from the ground or standing with their eyes also set on the queen.

Not long after the last of the fornicators had dropped, drained, from the corpulent materfamilias her expression finally changed. It underwent a rapid alteration in which a glazed countenance of smug, sleepy contentment morphed to a look of one who had just comprehended that a mutant rat with preternaturally strong jaws was gnawing its way to their brain through the back of their skull, and there was nothing to be done to retard its progress.

From each spot where a mudman had unpleasantly united with her, in chronological order of attachment, a small brown slug-like creature now burst like an exploding popcorn kernel, their trajectories shooting them across the heads of the hundreds who'd moments earlier climaxed while penetrating the tribe's leader, the protoplasmic bundles of just-formed mudperson landing scattered throughout the crowd, which observed the phenomenon with awe despite an expectation of the babies' advent.

No sooner had these infants landed, impact softened by their shock-absorbent malleable exteriors, than each crawled determined toward some destination—the arrival point for every newborn, it became apparent, the individual whose fluid injection it was the product of, every odd limbless babe slithering up the leg of its father and situating itself cozily in his armpit region, prompting the parent to shelter the pupal child in the crook of his arm. And then one was making its way through the crowd of progenitors—at their feet—to Calvin, crawling upward, finding haven snuggled against his own shoulder. And as the byproducts of the orgy that no party had enjoyed continued to shoot forth with a pop from the blob that was the horrified queen's body she emitted a long, relieving exhalation and evidently expired, her visage going slack but posture remaining unaffected, some neonates yet being ejected from her post-animate form.

29

B earded, twenty-seven-year-old Stanley Northrop—who in short order had come to appear to be closer to thirty-seven, or forty—had recently gained a wiry aspect, his musculature of late substantially less padded by stores of adipose. His beard was near black, curly, with sporadic patches of limited growth. Its untrimmed wild look, combined with erratic hair, a facial layer of grime and spots dark with dirt, served to make his overall presentation one of a man who'd regressed to a quasi-bestial state. And so he had—his last shower six or more weeks earlier, his last hot meal months prior, his smell a repugnant combination of aromas discernible from three feet, his interest in societal engagement (at the moment irrelevant) steadily approaching none.

He did, of course, nonetheless have sexual desires and by virtue of his lack of sexual activity (except occasional masturbation) sexual fantasies: often fantasies featuring passersby in the park that was and had been for much of his short time on the street his center of activity—where he generally slept, spent the majority of his abundance of time, and within which he consistently, diligently foraged.

Nearly always he was hungry, and he would have been depressed, had he not been so frequently outside of himself, mentally-emotionally. When rarely (before he was able to curtail such cogitation) he thought of his crimes, his serious and fatal lapses of judgment, he felt no anxiety however—and only tinges of remorse. Stanley knew or felt confident he was too far removed from normal society to be found if he ever came to be sought for his misdeeds. All that worried him was that he find himself in prison should he see the day when he was once again housed, working, a part of the system. As an ignored one, an invisible one, a rotting pariah whose existence was of no consequence he was immune from such concerns. Life was day to day, hour to hour—a pure survival game; a game it was his appraisal he was in the process of losing. An average day might go something like: hear another bum or two nearby in the night who was insane and talking to themselves; be woken by public noises around nine in the morning; unsuccessfully attempt to sleep for another two hours; with an achy body and empty stomach and thirsty wake and pull himself up to use the water fountain; lazily watch the goers-by for a number of hours while sitting on a blanket; scavenge for food scraps in the garbage; sit in various places around the park for another two to three hours while growing hungrier; check grounds and all park garbage receptacles for refundable containers, then walk a two-hour circuit seeking the same, possibly vomiting during this time due to an item or items consumed from the trash; if a dollar's worth of such containers acquired journey to nearest store that took such items to redeem them; using these funds buy a 99-cent fruit pie or more from the supermarket downtown, eating it immediately; return to the park exhausted, lay out the blanket that had been tied around his waist, and plop down on it, absently people-watching again; when there were no more people walking to a bush and mechanically ejecting semen into it while thinking of a perky-breasted twenty-two-year-old he had followed with eyes of focused desire in the afternoon, feeling pitiful immediately after his ejaculatory groan; laying down on the blanket and drifting to sleep, situating the blanket over his frame if conditions were windy or cool.

While his interactions with others occurred almost exclusively in professional contexts—he didn't even panhandle, was adverse to the notion, and didn't think he'd have much luck milking the denizens who seemed unaware of him in any case—his lack of isolation had, on at least one easy to recollect occasion, led to an unpleasant interaction with a man of his ilk, a fellow some twenty years older and a good deal worse for wear.

It was night, though not late—perhaps eight. In tattered clothing and smelling of sweat and urine, walking with a hitch, the fellow had approached Stanley from behind as he lay on his blanket, the young man dreading the encounter but foreseeing it from a mile. The stranger had a wispy gray and black beard that descended to the bottom of his Adam's apple, a bald pate, also long wispy hair falling from the sides of his head. His teeth were misaligned and yellow, his voice was raspy and deep, his wide eyes those of a very anxious and sleep-deprived animal. He had emerged from foliage in the center of the park.

"No can money?" he asked, Stanley spinning to face him. The man, about six-two, had stopped a foot from his body and towered over him.

For some reason Stanley interpreted his query as "Know can money?" and, after taking the inquirer in a moment, he said "Do I know can money?"

"No can money today?" the person repeated, standing over but not looking down at him.

Stanley backed away slightly and came to his feet, making eye contact with the older bum. "I got a little. You?"

"Didn't amount to a hill of beans."

"You didn't find any?" Stanley, perplexed, asked him, keeping his eyes glued to his face.

The other chuckled. "I didn't find enough to buy ketchup for a can of beans."

His face had softened, causing a reduction in Stanley's tension. "I assume you didn't actually have a can of beans?" he attempted to clarify.

"I haven't had beans since a long time ago." Another chuckle.

Stanley stood looking at his sooty face and prominent eyes, the man standing quite close. Confusion unabated he was trying to conceive an additional question to ask the person who had opted, perhaps out of loneliness or boredom, to have a conversation with him—while speculating that asking him anything might be futile due to his probable lunacy; while wondering whether the person's motivation was social or perhaps malicious.

"Do they make you fart?" Stanley surprised himself by asking.

The tall man flashed canary choppers as he laughed. "My wife used to fart. She said 'cuse me though and got embarrassed."

"Was she a pretty woman?"

"She was a brown-haired woman. Pleasantly disposed. Good smile. I used to call her cinnamon girl..." His eyes, looking sideways to the left, at nothing, seemed to indicate that he had gone else-where—was possibly recalling a happy time distant from his present circumstances.

"I don't have any money to give you, if that's why you were asking."

Unhearing the stranger said, "Her hair was curly and came down to her shoulders. She had freckles. We were married for five years. I was nineteen when we got married."

"Well," began Stanley, patience dwindling, "I'm sorry that you couldn't get enough money to eat. I'd help you if I could."

On an entirely disparate wavelength the man across from him continued, "She used to read beside me in bed, after I'd gone to sleep. Had a little lamp on the table on her side."

"Why'd the relationship end?"

"Our baby boy died and the depression got to her. That was 1992."

"That's rough. I've never been married, but my relationship ended because I murdered her. Probably worse."

"She cut open the veins in her arms in the tub. I found her when I got home from work." He was looking directly at Stanley now.

"Better than killing her maybe...."

"I would never have hurt a hair on her head!" said the other, sud-denly angry, into Stanley's face, spit flying.

"I never implied you would have." He met his gaze with arched eyebrows.

The man kept his face in Stanley's. "And if someone had tried to hurt her I'd have beat the life outta them!"

"That's good!"

"If some little shit murderer like you had touched her I'd have run my fist through the other side of their head!" He shook his right fist waist level as he yelled, nose inches from Stanley's, droplets of saliva landing on his visage.

"And if I had a knife and you were in my space and you refused to fuck off I'D STAB YOU IN THE NECK AND TAKE A SHIT ON YOUR FACE WHILE YOU WERE GUSHING BLOOD!" Stanley exploded, spitting on his fellow hobo, the veins in his throat engorged, the tendons there strained and taut.

Taken aback, genuinely frightened, the formerly upset vagrant took a few strides backward and turned away, going back toward the mid-park bushes. Stanley meanwhile stood shaking, his eyes locked on the stranger's back, fists clenched anticipatorily and whole body tensed, face red and warm.

That had been, to date, his worst experience with another human being, homeless or otherwise, in the brief time he'd been out-of-doors—about a month and a half. But one of the realities he disliked most about his predicament was the lack of privacy, the exposure. He couldn't help being anxious about the possibility of someone coming up on him during the night and attacking him in his sleep, just because he was helpless, out in the open. And anxiety likely contributed to his not sleeping well some nights, even if he thought it unlikely he would become the victim of a marauding psychopath.

It was ironic. He, a murderer, wary of being murdered. But the truth was being a killer didn't mean one was less likely to become another's prey, at least while they were off-guard, unconscious. And maybe he was more worried about such a possibility because he knew firsthand the relative ease of ending the life of a person who was weaker or unprepared for a life or death contest.

Hope had deserved her demise though. She was evil; her actions, her treatment of him, her revealed past had evidenced that. And what had that disfigured man in the bar, who had also called her evil, said?

He had called her Mary, he remembered that much. And maybe that was her real name, or had been. Maybe she had been living in Oswald under a false identity—perhaps because of whatever the cripple had been talking about.

Her name is Mary. She tried to kill me and she drove my mother crazy, and caused my dad to kill himself. But if the story were true what, exactly, had she done?

Maybe Hope—who was either going by Mary so the community she was in would know less about her or it'd been her actual name all along—had been the guy's babysitter; long ago, say fifteen years earlier. Maybe Hope/Mary had not been twenty-six but in fact a young-looking thirty-two. And so she had been seventeen and her accuser, who might have looked far older than he was, had been a boy under ten. And slowly, over the course of her watching him for months, possibly years, his dad came to lust after or was seduced by Hope. And she slept with him for a while, long enough to really get him hooked; and, though secretly not caring about the man but only about destroying his life—because having the power to ruin someone's life, especially doing so, gave her a thrill—she eventually told him to leave his wife, said if he didn't there would be negative consequences. But he couldn't bring himself to or didn't want to. So what did she do? She set his house on fire while his wife and son were inside. The wife escaped, third-degree burns to thirty-five percent of her body; the son was burnt worse and escaped by jumping from his second-story window, destroying a leg and its housing. The domicile and everything inside was lost, including the trapped family dog. And as the wife was lying half-dead on the front lawn, not far from her critically injured son, Hope—who'd been watching from the perimeter, having a good chuckle—came up to her and told her she'd been fucking her husband for months. "I warned him I'd do something like this if he refused to leave you. So this is all his fault," Hope—bent over her quivering, fetally curled body as she spoke into her ear—told the badly hurt woman, the arsonist's eyes glittering with maliciousness, lips a broad smile. And the man hearing all this hung himself within a month. His wife on the other hand lost her mind rather than her life, going from a long, expensive hospital recovery to living in a state mental hospital, while the son's recovery took many years and included nearly thirty skin grafts; and no matter how many surgeries he endured the boy was doomed to spend the remainder of his life a monstrosity.

Soon thereafter the self-satisfied culprit Hope (maybe Mary) left town, perhaps wanted for questioning as the prime suspect in what was determined to be an intentional fire. Only to destroy someone else a decade and a half later (and consequently meet her end). But god only knew how many other victims there had been in that time. The beautiful manipulator leaving human husks possibly across the globe, byproducts of a capricious machine capable of destruction though not creation, of indifference and never love.

30

For some months, since he had happened to discover the existence of such films by coming across an example entitled *Deep River Denizen* (a.k.a. *Blood Rites*), Calvin had been going through a phase in which he watched low-budget usually Italian horror movies, often of the cannibal subgenre—titles that invariably fell under the designation of "video nasties." And, that evening, his Michela having fallen asleep early, on the living room couch beside him—where she slumbered peacefully, cherubim-like—he started an b- or c-grade contribution to the cinematic output of 1984 (courtesy of Italy but filmed outside of the continent) called *Sacrifice for the Heathen God*, which motion picture he had added to his digital to-watch list eight or ten days earlier.

Ninety-one minutes in length and shot on location in Bolivia and New York, the story began by introducing the character of Linda Johnston, a Big Apple resident of approximately twenty-five; intelligent, ample-bosomed, perhaps five-seven, healthy and energetic; a writer for a magazine with a circulation in the tens of thousands.

Her affluent boyfriend, an adventurer and amateur anthropologist, having just returned from a South American jungle, beds the beauty then under the covers regales her with a tale of a tribe he encountered on his two-week trip that had apparently never had contact with the outside world. They'd seemed a benign people but had wanted him to stay in their community—from what he could determine believing him to be a god in human form.

Linda says it sounds like potentially a fine piece for her periodical and convinces her partner to make a return excursion, with her, the following month.

This occurs, with her boss's blessing, and the two—along with a pilot and a guide—are a few scenes later flying over rivers, valleys, and immense expanses of forest, their green canopies bushy trees fourteen to eighteen feet high and growing closely together, their branches abundant with noisy and colorful avian life, the unseen floors of these woods deeming with fauna often camouflaged, swift, and lethal.

As the lady and man are admiring the magnificence of the world below however the tiny plane experiences a malfunction, resulting in engine failure, and the craft begins a rapid descent into a dendritic sea that suddenly represents the threat of death.

Crashing through the trees, its trajectory joltingly terminating in the body of one, ten feet off the ground, the wingless and crumbled remains of the machine reaches its final resting place—the pilot dead with crushed legs and a branch extending through the front window and his neck. The surviving trio, scratched up but unharmed, push the outer-facing door from the frame and attempt to shimmy down the trunk—the indigenous paid helper and busty brunette managing, the latter's boyfriend though falling at the outset and spraining an ankle.

For some time the three make slow progress through the obstacles of the thick jungle, lost and aimless—Linda's boyfriend helped along by his significant other and the guide, an arm around the shoulder of each. They crashed not far from where they intended to land estimates the guide, and while they trek across vines and other underbrush, under drooping trees and among assorted serpents and screeching monkeys of colorful countenance, the fellow has his eyes peeled for the appearance of members of the tribe Barry, partner of Linda, had briefly lived among.

The group, banged up from their near-fatal landing and without water, grow tired soon—but not long after they begin to drag their feet a face peeks from amongst the foliage, painted with naturally occurring yellow and fuchsia; an inquisitive face, a face free of the lines of worry.

Eduardo, the native of another tribe, sees this visage between the trees and alerts the others to it, Barry visibly relieved by the sight of a member of the people whose name was unknown to him but that he called the *oculto gente*.

All were taken in to their small simple village and the injured man's leg wrapped. They were fed turtle meat, honeydew, and wine consumed from pepo shells, for which they did their best to express significant gratitude. Linda clearly captivated the tribespeople, particularly the young males; while she received no special treatment but merely stares Barry was given a crown, a jaguar pelt to wear over his shoulders, and led after being treated and provided sustenance to a centralized throne.

Following a firelit evening celebration of some sort and a night's sleep Linda was taken early in the morning by a party of four, despite protestations that woke her companions. As the boyfriend and guide watched held back by a crowd she was stripped nude, secured to a cross of tied together tree limbs.

"Tell them she's my queen," Barry pleaded with Eduardo. "She's my queen—explain it to them."

"This tribe speaks a tongue I don't know," responded the guide. "Even if I could communicate, trying to interfere with their customs would not be helpful. There is nothing I can do."

"Can you at least tell me why they're doing this, what they're going to do to her?"

He held eye contact with the impotent traveler for a long moment. "From my research I would speculate...that the people intend to sacrifice her to propitiate their god, which they must do every ten years to remain in his favor. They have probably chosen her because of her great beauty. They would believe this makes it more likely that the god will be pleased."

"We can't let her die, Eduardo!"

"Likely they intend to throw her into the volcano above us. There." He pointed. "If I am right this is their method for offerings. A living person is released into the volcano, which they view as the earthly mouth of the god."

While they spoke Linda, yelling for aid, was carried on the cross up a steep muddy slope by no fewer than twelve men. The slope leveled off, only to continue as a winding path up a small verdant mountain—the peak of which was level with the crater of the volcano Eduardo had spoken of. While the dozen trekked with their encumbrance to the formation's apex the duo below watched the restrained woman being borne out of sight and reappear over and again as her bearers brown and sinewy wound their way up, until at last the wooden frame was erected by the team some yards from the rim of the fiery pit intended as her ultimate destination.

The taut and bountiful breasts of the crucified Manhattanite glowed in the sun; nipples firm, the mounds of smooth flesh of which they were the centerpiece glistening with perspiration. Beads of sweat too spotted her lineless well-sunned abdomen and pelvis, below which was a small hair-ornamented evocative slit that drew the attention more even than the captive's perfectly situated mammary glands, protuberances that due to their substantiality, aesthetic excellence seemed a constituent of the physiology of a figure of dream.

A shot of Eduardo's eyes revealed him to be particularly rapt, and in a short time the feminine paragon's sexual appeal occasioned her salvation, for when night fell once more a native who had grown smitten with the powerless maiden as he bore her—a squat, facially unfortunate fellow with badly discolored teeth; a cretinous-looking man whose physiognomy revealed his insidious nature—crept up to where she hung semiconscious, sore, dehydrated, and enduring the pains of hunger and swung the lasso fashioned of vegetation he'd brought around one arm of the cross, pulling the device to the ground from a posterior position, its crash to the earth, jarring Linda, jeopardously audible. He then came around and began to cut the braided reeds that held her to the makeshift structure, her moonshine-highlighted body damp from the mist that floated through at the altitude of the vertex.

The man—so excited he was barely able to maintain quietude—stopped, however, once he had released Linda's lower body, her eyes wide now with a mix of surprise, anticipation and uncertainty, her various aches drowned by rekindled hope. It became clear, as the ugly native unfastened from his waist the animal skin that hid his genitalia, that his aim was not the rescue of the young magazine writer but access to her, to the root of her femininity. He put a finger to his lips and flashed his knife, indicating the price a scream would cost her, and—loincloth at his feet—aroused and ardent, he fell upon the object of his lust with a wide smile and beaming eyes, immediately entering and driving with fast-moving hips repeatedly into her initially unlubricated vagina; mechanistically, his consciousness ardor-altered, seeing nothing; aware only of the signals of his body, of its one strong signal: pleasure.

He gripped, roughly, her right breast—squeezing it tightly as he thrust, unable to extend his fingers over the whole of it, the other continuing to jiggle with his copulative action—and continued to grip it as his cranium went back on his neck, nerves firing delight while his eyes took in clear stars fulgent and sublime, his lids shuttering briefly so that all he could sense was the crisp night air coming in his flared nostrils and the heaven of the woman's orifice in combination with his organ; snug depth, teasing lips, and once more the warm pocket that fit him perfectly; a cycle of bliss, in a present he had authored, with a creature *de cielo* who was all for him, who existed in that present of mild night and carnal glory as if for him exclusively, for his enjoyment, attainment of a gratification more intense than what he'd thought the world held for him.

And at this moment, nearing orgasm, his loins hardly able to endure further stimulus, a long, curved silver blade, gleaming in the night, came through the middle of his chest along with a great deal of thick crimson liquid—the man holding the other end of it having pierced his back and pushed the weapon easily through his thorax. And the man was Eduardo, who'd used the machete he carried to hack paths in the jungle, the death stroke causing he whose coitus had been interrupted to utter the sonorous horrendous yelp of an animal killed unexpectedly and then to expire—collapsing wide-eyed with a frozen grimace onto petrified Linda, the murdered tribesperson's penis still within. Waking and catching sight of the dead fellow advancing on the immobile, nubile sacrifice-to-be the intrepid guide had snuck up on the rapist, reaching him only after he'd initiated his intended violation.

Eduardo pulled the bleeding nude corpse off the woman he shared a desire for and undid the remainder of her bonds, Linda afraid and confused, both (but particularly her savior) conscious of the village below stirring and rising for action, the death of he who'd taken liberties having roused the whole of them.

"Come on. They're soon climbing up. We must find some escape," he said to the silent lady as he clutched her to him, feeling the sensation of her skin against his like a kind of electricity that surged throughout his body with an effect enlivening.

The people furious were winding their way up the mountain already. Eduardo, girl's hand unconsciously taken in his, was looking about pressed and stressed for an exit, an answer. To the left was churning lava in a chamber of rock, before them a path up which the natives treaded. But behind them, past the cut path that spiraled around the low formation, was a frothing river, its cyan rendered a forbidding glimmering near-black by the night.

"We must try the river. It's the only chance," announced the guide, brave and energized, having swiveled around in the direction of his object.

The two moved to the edge, observing the fast current of the water body and mentally measuring their odds.

"It seems too dangerous."

"But when they get to us they will kill me for helping and tie you again to the cross. And sometime after the sun is up you will die."

Linda's gaze went from Eduardo's face back to the wild ribbon that flowed through thick jungle, her expression that of a daredevil moments pre-leap.

"What about Barry? We can't just leave him."

Eduardo looked to her, and lied. "He knew what would happen to you tomorrow. And even what was happening to you just now. ...He said there was nothing to be done. That you couldn't be saved. He wouldn't try to save you from a single man. A distracted man, a man of less than average size. He decided to continue sleeping as I came up."

Linda processed this intently, her countenance transforming from indicative of crazed flight-or-fight state to shock and sadness. Her eyes slowly found the river once more as if her heart had just been chipped away at. She was conscious of the fact that her nudity before Eduardo no longer made her feel uncomfortable, despite the fact she had seen him subtly taking in the contours of her form with perceivable yearning.

"Let's jump," she said, leading the other, sole ally in a strange land, down to the dirt walkway past which it was a straight drop seventy or seventy-five feet to the surging watercourse.

"Point your feet. Don't hit with your body horizontal. Go in like a missile," advised Eduardo, looking concernedly at his picture of an ideal female.

"I know," she said.

And the pair leapt simultaneously, landing with frames nearly straight and substantial splashes—the river cold, a system jolt, though not too cold; their bodies going deep, although not so deep that they'd neared the bottom.

But then the film cut to what really happened to Barry. In the moments between Eduardo suddenly gaining consciousness and espying the native on the mountain and his journeying up the mountain himself he had dispatched Barry as the latter continued to sleep. He stood briefly above him then plunged his weapon down into the man's chest.

The dying adventurer, curled around the machete, looked into the guide's cold alert eyes, glowing in the night. "Why?" he gasped, hands gripping the tool's handle but unable to extricate it.

"I will make your woman mine. I can't do that if she has you."

He two-handedly pulled the sword from his victim's belly, blood spraying, and stabbed again, the implement going into his heart, after a final exhalation the man's expression becoming blank as a mannequin's.

"I am your better," he added, unheard. "You don't deserve such a woman."

This parcel of information communicated it cut back to the duo struggling in the water, being swept briskly along, the natives having reached the top futilely directing arrows at them, the river growing calmer as the disrobed temptress and her murderous rescuer were carried further downstream from the angry tribe atop the mountain.

Soon Eduardo was able to hoist himself onto a large slick rock amidst the flow of water, pulling his companion up as well. Here they caught their breath and looked about, those they had escaped now seemingly far upstream of them. As he formulated a plan Eduardo gazed more boldly than before at the young woman who excited him, the sight of whom woke him internally in a way that a long drop into a rushing jungle tributary and even killing a man in cold blood did not, whose wet unencumbered form lit minimally by the rising star was like the masterpiece of an artist who specialized in the anatomy. And then, sun coming up above her shoulders, smooth full breasts so close he could take her firm pink nipples into his mouth by merely bending his head, he began not to think of what they ought to do in the next ten minutes, the next hour, but of how they could spend the following year, the following decade and beyond.

"Linda, my love," he imagined himself saying to her, "you know we need not ever leave. ...We could stay here, in the jungle, among the beauty—I don't know any reason we have to go back.

"The cars, the lights, the screens, the noise, the rude people—we don't need all that; the chaos and confusion, the anger, fear. I need only you. My own queen. I know that. Everything else...pales by comparison.

"I could make you clothes. Sew them from skins. I can sew." Eduardo was shown doing just that, crouched amidst vegetation, his brow furrowed in concentration as he ran a thread through an animal hide. He was seen crouched over a cauldron of roiling soup, steam making his brow sweat, one arm stirring the assortment of meat, tubers, vegetables of many shades. Seen hanging damp clothes, those of he and Linda, on a line of twine strung sixteen feet between tree trunks.

Cut to: the pair luxuriating in wood handmade chairs in a clearing, both smiling, Eduardo in voiceover saying, "You could bear my child. We would be a happy family, living simply. Worrilessly." Shots of Linda with an infant in the crook of her arm; Linda rocking the babe; feeding it from a full breast. The child, a curl-headed boy, now five or six, situated between his parents, a hand in one of each of his progenitors as they walked with him among sunlit greenery. "We could grow old here together. Maybe this is where we've all along belonged." A shot of Linda and Eduardo now sixty or so (the brown hair of each a bit gray), holding each other's hands, turning to each other and grinning with deep love and contentment. Cut back to: Eduardo and Linda on the rock, the former yet lost in fantasy, heart beating rapidly due to the pulchritudinous North American's proximity—his reverie suddenly, violently, interrupted via an arrow being sent into the middle of his neck, point coming out the posterior side of it.

The eyes of the stricken dreamer bulged, blood spraying on the shrieking Linda. Eduardo gargled, the sound terrible, his venous hands helplessly clutching at the projectile that'd speared his neck, warm crimson life fluid smothering them; the woman of his shattered trance unable to tear her eyes from him; the natives, four in a dugout, having found them, reached striking distance of them while Eduardo's attention was nonengaged, his companion's back to them.

The guide expired quickly, falling laterally into *el río azul* as the other on the water-surrounded stone continued watching, aghast at his fate and once more utterly vulnerable. Canoe gliding up alongside her Linda was promptly recaptured, retied to the cross that previously, for half a day, had been her home, and finally successfully sacrificed before the cheerful, raucous tribespeople—the misfortunate metropolitan magazine staff meeting her almost-averted end screaming horrifically as the cross was pushed into the bubbling orange lava; Calvin chuckling at these final moments in the dim living room beside his slumbering spouse.

31

*M*an—*I feel like a hobo from an earlier era right now*, Stanley was thinking, eating unwarmed kidney beans from a can with his grimy fingers. He cackled at the notion, teeth mossy with plaque, with bacteria eating them from his mouth at a leisurely pace.

Ha ha. Ol' chompers aren't feeling so well-maintained he considered with a smile, the fact failing to bother him except subconsciously.

He scooped some more legumes into the pit between his lips, sitting in a shallow grassy gully a few yards from railroad tracks surrounded by gravel. It was eighty-eight degrees out but there was a breeze and Stanley, t-shirt-clad, was not uncomfortably hot—though his own smell disgusted him, so foul had he become.

And sitting there, without responsibility, long post-hygiene, in the heat mitigated by the wind, Stanley—in the midst of alleviating his hunger via consuming the only food he had—rather than by the poor state of his teeth Stanley continued to think of and become disturbed by his odor.

It was one thing not to care, but the quality—the intensity—of his smell was causing him to pay heed to this aspect of his present condition, despite his overall self-indifference.

Maybe someday, maybe it wasn't so silly to believe...that someday again, perhaps, he could be one of the living—those who were both alive and had lives. One of those who practiced good personal care, who looked normal: a productive member of society; a person who showered, wore clean clothes, ate decent food with regularity, had a phone, had a job.

But how, pondered Stanley—whose life choices had taken him from low-wage modern serf to transient living outside of everything; even, it felt, beyond time—might he go about possibly having such an existence once more? Was there possibly a way in manipulating people, as Hope seemed to've excelled at? Did he really have any currency in society at the point he had reached—a point as low as that of his worst nightmares?

He would finish his beans. He would stand. He would go again to where he was among the people. He would go observe them, take additional mental notes, even if superfluous. He would study the members of his species who passed before his eyes with the specific object of determining what he could gain from them—any of them, one of them—and how. He would be a symbiote needing to feed, seeking entry to a host.

⸺◉⸺

Within an hour he was back in the park he spent the bulk of his days (and nights) in, lying on the grass propped on his elbows—his gaze cool, his body an aspect of the scenery; his mien probably to those who for a moment considered him indicative of mental illness, though not a dangerous kind.

The passers again were his television substitute, and they seemed as inaccessible as the actors he watched on the electronic box—in shows as old as the one about the activities of disparate strangers on the island on which they'd been stranded together and as recent as the thoroughly vapid and generally unfunny romance-centric *Rules of Engagement*.

One woman, twenty-eight or so, fifty, sixty pounds overweight, light brown locks in a pink hair tie—her buttocks much larger than her bust and overgarbed for the weather in gray close-fitting sweatpants and a lavender sweatshirt featuring the head of a smiling cartoon cat (ebony eyes rendered globular and single-line lips a squashed U)—walked through slowly with an odd lopsided gait, an asymmetrical expression on her face that gave the impression she was being bothered by a bad smell that she could not distance herself from. Stanley speculated her IQ was likely in the range of ninety and her vaginal maintenance was poor, that she perused websites and possibly magazines of little value but had read no more than ten books since high school. That she was a dull person though neither a virgin nor frigid and had once had a dull boyfriend for a couple of years, probably a guy who also toted a few score surplus pounds. That she lived alone or with a quiet and very shy female similar in age and had a dog of a small and obnoxious type that she didn't like to take out in public because it would attempt to attack every living being within reach. He was also aware that despite all this her unclothed body would somewhat arouse him and in his current state he would happily fornicate with her given the chance. In fact he even involuntarily imagined what her nude posterior and breasts might look like.

Then came a helmeted someone brisk on a bicycle designed for speed, a person in compression shorts and a sleeveless shirt; following behind the cyclist was a man maybe sixty-two or -three, shoulders a bit bent forward, hair gray and disheveled, his arms thin and moderately hairy, the skin of his elbows loose as those of the aged always were. He was dressed in a plain olive-green tee and worn gray jeans and seemed particularly unaware of his surroundings, restless eyes in deep pools of sleep-deprived gray directed at a point about three feet above the walkway pavement, his mind turned—it was Stanley's impression—toward the inside; ruminating perhaps on events of twenty years earlier or worried half to madness about a present crisis.

Some hundred or so seconds later amateur sociologist Stanley sighted a lonesome-looking woman of sixty or so going by on the path, a woman who came across to him as wanting, conscious of an internal emptiness she felt only another might fill, as a morose individual leading an existence of sedate endurance; and almost immediately he struck upon a plan—albeit a plan he had little faith in the efficacy of.

The watcher stood, with no plan but to approach, nonthreatening, nonvexatious, noninvasive. With a plan merely to devise one in the midst of spontaneous action; with the idea to seize a moment deemed opportunity-rich utilizing whatever powers of manipulation he could muster.

"Excuse me, ma'am," he said, coming up on her right as she steadily promenaded toward a destination unknown, Stanley's lack of a course of action racking his nerves.

"Yeees," responded the wrinkled woman, trepidatious, turning toward him but not slowing.

"I'm sorry, but I was wondering if you know the way to city hall?"

She looked him over quickly, stopping. "Oh. Well, it's south of here some ways." The lady looked in the stated direction, the conifers of Stiles Square Park in her view, beyond which were the streets and buildings.

"How far would you say?" He was trying to appear, and he judged succeeding in appearing, normal and of pleasant disposition.

"Twenty blocks," she answered frowning.

"That's not that bad really." Stanley peered in the same direction, right hand at his forehead as a visor.

She took him in a second time, with an eye to details. "What is a nice young man like yourself doing in such a bedraggled condition?" the lady inquired compassionately.

Making eye contact, predatory psyche secreted by a mask of amiability, the unhoused perpetrator of numerous local homicides—five in total (or had it actually only been three?)—thought: *Bingo. Dipteran is in arachnid web.*

"I'm, I guess, a less than fortunate victim of circumstance," responded the devious young man with a smile; which could have been read—had the other known to whom she spoke—as the malicious grin it was, rather than as winsome.

"May I ask," she began, probing his face visually, "what undesirable happenings befell you?"

He liked the way she used the language. It made him want to speak similarly.

"I was initially entangled, one-sidedly, with a woman who proved to be a quite reprehensible human specimen. A person who doubtless suffered from a personality disorder. But the sort of disorder that led more to the suffering of those she came in contact with than her own."

"I see." The aloneness-radiating lady's body language indicated she was fully engaged.

"She died—it was a drug thing; she dabbled with those, sometimes in dangerous combinations and quantities—and when she did I was left living in an apartment she had paid for; jobless, impecunious, and distraught. And soon afterward was evicted..." he sighed, "for rent nonpayment."

"Oh, how awful!" Tears, Stanley was amazed to behold, began to form at the base of her eyes' whites. *Hook, line, and sinker!* thought the storyteller, pleased his tale, which partly due to practicality he'd kept close to the truth, had had the effect he'd hoped it might. "How long have you been living in this manner?" she inquired sweetly, inhibiting her emotion.

"It's been...in the neighborhood of two months I estimate."

"Poor dear." The woman lightly patted the sleeve of his tee, the shirt these days akin to a second skin. "Poor young man. ....And what do you need to do at city hall?"

Stanley cogitated quickly. "I'm trying to file a restraining order, against a frightening fellow homeless man who tells me he's going to exterminate me on every occasion I encounter him. I can't think what else to do. He always finds me."

"Good heavens!" cried the stranger, vivified by the sudden alteration in the day's direction, by bold action. "That's it. I've heard enough. I cannot in good conscience permit a good-natured young gentleman to both rot in the out-of-doors among all these apathetic so-called people and to be persecuted and threatened bodily by a man who shares a similar misfortune." Her perturbation caused the tendons in her neck to become strained as she spoke with wide, wet blue-gray eyes looking directly into his.

"I have a large house. Anymore I am the only occupant. Therefore you are quite welcome to stay there with me, if it suits you, until such time as you have managed to financially extricate yourself from such a dire state—or for as long as you choose." She resupplied herself with a considerable inhalation. "I believe you'll find me an easy enough person with whom to tolerate the sharing of an ample domicile." Gently, the woman took his elbow in her palm. "Does that sound agreeable?" she inquired hopefully.

Stanley's eyes were shining, both due to genuine surprise and felicity as well as his knowledge that a show of shock and happiness was the anticipated response. "Why of course that sounds agreeable, ma'am! All I expected from you was directions to the building that houses the city government offices!"

They began ambulating at a slow pace side by side. "Well, my beloved Jackson died some eight years ago now—throat cancer, inoperable, he was fifty-six, rather young for the great equalizer—and ever since I've had a big house to myself...and been admittedly a wee bit lonely, in quiet moments. ...He was a great man. Vietnam vet. Wounded in action. Worked for a chemical manufacturer for nearly thirty years. ...We had one child together. Susan. She passed away fifteen years ago. Drunk driving you see." She glanced at her newly acquired housemate.

"Very sad."

"Well, and since then I guess I've come to try to make the world a better place, in whatever small ways I might. For while I may be incapable of unburdening my heart of a heavy sadness I can perhaps nonetheless relieve the sadness of others, or at least ameliorate their circumstances."

"Seems like a positive approach." They'd reached the terminus of the path and were crossing a trafficked lane. "I never saw myself in this predicament," Stanley said in earnest. "And I certainly never thought I'd meet someone who would be willing to take a chance to aid an unwashed stranger with nothing to offer but his company."

His just-acquired companion grinned warmly. "We'll get you washed up and smelling lovely in no time. I'm not so far. Just four blocks up from here."

***

"It's this light-yellow two-story with the wrought iron gate on the right," said Stanley's companion pointing as they neared her abode.

"I shall proceed to give you the lay of the land," spoke the woman shortly after they had come in the thick, squeaking front door, a rush of stale air hitting him in the face as it'd creaked open. "Don't mind my feline associate, naughtily named Fritz," she added, a cat brushing itself against one of the young man's legs as the pair ambulated from the front corridor to, on their left, the living room—a site of plastic-encased couches and an organ coated in gray dust, in which the sun was brightening stiff ancient-looking mustard-colored curtains and via the three inches separating them shining on the hardwood floor, its slender beam briefly striping the bodies of the entrants as the woman circled the space.

"Not much to see here. As perhaps you have already ascertained it's not a section of the house I much utilize. If you play the organ though have at it." She laughed, revealing what Stanley suspected were dentures. They moved out and down the hall into the kitchen—a spacious, neat area in which there were dual sinks and an industrial-size microwave, a superfluous toaster oven, a clearly disused blender, and no dishwasher. "I'm the one who'd once played. But I stopped having the desire. Haven't touched that dusty old box for well over a decade I'm positive. A part of me I let go."

She elevated an arm, freezing a hand indicatively in the air. "This is the kitchen obviously. I try to keep it well-stocked and welcome you, my new guest, to make requests. Everything one might require for meal preparation you should find to be present within its cupboards and drawers.

"Bathroom off to the right here. This is the smaller one. And beyond that the back door. Big yard. You could do some gardening out there if you chose—down the line." They gazed at it for a minute, screen door banging behind them. The grass had probably not been mowed for three weeks but other than assorted weeds thriving along the lumpy lawn's edges it was tidy.

"I pay a young handyman-type a small stipend to mow both front and back once a month. But—if you wouldn't be opposed—I'd appreciate it if you took up the task for me. Only makes sense. No point having an able-bodied fellow make a trip over if I have one occupying the residence."

"Definitely be no problem doing that. It'd be my pleasure," said Stanley in an upbeat cadence, his eyes locked on the tall stalks of a patch of an invasive genus, its appearance exotic and inexplicably unsettling to him—the plant's uppermost spiky bulbs in his psyche alien, ugly, predaceous.

"And now the bedrooms," announced the houseowner, name still unknown to her new resident, after they had cautiously mounted the stairway that opened onto a landing of varnished fitted-together rectangles of sturdy timber like the rest of the home's flooring.

Hers had the same musty aroma as all the dwelling's other areas. The bed was a queen-size, with a carved headboard and posts rising from each corner. Before it was an armoire, a large oval mirror centered atop it; a number of framed photographs were also situated along the top of this bureau—one showing a substantially younger and not unattractive version of the lady of the house, and another featuring her and her late husband on their wedding evening, both smiling widely, the former so youthful as to be barely recognizable.

"You know I'm embarrassed to say I never got your name," said

Stanley as they stood quiet, side by side, in the stillness of the dim boudoir.

"Oh, it's Charlotte, dear. An old lady name for an old lady." She chuckled disingenuously. "What is your name, sweet prince?" she inquired, offputtingly.

"Stanley."

"Ha. And you have an old man's name. That's perfect. I love the irony," Charlotte said, leading him toward the room he was intended to sleep in. "I hypothesize this is the beginning of a beautiful relationship."

The chamber was ample in area, like the homeowner's, but unlike his host's room had much more available floor space, the firm-looking bed, swathed in white linens—while still large—not monopolizing the length of the cube with its mass.

There was nothing on the walls; one throw rug on the hardwood floor; an oblong dresser, abdomen-height, facing the box spring. Generally, the room had a starkness, a loneliness about it.

"I do hope this will work for you, Stanley. Spare on the interior I know. But feel free to do as you like with the environment—hang things on the walls, bring in furniture. Honestly I wouldn't mind if you wanted to paint it."

"Oh, it's great, Charlotte. Good size." He turned to his benefactor. "Thank you!" he said earnestly, beginning to visualize possibilities substantially less grim than his current existence—to formulate images of theoretical states of being that, as before, weren't characterized by deprivation; lips forming a slight grin as he did.

32

After Stanley had showered, changed into some ill-fitting clothes of the woman's husband's, and brushed his teeth using an unopened toothbrush she'd had in the bathroom, the duo had an early dinner, seated across from each other at an oaken table—a two-course meal of Charlotte's devising that was functional though not flavorful, but that as Stanley's first hot meal in months was like the satisfaction of a long-present unconscious yearning; which while it was only salad followed by baked chicken and French-style green beans with tap water on ice was a reintroduction for Stanley to what food could and was intended to be.

He had asked her what she did in an average day and she had informed him she was retired, living off her late spouse's life insurance, and collecting social security benefits (for an unspecified mental malady), and therefore spent the days tidying up around her house and doing various errands and other than that little more than watching a lot of movies at home, occasionally volunteering at a soup kitchen, and—for exercise and air—taking early-afternoon strolls usually through and around the park where Stanley had encountered his prey.

She in turn had asked him what he had done, when he'd last had a job, before the world desiccated him, before his personal world imploded; what his late girlfriend had been like, more specifically—and he had truthfully answered the first question and said of Hope she was beautiful, but not that she was a prostitute; was intelligent, a musician, an artist, but also a probable sociopath; had kept the fib going that she was into drugs harder than marijuana and this had been the cause of her demise; had said she'd taken him down with her not just emotionally but by offering to support him and then throwing her life away.

That night, his first in Charlotte's house, tossing in his sleep in an unfamiliar room in an unfamiliar house, sleeping on a bed for the first time in some time—no longer comfortable on a bed, acclimatized already to the hardness, the bumpiness of ground—Stanley had a dream of no minor degree of unpleasantness: He was living in a United States that had elected a fascist president, surname Druce: an obese fellow in his sixties who enjoyed some popularity, despite or because of his tactlessness, his seeming narcissistic personality disorder—a fellow who after a few years, using as a pretext an infinite war precipitated by a false flag, issued an executive order that made him president for life, and proceeded to transform the military into something uncannily similar to the armed forces of the Third Reich (indeed they were the troops of the implicit Fourth Reich).

They were soldiers black uniform-garbed and assault rifle-equipped, and with these weapons strapped to their backs and armbands on the left arm of their simple costumes, red letters that read 'NA' for New America on a white background in a red circle, they stalked the land terrorizing and often arresting undesirables—anyone who they could make a case was a potential political enemy or any type of criminal, or an abettor of either, according to some quickly drafted new legislation. It created a predictable general atmosphere of anxiety and many who were able left the country for greener pastures, which meant practically any nation other.

Stanley—who had frequently and publicly expressed his unfavorable views of the administration that had become a dictatorship—was in his disheveled apartment, on the fifth or sixth story of an apartment building, and was aware some number of government troops were coming, that he had to evacuate posthaste or be left at their mercy, be in the hands of sadists with the legal and practical ability to kill at will. But—not knowing how long he had and taking an unnecessary risk—he decided to shower first, unsure when another opportunity would arise; for he had nowhere to go upon vacating his domicile.

While he showered, ruminating on the destruction of his comfortable existence, Stanley heard the dreaded NA men enter, heart plummeting. There were two voices—the voices of two strangers sounding comfortable in the apartment they had just entered by force; the sanctuary of an unknown, a better man, a man who had committed no wrong; who was not a follower, not brimming with malice, not an enemy of his homeland or its citizenry. He got out and dried himself, dread-filled, eyes on the door he would in moments be opening to likely doom. On the other side of it, waiting for him, was a young blond officer, blue eyes blazing. He wore an evidently fraudulent smile and came nonaggressively though unrelentingly toward emergent Stanley, who walking backwards at his approach found himself back in the steamy w.c.

"Hello there!" he said as he advanced.

"Have you ever tried this after a shower?" he asked after the apartment's tenant was pinned, wearing a mere towel, within the room he'd briefly exited—the uniformed man's hand pulling a fold-in knife from a pants pocket.

Stanley became stony-faced, aware of his petrification by cold, animal fear.

"You just prick yourself repeatedly with it," the other said, flipping from its black metal encasement a long, thin, double-sided blade. "It's very invigorating. Purifying. Like the bloodletting the middle ages people would do."

The man slashed at him, mouth opening in a toothy malicious grimace, revealing yellowish and crowded choppers. The blade made contact, cutting him shallowly, creating a crimson line three inches long on his left arm. As he processed this another slash came and another, the dark-suited soldier at a perfect distance to superficially wound Stanley with each quick-succession swing of his item-wielding appendage—striking his victim twenty, twenty-two times, none of the openings deep or serious, in little more than a minute, bright eyes flashing hate as he did.

His own eyes wide despite a mind dulled by ordinary horror, un-clothed Stanley stood in the humid small room, his many epidermal breaches centered between his shoulders and waist leaking but not dripping, as the psychopathic military fellow seemed to tire of his game and turned toward the rest of the apartment, leaving his human toy without uttering an additional syllable.

He felt sapped of energy, perhaps due to the many just-acquired injuries, more psychologically than physically impactful; however, quickly the prisoner of his own homeland began to ponder the plausibility of escape, to formulate means of evacuating below the noses of the criminals to whom humanity was a technicality—adrenaline coursing in him, oppressively aware that his demise or continued life (of some quality) depended upon the trajectory of the next few hundred seconds; aware too that the many sharp-rendered openings, initially similar in appearance to lines drawn with a red ink pen, had started sending up low-level yet cumulatively unpleasant pain signals all at once.

Across the miscellany-strewn living room from the bathroom was an open window, and below the window were buildings—buildings that to memory were high enough to be accessible. And so driven to rash decision he darted, almost without producing sound, from the white washroom to the portal hanging in the far wall, three and a half feet in length, via which mid-afternoon sunlight was falling on books cracked open on the floor, a many-colored afghan, scattered CDs, the right arm of a sofa he had sometimes fallen asleep on while viewing a movie, and a backpack with an important item in it that was the only possession he cared about taking with him. He closed the distance with necessity-born swiftness, efficiency, and—while the sadist and his partner stood in the kitchen talking, oblivious—exited into the brightness and air by jumping (following a single moment's hesitation perched on the sill, the bag on his back that with a sweep of his hooked left hand he'd grabbed) onto the roof of a structure below, a lower wider apartment house, the wind taking the towel from his body mid-leap. His landing was hard but Stanley remained on his feet, began jogging nude along the length of the tenement's canted tile top toward the next rooftop, that of a store for secondhand goods run by a kindly couple. It was a story lower, bringing him to three from the ground.

He managed to reach the concrete of the city sidewalks, looked about as people reacted wordlessly to his nakedness and saw no sign of the blackshirts, and immediately went into the thrift shop he'd been running along the peak of minutes before.

"I need to take some clothes. I was just assaulted in my home by Druce troops and had to leave like this," he said, sweating, to the bug-eyed fiftysomething proprietor at the front. His feet hurt from the heat of the rooftops and the numerous impacts hopping one to the other.

"Take it. Take whatever you need!" responded the owner as Stanley was already in transit to the racks of clothes under oblong fluorescent bulbs.

Stanley reemerged into the street in ill-fitting clothes, pack over one shoulder, with the simple objective to locate his half-sister, Clara, who he knew was also vacating her home that day.

The accomplishment of his single goal though would require continued good fortune; for the city was large, and the time of her departure, her departure point, or whether she had left, was in the midst of doing so, or was still at home were all unknowns to him.

He approached one of the riverside vicinity's many ports—the yellow tee he wore, a NCAA basketball team's logo emblazoned on the front, two sizes too large; his pants, gray slacks, loose at the waist and short in the legs—cursing himself for having lacked the presence of mind to take footwear from the store, considering the unlikeliness of finding Clara at the port, yet intending to look there for her.

Three small vessels were docked in the gently swaying water, all objects of wood with room for eight to ten individuals—two of the group already loaded to capacity with human beings of both sexes and all ages wearing nearly universal doleful expressions. Among them, to Stanley's substantial shock and relief, was his beloved relation Clara, thin lips in a frown, flowing black-blue hair played with by gustiness.

He hurried to her, the boat apparently about to be untethered and begin along the waterway to a site unbeknownst to him; he was unzipping his backpack, pulling a small rectangular parcel from it as he went to the watercraft loaded with mostly women, crying "Wait!" to a worker standing on the pier who had now untied the thick rope attached to a dock post and was about to start helping to shove the people-laden vessel from its mooring place.

Stretching, just before she was out of reach, her brother passed the package to Clara, whose face lit up with a combination of love, relieved anxiety, and bittersweet sentiment.

"Guard this as best you can. Besides you this is all I care about. I love you. Be careful. Survive this."

"I don't know where we'll go."

The saline wet of tears formed above her lower lids. And Stanley watched her quiet, sluggish departure from the city, out north into the undulating blue, unaware of when, how, even if he'd see her again.

And then it was quite a while later. Visibly older, more tired, depleted, Stanley—no longer in hiding despite residing in an America still under the reign of geriatric Druce and his blackshirts—was in a gymnasium replete with plastic fold-up tables and chairs, two chairs stationed on either side of each two by two table. It was a speed-dating sort of event, and the internally necrotic former online government critic was among those seeking romance and/or sex—and as such was essentially being interviewed by a string of women for the position of boyfriend.

The weary Stanley, baggy-eyed and morose-looking, was seated on one white plastic on gray metal chair while across the table sat a woman four or five years younger, about eighty pounds overweight, with a short haircut and a prominent mole. She was talking—describing her family's long history in the agriculture in-dustry—while Stanley, unconsciously, as if hypnotized, stared at her completely unremarkable teeth.

While attempting to focus enough to both be aware of any ques-tion that the woman might ask and to also initially apperceive the question the dazed blitz dater found that he had begun, with an in-ternal shudder, to imagine French kissing the lady droning feet away, to envision to visceral effect his tongue exploring her mouth, her pale carpeted tongue meeting his, to imagine what it would be like to be unrestrainedly exploring the moist warm dark orifice in the face of a female he did not, likely could not, feel the slightest twinge of desire for—despite having been alone and wholly sexually de-prived for more than two years. And while evoking strong inter stir-rings of repugnance via this method Stanley's consciousness tuned in again to what precisely the near other, her eyes at some point just north of his left temple, was discussing; it surprising him some-what to realize she was discussing a time when her father taught her about a combine, during her Iowan upbringing—despite the fact they had only ten minutes together to acquaint themselves with the individual opposite.

The next woman, as the previous two, was also obese, also un-attractive—but as the others verbally rejected him (one of them saying he was too quiet, despite his having hardly had a chance to speak; another explaining he was not her type physically). And then a woman seated herself in the chair across from him who had a slight moustache; was overweight, but not to the degree of the three ladies who'd preceded her; had gigantic breasts; and for some reason wore neither a shirt nor a brassiere, her huge mammary glands hanging low over her stomach (which fact everyone appeared to be oblivious to or indifferent about)—breasts that despite everything roused his sexual appetite.

"You can be with me if no one else wants you, but I don't want to hear any complaining," she said to him within the first sixty seconds of their exchange, her expression blank and inscrutable.

Stanley told her he wasn't ready to make a decision.

"Let me. I'll be here. I'll take you. I will *accept* you."

The man addressed sat looking at her queerly, his eyes within moments soon being drawn down again to her full breasts, Us of fatty flesh terminating in brown nipple pads that activated a primal drive deep inside.

He was interviewed by a few others, not all so strange or self-involved; yet they continued to be people with obviously horrible personalities who evidently found him unappealing too. And so—feeling warm, thirsty, cooped up, bored, antsy, exhausted, out-of-place—Stanley left his chair and walked over to where the one who'd expressed willingness to be his partner sat alone, the chair opposite her having just been vacated by a rotund man with tufts of neck hair.

"I am opting to accept your offer."

"You are desperate. But that's okay. It's okay to need people. I will be your emotional support. If at any time I feel you don't appreciate me, however, I'll quickly bring our arrangement to an end."

"I understand. I'm really grateful for what you're doing for me." He attempted to read her face. "Do you mind if I..." he asked standing and coming around to where she sat monolithic and impassive, then lowering himself to his knees and plunging his head between her massive teats and embracing her tightly.

The sweat from between her feminine outgrowths moistening his cheek and nose with biologic salt, lips forming a smile originating in resigned contentment, he said "Thank you for taking me," and began to sob.

"I lost everything when the New America party was created."

"Many did. I know. I know that you are a fractured survivor of the horror that goes on. I empathize. You have a home in my bosom."

And then in the final scene Clara's fate was shown: long black hair splayed across vivid trimmed grass, firmly gripping Stanley's parcel in one hand, she was seen being energetically raped by a demonically grinning blackshirt in his twenties, open mouth displaying teeth saliva-dripping and fang-like. As Clara squirmed, alternately screaming pathetically with a hoarse voice and grimacing as if being scalded, her assaulter ejaculated loudly within her and was hustled out of the way by another blackshirt, a stern-countenanced fellow with his pants around his knees and penis jutting out in enflamed readiness. And as the supine captive writhed her mouth ceased to emit sounds though it opened; and then it remained open, becoming part of a mask of resignation to the worse potentiality that might have occurred, the end of dignity, hope, emotional and physical eudaemonia—tears making a laggard pilgrimage along her apple-hued cheeks. And the blackshirt pressing down on her ripped open her blouse, revealing a lavender bra he pulled at until a plump breast was exposed, the man gripping it ungently as he moved his hips at a brisk clip to completion—another of the soldiers who had been watching, masturbating, replacing him; and eventually another, the person-as-object's womb viscous with much mingled seed; the acceptance of a destroyed woman named Clara conceived a quarter-century earlier by progenitors distant or dead finally rendering her eyes lifeless, her appearance that of a hideous five-foot-five doll, long wig shining in the sun. A mannequin with a hyperrealistic face contorted to give it a grotesque aspect a succession of costumed boys were employing to self-gratify—frenziedly, homoerotically, half-clothed in the color of their souls in a field devoid of witnesses, too animally engaged even to judge themselves.

33

"How many trips have you made around the sun, young Stanley? I've thus far neglected to ask you."

He laughed. They were sitting at table for breakfast, ham slices and over-easy eggs. "I love the way you phase things."

Charlotte beamed.

"I'm twenty-seven," he answered. "I've never asked you the same question. Though I know it's considered untoward to ask a lady that."

"I'm fifty-nine, my dear. More than old enough to have birthed you!" Charlotte cachinnated cheerily. "Which makes this, the way I've been feeling, a bit awkward—at least for me!"

"What do you mean?" inquired Stanley, fork poised with a chunk of pork on it, fearing he already was aware of the answer.

"Oh, just silly talk. Never you mind!" Her eyes lowered to her plate. "Do you like it?" she asked after a moment, perceivably blushed. "I know I'm no Julia Child. I can only concoct simple things."

"It's great, Charlotte. What you've done for me...it's hard to express sufficient thanks for. Home cooking is a cherry on top."

Stanley was swimming in the woman's dead spouse's decade-old attire, which Charlotte had kept the whole of. He wanted to ask her if he could have some money to buy clothes of his own, or ask her to, but was embarrassed, and predicted he'd likely never bring himself to.

Eating silently, the formerly lonesome postmenopausal woman's eyes intermittently on him, Stanley was troubled by her apparent romantic interest in him, which had either developed quickly or been from the outset of their acquaintanceship simmering.

He found himself speculating as to the appearance of her nude body, and was not fond of the picture his mind painted. He wondered whether—if he decided it would be unwise (for fear of alienating her) to decline her advances—if a proposition occurred he could make himself sleep with her, could force himself to perform such an act and do so without her ascertaining that he found her sexually repellent.

Had she been thirty years younger, if her current body was that of the version of her captured via the photograph atop her armoire, he'd have had no issue—would given his state of sexual deprivation leap at the chance to achieve release between her hairless white thighs.

How he wished she were still young, thirty or below say. His groin missed the silkiness of woman, just as he yearned too for the feeling of taut skin against his, the sensation of a warm other in his arms, of slumbering sweetly with his body pressed to a soft and lovely partner, of waking that way—and as a result waking with a sense of everything being good and correct in the world, of being insulated from the cruelty of assorted unavoidable realities at least until he had risen.

Finally, chewing a last, Tabasco-dotted section of dark pink meat, Stanley made and held eye contact with his host, his housemate—and the lust was there, palpable, near alarmingly so, in her smoky eyes, despite his having been there merely eleven days: a perverse, intense longing of a kind; perhaps more for her companion's essence, what he could (theoretically) give from within himself, than for his body.

It occurred to him—what he read from Charlotte said to him—that the act, the possibility, he had speculated might transpire down the avenue of time would, for a fact, take place. The withering woman with the good heart would overtly come on to him; and he was confident this would happen soon, not within months but inside a week. It was a bridge that would be crossed, for better, or worse. The question was only: how would he tread?

————— ⋙(0)⋘ —————

A few days later he was out-of-doors, bored, walking aimlessly in the direction of the park that'd been his last home.

"Know anybody who wants to buy some acid?" asked a man of approximately twenty-five wearing a knitted beanie despite the heat, dreads spilling from below it and framing his brown face. The man was standing on the edge of the park and seemed trustworthy enough, for an unknown drug peddler hanging out in a public locale—despite the fact that his eyes did not remain in one place for longer than a few seconds.

"How much?" asked Stanley, interest perked, despite having no more than three dollars (given to him by Charlotte) in his pocket. *I've never tried LSD* he thought. *As good a juncture as any.*

"Five for a hit. I've got eight."

"Shit. I want to actually. But I only have like three bucks."

"Sorry, dog."

"Yeah." Stanley was about to continue on, then redirected his attention to the darting-eyed fellow with the backdrop of the site's verdancy, grass close-clipped, stretching behind him over rolling ground to a row of trees garbed in coats of thick brittle bark. "What if I came back with more money? In twenty minutes or so. Enough for two or three hits."

"Sure, dog. I'll be here. Come back."

And so Stanley returned to his large new home, home with a mold smell and neat, sparely utilized rooms—one of which was his room with the hard bed and nothing within that personalized it, this space situated across a hall of hardwood from a woman who evidently wanted to have sexual congress (or at minimal a romantic bond) with him; a kind woman, a generous woman, a woman to whom he owed his recent modicum of regained normalcy, but a woman of approximately sixty.

Finding the benefactor in the living room, quiet and reading something in hardcover he couldn't make out the title of on the faded spine, he asked her for funds to spare—for what he didn't say. The widow, immersed but alert, looked up at her housemate from a plastic-sheathed sofa, her furry follower Fritz observing him from the floor, and said, "How much do you require, dear?"

"Oh...fifteen dollars, if you can part with it." He looked around. The curtains were parted for light enough to read by though the area was nevertheless dim. "I've noticed you've started using this room more."

"Yes," Charlotte responded, a shininess to her eyes. "I've felt like reading more lately and the den appeals to me for that."

Stanley judged the expression she was displaying to be indicative of happiness. "Well, that's positive. Good to see more use being made of it."

"Indeed." She smiled. "I suppose for a good while, possibly years, I might have been too melancholy to feel like reading much for leisure. Now—that's changed."

Stanley smiled back at her, adding her words and behavior to an expanding mental tally of reasons to hypothesize his host was possibly falling in love—or becoming obsessed—with him.

"So. Fifteen dollars," she said, finger in her blue mystery novel, switching gears.

"Only if you can part with it. I appreciate it," he said, Charlotte unclasping and inserting a thumb and forefinger into the small money purse she had extracted from the larger purse on the floor at her feet. "I just need a little spending money. I plan to start seeking a job here soon—now that I look presentable, smell agreeable; thanks to you."

"My dear," began the woman, a few bills clamped in her hand, "your health and happiness is what I am concerned with. Not your employment status. It brings me pleasure to be of any aid I might to someone who has less than I." She outstretched her arm toward him.

"Thank you again, Charlotte," Stanley said, taking a ten and a five from her hand. "I'll be back before long."

"Come and go as you please, darling. As always." She picked up the book that she had laid splayed on the table to her right.

Stanley opened the door, which creaked, and was back out in the larger, brighter world. It was a Saturday afternoon and tolerably warm, the picture-book clouds above seemed somehow benevolent as did most of the faces he saw; the month was now August, and as he walked the young man with no responsibilities but no longer stinking and scavenging for meals reflected on how quickly the reality of his day-to-day existence had shifted substantially toward the better.

"Hey, bro," he said, approaching the antsy peddler standing to the side of the main walkway, who was now dripping perspiration. "Got what I said I would be."

"Sweet, dog, sweet. How much you getting?"

"Three hits, brother. Please." Stanley discreetly handed the man, maybe on methamphetamine, two thrice-folded strips of currency.

"Alright." He reached into a shorts pocket. "Sounds good."

"This stuff is real, right? You aren't going to sell me bunk?"

"Oh it's real alright. Real as this garbage can." The guy with the ceaselessly moving eyes gestured beside him. "It'll get you there—where you want to go," he added, extending a cupped hand below his waist to pass the other a small, thin bundle of folded paper. "Three doses should take you to the place and then some, dog. I've sampled and enjoyed."

On meditation the dealer's use of the nondescriptive term *the place* appealed to him; he liked the mystery of it. *What exactly is "the place"? I'll soon be finding out.*

"Thanks." He began walking past him.

"Happy travels." The fellow continued moving his feet in place, eyes looking in a hundred places a minute and seeing nothing, as his customer moved his along the path, on a trajectory away from

Charlotte's, to spend more time under the sun and among the assorted and the young before returning to the house he found somewhat dreary, that felt a bit empty, even with two inside.

34

And then it was Sunday. A groggy Calvin, alien, Earth prisoner, was awakening, gradually, both he and his wife having made it upstairs to their bed during the night. The sun drenched the room, the comforter was soft, and Mister Chaulk was looking forward to his second day off—to the activities he had planned.

The somewhat overweight man, gray whiskers showing along his jaw and mouth, reached an arm out to deactivate the alarm of his bedside personal assistant, its digital face informing him the time was seven fifty-six and therefore he'd woken in advance of its sounding—which fact made sense given that he had fallen asleep before midnight, and meant he'd slept a bit longer than he would've liked. Beside him, cherubimic Michela stirred but still slept, based on her intermittent wiggling ten or so minutes from joining him in consciousness.

Departing about eleven-thirty at approximately noon—as per usual—he would show up at The Cellar, he cogitated, descending to the foyer. The Cellar, his nickname for the site, was not truly a cellar but an enormous, rectangular storage space of sheet metal; subterranean, secreted in the forest outside town, encased in a wooden framework, supplied with water, sewage, and oxygen by means of pipes, and wholly insulated from the outer world: no noises escaped the enclosure and feet of soil above it and even if a captive freed herself from her bonds to reach the above-ground, especially without the use of tools, was nigh impossible.

The genesis of the notion of having a place to keep living young women had occurred something like eight years earlier while Calvin was considering that he, out of necessity, was commonly disposing of those abducted before he'd finished having his fun with them. And over the next nearly two years he had laboriously worked at the creation of the many-sectioned cell—finding a sufficiently isolated spot, drawing up a plan, gathering materials, and building; sometimes spending two days a week at the place in the thickness of towering trees, as much as six hours per day.

In the half-dozen years since the site's completion Calvin had had twelve, as he called them, pets—seven having died in captivity (only one though because of poor health, the others dying due to torture or having been killed outright).

Calvin prided himself on keeping his pets alive as long as he wished them to be. He was gratified by the feeling of being the unfortunates' god, and of doing a good job of it, determining to the minute in every case if possible each captive's lifetime.

One aspect of visiting The Cellar he was not fond of was the minor ordeal of gaining entry. This was only accomplished by shoveling a good deal of dirt and organic material off a hinged vertically opening shutter. For this purpose he placed a shovel from the garage in the trunk of his vehicle prior to departing each Sunday.

There was substantial physical and circumstantial evidence via which Calvin could be linked to his repository for the kidnapped and subsequently abused were its existence ever to be discovered. And yet he could of course quite easily avoid capture or escape should he fail to. The problem was such a potentiality would entail abandoning his well-lived-in Calvin Chaulk persona, his wife, children, home, job—the whole of the life he had constructed bit by bit over twenty years.

Today, once he had relocated the soil atop the door of lumber and thin steel and pulled up on the storm cellar-like door, then descended a set of wooden stairs numbering ten or twelve, he was greeted by both a smell of excrement and stagnancy, of body odor and bunched together bodies, as well as a view of the darkness those whose lives he'd destroyed—and permanently, given the near impossibility of escape—now lived in. And though all inside were no doubt awake, due to the sounds of his coming down, the moments of daylight, this break in the monotony, the horror, of complete blackness, of wasted activity and inactivity, he could not see their eyes, any of the twisted visages, the bodies aching due to long being boxed in and for some, to various degrees, pocked with sores—those of the bedridden—or marks associated with disease, malnutrition; the self-injuries of the insane or desperately bored or suicidal.

The weekly entrant went forward a few paces and reached up by memory for a dangling cord of beaded metal his hand at once found, tugging on it gently. A ceiling-hung bulb blinked on, emitting yellow light from the coiled U of its filament. White orbs in soiled and somewhat recently washed faces—some of the young woman being more in the habit of or interested in regular hygiene than others—were by lids top and bottom sealed up at once; following this initial reaction revealed partially again and again, until remaining exposed, except those of the few who chose to ignore Calvin rather than observe him anticipatorily or gaze elsewhere; staring perhaps at a wall of gray sheer barrier as if entranced or mindless.

Left to right there was a crouched woman of twenty, her face between her knees, directed at the floor, medium brown hair approximately to her shoulders matted and bestial. Her bare feet and visible lower legs were dirty and she rocked almost imperceivably as she sat perched, buttocks a few inches from the ground. Her name was Katherine, Kathy, and he had lured her to doom as she was on her way home from college early one summer two years ago. She had not fared well psychologically over that time, and for reasons related he found less enjoyment in raping her than most of the others he currently held. On the other side of a chain-link partition there was Charli—blonde, full-lipped, manipulative, but lately growing progressively more resigned, though not yet to his judgment depressed. She had been among the others of The Cellar for five or six months; therefore was a comparative newcomer. He tended to rape her roughly, and she had stopped crying during early on—perhaps accustomed to the pain, emotionally adjusted or numb, or both. She still kept herself looking more human than animal, and was among his better-looking catches, so he was more aroused by her than most; yet her unbroken spirit irked him, and this factored into his treatment when he used her for ejaculation. In the pin beside her was Tera—voluptuous, redheaded, five-six, in a state of abject misery the last half a year. She ate little yet her body mass index seemed to've reached a point of stasis at around one hundred eighty-five pounds. She had very large breasts and sometimes, in the past, when she was not so given up—which reflected in her looks—he would rub his crotch in her face, pressing his groin into it via forward pressure to the back of her head, though never going so far as to attempt to force fellatio, for fear of her injuring him (despite their both knowing this would result in her, probably awful, demise). Calvin had intercourse with her somewhat frequently at first, even favoring her the first few weeks; but now, rarely. She read as too internally dead. Her internment stood at sixteen, seventeen months.

Further right was Willow, with curly light brown hair and eyes hazel, perky small breasts and a pleasantly snug vagina—which captive he raped often and had for the almost three years of her occupancy (though typically miscarriages due to poor health were the result of incidental impregnation twice she had had his baby come to term, the infants being summarily thrown away). Who rather than resigned was by comparison full of life; likely determined to live—regrettably, as the twenty-one-year-old would only so long as allowed, as it pleased her god and master, the monster Keimut, keeping her secreted in stale darkness below feet of earth and padlocked within multiple boxes of steel.

And then there was his long-timer, Bree, five-year resident, long ago lost completely to madness. Bree, raven-haired and slim, who engaged in picking behavior and regularly had outbursts; who raved and paced but other times was an internalized statue. Who he still forced himself on with semi-regularity but only as part of her torture regimen, not due to any measure of surviving attraction—spitting in her face when he was inside her. Bree from hundreds of miles south, whom he had three years or so ago decided to utilize for torture (physical, emotional) rather than mainly for sex; her selection being based upon his tired familiarity with her but also because she possessed traits—some passive, some willful—that roused inside Calvin a desire to victimize her, differently, with more focus, augmented cruelty; to see when, how she would break (as she had), how she would continue breaking. As an interpersonal experiment of the blackest sort, his no-boundaries long-term experiment in the woods.

As he watched Bree, head bent, clawing at her right forearm, oily hair obscuring the pallid skin of her forehead—observed the woman, twenty-four or twenty-five now, that he'd brought to and past mental collapse merely because it was possible, for his amusement—he determined that he would first relieve himself within Tera, as it'd been months, and then think of some short-lived form of torment for Bree, who scared him a bit but who he nonetheless terrorized relentlessly; partly driven, he speculated, by a curiosity as to how she might further respond to the bodily and psychic stresses of ongoing abuse of all kinds. Then, having finished with the two, everyone would get their time with the sponge. And he'd go back up for their week's worth of food to be rationed—this time, as often, white rice and refried beans, a loaf of bread—and their jug of water each. Enough water that they were unlikely to become thirsty, if they managed it well; but not enough food that they wouldn't experience hunger every day, or be sustenance-less toward the seventh.

The girls' enclosures had crude toilets but neither sink nor shower; however, there was a simple shower at his posterior, a spigot over a plastic tub as well, and he turned his back to the imprisoned, Willow along with Charli watching him, and turned the water on—its cool flow being caught by the tub below, in which a yellow sponge began to float. He approached the redhead's pin, dripping sponge in hand. She turned her head to follow his movements with eyes drained of vitality in a face gone white, the skin around the eyes gray and cut by thin lines as those of an insomniac.

"What're you going to her for?" called out Charli, not jealous but as ever trying to work an angle, to make her nemesis develop at length some emotional connection that he never would. "Not in the mood for a hard fuck today? You know I'm good for it."

He made long eye contact. "Got some of your vigor back lately, Charli?" he inquired, squinting suspiciously.

"Maybe I want you in me, baby," she replied, attempting seductiveness. "Maybe I like the way you do it to me."

"I'm not sure you like anything anymore," said Calvin, unlocking the cage beside hers and going in, Tera not moving from her position seated on the ground but staring up at him warily. "Keep fucking with me though and I'll give you something besides a dicking." He laughed.

"Been a while, huh?" he said to a blank face from which no response issued, the addressed slowly undressing, as he massaged his penis through his pants.

Now standing, the young woman removed her underwear—which along with her other clothes, and everyone else's, the being from Volfokia periodically replaced with items from the large corporation department store in town—and nude and motionless, situated a foot in front of Calvin, her eyes set on a point on his upper thorax, he handed her the sponge.

Her captor continued to stroke and tug gently at his member as Tera cleaned herself thoroughly, unselfconsciously; eyes sparkless, sickly visage a phlegmatic mask—the weekly sponge bath a respite from her accumulated foulness that she no longer, conscious of the static bleakness of her reality, looked forward to.

Efficiently completing her task she returned the wet item to the hand of the other, who had unzipped his fly, pulled his protuberance from his trousers, and was masturbating with slow precision while staring at the middle of the woman's body from pink-nippled breasts to V of wayward dark orange hair atop two white plump thighs.

He threw the sponge behind him into the sink. "Turn around," was the command the captive seemed to await, the long-caged one complying (existence reduced to an animal one, her only functions to act as a vessel for the pleasure of he who'd imprisoned her and survive hopelessly), revealing round ivory buttocks Calvin gripped by the sides, steadying, the probing head of the manlike entity yet accustomed to entering her fast finding the envelope of flesh it sought, her womanhood moistening around him as he thrust toward the accomplishment of his task.

In a few minutes Calvin was groaning primally, semen being ejected from one body to another; and seconds after his spasms ceased he pushed Tera forward, sliding her free of his red append-age, a line of sweat globules having formed along the crest of his forehead.

The woman remained turned away, her priority not to glimpse the face of the creature that had again aggravated the nightmarish situation she knew as actuality. Who repeatedly, during an intermi-nably long period she had not been trying to measure, had violated even the sanctity of the inside of her body. Who while endlessly de-priving her of family, friends, a partner, goals, a raison d'etre, would also sometimes deprive her of the freedom to choose who could par-ticipate with her in an act that was meant to be something entirely different.

And as she was processing this latest crime, more physically than psychologically, Calvin was opening the pin of the most unfortunate of them all, his exposure reversed, perspiration wiped by the back of a hand.

He didn't really have any tools with him he was thinking, There was a lighter in the glove box. He could use that. But then he'd re-ally have to restrain her first, which he wasn't prepared for and didn't want to. And he didn't much like contributing to her scars anymore. There were plenty from him. Not that he felt bad; he just didn't want her to be a physical monster. Already she was one internally. And he was sure she always would be, even if her life were not to end within his handmade dungeon. She was a ruin, more so than the others. He was a god of destruction. Whatever he might create had as its purpose, its end, reduction, decimation. Chaos, unjustifiable cruelty.

She had not looked up or ceased to self-mutilate, gradually, with unclipped nails, dirt lodged deeply beneath them, when he'd entered—nor had Calvin solidified any plan. Merely he had resolved not to contribute any new marks, testaments of pain, to her frail, much-injured shell.

Bree was not substantially, he knew, out of touch with reality, though she was certainly disturbed. The girl was aware of his standing before her, cold orbs locked in placid observation of her psychotic behavior, just as she was doubtless aware that soon, in the near seconds—for some span, of some kind—pain would come; and she would take it as she had for years: as an abuse absorbent; stoically; retreating inside herself away from site of contact, her location within the world, from her world of the cell.

35

Quiet in his still unpersonalized room, Stanley unwrapped the fifteen-dollar bit of paper he had purchased two days prior but only recently remembered he possessed; gazing down at its contents, was thankful there was something inside, something that appeared to be what he'd paid for. It was an oblong strip of absorbent material, white, without design, sectioned into thirds by perforation.

Smiling, almost thoughtlessly, anxious to discover whether the rectangle contained potency or disappointment—and if the former what the quality of the mental excursion would be—the young man, sitting on the edge of the large bed, popped the whole into his mouth then plopped backwards onto the mattress, anticipation sending visceral waves that felt electric throughout his body, legs still hanging off the edge. Eyes directed at the stippled ceiling, happiness yet forming his lips into its indication, within minutes there was a knock at the door.

The recollection that the day before Charlotte had had a new television delivered and placed in the living room, which she'd rearranged to accommodate it, raced across Stanley's mind ("I thought about how you communicated to me you were in no small measure a cinephile," she'd said. "So I decided to visit the electronics section of a nearby department store, where I chose an apparatus to view films via, along with of course a DVD player—since I, unlike most, had no such devices in my home").

"Yes?" he responded to the sound's entreaty, conscious of a

slight dread.

"Sorry to bother you, dear. Hope you're not busy," she said on the other side of the opening. "Remember how I told you my favorite picture, going back to when I was wee, was a John Wayne one called *Hondo*? Well, I didn't mention earlier I obtained a copy along with the other items while I was out yesterday." Listening, Stanley sighed. "And...I was wondering, sweetness"—at this word the addressed cringed—"if the handsome young man within my walls mightn't be willing to and interested in sitting down to watch it with me this evening, at his soonest convenience? I myself haven't seen it for some time—five years easily. And I know you informed me you'd viewed nearly none of his oeuvre."

He rolled his eyes, returned his upper body to the vertical position. "Sounds great, Charlotte. You are always thoughtful. I'll be out and down momentarily."

"You're a handsome young gentleman, Stanley I-Don't-Know-Your-Last-Name. I truly enjoy having you here. The isolation I experienced in this large house prior to your habitation was honestly quite oppressive. It had been wearing on me for years. Making me I daresay ill. Emotionally ill—from prolonged social-emotional deprivation. I wanted to share that with you."

Stanley had just sat down beside her in the living room. *Christ*, he thought. *You're pathetic. You're kind of scaring me.* But the truth—a truth he was aware of—was that he actually didn't find her pathetic. He understood, could relate to, her loneliness. Could understand wanting what (who) you might not have. Knew that being chronically alone could come to be oppressive, could led to mental poor health. For the human being was, by and large, a social animal, no matter that humans were capable of substantive heinousness toward their own kind.

Neither was he frightened by her emotionality, her openness. She was not an alarming woman, in any sense; and he would have been largely indifferent to her feelings, her expression of them, if not for the fact that he worried non-reciprocation was likely to have negative repercussions for him apropos of his housing situation, his being in her hands.

"My last name's Northrop," he said.

"Oh! Wonderful to finally discover this," responded Charlotte mirthfully, gleaming. "Mine's so dull, young sir. It's Owens."

"Good to get to know you better, Missus Owens." Stanley smiled winsomely.

She beamed. "Ready, sweetheart?" she asked. "The film's already in the mechanism drawer."

"Do proceed," said Stanley, still smiling.

"John Wayne—the Duke—is my all-time favorite actor," she said, to no response, as the opening credits began to roll. "I've seen most of his films. And there's a multitude. Maybe near a hundred."

"Hmm," he said, not looking forward to the next ninety minutes to two hours. "I like movies, but when it comes to Wayne's work I'm quite uneducated. It's partly because I've really seen few Westerns."

He remembered then, as he was intermittently, about the acid he'd ingested—and the quite significant question formed in his mind of whether it was going to be an unpleasant experience being under the drug's strong influence while engaged in an activity he didn't want to be. And next he wondered, knowing it didn't take long, how soon he could expect to start to feel the effects.

Who is this old woman? Stanley found himself asking, not really knowing what he meant, looking every few minutes furtively over at her, not long after the movie had commenced—its beginning section having to do with the character (akin to all the star's characters, to Stanley's knowledge) making the acquaintanceship of a woman and child living on the frontier.

He found himself comparing his lack of attraction to her to his lack of attraction to the twenty-some years younger actress of the film, despite his knowledge he thought Charlotte pretty at the same age.

His awareness of his absence of sexual feelings for her was not new to him; but what was it he was trying to ascertain about her by asking who she was? Was it secrets he sought to know, of the unique organism she was, that perchance none had ever known? Did he want, despite his romantic disinterest, to discover all he or anyone theoretically might about the woman in the large house with the dead family, whose loneliness he had been brought into the home to assuage?

On the screen, Stanley barely consciously absorbing this, Wayne went in for a closed-mouth kiss, the blonde lone mom allowing it but not kissing back. "You remind me of my late wife" or something similar he said in the seconds before his bold action. Just then, Stanley seeing peripherally, Charlotte closed the ten or twelve inches between them, stared at her guest's profile a moment, and then brought her face around to kiss him.

He was surprised, the widening of his eyes betrayed this, and internally repelled to a degree by the mere glimpsing of her lined lips-puckered countenance, though the room was dark, from so close a distance.

Then the lips made contact. They felt dry toward the outside, wet toward the inside. Her lips were thin but there was substantive pressure to her kiss, and Charlotte's mouth being fully, firmly on his own, almost forcing his head back, caused him to want to beat a fast inner retreat; only what happened—quite unexpectedly, embarrassing him, the fact of it undeniable—was a quick firming up of his penis into a wholly viable erection. And this reaction was a worse reality due to the fact the homeowner's hand was draped over his thigh and felt movement, and so her fingers moved slowly up to the throb within his pants as she held her lips to his—tongue timidly opening his mouth, her hand concurrently coming to lightly grip his inexplicably awakened appendage, her attention to it and likely the fact of her tongue seemingly drawing more blood to the organ, red-pink and pulsing beneath fabric that had once been on the body of the woman's husband, housed many years in a cemetery.

Indeed Stanley's half-conscious speculation—while his manhood was held by a dim-lit quasi-geriatric probing him orally—was that his physical response was due to the unexpected aggressiveness, confidence, her pure desire; this paired with his months-long sexual deprivation. It occurred to him too that Charlotte, still evidently a being of such wants, had herself been so deprived for exponentially longer; and as this thought traveled through his brain a bony hand, its small blue veins hidden by the dark, unzipped his fly, retracting the erection, warm in the warmth of her palm.

"Wait," said Stanley, not expecting himself to speak, or to act at all, as he put his hand around hers on his penis and directed it away. "I just want to watch this movie right now. Maybe later...we can do this."

She looked into his eyes with her wide, uncomprehending own, their blue-gray hue lost in the dark.

"I haven't thought about you in that way. And I will have to—have to consider my feelings—before I would feel...comfortable interacting with you like that." He faced back toward the TV, Wayne dismounting a horse at some sort of military base, large tents everywhere and men with substantial moustaches in creased tan hats.

"Okay," Charlotte, much quieter than was her habit, said and turned to face the same.

He sensed his action, spontaneous, unconsidered, had been unwise, that he had hurt his benefactor's feelings; yet, acid kicking in in a fuller, unignorable way, he felt himself sinking into a pleasant state of acceptance of his behavior, his life as a whole. He was in the right. He was in control of his destiny. And, maybe, now, he would direct his life down a desirable path, pilot himself toward a mysterious though felicitous future.

But—his mind seemed to at once shift gears on him—what if she, an aged, unattractive woman who lived in a stuffy palatial house, was exactly what he deserved; just as someone as attractive as Hope had been what he'd perhaps deserved but only if she was a sociopath and a peddler of her flesh, as he had discovered her to be. What if, for some reason, Charlotte was his destiny, as the other woman, the life-destroying one, had been? Because someone like Stanley did not get to be with someone good, generally a correct fit for him; because his correct was a person there was something wrong with, whether it was that they were not attractive to him or that they'd sit on anyone's penis who had a hundred dollars in their pocket. And as Stanley pondered this possibility, though not understanding what exactly was wrong with him—thinking maybe he would make himself available to his admirer seated beside him, for the sake of sexual release if not just general resignation to being with undesirable partners—he suddenly was struck by a lower intestinal sensation that told him he immediately needed to evacuate his bowels.

"I'll be back soon," he said without looking at her as he rose and headed to the back bathroom, a mass of refuse feeling as if it'd been released from a higher point in his body and now was barely being kept from emission via his consciously sealed anus in one foul amorphous pile.

⸺◦⟨◉⟩◦⸺

In the bathroom the discharge was repellent, substantial, immediate. His mind was at first on the feeling of the repugnant semi-solid product of his body coming out of it, on its businesslike release of odorous ooze; then on the essence, the composition, of the stuff itself. But he noticed his skin had gained a very strange quality; it was overly responsive to touch—he gently poked his forearm and a number of nerves seemed to leap to life. He brushed his palm over the tops of the small brown hairs there and a shock of stimulation was sent up his spine—an unpleasant sensation, one of a nervous system that without permission had had its controls adjusted, set to hyper-responsivity.

The feces came out of him all at once, in a tapered pile, and when he realized he was sitting above it on an open opal for no reason thinking about his arm he began wiping, conscious as never before of the unalterable fact of his animality, the disgustingness of his nature as a beast.

When after what seemed an abnormally long time for the act he journeyed back to the living room—finding that Charlotte had paused the film and been sitting in darkness, probably thinking of him—Stanley lowered himself to the temporary parking place that was the couch, the feel of its plastic skin an unusual tactile experience for him. It now, the insulated furniture, was sticky, out of place, and there was a textural intensity to it. It seemed to grip him, hold him there, matter of an extraterrestrial or supernatural nature, maybe even sentient, but its action and effects definitely unwelcome.

Three hits was maybe too much said Stanley in his mind, his internal voice sounding slurred, drawn long.

He looked over at the woman beside him who, blue-lit, he found to be back to looking at him intermittently, though a second after their eyes connected she returned her questioning gaze to the television screen.

Stanley directed his own eyes to the same; however, what he saw no longer made any sense. It was a visual puzzle, and its confusing nature rendered his experience of the world unpleasant in short order, for the movie seemed an enigma he would never unravel.

It, the movie *Hondo*, had become its own reality, one that Stanley could not be sure was fictional; a window to cowboy hat- and feathered headdress-sporting stern-faced one-dimension electronic people who seemed to speak another tongue and he judged could not be processed in any truthful way unless they stepped through their world of old, distant color in the box into the dark room with him and the sixty-year-old whose lips were a half-inch parted and moist eyes divulged her nonengagement with her favorite piece of cinema.

It might not be so bad the young man thought, glancing quickly over again at his housemate, as a wave of general sexual longing passed through his body, brain to toes.

She has what I the animal long for he further cogitated darkly. *You could just give in. Could just kiss her now. Scoot a bit, lean over, press your lips to hers.*

Charlotte would be all receptivity. Would probably be sexually at your disposal within minutes. She would open her legs and maybe could, would, even be wet. You could get hard. Could eject the seed built up in you. You could groan and scream ejaculating it. Only in the next seconds feeling ashamed of your actions. After you had purged.

Maybe she isn't even real. Maybe she is entirely a figment of your mind, like that alien shapeshifter, the seventeen-year-old who kills skunks.

Maybe I am the mental invention of a godlike entity, who made me godlike similarly, on a smaller scale, in its mind. ...How can I really be sure I am alive? wondered Stanley, sitting on a squeaky plastic-covered sofa beside the woman who was newly a significant part of his life, John Wayne, visage grim, speaking from a glowing cube, but not to him.

And he began thinking, perhaps simply due to the substance that had altered him psychologically, of the lyrics to a song by the artist Peck he liked but did not understand at all. In fact he remembered very little of the lyrics, though they—the ineffable feeling or conception they stirred in him; or was it merely that they stirred his imagination?—were what he primarily liked about the song, a song from the nineties. One of the couple of verses he did remember went something like: *In the era of monkeys I was an ape.*

But wait—isn't that like saying "In the time of humans I was a person"? What's he saying? pondered Stanley, sunk into the sofa, his buttocks and whole being progressively, unperceivably, going deeper into it—time no longer real but affecting all despite this.

The other part that'd stuck in his mind was something along the lines of: *And my time is a bit of beeswax cascading down on a termite/ that's coughing up splinters.*

My time is a bit of beeswax... What the fuck did that mean? What was his time? What exactly was time? Merely make-believe—just a utilitarian construct?

But maybe he couldn't break the sentence into parts, maybe it didn't make sense that way and to comprehend the lyric he had to analyze it in its entirety. ....*My time is a bit of beeswax cascading down on a termite that's coughing up splinters.* Why would time be wax though? Never mind that time meant nothing to him anymore or currently, that its concept was beyond him or nonsensical—why would one equate the notion of time with a substance produced by bees from a number of special glands for the purpose of storing honey and in-sulating young? ...Forget it: time is wax, but liquid wax that's falling onto an insect—a wood-eating insect hacking up its food. So...time is: the strange symphony of life, all of which is interconnected. But why would the wood-eater be physically rejecting that which it is designed to consume? Perhaps just for the reason that a person can (and people sometimes do) choke on a bologna sandwich. Because bad things randomly, albeit logically, happen in life. Because nature is cruel and existence a struggle. Therefore: the construct *time*, the nonphysical infinite arena during which all that ever has happened or will happen occurs, is one with all that does occur—the ongo-ing, presumably never-ending, all-correlated reality of that which is; the whole of the unfathomable indifferent universe. Made sense, he thought; although he felt fairly certain the lyrics he could not recall (which was the bulk of them) pointed to a different meaning entirely, probably one that was not nearly so broad, yet perhaps was esoteric or abstruse.

No sooner had he devised an explanation, whether correct or utterly baseless, of the line he'd zeroed in on from that popular song than another track came to his mind, without his definitely knowing why (perchance because it lit some small fire in his mind)—this time an unpopular composition by a man known better for his contribu-tions to American cinema; a spoken word piece by jack-of-all-arts David Pinch entitled "Weird and Unworthwhile Thinking."

It was a brilliant non-song, that was evident immediately, though he was well aware he didn't understand it in toto—as was true of some or all of the man's films. A sort of monologue comprised of run-on sentences it began by talking of the possibility of the human species realizing what it called the overarching objective of internal evolution—the result of which would be limitless happiness and preternatural consciousness.

According to Pinch's piece said evolutionary apex was the giving of one's being utterly to the true, above-animal, ascended self; such submission had for millennia been the object of Homo sapiens' yearning, and this self had for long years laid dormant, at times slumbering, causing brief thoughtless (or near-thoughtless) states in the organism that were periods of non-reflexive consciousness—of consciousness pure and all-embracing.

It went on to posit the meeting of negative and positive energies was propelling the human race toward enlightenment (for dark and light—forever at war—were both necessary for either to have meaning, for the species to grow educationally, spiritually), toward an endpoint the species in its collective soul sought with a deep hidden intensity—on to a developmental stage each member of the species had a long-standing hunger to reach.

Sometimes, Pinch stated in a modulated voice, in the song that was musical but was not a song, sometimes at night the woods would emit a sensation that could be perceived by the attuned, the hyperaware; the innocent, the awake. All light would dissipate into pure black, and sensorially all that remained would be a faint aural stimulus entering into the body via the orbits. Small mysterious fauna unseeable, consciousness on a non-knowable other wavelength, would scurry into the earthy hills, plump with soft umber dirt, where trees trussed in endogenous armor bled a molasses-like secretion, its exposure causing it to on the outside become indurate, protectively—the viscous fluid sheltering alike the genuine nature of all and everything; the fluid that of life, reminiscent of a truer home that was not spatial, from which we were birthed into the physical, over and again; into the land of trees and greenery that we'd separated ourselves from, detrimentally. From the nothing into the solid and visceral—thrust, crying, into the brightness and bustle. The pinpoint in the airless fabric of the void where the asinine animals roamed, made one do the things they did—live within their manufactured circus or live poorly, live unfree or moan insane on concrete unloved and invisible by will.

And as we were largely divorced from nature and harmed by our imposed removal from it, our inaccurately perceived conquest of it, we too had been dealt self-inflicted injury by our belief that our genesis was from other than the vast nothing of the universe, a belief that had formed the foundation of centuries or more of backwards thinking and faulty conclusions—that had benefitted the agents of malice that sought to keep humankind benighted, perplexed, and afraid. To transform each unit of the population for good and all into a disoriented ape ripe for manipulation—by being fed church, and avarice, and sports fanaticism, and ills and fallacies political and social. To keep the whole, or as much of it as they might, unaware of their real, unique, noncorporeal essence; from looking up and in and realizing they were gods of the cosmos; that just as they were within the external infinity it too was within them—and meaningfully all was inextricable from all. To stop every last one of the plebs from tuning in to the ache inside that was their spirit's way of notifying them something was amiss and missing.

These powers wanted people not to acknowledge their toothache, not even to feel the incessant throb of advanced caries or sharpness of revealed nerve. But perhaps there could be a world where no one suffered this way, from any malady of the teeth or mouth. Perhaps, postulated Pinch, this simple absence of a common physical problem would mean the absence of the fear of one of the body's most important tools: pain. Might mean no longer experiencing an unbeneficial fear—fear that was irrational, that resulted in stress and mental poor health—of the most natural and helpful of sensations bodily. Could mean people stopped worrying about the specter of decay and destruction and all that accompanied having teeth with practical or cosmetic issues. That they ceased fixating on a nuisance that caused an unfortunate disquietude where there had been ataraxia, that became an obstacle to happiness and ascension from rootedness in the corporeal shell and the material realm in general—a minor nagging ailment, bothersome truth, that occasionally acted as a catalyst to weird and unworthwhile thinking.

He had known or crossed paths with at minimum four or five individuals over the years who had been unpleasant and also had terrible teeth, who'd seemed to have poor oral hygiene. Was there a correlation? Were they bad to others, without those others having been bad to them, because they didn't like themselves—and did they allow their teeth to go to rot because of a lack of self-love? Were they sociopaths whose apathy toward humans extended to themselves?

I'm glad they had horrid mouths. Serves those awful idiots right. I hope their teeth got progressively worse until they were moaning in agony, barely able to focus, thinking Why did I rarely brush my teeth? I knew I'd regret it later.

I hope the people who were mean to me as a child whose teeth I don't remember have bad teeth now too. Or chronic injuries. Or had a child with Down's syndrome or Harlequin ichthyosis. Or their wife is obese, has a moustache, and is slothful and demanding.

...Too there was a song, partly having to do with the lost wonder of childhood, that'd always appealed to him in a way he didn't fully comprehend. A very famous song by a very famous group, British. How did it go?

When I was a boy/
I spotted something in my peripheral vision/
That I could not identify.
I looked straight at the spot/
Where it'd been/
But I could not see it there.
I'm unable to name the thing/
Or the feeling it roused.
For the kid's matured/

Turned into a man/
And the youthful dreams nightmares.
I am a nothing from out of nothing/
My heart withered until it vanished.
Nothing touches me now/
All the mysteries are gone/
Or don't pique my curiosity.
I'm much like a mannequin/
Empowered by magic/
To talk and move around.
My blank eyes can be seen/
Though can no more see/
Than a pair of marbles.

His mind was an internal rollercoaster, twisting and making loop-de-loops at high velocity, completely beyond his control.

And there was that extremely overplayed song from '78 or '80 by the band Excursion—the song he unfortunately heard on the radio every time he was within earshot of one for fifteen minutes or more—with the line that nonetheless (still) resonated with him, particularly while he was on acid in the year 2014 with John Wayne emanating from a glowing rectangle in front of him: *The film never ends—it goes on and on and on.*

Why though did it resonate with him? Because it was true. The movie referenced was life, the movie of one's life. And life seemingly did go on infinitely—though he of course knew it didn't actually; that is, that each lifetime terminated in death, even if it (likely) was followed by another.

But life felt as if it lasted for an extremely long time, interminably long. And as with the best films it was unpredictable, and over its length generally much transpired, outside, in-. There was no lack of change, at least in his recent past, and the course that the metaphorical film in question took, the events that occurred in it, the transformations that the primary character experienced often legitimately were cinematic, and generally stranger than the material devised by clever screenwriters.

In just six months he, Stanley Northrop, average guy—single, twentysomething Caucasian male, a guy with a modest apartment and a dull nine-dollar-an-hour non-career, a man of (he thought) sound mind and body leading a wholly unremarkable existence—had become a spree killer who dispatched his own girlfriend; unquestionably mentally ill; a job- and homeless person recently rescued from that fate by a woman his parents' age who was seemingly romantically infatuated. Who presently—not sought for his murders but his whereabouts unknown regardless—sat quiet and abnormally introspective in a large, vaguely eerie house while on an intense inner voyage powered by ingestion of a substantial quantity of a psychotropic substance, beside him the quinquagenarian who had selfishly saved him, which television-illuminated individual kept for some reason (attraction, curiosity, concern?) discreetly glancing over at him, oblivious to his altered consciousness.

He directed his attention to the woman, chancing to meet her eyes. Contact held, the poorly illuminated orbs glowing within her face emanating emotion—though what emotion he could not be sure—he asked, quite spontaneously: "What are we, Charlotte? What are you?"

"What?" she asked with widened eyes, eyes that appeared so wet as to be on the verge of emitting tears.

"Do you ever ask yourself that? Have you ever?"

"I am...a human being of course. What...is your meaning, sweetheart? That expression..."

"We are animals, of the type called human. But, what does it mean to be alive? Do you know what I'm saying? What is this...experience? What am I? What is consciousness? What is the purpose of this experience? Or is it all happenings of no consequence at all?"

She stared. "To learn. To feel. To be. Growth, I suppose, darling. ...What's gotten into you?" Charlotte took his hand in hers, her palm soft, paw compact. He looked down, uncomprehending, at their paired hands.

"What am I?" Stanley was no longer seeing the hands, or anything; his eyes, open, were not processing with consciousness. "Am I merely a small, fragile creature in the midst of an infinity of colorless space? What is an 'I'?"

"Stanley, dearest—have you ingested something this evening? A sort of consciousness-affecting substance, say?"

But there was no Stanley, not now. Not anymore. No more than there was any little woman sitting next to him.

"I am not a person," he met her eyes again, which brimmed with concern, "but a thought. A possibilities generator. ...Like you."

She observed the speaker, in a silence ruined by the movie voices of the dead.

"Time is nothing. My life is over, and has not begun—but always will. Don't you see?" the young man asked a blue-lighted visage bathed in incomprehension. "The entirety of my life is occurring now and also has already occurred, no matter what age I am.

"Age is meaningless, the terms *past* and *present* are meaningless. I may as well have intercourse with you, right now, on the living room floor, because there is no 'me' either. There exists no separation from you anyway. The idea that we are separate units is not even a biological fact, and certainly isn't spiritually accurate."

His eyes were inside of him, took in a panoramic view of the room but were unaware even of the television in front of him, a yard and a half away. There was no more Marion Morrison arguing, fighting, wooing from a radioactive square. His psyche was open but highly selective, tuned in but to the inside only. Charlotte had interlaced their fingers now, and their joined hands were two inches from his crotch.

"I'm not twenty-seven. That has no meaning. There is not old, young. There is only humanity, in all the shapes, colors; in all its variegation, complication. Like a blob with fourteen billion feet.

"We shuffle along, dance, prance. We are the great show. It all is. And there are more of us elsewhere!"

Charlotte stared at his profile, curves and angles of medium blue and near black. "Would you have sex with me on the floor?" she asked, expression bright with want.

He looked to her. "I've never had sex on acid before," said Stanley.

"I knew you had taken something, my love," she said. And she released her housemate's hand, rose, approached the DVD player, and turned it off. Electronic light from the imageless TV continued to minimally illuminate the space near it. "I'll be right back," Charlotte told the young man, swimming in his skull, as she left the room headed for the staircase.

Returning minutes later with a folded thin blanket, a disused blanket that had been in her bedroom chest, which she meticulously spread across the living room hardwood before the entertainment setup, she said, "You know, I'm not like an old maid when it comes to coital matters. I become lubricated easily and substantially. Right now, I can feel, I am already quite wet, anticipating your manness within me. ...Come." She took his hand, pulling him down on top of her as she laid supine upon the teal blanket meant to provide comfort, a degree of decency, and to protect their epidermis from being rubbed raw by the material of the floor.

Laying atop her his erection had returned. He lined it up with the tops of the small widow's thighs as he looked down at her receptive face, appearing smoother due to the lack of light. "I am moist," she said unfastening and pulling down her caramel-colored slacks beneath him. "Take off your pants too."

Complying, Stanley opened the belt that kept her late spouse's overlarge jeans on his hips and tugged and shimmied till the denim garment enlarged the clothing pile at their feet.

"I have been looking forward to this act since you joined me here, love," Charlotte informed him with shining eyes that seemed to be bursting from her skull as she extracted his primed penis from the boxers he wore and guided it into the slick vagina she had exposed by drawing her underwear to the left with two digits. He went in with a sigh, the fit loose but the damp of her orifice appealing tactilely to his organ. Moving above her in a slow rhythm he saw that the woman's face had gained an angelic, unnatural quality, as if he were seeing her spirit manifested through her visage, which was as a result transformed into more than a mere face, became the luminous face of a deity, whose essence he was enabled to glimpse simultaneous to his feeling the inside of the organism that was very much her but also quite apparently a mere vessel through which the god could function, could sense and be sensed. And the combination of these inputs further aroused Stanley, but also made him regard with a new mind the entity whose lower body his was connected to—viewing her as a version of a great mass that was everyone, a configuration that he was privileged to be able to experience in a fuller, more accurate way than he previously had an other.

She elevated her arms, knitting her fingers around the back of his head as he sensorially took her in, enraptured, having forgotten himself as the doer, a separate creature.

"You are perfect, like all the rest of the universe," he said, vision locked on her face, electrically azure, gleaming, its angles presently swimming within the oval of her head. "I see you now as you are. As everything is. Ever in flux. Collected molecules that make shapes that camouflage the fact we like the blackness that surrounds us are essentially empty space."

She stared, knees up at his ribcage. "I want you to go deep inside me. I want your semen inside."

His gaze was on nothing, on the wall across the room. "Every action is correct. The whole of history was written in the past. None of us can commit a wrong because there is no meaning of that term. Even Hope, what I did to those people, was nothing to regret. There was no other outcome."

"This was right all along, Stanley. I want to be possessed by you often. I want you making me sore daily."

"Your face is like a midnight sun, frightening and beautiful." His eyes had returned to her. "Being like this with you is a fulfillment of destiny and fulfills my body also."

"What people...what were you saying, dear?"

"I'm getting close." He appeared strained, in pain. "What?"

"What you did to those people you said."

"I never...expected to meet anyone like Hope. And I thought it was bad luck. ...But there's no such thing. Oh god."

An explosion, the jettisoning of built up body fluid, occurred internally—Charlotte conscious of each individual discharge, each jet of seed; Stanley groaning animally.

"That was so relieving, so...life-affirming," he said after a moment, mostly recovered from ejaculating, propping himself up but having not yet withdrawn.

"That was a fulfillment for me, too, Stanley. Of what I'd desired for a fortnight. You. And, another ideal aspect of us as sexual partners: you don't have to worry about pregnancy."

Stanley came to his feet, flipping on the main light, the dark suddenly upsetting to him. His eyes found his member, slimy with the byproduct of coitus, brain as if on a merry-go-round half-hidden in early afternoon fog—processing zero percent of stimuli consciously though deluged by sensation, the familiarity of his surroundings substantially diminished. "Who is Hope?" he heard Charlotte, leaning on one elbow on the floor, inquire. Her voice sounded far off, words drawn out.

The woman I murdered he thought. *One of the women I murdered. The woman I loved who I murdered.* "A trollop who was a god, who earned another god's disfavor and was smitten." The words were emitted unknown in advance. Meanwhile patterns, highly ornamented diamonds, were popping out from the walls at him. Each was identical, seemingly containing all colors. They were alive and throbbing, like hearts—nonphysical pumps that lived in the room's sides but had emerged, in his state, to show their nature as akin to mechanical cuckoos, the walls (which seemed striped with wrongly hued rivulets) cuckoo clocks.

He tried to force the visuals from his mind, finding his pants and re-garbing ungracefully. Charlotte meanwhile came to her feet and slipped back into her own pants.

"The room seems to be alive," said Stanley, glossy-eyed and ill at ease.

"That was wonderful, what just occurred. You have me worried you took too much of that lysergic acid diethylamide. ...It's not candy, that. Caution must be utilized. A boy I'd gone to high school with—I came of age in the seventies and a multitude of my peers had such experiences—once overdid it, or his mind could not cope, and he went for an ill-advised drive, seeing objects that didn't exist, and never came home. He went through the windshield at fifty miles per hour or so and was badly torn up. ...Personally I've never been so bold—or I daresay foolhardy—to experiment with a chemical of that sort. There was some similar story about Art Linkletter's daughter too I seem to recall, poor man."

"She jumped from a high window. A bad acid trip or more may have been partly to blame. ...It's so bright in here. I know it's my current state, but I feel like my retinae are being deluged by luminance, negatively, like I could be blinded—that is if it weren't all in my mind. What did we just do?"

"We made sweet love finally, sweetheart. Don't you know? You enjoyed it a great deal. You told me I am perfect. You referred to our lovemaking as 'life-affirming.'"

"That's okay, I guess. That's alright. Maybe again we can also. Another day. Maybe that can be an activity we engage in now."

"I certainly hope so! You're all I want, Stanley Northrop."

He directed a perplexing expression at her face. "There is no Stanley Northrop. That is only a name, and without meaning, but there is no me either, if you'd been listening. I am an idea. An illusion. A figment of the universe's vast imagination. You and I are one. That is why fucking doesn't matter. It's a coming together of entities that are already connected."

"Yes... I understand."

He began to pace. "The brightness is just so piercing. And the walls are dancing."

"Do you need anything, Stanley dear? A tall container of cold water? A nap? Can I do anything to improve your interior condition?"

"I couldn't take a nap!" replied the pacer, slowly yoyoing between the front and back of the room, his eyes communicating that she had said something ridiculous or stupid. "I am seeing this space as it must truly exist. As an aspirating, sentient chamber, expanding and contracting around us. ...But it doesn't have the capacity we do, as so-called higher animals—the ability to love." He held her eyes, forehead furrowed by the intensity of his private world. "I love you. I love everyone. Everyone is *correct* in their being. That is the point at which we are meant to arrive. And I am there now. But when my mind is no longer wide open I will descend again into primal blindness. I know this. And I doubt I'll be able to feel this again sober, this encompassing love and acceptance."

"I love you too, darling," said Charlotte, standing in the middle of the hardwood floor, saline secretion built up above her lower lids.

"No! I don't mean it like that." He was swarming inside. "I mean I love you because you're a person. Because you're part of creation. The everything that came from nothing. Love is the answer, like all those prophets were saying. Any other reaction, because we are one god split up into a trillion parts, is unnatural."

"Okay. I understand, darling," responded Charlotte sheepishly, observing her housemate with impotent concern.

"I need to go back to my room and be alone. The enhanced stimuli, and you, are too much for me all of a sudden. I'm sorry." He turned, headed for the staircase, the bemused woman left staring after him.

Within the quiet of his stark room, as he sat on the bed, back against the white wall, his mind was anything but quiet and everything stationary was subtly in motion—and the effect of this made him somewhat queasy.

For a time, a minute, five minutes, or maybe mere seconds, he thought he was unconsciously voicing his thoughts, but then realized they were contained in his head, that he was hallucinating sounds. He was thinking in loops, frenetically. Thought: *There are two me's. I am not one but two. Not one entity but two people inhabiting a single body. Two programs simultaneously running in the computer that is my fragile little body. There is the me I know and that which I don't know, that I hardly know. The me I get only glimpses of. When tired, when drunk, when sufficiently disinhibited that ol' lurking other me comes peeking out.*

"Hello!" it will greet me.

"Oh, good to see you!" I'll say in return.

"You've done the right things to release me!" it will say.

"Well, I wouldn't want you not to get any exercise," I'll respond.

"I'm the one who murdered Hope!" it might say.

"Oh. So you are!" I could say back.

"Did you like that I did that?"

"No, I don't. It's only you that thought that was good."

"Oh, that's right. Silly me. ...But she's gone anyway, isn't she?"

"You know she is. No takesies backsies on that action!"

"No, no. No indeed!"

"And it seems like they'll come looking for me. Especially if—when—her body is discovered. The live-in boyfriend who's disappeared. They must be able to link me to her."

"I wouldn't worry about it, champ."

"And why not?"

"Because I never worry—about anything!"

"But I'm not you!"

"Oh yes you are."

On and on the imagined conversation between him and himself went, the nausea not subsiding but worsening, the walls and furniture continuing to shift and wobble and flow, auditory signals entering his mind that were either barely perceptible noises from

Charlotte ascending and coming through a door or else were wholly conjured by the command center that processed them.

But then there was the definite and, he judged, quite real sound of footsteps on the wooden stairs. And soon, very close and certainly not a mental invention, there was a series of three knocks on the door that segregated him with his chaotic psyche from the rest of the house.

"Stanley?" entreated Charlotte mild-manneredly.

"What do you want, Charlotte?" He shut his eyes in annoyance, hoping this might precipitate her disappearance.

"Dear...I'm sorry. I am aware you expressed a desire to be alone, but we live together...we're great friends...and we're even lovers, and...something you said minutes previously has really lodged itself in my mind—in not a positive manner. 'A trollop who earned a god's disfavor and was smote' I believe. ...Stanley? Can I come in?"

"No. Not now. I require some time. It's this drug."

"Please though. I'll go away. Just tell me who this Hope is, what you were talking about. The way you were talking you alarmed me. I know it's nothing."

He sighed heavily, unclenching his eyelids, iciness in a gaze that was unseeing. "Hope...was a previous girlfriend, who was an emotionally abusive whore. And I got drunk one night, and accidentally strangled the life out of her. She's under dirt and I don't want to talk about it. Leave me in peace."

Stunned, Charlotte slunk away as if broken, psyche flooded with chemicals tied to an altered impression of the previously idealized Stanley, who while she could not be certain wasn't telling her a fib was now a potential murderer, ergo a possibly dangerous roomer.

What would she do now? she wondered while creeping downstairs, newly concerned for her welfare. At the same time the subject of her thoughts, experiencing no anxiety about what he had divulged, felt wave after wave of warm invigorating energy hitting him bodily, passing through his frame and quickening his heart. He pulled himself to the edge of the bed and stood, not wanting to leave the room and encounter Charlotte but not wanting to be sedentary. And then he was pacing, the whole of the visual stimuli substantially sharper than normally, such that his sight seemed to've been rendered superhuman—the distinctness of every color, border, texture, detail inundating his mind with a clarity he experienced as each object, whether an item (what few there were) or just a wall, popping out at him; rushing at first perception at his face, into his eyes, so that merely seeing was sensorially overwhelming.

It was like he could reach and touch the rectangle that was the dresser without moving toward it, though it was situated ten feet away. Like every quality of that piece of furniture was being beamed into his mind, crowding it with a bulk of information that was of no practical use but made him a god of information in his self-image, an Über-man whose human brain had been split wide enabling him to know what other mortals mightn't. To be able to sense (or vividly imagine, akin to being present with her) that Charlotte was in the bathroom below crying—confused and scared, a weak animal trapped with a deranged stronger one by her own foolishness.

His mind was moving at million miles a minute, thoughts too rapid to process. But he was fully cognizant of the stream of them, a river of disconnected cogitations possibly akin to that of a schizophrenic being, again and again the hyperactive processor in his skull returning to thoughts of, burgeoning unease about Charlotte's probable reaction, whatever it was certain to be highly negative—realizing that he had imperiled his new, substantially preferable living situation and himself generally. That he now, he might rationally suspect, had one foot out the door and the next step would be into prison; prison for the remainder of his life, maybe some sixty years. Prison because he was a ne'er-to-well gone all the way to the dark, though he blamed this development mostly on the former Hope, slumbering eternally beneath soil and the organic detritus of the forest.

Time had by his perception long been an idea without correlation to the life of Stanley Northrop of the spacious sepulcher-scented downtown home. If it was a reality-based concept he was beyond its power. He was seven again in a childhood shed, spying on across-the-street strangers, taking in the faces of passing bicyclists, experiencing pre-sexual feelings for a neighbor girl the same age. Was spending a morning in a retail clothing store, folding overpriced merchandise and offering aid to those well-heeled people who came in to browse it. Was looking up in the rain at gargoyles perched on a cathedral on a school trip to London at sixteen and then beside him a stringy-haired brunette probably five years older but who was spotted with open sores, skeletal, and looked thirty was saying "You wanna get high? You wanna fuck? I like a young cock. You wanna smoke crack with me and get fucked? I wanna fuck. Fucking on crack is the best sex, baby. I can go hours..." He was rhythmically penetrating supine Hope, a knee bent on either side of him, thinking of the silkiness of her womanhood, a warm, moist, visceral version of heaven; dually focused on the perfectness of his present and on holding at bay ejaculation.

He was many selves, at many moments. But he was ultimately the still bearded, drug-altered one who was wearing the overlarge clothes of an older woman's long-dead husband, which version of himself had been unemployed for something like half a year. And he was of course a criminal, and his acts deserving of the worst punishment. But he didn't think the authorities knew that. ...But then wouldn't he be the prime suspect if Hope was declared a missing person, if her body was found? And hadn't someone likely seen him leaving the bar with Delilah? Perhaps he was only free because the police didn't know where he was. Maybe he shouldn't look for work, and therefore could never be a real person again, who was a part of society. And what about the new problem of Charlotte? No—life seemed good, better, for a moment but in actuality he had nothing. His slayings would be linked to him and if something wasn't done about Charlotte she might become the reason the cops apprehended him for Hope's disappearance.

The room was spinning though he wasn't sure whether his eyes were even open, wasn't sure whether he was standing or lying in bed, was uncertain as to where he was—a stark room in oblivion. And soon he had passed, unaware of the transition, into a slumber of dreams he would recollect the emotions stirred by but not the content of. Though Charlotte, downstairs, would remain awake, her anxiety-ridden psyche, seeking a solution, unable to shut down.

36

When he had finished at The Cellar Calvin went immediately to an uninhabited part of northern Iceland, where he had learned only the day before a large volcano had for days been steadily releasing a cloud of odorous black ash.

He arrived, at a rock-covered incline, near the crater—though not so near as to risk personal injury, glad of having no need for caution as nobody was there to see him appear—to find trickles, little extremely hot rivers, of exposed magma flowing from all sides of the irritable mountain of fire's wide emission-issuing mouth.

The heat radiating from its center the shapeshifter felt fully on his face, as if he stood mere yards from a powerful heater or fronted a sauna being run at the highest temperature setting—an assaultive heat distinctly in contrast to the current meteorological conditions, a chilly thirty-three degrees that evening in that region of upper Iceland, at a remove of nearly forty miles from any real settlement.

Always conscious of his mortality, his vulnerability, the man who was something other imagined dipping an exposed foot's toes into the lava, seeing and feeling them become immediately and irreversibly ruined, nerves going haywire. And the next moment he was consciously enjoying the beauty of the sight that so few could access at such proximity and none so easily; his knowledge of powerlessness over this geological phenomenon of the Earth, that if he so chose his estimated two hundred years on the planet (of which a hundred eighty remained) could quickly, horribly come to a premature end via heaving himself into the ferocious opening—this though, self-termination, an option by any means Calvin couldn't imagine himself selecting (for he was, here, in his world-sized penitentiary, a superman, and relatedly had been having a great deal of practically consequence-free fun).

But he didn't linger long being blasted with heat, on the slope standing atop the innumerable small porous stones, inexorable streams of cerise lava approaching his legs, vulnerable as anyone's. He jumped, still wearing his common costume, the flesh of Calvin Chaulk, into a city of moderate size way down south of both the cold-night volcano far from anyone and his home of conveniences in suburban Maryland—a city some forty-eight hundred miles away, in Michoacán, Mexico—standing within minutes (after reconstituting behind some accumulated rubbish in an alley it fronted), as planned, before a cantina he had visited a few times before; the time after-noon again, a hooker standing outside the bar, though not the one he hoped to find.

This working woman—wearing a coruscant skirt violet in hue, elevating shoes, garish jewelry, and very much at ease; height about five-seven in her heels and her hair upright with copious chemical—was substantially less attractive, more used-seeming, icy-seeming, than the beauty he had enjoyed during his previous leisure jumps to this bar in this wide, wild nation he had developed a fondness for. The prostitute stared, futilely appraising the gringo, desirous of his business, brown eyes rendered impassive by experience, portals to an abyss that none wanted access to. The object of his longing, however, was a size-six twenty-eight-year-old with taut B breasts and a sup-ple bottom who spoke a good amount of English and whose name was Valeria, with whom sex had felt less businesslike and more like a rendezvous between two new lovers, the sensations of her aestheti-cally impressive nude body viscerally summonable.

"Dónde está Valeria?" asked Calvin as he approached the wom-an who leaned on the establishment's concrete wall, its coat of pale green paint flaky from long exposure.

"No sé," she said as if oppressed by ennui. "You want date?"

"Tal vez. Maybe if I can't find Valeria."

He recognized the prostitute and he guessed she recognized him, but never had he paid for her service—and though he did not particularly find her sexually appealing he nonetheless wondered what she might feel like, and in fact planned to take her if the search for the beauty was fruitless; but also he wanted to see her reaction to pain, to hurt her, to injure her badly, perhaps even to render her unbreathing.

Beside the watching whore he pulled the cantina's heavy door open to the left and strode into a wide room of low-lit hunched drinkers, all seemingly natives of the region. Most of their pairs of eyes found the extraterrestrial's visage, then quickly left it.

Calvin walked to the bar. A man in his forties with a bushy mustache and serious gaze questioned his face. He couldn't recollect this bartender. "Do you know Valeria?"

"Valeria? Conozco a Valeria. She is not work today. Martes."

"Martes? She work martes?"

"Sí." The man began washing a beer mug. Down the bar a fellow on a stool had been staring at Calvin. "I know Valeria," this individual now said. "Good fuck. Muy hermosa."

The traveler met his eyes, which were animated unlike Calvin's. A tall beer, a half-inch of froth, stood before him. The man, good-natured he sensed, looked to be some six inches shorter than the outsider in his current and usual form. "Sí. Muy hermosa."

"Take Marta," suggested the other, ingesting a bit of the beverage while maintaining his embracing stare.

"Marta? Outside?" He motioned.

"Yes. Al frente."

Calvin sauntered back toward the door, watched by barkeep and stool-situated customer. Outside the daylight had become a system shock. Marta to his immediate left regarded him with a clenched countenance that communicated suspicion. "What you want now, gringo?"

"Valeria's not around today. I guess I will sample your wares."

"What? You want me?"

"I'm going to try you."

"Cien. Come with me to mi habitación." She took his hand roughly into one ornamented by long fake nails, pulling him forward and around the corner toward the rear of the cantina.

"A hundred? No. I'm not some stupid foreigner. This isn't the first time I've fucked a whore in Mexico. Fifty."

She halted, directing a harsh look at him. "Sesenta."

"Yeah. Okay." He began to be pulled along again.

━━━◦《◉》◦━━━

Behind the bar there stood in a condition of dilapidation a five-story apartment building separated from the tavern by a courtyard of sand in which presently three children no older than six played. Two of them chased a chicken around while the other observed and picked her nose. Marta and Calvin climbed to the third floor where she stopped before a unit with '33' stenciled on the door and unlocked it. Briskly she undressed to her brassiere and panties, throwing shoes, skirt and blouse on the floor beside the bed. "Una hora. Money now."

Calvin fished for cash in his billfold. "I have a fifty and a twenty."

She reached for a pile of loose currency on the low table next to the mattress, under a switched off lamp, handing him two bills totaling one hundred-fifty pesos. Staring at him, she slid down her underwear. "I have condom. You want suck?"

Calvin gazed between her legs, half-hard, seeing the top of a slit below a patch of black hair. "Just touch it."

He seated himself on the bed and unzipped his fly, extracting his penis; Marta sat beside him and proceeded to tug on the appendage, brass bracelet jingling, while Calvin squeezed and ran a hand across her bra-contained C-cups.

"Uno momento." Marta reached for a condom on the table with the money, opened the package and slid the manufactured membrane over the protuberance of flesh.

"Ready?" she asked.

"Get your panties off your ankles first."

She released him and complied, kicking them—a simple black pair—across the discolored linoleum floor; laying back on the bed with her knees up and legs parted, a trimmed patch of curlicues above a surprisingly attractive opening.

As he crawled on top, entering her wetness with his engorgement easily and finding the fit, the feeling—similar to a loose, very moist and soft glove—wholly appealing, Calvin noticed between the hips of the woman of the hairspray-hardened coif and emotionless eyes the presence of a C section scar.

"Do you have a boyfriend?"

"No."

"Before?" he asked, still becoming acquainted with the sensation of the warm canal with which he was connected, a shaven thigh in contact with the outer side of each of the penetrator's clothed unshorn own.

"Yes. Before. Now I am married."

"Oh, you're married?" His pace and pleasure were gradually increasing. "How long?"

"Many years. Diez años. I have not seen him en mucho tiempo. Él vive en Jalisco. He is un fontanero. He drinks too much."

Calvin looked intermittently at her face and above it, where her raven hair was splayed beneath her on the top sheet-covered mattress. "You know...I wanted to hurt you. To see your expression transform. To see you wide-eyed and helpless as thick dark blood poured from you. But now I just want to fuck you. ....I don't think I want Valeria so much anymore. I think I want you." He moaned, beads of perspiration on his hairline; his penis inside her seemed uncommonly rigid, drenched by her secretion. "Ahh...bitch," he uttered, sensing he was near climax. "Your pussy is wonderful."

"Qué? You want to hurt me?"

With a loud, guttural utterance the alien man came, powerfully, his toes curling, feeling at home, as below a cockroach scurried from the kitchenette area—a dim alcove with a decades-old refrigerator against the wall—to under the bed. "So good," he said, propping himself above her, his shrinking penis yet within.

"Hurry and get off," she said pushing him lightly. "Be careful." Both arms went to her vagina, fingers on each hand finding the top of the semen-filled condom, Calvin's own hand without being verbally prompted taking over. Gingerly, he pulled away while holding the condom sagging from his member in place on it.

"You want to hurt me?" he heard Marta saying as he disposed of a tied off jellyfish-like prophylactic in the bathroom wastebasket.

"No. Wanted to. But I decided I like you too much. Don't worry."

"You don't hurt me," she said, eyes suddenly so wide they looked ready to pop, eyes intense to the point of appearing to glow. Sitting up in bed, a spot of warm ejaculate that escaped the receptacle between the inner tops of her legs, her jangly right hand searched for the handle to the bedside table's drawer, opening it as the returned Calvin was closely watched.

"No—I said I wouldn't. I said not to worry."

"I don't worry!" she said heated, with a rapid movement taking a silver revolver from the drawer and aiming it at the vicinity of her customer's balding cranium. "I have this—idiota!"

Calvin, standing at the foot of the bed, at once envisioned his death on the foreign planet he had been condemned to—seeing his skull burst, blood and brain flying up toward unmoving ceiling fan and hitting the plaster behind him; seeing his limp frame collapse and crumple on the dirty floor of the cheap room in Central America, the domicile of a run-of-the-mill hooker he had found he was oddly fond of (and what then? Would he fly? Would a spirit that had animated his body in fact look down upon a shell of flesh that was like a discarded puppet? Followed by?). Considered, the pistol trained on him, that another hundred and seventy-five, hundred and eighty years of raping and pillaging, homicide and general chaos, could quickly be prevented—the world being much better for it—by a prostitute with apathy in her eyes firing a projectile into his all-too-organic head just above the left eye socket.

He saw this potentiality and was worried, in fact was afraid. Staring into the lightless interior of the tool's barrel he knew that his chance wasn't to try rushing her but to talk his way to freedom. After all, he was no threat to the woman with the weapon; her being armed didn't change that. His task was simply to convince her of that truth.

Or, like her though he did, he could always play it safe and dematerialize. Which would necessitate quickly killing her, since he was disinclined to start letting people say they'd seen a man disappear before their eyes, no matter how crazy that sounded—couldn't start doing it in front of people, whether or not their report would be dismissed as delusion. He regarded one exception as too many. If he teleported to save himself he would be forced to immediately murder the woman, probably coming right back behind her and bashing her head.

"Marta—"

"You don't talk to me. You get out. You go." She motioned with the extended weapon, mingled anger and anxiety in wet jelly orbs with brown centers.

Calvin complied very slowly and keeping his arms at his sides, relieved that she would survive him but irked that in order to enjoy her again he would have to take a form he was unaccustomed to.

In decelerated motion he opened the door just enough for his body; maintaining eye contact exited, taking the walkway and the stairs at a similarly laggard pace, despite Marta apparently not observing his departure from the building.

"Goodbye Marta," he said semi-audibly to himself as he crossed the rectangle of sand in which the children played, a stalactite of yellow glistening snot extending from one's—a five-year-old, male—nostril.

He resisted the urge to walk back into the cantina for a drink, out of concern he would see once more the rageful bawd. His head was high but he felt low. He almost regretted having come.

37

When he spent his time this way he often, on being questioned by Michela as to where he'd been for hours on a Sunday or Saturday, responded that he'd been playing golf (or engaged in some other such activity) with his work friend Peter.

In reality though Calvin was a terrible golfer (and felt he would not have had any interest in the sport even if he'd had a knack for it); and though there was a real Peter, and this person was someone who he knew from work, he was more a business associate than a true friend. For Peter from work was a man about forty with whom he had an agreement—an argeement that was around fifteen years old. The arrangement was: Calvin would present Peter with a thank you stipend of a thousand dollars every year so long as Peter, if circumstances led to his being asked, would tell Michela that on the day in question, during a certain period of time, Calvin was with Peter doing whatever Calvin had instructed him to say they'd been doing: nine holes, lunch at a bar and grill, watching a game while putting back some brews. For this thousand dollars Peter would accept any responsibility for whatever unlikely negative repercussion could result from his occasionally lying.

Peter, like Calvin, was a sense center installer, which career the Volfokian had held, after a rigorous training period, for going on eighteen years. He had come, over that time, to be trained in the maintenance and repair of the devices as well. In fact, Calvin would say, there was little about sense centers, regardless of model, that he didn't know.

In the nation of Patriopia, a sense center was, by law, installed in every dwelling. These viewing, hearing, speaking, smelling devices—that were also internet-of-things connected—were machines with which a domicile's residents had an open line of communication and the purpose of which was ostensibly to perform tasks for the residents of a home, to make their lives easier; sense centers were an aspect of daily life accepted without question by most and even appreciated. People interacted with the items and the items interacted with them; however, the devices additionally immediately reported whatever fell under the definition of antigovernment activity to the Patriopian agency that kept records of such behavior.

Every house, apartment, or other place of residence had a sense center within, just as each citizen at birth had a microchip containing all their crucial information implanted below the skin and among the tendons of their left wrist. Bodily chips and sense centers had been facts of existence as a Patropian since at least the year 2000, when legislation was passed due to the stated threat of the other that ensured a greater degree of control and surveillance of the population.

As the plebeians of Patriopia moved through life increasingly more information was added to the chip, the body wallet, including funds and debts; credit; medical, criminal, and rental history; records of marriages, divorces, offspring; and of course all matter of credentials and licenses. There was besides a voluntary procedure some chose to have in which a chip of the sort was introduced into the cerebrum that would then communicate any relevant desire to their sense center telepathically (but any antigovernment thoughts they might have too). Sufficiently serious or persisting antigovernment ideation resulted in the deviant being required to attend weekly meetings with a member of the official education and psychic wellness squad, meetings that were to continue until their sense center no longer registered such thinking.

On the worst end of the spectrum extreme antigovernment

acts—either caught on-camera outside the home or recorded in the domicile by a sense center; or otherwise proven, perhaps by an investigation commenced following testimony—were penalized by State-mandated summary executions. Such executions—by means of being burned alive, one individual at a time, in special fireproof chambers (trial boxes)—were referred as to trials and the execution-ers were called trialsmen.

Calvin's best friend Victor—a handsome, happy, energetic man of thirty-six—happened to be a trialsman, and he sometimes allowed Calvin to watch a trial, an activity Calvin enjoyed. Calvin, a fascist, was a staunch supporter of the status quo in Patriopia; he could have been antipodally different politically, a State enemy, and the fear of death, the fear aroused by merely hearing the word *trial*, would likely rarely or never have been a part of his experience in Patriopia, given his abilities. He liked his country. He was a true patriot. The State was, for him, the master he felt gratitude for; the omniscient father with his many children's best interest at heart.

Calvin had been asked by Victor if he wanted to view a trial four years earlier. He immediately accepted, and the following week on Monday took a long lunch and drove over to the nearby transfor-mation center, the sole purpose of such buildings—of which there were between three and a dozen per state—being to house (for a few days at most) criminals to be punished by trial and the performance of the trials. Each transformation center was therefore a dual jail and honeycomb of trial boxes, the jail section being merely ten or so chilly rooms with cots and steel toilets; the number of trial boxes within each was always greater than there was any purpose for, espe-cially considering the maximum duration of a trial was no more than a few minutes, each condemned individual being flash-burned—the eight by eight trial boxes, just specially insulated fire-impervious rooms situated above an enormous incinerator, designed such that at the press of a button (one of Victor's few jobs being to push the button) hissing fountains of orange flame shot up through multiple openings in the floor the shape of compressed ovals.

In an effort to augment the terror of those imminently to be killed four or more people were sent at the same time to await their fate. The criminals were led nude to a corridor outside a line of trial boxes where they waited in a queue, naked, with others of all ages and genders to be killed, hearing the brief animal screams of those who had been in front of them dying one at a time until it was their turn.

There were six people waiting in the corridor of the transformation center downtown the day Calvin first witnessed the trial process. Whenever he recollected the experience he could hear again the first man dying, the worst sound he had ever heard a human being produce, a sound that had stirred a sensation of glee in him. (For a mere thirty seconds the creature within the room of fire possessed the biological capacity to scream. Ninety seconds later another button was pushed, by Victor, and a heavy door with a small window hissed open, retracting into an opening in the wall. Then came the unpleasant duty of removing the corpse—a charred, fetally curled object that looked like some black, minimalist sculpture of a person—and this was Victor's duty too. There was a kind of enormous spatula that attached to one side of the exterior of the trial box and Victor would scoop the brittle, charcoal-smelling shell of a prior organism onto this implement, its former weight now substantially reduced by what the good-natured executioner sometimes humorously referred to as a "trial by fire." The byproduct, the smoldering compact erstwhile human, was then manually transferred onto a self-driving flatbed vehicle, oblong, only a foot in height, which Victor referred to simply as a "mover," and this machine transported the cadaver to another, larger incinerator elsewhere in the building, depositing it into a spacious receptacle of such corpses, all to be burnt fully to ash once per twenty-four hours.)

Too, he readily remembered, thinking back on that afternoon, the sight of the third person in line for trial, a pretty woman of twenty-eight or -nine, who'd been shivering, her haunted eyes set back in gray-brown caverns—shivering though outside the boxes one could feel the heat. She had seemed so broken, so traumatized, so tragic and innocent. Icy-hearted though he knew he was Calvin had felt something akin to pity for her. It was though she did not belong there, awaiting an execution booth; like the taking of her life was conceivably a crime itself.

As enriching as his reality was, Calvin, like most with a reasonable income, owned an in-home virtual reality chamber. They had become affordable (to the average middle-class person) and then immediately popular eight or so years earlier, and that was about the time the man who was not a man had purchased one—the user-friendly Imaginator 1000—a decision that hadn't made Michela overly pleased.

Had his spouse known how Calvin was using it their divorce may have been the ultimate consequence. At least twice a week for the first six months he was having simulated sex with avatars of his devising in it. For nearly two months he experienced practically the same threesome with the same pair of similar blonde college-aged girls designed according to his idea of physical perfection, the cognomens he'd given them, of course obligatory, Tessa and Tiffany—the girls based on a pornographic video he'd watched online and masturbated to many times before he ever had VR (though with the impressive technology he had in the basement at his deposal his was now the penis entering the smooth-skinned, taut-bodied beauties, unreal but wholly authentic in appearance. He was the man taking them from behind, missionary, one riding him facing him and nude while the other balanced on his face, being tongued. He was tasting their nectar, kissing their nipples, squeezing their busts, buttocks; inhaling their scents, working up a sweat while ravaging them, spraying seed on forms he had told a computer to fabricate; the good-sized and reliably functioning member he'd provided himself in his Calvin

Chaulk costume being fellated deeply by both, being the cause of erotic moans, being able to consistently withstand fifteen minutes of nonstop pleasure via ideal partners in fornication—there for him but as carnal objects, to be summoned as he desired; immediately receptive, seductive; smiling, biting lips, fingers moving for his zipper, working as a team; in short shorts and too-small tanktops, in a well-lit room that was seventy-two degrees every time and existed outside of worldly turmoil (due to not existing at all)).

An associated development, none to his surprise, was that his wife periodically dropped hints and eventually confronted him about the frequency of his use of the machine; by which point he was already well aware he was addicted to the technology, as so many others. And following that conversation he resumed having most of his sex in the real world; occasionally with Michela, occasionally with prostitutes, fairly frequently when raping people while disguised, and (if he were to say it counted) sometimes by copulating with the corpses he created—in many states, in many nations. He continued to entertain himself via the VR chamber, but was no more than two hours a week within the machine—that was his self-imposed limit (and anyway in there he received a degree of radiation exposure, radioactivity being something Calvin was certainly not immune to).

Pathetic though perhaps it was, after so much time at least once a month when he stepped into the Imaginator he was still having sex with the same fake twenty-year-olds, his hyperrealistic coitus with his eternal, enthusiastic creations—typically transpiring on a couch of brown leather—a fantasy experience eight years running.

He'd never stopped indulging in cocaine either. He saw no reason. And now and then when he was somewhere in the world copulating with a sex worker or even randomly taking a life he'd have snorted a line or two just prior. Calvin had retained the same connection for years—a fellow of many tattoos (and substantially widened earlobes) in his late twenties or early thirties, Gary—and this dealer was a no-hassle sort, always supplied, easy to get in touch with. There seemed to be no risk and he staved off addiction by partaking with moderation; never doing it more than once in a week. Even Michela didn't catch on. It was just another of his many clandestine vices. Another amusement that kept Earth time from being a term of drudgery, a series of psychologically gray days that would stretch on for two and a half human lifespans.

PART III

38

Charlotte and Stanley sat facing one another at table the evening following the latter's experience of drug experimentation
in her (their) home. There was a weighty silence, neither having seen
much of the other throughout the day up till supper. Before Stanley
as well as the dinner's cook was a bowl of minestrone soup and a
small plate with two buttered rolls on it.

"I hope you like the minestrone," said the woman, taking her
spoon into her hand for the first time. "It's been a good while since
I've fashioned a batch."

"It looks tasty. Smells appealing too." Stanley followed her lead,
preparing to eat. He stopped, spoon poised above the soup, which
had gone from hot to warm in the time they'd been sitting there. "I
hope..." he began.

"Yes?" Charlotte looked up at him, having just consumed a
spoonful of her main dish, something uncharacteristic about her
demeanor.

"I hope you didn't believe what I'd said about my ex-girlfriend...
last night. I was making up a story. I was temporarily out of sorts.
You know I'd taken a powerful controlled substance—and I'm sorry
for that, for doing that here. It won't reoccur."

"Oh, don't worry, Stanley. I knew you were just being strange.
Because of the lysergic acid ingestion."

The young man's mouth became a transitory half-smile and then
he started in on his soup, hungry due to having eaten little since

finally waking around noon.

Masticating, ingesting broth, the junior diner was fully unaware that early the previous morning, sleepless, a plan at last had been devised by anxiety-riddled Charlotte, her image of an idealized housemate shattered irreparably. She'd lighted upon an idea she believed in and then driven to a twenty-four-hour department store, purchasing eight or ten boxes of over-the-counter sleeping pills. Then in her kitchen, drowsy but determined, she had turned every last baby-blue pill into powder using a mortar and pestle; and this blue powder she had stored in an envelope until she had prepared the minestrone during the five to six hour—the whole of it being carefully stirred into Stanley's portion.

Charlotte's loved one turned feared one sat across from her for around twenty minutes, consuming everything that'd been presented him. Thereafter, with a thanks and eyes that had begun to look weighted, with an appearance of powering down, he trod up the stairs, returning with sunken posture to his room.

Thirty-some minutes later the homeowner was quietly opening his bedchamber door, not having knocked. She was excited and nervous; and felt devious, picturing herself an arch-browed villainess, features sharpened by being partly in shadow, as anticipated finding the suspected murderer to be evidently deeply asleep, his fully clothed body sprawled awkwardly across the mattress she good-naturedly had allowed him to use, one leg dangling.

As she stared at the lifeless body a moment she mentally envisioned what was to come next. The other part of her plan she had put into motion early in the afternoon, around the time groggy young Stanley was beginning to stir upstairs. This had involved a trip to Home Depot for numerous pieces of thick lumber cut two by four that a store associate of around twenty-five had loaded into the back of her vehicle—these and some long nails. A hammer she already had; and though it was an item Charlotte rarely used she knew exactly where it was located. Her only fear was that the sound of driving the nails through the wood and wall would wake the slumberer, drugged again the day following his acid-ingesting recreating.

It didn't bother the woman as much the thought of what to do with the presumed homicide perpetrator once she had him trapped in the bedroom. He would react poorly of course, but she felt the screams would be ignored by the neighbors even if they heard—and besides, she didn't judge Stanley to be the screaming type. She pegged him for more of an internalizing sort. He would starve though, or actually first die of thirst, if something wasn't done to prevent that. So she would have to devise a life-sustainment strategy, or be open to becoming herself a murderer.

There's an ax out in the back she thought, forefinger to her lower lip. *In the shed with the lawnmower and the various gardening implements. I could grab that, make a little notch in the door large enough to pass foodstuffs and water through, and thence have solved that dilemma.*

Already, as she considered this, she had exited Stanley's room and was headed back down, for the lumber that was still in her car, which she would carry up a single board at a time. And she would board up his door, and then she would make an opening; and that way would only have to worry about having a killer kept as a prisoner in her home, rather than about the possibility of extinguishing his life. She would become a criminal, guilty of false imprisonment—should the man's captivity be discovered—but that was nonetheless substantially less serious than being responsible for his demise. Maybe twenty years tops as a penalty versus life. But then again...a score of years was perhaps all that remained to her. Plus: what, eventually, would she ever do with him? She couldn't very well forever leave him to rot in there. Also, he might escape. A human being was quite resourceful when it needed to be, and he seemed like a fairly intelligent fellow, and was probably reasonably strong.

But it didn't matter. She couldn't just let him roam free, constantly fearing for her life, nor could she kick him out. For if he left, tail between his legs, never to be seen again, she would miss him terribly, would pine after him endlessly; for she nevertheless loved him, desperately, murderer or no—despite the fact there would never be another occasion that she would feel the heat and pressure of his body on hers, him inside her, his warm spray filling her deeply.

She was doomed, it had been decided very recently in her busy brain—destined to keep him as a lepidopterist a specimen of rarity and pulchritude. Except never could her find be espied by another, and never its presence be mentioned.

Stanley's abrupt unconsciousness spanned six and a half hours, but the houseowner had only required around three to accomplish her task. He awoke very groggy, disoriented, at a few minutes before two A.M. and, yawning, eyes slits, headed for the door. Though it opened inward the man faced a wall of aligned horizontal boards, so unexpected that in combination with his being half-asleep his nose made contact with a face-level one before he really visually processed their presence.

"Holy fuck," he uttered, backing away to see the new obstacle in its totality. His eyes bugged. "Uh...Charlotte?"

But she who the young captive called out for was soundly asleep in her own chamber, restoring herself after an unpleasant span of anxiousness and activity.

There was a chunk of wooden barrier missing—triangular, about eight inches across and no more than three inches from top to bottom—at about mid-thorax level that looked as if had been hacked incautiously out of the unanticipated timber barricade. Stanley peered through this rough opening but saw only the linen closet door, hardwood floor, to the far left a bit of oaken balustrade. As he considered his circumstances, quickly deciding his sequestration was the bizarre and irrational consequence of Charlotte's fear, he was reminded of a made-for-TV film he had seen some years ago—*Bad Timothy*—about a sociopathic teenage boy who one day inadvertently injured and then executed a young neighborhood girl who was on her way home from school. The awkward acne-ridden youth in a panic informed his overprotective mother about the incident and in an effort to save him from long years in an institution hit upon shutting him up in the walls of their home and then telling the authorities when they came looking he had run away. Once secreted in the structure's skeleton though another tragedy occurred: Timothy's mother suffered a fatal heart attack. Soon, her demise was discovered by a deliveryman, catching sight of her petrified corpse with its gruesome gaping maw, and the house was placed on the market; the teenaged killer watching all from discreet holes drilled into every wall that afforded him a view of most of the downstairs areas. As the weeks passed, the supply of water and canned goods dwindling that Timothy had been left with, the place was sold to a typical-seeming family of five; the children three girls ages twelve to seventeen. And the secret sixth dweller, grimed and stinking—already absorbed in a distressing fantasy world he documented in crayon on the inside of the dividers that formed the boundaries of his narrow, mazelike enclave—began to lasciviously spy on and incorporate into these fantasies the pretty daughter middle in birth order, which idealized fifteen-year-old became the queen of his mentally extant kingdom.

Now Stanley was the hidden (the dangerous, the shameful), hidden without consent but for the same reason: he was a murderer. And perhaps, should he ever escape, he would take life once again, raise his tally to four—for dispatching Charlotte, whose home to his knowledge his presence in had been revealed to none, could save him from his responsibility for his vile ex's demise being revealed to the police. She clearly was no longer his ally, could no longer be trusted. She was, showed the circumstances, a liability at the current juncture; and anyway he had already multiple times committed the ultimate crime—the crime of those who play god—and had nothing to lose other than the shelter of the house he had become a prisoner of.

A plan began to form in the young man's psyche. How had he come to be here in the first place? Trickery and persuasion. And so perchance he could use his manipulative skill to again put the lonely widow in his crosshairs. And knowing her romantic and sexual feelings for him that would be the homicidal arachnid's avenue of approach.

———))(((•)))((———

Hyperalert, Stanley—supine on his bed, not yet bored for his mind's meanderings—five or more hours later heard Charlotte's footsteps on the wooden stairs. Then her head was visible in the chopped out section of the boards. "Here." She handed a bowl of steaming oatmeal through to him. "This constitutes all you'll receive till noon. I cut up an apricot and stirred in the pieces. I will return in a moment however with a glass of water."

"Charlotte..." Stanley started after he had placed the white ceramic bowl at his feet.

"You don't need to speak. I know you have questions about your captivity and/or want to plead your case; and so I'll respond preemptively. You are being kept within this bedroom indefinitely because I am afraid of you but am quite unsure what else I might do with you—other than inform the authorities of what you chanced to reveal to me, which option I am not inclined toward, due to your place in my heart. Silly or unideal as it may be I love you. That is a reality I must cope with. In light of the recent revelation I am coping with it by restricting your freedom. This is likely a maladaptive response, yet it is for better or worse the solution I've opted to adopt. We shall both discover how it works in the long term."

Stanley saw her turn away, but a moment later she pivoted to face the blockaded doorway again. Her expression exuded a mix of toughness and purpose her captive had not seen from her.

"I know you would like to attempt once again to convince me you'd told me a tall tale, to petition me to release you, to rethink this action. But, that would be a futile expenditure of your time." Charlotte seemed about to head for the staircase. "Speaking of which," she said, shoulder to the window in the timber, "I intend to pass a book in to you soon, and every week or so—and I'll be receptive to requests. My dear—my motive is not to in any sense torture you, not even by ennui; it is primarily to protect myself. Because I believe what you told me. I think it was a slip, a fated one. It fits, in my mind. I can see you as that, a killer. I'm not certain why. Perhaps it stands as an answer to my many longstanding questions. In this head of mine—silly as possibly it is—you communicated legitimate information; its nature altered our relationship irrevocably. The present we have arrived at is one in which I can see you only as a killer...that is, in addition to the person I love. Despite what I would wish; this is no chosen outcome. Due though it might be to my status as a maudlin, pathetic, older individual, lonely a long time, in a reeking house spacious enough for six or seven. ...I have such self-knowledge, such consciousness of my environs."

Finally, soliloquy concluded, Charlotte—her gaze directed at her feet, strapped into low simple white canvas sneakers—did go off, descending slowly, steps soft on the wood passage, leaving Stanley's mind to work in silence and isolation, for a duration left up to the one who kept him, the unassuming woman whom he had disquieted.

39

He lay supremely bored on the floor of his bedroom, aware of his own body odor. It had been days since Charlotte had explained herself; he wasn't sure how many. Time had, again, a different meaning—a less meaningful meaning. It was a fact still but was more difficult to track, had less relevance to his day-to-day existence than points previous. He found himself dreaming frequently—sometimes the sort of dreams had by those who are awake—and spending long hours in the recesses of his mind, which seemed to have undergone a variety of deterioration that he could vaguely perceive. It was there (among mental caverns, sitting around the prison of the room in the palatial residence of a widow) one afternoon or possibly morning that he recollected an event that had perhaps not really occurred, or that unfortunately had and he had until now repressed the memory of.

It was some time between when Hope died, was murdered, and he'd been required to vacate her apartment—before Stanley had resigned himself to the streets, another homeless no one who the eyes of strangers cold in deposition hardly saw. Before he'd walked out the front door into the void that was the urban environs of a 2014 America, that was late-spring Oswald; thoroughly peopled, though none of them accessible.

He had taken a blanket with him, only a blanket. Not a particularly warm blanket. A blanket he would lay on, would use like a cape. Due to the weather, the season, it didn't need to be warm. (And so he became a part of the landscape. An invisible man. An invisible murderer. The best kind of murderer to be.)

It was before that. Before the existence that was smelling bad and typically being without necessities and exposed to all the passers (who were primarily blind and/or cell phone-distracted) and being conscious of self-decay and generally desperate and being so alone as to in itself drive him to madness—before the vagrant experience, his *bumdom*, had begun.

There had been a knock. Perhaps it hadn't been the first time, but it was the first time he answered, looking out the peephole and seeing blond dreads.

It was Chelsie. He recognized her at once, despite his poor psychological health. His mind flashed her gorgeous nude form, snippets of the sex they had had, with Hope's consent, under her observation, many months earlier—during what now seemed the life of some other, a luckier life. The young woman's stomach was sexily exposed, as it had been the night they met, the day he'd met Hope, the beginning of the track to unsoundness and destitution—the unforeseeable nightmare of the present. (Hadn't it only been about four months since the threesome at her apartment that night? How incredible it was that in such a brief span his life had changed so dramatically.)

He cracked the door. "Hi," she said in a friendly manner as they locked eyes through the daylit slit.

Stanley continued expanding the door's arc slowly. "Hi," he uttered reticently, reiterating her greeting with little thought.

Door fully open, the lone tenant stood staring emptily at her as she stood on the threshold. "I'd like to come in for a second if that's alright."

"Yes. Yes." He was embarrassed by his failure of social intelligence, although simultaneously confused why he had not become indifferent to adherence to etiquette.

The person from a better time walked in—stopping a few feet into the front room—exuding organismal health and ideal self-confidence, cheeks just a bit ruddy, body and attire communicating cleanness.

Stanley shut the door at her back. He felt hunched, saw himself as appearing vampiric. He could not recall the day of his last entry into the sun and the larger world. In Chelsie's eyes he imagined himself an obvious monster, a housebound pallid wretch of poor posture who might offer the irregular guest lukewarm mint tea and a platter of stale porous crackers, the visitor sitting uncomfortable on a musty couch in a dim parlor.

Chelsie stood awkwardly idle. She seemed not to know why she had come. Then she turned toward Stanley, who was behind and to one side of her, observing and slightly on-guard.

"Where's Hope?"

"...Well...it's a weird thing," he began, inhabiting deception. "A couple weeks ago she left town, apparently. She didn't even say goodbye to me. Just left a note. Said she needed a change of scenery. I've been pretty depressed since. Been holed up here. Rent's due soon and I don't even have an income. She really blindsided me."

"It's definitely peculiar that she'd just leave town without saying anything to me." She peered at the surroundings suspiciously. "Looks like shit in here, Stanley. Sorry to say you somewhat look the same." Chelsie was making eye contact with him, lucid intelligence in her gaze.

"Like I said, I haven't been at my best. I loved her. For her to up and split like that..."

"'Loved,' past tense," the woman noted softly.

"What?"

"I understand," said the visitor, still scanning for clues. Then she quickly looked back at him, having recollected some disquieting event. "They showed a sketch of someone who kinda looked like you on the news."

"Oh strange." He felt his eyes shifting guiltily side to side. *Get her away from an exit—then attack* he heard himself think; the mental voice, to his perception, some other entity's, not his own.

"You know," his eyes widened, "she did leave a note for you too come to think of it. It's back here. Follow me," he said, aware of his speaking but separate in consciousness from the act of doing so.

With a quizzical countenance Chelsie—on a single occasion not long ago his partner in fornication—wordlessly complied, following him to the bedroom.

He opened the door, smelling that the air within had an unpleasant scent, but immediately realizing that in fact the entire domicile did, because he had not been letting in any air from the outside, not even to go outside (since he hadn't been); hadn't been cleaning within whatsoever; and had rarely been showering—which meant, he quickly reminded himself, though he had seen no indication from Chelsie, that he also smelled foully; and he was not yet psychologically immune to self-consciousness, particularly in the presence of a woman of physical loveliness to whom he felt a strong attraction. An attraction amplified by his sexual deprivation, by his having experienced the pleasure of carnality with her. He was hungry primate, she slab of meat—naturally perfumed, genetically graced. A creature of suppleness and strength, effortless vitality; and here she was in the appropriated lair of a visibly decaying creature, to whose mind he was a bent Nosferatu, with thinned shoulder-length hair gone silver and four-inch inward-curled fingernails, xanthous, veined with fine cracks. Preying, eyeing, his uber-vigilant jelly orbs gazing from the posterior side of his skull at the trailing quarry, just now so close to mortal peril—and apparently unwary despite any incertitude. Confident that life would go on for a half-century more and never wrongly be stolen.

The young man who felt like an old one reached into the tiered bureau on which assorted items were strewn, Chelsie at his back, knowing there was nothing within he could present to her and having only the vaguest of plans.

And then he withdrew his hand, clenching it tightly while swiveling and striking the mandible of the room's other occupant, hard, with near to his maximum of force, stunning her—the blow a shock that created a bone-on-bone sound while pushing her head to the right and approximately to the level of her navel, her neck bending unnaturally. She began to correct her posture, by instinct, and Stanley directed another punch at the head of flaxen dreads, connecting with rouge cheek and causing her cranium to hit but bounce up from the carpeted floor. The assailed rose rapidly to an erect stance and at the same time put a wild upper cut he saw as a blur of flesh into Stanley's own jaw, his teeth snapping together with a click that made him wince; then he felt another jolt in his nose, a stream of blood starting from it at once.

Seeing her turn toward the threshold of the space he reached out for both legs with arms widened as if about to give a bear hug (his hug deathly—his embrace not that of love or acceptance; a hug of malice, meant to do the deed of a god and to extinguish what had being, value; Stanley, life's antithesis, functioned too as the nemesis of the living).

He grabbed and Chelsie fell, the movement of these limbs restricted by the man's two interlocked upper own—fell with much of Stanley's modest weight falling in tandem upon her lower half. Her frame was similarly not bulky, was about twenty pounds less than he she fought, but her legs were strong, and Stanley experienced a sensation he postulated to be something like anchoring oneself via will and strength to a vexed steer as he squeezed and the personage beneath presumably tried to kick him injuriously in gritted teeth; adrenaline pulsating her incarnadined cranium, blood vessels in her forehead (above watery eyes) engorged vines.

Holding her thus, cognizant of her puissance having been sapped by his strikes, he surprised himself by biting her back—and clamping on to a substantive portion of flesh—approximately an inch to the right of the middle of her spine.

Chelsie yelped. Stanley punched again—without much power, due to the angle, wanting to maintain his connected-arm restraint—knuckles going into the region of a kidney. Then, pulling himself higher on her, so that most of him was atop most of her—high enough that his head came up to her shoulder blades—he punched twice more, forcefully as he could from the position; punched the side of her head, causing the attackee to briefly lose consciousness.

And then a panting ape lay a few moments on an incapacitated other ape. A weaker one he had unimpressively vanquished. His head was flooded as if by fire that was sentences moving too rapidly through it to fully process (their subjects dread, uncertainty, horror); it felt hot and he had a sense of the evil he was responsible for, the compounded malevolence he was in the process of augmenting—and it felt like a weight, like a thing that outweighed him by two hundred pounds was slumbering across his body just as he was draped across Chelsie's; like a psychic stabbing he would all the rest of his life have to suffer. And brain figuratively in flames, conscious of being crushed by the consequences of his animus, he began with a visage vacated by expression to terminate the lifetime of the person below him—doing the deed he decided now, since attacking her, needed to be done. So his hands went to the sides of her neck and he began to squeeze with all mustered might.

Women make life but I take life; we are both deities—one is a fecundity figure and one, I am, a bringer of death he was thinking as she awoke squirming hopelessly and he maintained the pressure, knowing in a manner this was accurate. *I am a Yama or Mors.* Chelsie was in her final spasms. *Whether exterminating the black-hearted out of rage or those who are decent, deserving of no such fate, in order to protect myself I take from Earth those whose lives I have no right to—and am thus transformed into a malicious entity. No longer human. Instead existing at once within and outside humanity.*

The individual presently, this second, was no more; maybe her spirit was up somewhere just above Stanley and the vacated shelter of flesh and water, blood and bone, gazing possibly in horror or anger at the tableau. And as it quite possibly observed, unseen, unattached, untethered involuntarily from the reality of the physical and its visceral pangs and pleasures, Stanley—the murderer four times over—began with an upsurge of understanding to ruminate on the quality of the organic product of his metamorphosis.

He dismounted the corpse, turned its bulk over so the front faced him. The eyes were open wide, staring frozen past his forehead at the ceiling. They were a medium blue and dotted with specks also blue but far paler. These were the eyes he had rendered forever unseeing, he thought. The eyes he had consigned to rot. They were beautiful. They had been, when lighted by sentience. This was the body, post-animation. Full-breasted, with feminine hips and muscular thighs. A body beyond function—that had been vehicle to a vivacious fellow specimen, that'd had perchance as much as seventy-five years left to it. A young person from whom all, with one action, had been robbed. A person who presumably had wished him no ill, unless knowing what he'd done.

But then he recollected that she had been unfaithful to her boyfriend, that the manifestation of lust the trio, two-thirds deceased, had participated in months earlier had been an illicit one. Was it possible that he had already, in dim caverns of his mind, knowing this, labeled her a tramp as he had Hope—and therefore deemed her life to have less value than another's might due to such a subconscious designation? Had he made this assessment and passed this sentence despite realizing the injustice and in fact hypocrisy of it, despite realizing—at some mental depth—that he was far more immoral, as a multiple murderer, than Chelsie or Hope ever were due to their sexual choices? Just what were the specifics of his psychological ailment? What variety of sad little demon was a Stanley Northrop? Stanley Northrop was a twenty-seven-year-old male human resident of a city, Oswald, in northwestern U.S.A.—but that all constituted inconsequential data. He was a malicious animal, a practitioner of homicide; and what could inferentially be stated about his internal condition—plausibly that he was as lifeless within as the warm cadaver with which he shared a space? A sick, scared sneak thief of life, with an especial antipathy toward those he judged to be particularly brimming with it; because he both envied and was perplexed by them, was frustrated by the fact of them?

"Chelsie—I'm sorry!" the man, alone in an appropriated apartment, stale air matching his stink, yelled into a grim death mask of tissue. "I oughtn't have taken you!" he lamented, aware the noise of his cries would go unheard or ignored. "You belonged here. I do not."

"I am the monstrosity, the aberrant," he said, pulling at the collar of her shirt, nonetheless remaining fully cognizant that he was communicating with what had been rendered no different from a ventriloquist's dummy; a shapely, ten-stone puppet with the quality of a permanently broken machine.

Laying his cranium on the created puppet's bust he began sobbing, equally aware of the ridiculousness of his feeling sorry for himself for being a killer and so all the more emotional; his penis stirring despite his inner turmoil—mixed regret and self-pity—in consequence of pressing his cheek to the pleasing breasts that no longer heaved with each breath.

Alone with himself, as he always sooner or later came to be, Stanley hugged the corpse, salty secreted fluid wetting the tee the evacuated shell beneath him, emblematic of his destructive nature, was clad in. He glanced down at his erection, eyes traveling thence to the exposed navel planted in a flat abdomen that further provoked desire.

Though expired, Stanley accepted the obvious fact of his unabated lust for what had ceased to be Chelsie; and sensed too his desire, increasing steadily since Hope, for the company of another, a female who stirred him interiorly; knowing of course that this the surrogate available other—actually a doll in slow decomposition—could not provide.

He pulled himself upward, using the deceased's shoulders, till his groin was lined up with its; then Stanley began to hump her, the thing, through their clothes—as if in mimicry of a half-forgotten memory of animal pleasure. But, anticipatedly, it was not sufficiently satisfying. It wasn't satisfying at all. It was merely concupiscence-intensifying.

A sick fuck is the kind of individual that engages in intercourse with a lifeless body, thought the man who had let himself go—who occupied a room, a number of rooms, carpeted boxes, an apartment alone with himself and his myriad, meandering, wild thoughts, the thoughts too of a person thoroughly unwell; and uncared for, unknown.

He had never possessed Hope—not in any way a human being can be said to be. She had always been apart, for others in addition, for others more than for him. Neither her genitalia nor her psyche nor soul had been his. She had been a pretty focus of lust, of emotional longing. She'd been an illusion—in the way sex with a feeling-less, nonmotive, warm object was illusory; playing sex but not having sex. Just as he'd falsely believe there'd been a connection with Hope sexual union with Chelsie now, secreted in this enclosure, would be make-believe, his act of necrophilia consciously masturbatory.

But, he decided, the substitute was preferable to the total lack. Watching a movie better than staring at a wall. And anyway Hope had been a soulless soul-destroyer. A sociopath on a lifelong rampage. And he had done the world a good turn subtracting her from it (himself a bad one by associating so intimately with her). And now he would play husband and wife with her dead best friend, so that he could taste again (but not actually experience) the reality of carnality with her, the reality of intimacy—felt once with Hope, another dead woman. Dead at the hands of a serial killer.

I've been made, not born. I am a nurtured non-psychopath serial killer. Just a mentally ill guy. A crazy, thought Stanley, unbuttoning, unzipping, pulling the thin pants from Chelsie's hips.

Her panties were pink and silky, with white ruffled edging. He pulled the pants away from her ankles and brought down the under-wear, seeing once more a pleasing envelope of flesh topped by a tri-angle of close-cropped light-yellow pubic strands. Inside the panties was a blood-soaked pad. Extending his arms he lifted her medium-blue crop top over the mounds of lobules and adipose that were her breasts, concealed within a white cotton brassiere.

The shapes were all pleasing of this one he had killed. All that she was now was a shape. But of course it was the shape of a person he saw walking down the street that attracted him first, and secondly perceived demeanor, an idea he might develop of who an individual was. So this shell, robbed of being, still held the important function of being a pleasing shape—and inanimate though she was her form continued to hold power over his primal mind, evidenced by his firm penis, which presently he directed into her aesthetic lower lips, entering with ease into the moistness past them.

Stanley sighed with pleasure, collapsing onto her for a few moments to reach beneath the body and unlatch her bra with both arms, then—staring at the exposed mammary glands—resuming the one-sided intercourse, a suctioning sound resulting from some inches of his erection going within and being withdrawn from her viscous womanhood, the veiny flesh of his phallus coated in the product of her menses.

There was a ghastliness to Chelsie's eyes, dead and locked on the void, netherworld, that kept his from traveling to her face. Seeing them would diminish his arousal, would crowd his psyche with the reality of being an agent of death, a being on the wrong end of the humanity spectrum, a man who was copulating clandestinely—and to his satisfaction—with a corpse yet warm from a lifetime prematurely concluded.

Really the whole of reality was at this point in his story a pain to him. Including the fact he was all too conscious of that he wanted Chelsie, in life, anyone who might fit the bill, to ease his pain of aloneness. That was how the tragedy of Hope had come to occur. Though with her what was in store he had not even suspected. But he ought to've. Because his notion of her constituted an instance of too good to be true. And in no way had she been true. He could hardly be certain the present was true.

Had Stanley Northrop transformed in mere months into a murderer and necrophile, residing in a ruin of a distinctly empty-feeling apartment, an apartment that had belonged to a victim and onetime lover?

Stanley could not be sure. He could know only that his experience now felt in no quality distinct from the bulk of lifetime he had previously lived, except for the character of the events. If he pinched his arm he did not wake from the horror, sweat-drenched and re-lieved, hyperventilating and disoriented.

Chelsie's vagina seemed as titillating a place as it had once before, but the fact of her existing as a mere object deducted the elements of the equation that truly mattered, leaving merely the visceral—a feel-ing of his being nothing but a beast satisfying a need, a fur-covered quadruped ripping into carrion; and the consciousness of the lack of fulfillment derived from coitus with a body, his awareness of a dearth of joy, led inside seconds to an awareness that the act—as he continued toward climax—was resulting in an emotional upswell of a sensation quite the opposite of happiness: a sadness, a palpable, op-pressive sense of emptiness. A recognition of the emptiness within him amplified and augmented by the dead Chelsie, by his sequestra-tion in the room with the cadaver, the apartment he was by another act of murder the sole occupant of—by the solitary, masturbatory, demented nature of his act with the remains, the reminder, of the erstwhile human.

He was aroused by his possession of the woman's body but in-capable of being fulfilled by a lifeless husk. A currently copulating monster had rendered the person below it a thing akin to a warm sex doll, a ghastly puppet—the ways in which the carcass that was Chelsie was real to it outweighed by the fact of its not being any more than a mass of animal meat.

Stanley could have an object—the item; malleable, controllable, imitative, substitutive—but an individual he was not permitted. They left or were taken (even if by himself) or were never his—and after he was worse off, more broken. No, these were for others, these people.

Cerebrated Stanley, *We all have a destiny; for me it's my mind.*

His destiny was the memory (famously faulty), or the corpse, not the clear and current—the animated flesh, the organism with a personality and needs and the ability to analyze and experience, to feel and be a receptor of being felt. To Stanley came death, the dead being; he deserved or created death, he was death. Life, the living, were for the extant who had not died. Inside Stanley Northrop there was an abyss, vacuum. Light could penetrate but was always lost within it. Stanley was he who had plaque-coated teeth and a freshly deceased human in his embrace and his penis in the body's vagina, the active coitus gentle, indicative of genuine intimacy (this an obvious fraud, because it took two to copulate).

What he was engaged in was rather an elaborate form of masturbation, oneiric onanism. The tableau was a pathetic manifestation of unalleviated desire. The circumstances that of a somnophile's heaven (and a somnophile was a masturbator who wanted only a representation, not an organism). However, for this man inside this dead woman it was a picture of a monster occupying a self-devised hell—one of its myriad iterations, aspects. A nightmare chamber among many he currently inhabited, all having been invented by the creature imprisoned in the labyrinth of them. Boxes of fantasy below which was no floor above which was no ceiling though from the honeycomb of which was no escape. Because the sole exit was via the psyche, and his was not sufficiently sighted.

It was a room of horror, he thought in his exertion, his rhythmic movement jiggling beneath him the body on the carpet. And then, with a brief groan and followed immediately after by intense discontentment, Stanley ejaculated.

www.ingramcontent.com/pod-product-compliance
Lightning Source LLC
Chambersburg PA
CBHW030933020726
47498CB00001B/227